"THE GOLDEN PORCUPINE

has the ring
of historical authenticity . . .

The Duke of Orleans gallops across France, calls on the
Pope for help, leads armies in revolt, languishes in an iron
cage as a royal prisoner, and falls in love with both the
king's daughter and the Queen of France. In the end it was
not Orleans which passed to the Crown, but the Crown
which passed to Orleans. The Duke became . . . Louis
XII of France."

The New York Times

"THE GOLDEN PORCUPINE holds its reader not by
mere vigor or brash effects but by deft construction and
grace of style . . . artistry pervades the entire novel . . .
a novel of modern love and marriage boldly placed in the
early French Renaissance atmosphere of Louis of Orleans."

The Saturday Review

THE GOLDEN PORCUPINE

MURIEL ROY BOLTON

AVON
PUBLISHERS OF BARD, CAMELOT AND DISCUS BOOKS

AVON BOOKS
A division of
The Hearst Corporation
959 Eighth Avenue
New York, New York 10019

First Avon Printing, July, 1977

To
MY MOTHER

1

The King of France stood at the altar rail, holding his squirming, newly born cousin and godson in his arms, and fervently wished he could drown the little bastard in the silver bowl of christening water! That it was a bastard he had no doubt, but proving it—well, that was something else again.

King Louis XI's malevolent gaze traveled across the high-vaulted Orleans chapel, past the murmuring figures of the priests in their brilliantly embroidered vestments, toward the supposed father of this lustily kicking boy. Charles, elderly Duke of Orleans, stood in a happy trance, acting, the king thought viciously, as though he really believed this was his son, blood of his blood and flesh of his flesh. The summer sun shone in through the big stained-glass windows, its soft yellow and rose beams slanting down to illumine Charles's thin, gentle face and faded blue eyes glowing now with restrained exultation as he watched the baby's christening.

The senile fool, the king thought bitterly. Past seventy, he was, with nothing to show for all his years of marriage but one little daughter with dainty pinched features like his own! What right had he to think he could fool anyone into believing this husky piece of male flesh was his issue? That it bore his name—and inherited all the vast lands of Orleans that *should* have come to the Crown and been king's property when Duke Charles died without male heirs—that was rank injury enough, but the pretense that it was actually his son was the final insult that made the king bilious with inward rage. His stomach, ulcerated by driving ambition and nervous impatience, contracted in pain as he considered what had obviously happened.

Anyone with half an eye could see that the young duchess, either with or without her husband's consent, had lain with a younger, stronger man, and this—this small impostor

1

struggling furiously in the king's arms—was the result of that union.

The skinny, harsh-faced king, a sour smile on his lips, steadied the wriggling child on the satin christening pillow and looked around the crowded church filled with kneeling nobility that had traveled to Blois, in the province of Orleans, to attend the christening of Louis, young heir to the Dukedom of Orleans, heir apparent to the throne of France, and godson to King Louis himself. It was a colorful assembly, the men in their ermine-trimmed green or blue brocaded jackets flaring out from their tightly belted waists over forest green or brown tights, their puffed turbans of scarlet and gold draped silk in brilliant contrast to the women's tall, conical black velvet hennins. The assembled titles were as brilliant as their robes, for all the neighboring dukes and duchesses were there to do honor to the House of Orleans, and to a child who might, one day, be a Valois King of France.

Not cheered by this brave sight, the king's black gaze came to rest on the pretty bowed head of the baby's mother, and should have withered the joyous prayer on her lips. But Mary of Orleans, sweet and young, and looking, as her husband had always described her, "like a gleam of sunshine on a country garden," devoutly prayed, undoubtedly thanking God for the son He had finally sent her. Her long blond hair was drawn up and hidden under her tall hennin, which exposed her small pink ears, her smooth flushed cheeks. She wore an azure-blue velvet dress, tight but demure of bodice, with a wide skirt, heavily embroidered with gold thread. Blue was her favorite color. It accentuated the deep blue of her eyes, the coral curves of her unpainted mouth. Her piquant nose, she feared, was beginning to shine a little with excitement, and under cover of the cardinal's long prayer she bent her head lower and took a quick glance into the shining disk of silver that hung at the end of her jeweled belt. It was the fashion, ornamental and practical, to use these little silver disks as hand mirrors. Yes, her nose was beginning to gleam, and she wished she had dared to use the white lotion one of her maids had bought from a traveling Italian perfumer.

The prayer ended. Quickly she dropped the mirror and reproached herself for her vanity at such a time—when her son, her son and Charles's, was being christened! Happily she looked toward her husband, standing near the altar.

Why does she look at him? the king sourly wondered. Why doesn't she turn around and look at the man who *really* sired her brat? For it was common gossip that the father was Alain de Mornac, steward of the House of Orleans.

When the astounding news had come to the king's court at Tours two weeks ago, the courtiers had roared with laughter at the jest, that Mother Nature had favored a natural union where it had failed a legal one.

"Have you heard," they sniggered, "that the Duke of Orleans has a son?"

And the answer came quickly: "You mean the *duchess* has a son!"

"It is very nice," they meditated, with mockery in their eyes, "that God has answered her prayers at last!"

"I hear that God is quite handsome," was the retort. "A dark, swaggering Gascon with an unusual talent for answering a woman's prayers!"

"So?" Malicious eyes would gleam. "Then I must return to my devotions. I could enjoy worshiping a God like that!"

Had it been anyone else, the king would have been amused also, but this birth took too much from him to give him any enjoyment. What rankled most bitterly was the thought that he could have prevented it. He should have kept his elderly cousin, Charles of Orleans, with him at court; under some pretext he should have kept husband and wife apart. The duchess would have borne the brat anyway, but it could have been proven bastard and kept from inheriting. He should have thought, the king told himself reproachfully, that something like this might happen. It was the sort of thing he would have done himself if he had been in their position—morals had nothing to do with it—but to see a bastard take the lands that should be his was hard to endure.

Most of the women in the church were twisting their silly necks, the king could see, to look toward the back of the church where the Sire de Mornac stood; the tall hennin hats, with their dangling overdrapes and sheer veils, turned restlessly as the women angled for a better view of de Mornac. Disgusting for him to be here at all, the king thought, and twisted his own neck to look at the probable father of his infant cousin.

Yes, the king growled in his bitter heart, he looks like he has sired an army of bastards and will sire more. A dark Gascon, strong—a stallion of a man, he stands there like a rock, an impervious look on his blatantly masculine face— pretending he doesn't see the women peering and tittering . . .

"God's death!" King Louis exclaimed suddenly under his breath, but loud enough to startle the closest priest. He hastily shifted the pillow, but too late. The baby's warm, wet trickle had gone through the pillow and stained the front of the king's robe, his new and extremely fashionable houppelande. This long surcoat was a favorite of King Louis, covering him from neck to ankles in heavy-lined velvet, hiding his thin shanks that were too chilly in just woolen tights, the full, purple-lined sleeves falling over his cold hands unless he chose to turn the scalloped edges back over his bony wrists. Altogether it was a wonderfully comfortable garment for a man who suffered from poor circulation.

And now this miserable infant, adding final insult to enormous injury, had stained his best robe!

After the ceremony was completed the king stamped angrily into Mary's room, where she had been put to bed again. "Madame," he said bitterly, "your little brat has wet me to the skin and ruined this robe of mine; tell me, what is that a portent of?"

For the king, sharp and worried and superstitious, looked for signs and meanings in every smallest incident.

It was so unexpected that Mary laughed, in spite of his obvious annoyance. She was so happy, anyway, that everything seemed funny. She leaned back against the satin pillows and laughed till her ribs ached.

Charles, older and more controlled, but still amused, hastened to speak. "I think it can be taken to mean that since you were so kind as to give him your name, he wanted you to have something of his also!"

"Is that what it means?" the king accepted Charles's explanation and Mary's laughter coldly. "Then thank him for me, but tell him I will do without such intimate gifts in the future."

"He has so little else to offer," said Charles, and Mary laughed again.

"He has Orleans, and that should be enough!" The king spoke sarcastically. "I have not congratulated you yet, madame. It is not every woman who can present her husband with so unexpected and timely an heir."

Charles was suddenly grave, and Mary's laughter died away as she accepted his congratulations and ignored his double meaning. They had heard the gossip too.

"Thank you," she said. "It is something for which we have longed for many years. And I haven't thanked you yet for so kindly acting as godfather to our little Louis; that was also unexpected."

"Little enough to do for my small cousin," the king answered shortly and ungraciously. "I am proud to be counted among his fathers."

He enjoyed Mary's flush of annoyance and felt a bitter revulsion against making them the promise he had come to give, the plan he had decided on, even while he had held the child in his arms and promised the priests to be its second father.

The first hope of the godfather was that the child might die. There was always that chance, but no active way to help the baby to that desirable conclusion, for he was heir presumptive to the throne. If the king died without a son, this child of Mary and God-knows-who would be King of France, and if anything unnatural should bring about his death, there would be many to suspect the king and the resulting storm might even blow the king from his throne. So there was no solution in that direction, except to hope the child might be frail and weak, its weakness ending in a fatal malady.

The king smiled at the Duke and Duchess of Orleans, making his hawklike features as benevolent as he could. "I plan to guard the little Louis's interests most actively," he told them. "Your son is my cousin and my godson; I have given him my name, and I mean to give him more than that! I plan to give him my daughter!"

He saw the amazed exultant look that passed swiftly from one to the other and he hated it. He wanted to strike it from their rejoicing faces, but he went on:

"In a few years we will betroth them legally. I wish him to be often at my home at Tours, so he may be acquainted with my family and I may see how his education progesses."

He received their fervent thanks with controlled civility

and left them very quickly, for he felt he could not bear very much more of their joy without strangling them.

After he left, Mary lay back in her large canopied-hung bed and tried to soothe her vigorously howling son, who was protesting against a world where innocent babies were taken from their soft beds and held against a bony man's chest while cold water was dripped on their foreheads.

"SSH—shh," said Mary tenderly, and thought she had never been so happy as she looked from her bawling son to her husband, who stood at the window gazing out at the land that was a part of his ancient name and would pass on now to the son he had feared he would never have.

Charles stood there in a dream of memory, remembering how he had yearned for a glimpse of these lands the long twenty-five years he had spent in an English prison after he had been captured at the muddy Battle of Agincourt.

Twenty years old, he had been, when he had led the confident French Army to disaster, a boy whose knowledge of battles was confined to the poems he wrote about war. But in spite of their leader's youth and inexperience, there had been no lack of confidence throughout the laughing ranks of the army of France.

It had been enough for them that he was Charles, Duke of Orleans, second in rank after the king and the dauphin. In the glittering splendor of his battle armor, Charles had sat astride his great horse and surveyed his personal position and the position of his army with swelling pride. A pride he remembered forever after with wincing distaste for his complacency. Smug pride before a disastrous fall. But that night, the night before the decisive battle, he had felt certain that tomorrow, the twenty-fifth day of October, 1415, in the gray dawn on the fields at Agincourt, Henry V of England and his ridiculous pretensions to the French throne would both be crushed out forever.

All of the mightiest names of France had been there, save Burgundy, whose allegiance wavered between the kings of France and England and who had wisely decided to sit at home and await the results. The front rows, the positions of honor, where death struck first, had been reserved for those of the noblest blood. Charles of Orleans, on his restless horse, had stood at the very center and front of the great mass of heavily armored lords; on his right was Louis de Bourbon, and on his left was the Constable of France, d'Albret. Alençon, Nevers, Dammartin, Saveuse, Vendôme, and Brabant were only a few of the others who surged around him, laughing and talking of the prisoners they would take on the morrow and of the great things they would do toward the coming humiliation of Henry of England.

Bourbon chided them with mock solemnity: "Treason! Treason to speak so of the good King Hal, who only comes to claim his rightful throne and his loyal subjects. He is stunned with hurt, his heralds tell us, that he has met with resistance when he had expected arms open in greeting!" He joined in the shouts of derision.

Saveuse's smile was bright and fierce with savage eagerness. "He shall see in the morning how we greet him!"

Charles of Orleans spoke wryly: "Those English—a talented nation. To state their foolish claims to France in such a sober way. It's a jest without laughter."

D'Albret spoke shortly: "And the jest is turning sour with time. Pretexts to snatch what they can."

There had always been a quality of aloofness in Charles's mind that enabled him to see things with detached clarity. "Of course, but they do it so well. They never allow a ray of mocking comprehension to shine through the false sincerity they have laid upon themselves and their foolish claims. I admire their control——" But whatever else he admired about them he wasn't allowed to say, for his friends refused to hear him out, feeling with thorough singlemindedness that there was nothing admirable about the English, except when dead.

They were all ready and eager for the battle, and although it was not to be until dawn—and there were three hours to wait—none of them thought of going to rest on the straw beside the field or in the few tents that had been erected for the leaders. They were too exhilarated; they wanted to be with their fellow companions; they wanted to sing and shout, and if this was to be their last night on earth, they did not wish to pass it in sleeping. Besides, they were all in their heaviest armor, and it was such a task to get themselves in and out of it that they preferred to remain upright. It had begun to rain a little, and the long torches of burning pitch sent up black columns of solid smoke and hissed as the rain fell upon the blazing ends. Sizzling and sputtering, they struggled against the dampness and the

night, flaring up now and again into a bright light that
brought into sudden vivid color the brilliant surcoats, the
gold and silver armor that flashed and reflected the tossing
flame. Then the light, with shivering speed, ran up the round
spear handles to the shining spear points and illumined the
embroidered banners that hung limply in the rain. The sacred oriflamme of France was not among them, but it would
be in the morning for the moment of attack. When the unsteady flame had dampened again to only a faint glimmer,
the surcoats were dark and the armor was somber in the
blackness; only the faces and the eyes of the French soldiers
still gleamed with their own eager light. They had seen King
Henry's ragged army as Henry had gone northward to
Calais. The French Army had outdistanced him, cutting off
the possibility of his retreat across the Channel to Dover, so
that now they stood between the English and England, and
Henry would be forced to fight his way through if he would
see his home again.

Had Charles of Orleans and the other leaders been more
experienced and cautious, they would have continued to
stand there, blocking Henry's retreat, and the English Army,
cut off from supplies and greatly outnumbered, would have
had to agree to a most humiliating peace. Henry had already
sent messengers to ask for peace, promising to repair the
damage he had caused in Normandy if he and his army
might be allowed to return to England, but his representatives had been almost blown from the French tents on the
insulting gales of laughter that had met their request. France
would have nothing to do with so listless an end to the war;
a decisive retraction of all King Hal's idiotic claims to the
French throne was what they wanted, and they had expected to have it by Friday afternoon, October 25, 1415.
There was nothing in the songs of battle and the lessons of
chivalry about caution. Reckless courage and the daring of
brave men had always been worshiped by the lords of
France, and a cautious victory did not even occur to Charles
or the Constable of France.

Charles had looked across the fields toward the quiet
darkness in which the enemy waited, and once more he had
considered the plans for the morning. He saw himself leading the cavalry in a sweeping charge, cutting through the
lean shabby ranks of the English, in which there was no
cavalry left, plowing deep into the mass of soldiers on foot.

After his horsemen had gone completely through the English lines, like a hot sword through a melting candle, they would turn and attack from the rear, and before it could be realized, almost before it could be accomplished in his mind, the enemy would be completely surrounded. When the six thousand men who made up the English Army were surrounded by the forty thousand Frenchmen, it could not take long to conquer them.

In Henry's army there had been no laughter and no exultation. It was a weary army, desperate for home, kept sober and pious by Henry, who had changed from a profligate prince into a cold and austere king almost overnight, and who had come, at God's command, to punish the French for their frivolous wickedness. He, too, looked across the fields toward his enemy and saw the flaring lights of the French campfires, heard their shouts of laughter and song, and knew with what confidence they expected victory. He had relied on their restless, youthful excitement to force a battle instead of starving him into defeat, and although he knew the odds against him, he made his own cautious plans that had nothing to do with chivalry or poetry.

The dawn came, but it did not bring the sun, only a heavily lowering sky that drizzled a steady cold rain down upon the fields of Agincourt. The French Army, seeing the oozing mud, for the first time had felt a flickering of uneasiness, and they delayed attacking while the leaders talked excitedly among themselves. Perhaps, although they didn't see or hear him, a pitying ghost from the Battle of Crécy whispered among them, "This has happened before. Remember what happened at Crécy!" And a chill foreboding touched them all for an instant.

But Henry, to whom the nightlong rain and the soaking fields were signs of God's encouragement to him, rode to the front of the line where he had placed his English and Scottish archers. He sent his thoughts to heaven for a moment, his ruddy face bowed and serious, and then he cried out, his voice ringing with that vital strength that made him so magnetic a leader, "In the name of Almighty God and St. George, forward, banners!"

The banners of St. George were raised high to the dripping skies and the archers knelt, each taking up a small piece of the soil of the field and placing it in their mouths to signify that dust they were in God's sight and to dust they might return in the coming battle. There was nothing to stir the blood of the French to enthusiastic fervor at the sight of the archers; there was nothing romantic or poetic about them in their drab leather armor, their bare legs and feet muddy, for they had taken off their shoes so that their bare feet might better grip the soil and enable them to move forward at their king's command.

Charles of Orleans, Bourbon, d'Albret, and the other princes in the first rank had dropped their visors and bent their heads so that the arrows that came toward them like eager, venomous birds should find no vulnerable spot. Orleans, pausing for a moment to survey the English line before he gave the order to advance, saw with some bewilderment that each archer had taken a long, pointed stick, several feet taller than his head, and had planted it before him deep into the soil of the field and then stood behind it, like a man trying to hide behind a slim tree without branches. As each archer planted his stake, the front line, spread out across the entire field, resembled a long fence of sharp sticks, about two feet apart, and behind each one a man was standing. A laughable defense, surely, against the mighty cavalry of France, and yet not Charles nor Bourbon nor any of them laughed. It was a sinister and ominous sight, the sharp sticks wet and gleaming in the gray light, the men silent and waiting, their long bows ready.

Charles had roused himself, raised his spear high above his head and called out, his voice shaking with emotion, "In the name of God, forward, France!" And the mighty, thundering charge that he had planned was released.

But the cavalry charge that he had planned and the cavalry charge that took place upon the fields of Agincourt were not the same. What was to have been a hurtling of fast-moving bodies was a slow, heaving, straining crawl. The horses sank up to their knees in the sucking mud, and it was only the pain of the English arrows that forced them to move at all. When they moved it had to be forward, for the ponderous weight of the pushing mass at their backs was growing to be more of a menace than the enemy fire. France moved forward slowly, each man thinking less now of attacking the English than of the more immediate danger of falling. If they fell, in the weight of their splendid armor, under the inexorable push at their backs, it meant inglorious, muddy, suffocating death. The foot soldiers in the rear lines, more mobile than those in front, pushed themselves forward, not realizing they were prodding their leaders on to drown in the sea of mud or, escaping that, to press against the English fence and die there in slippery helplessness.

Horses and men, fallen, struggled to raise themselves and were forced back into the black slime by another line of men and horses who stumbled and fell upon them. The loss was appalling, but nothing could withstand the slow-moving but ponderous French juggernaut, and finally the English fence gave way and the English lines fell back. Charles, fortunate to be still mounted, saw with exaltation the banners of St. George for an instant in the hands of Saveuse, who had flung himself at it. But he did not see Saveuse fall to the ground with a dozen fatal wounds, nor did he see anything else, for his horse slipped and heavily crashed to the ground. Although the animal twisted and pawed the ground with its forelegs, screaming from the pain of a broken back, Charles did not even try to raise himself for, rattled about as he was in his heavy armor, he was unconscious.

The battle went on for hours, but the blue eyes of its twenty-year-old leader did not see it. Although the English had fallen back, it had not been a retreat, only a strategic withdrawal from the deadly pressure that was proving an invaluable aid. The French cavalry literally destroyed itself; the French archers had been placed in the rear, due to their lack of royalty, and so had not much else to shoot at but their leader's backs, and when the English soldiers, supple in their bare feet and leather armor, came running out of the woods on either side of the field and fell upon the French men-at-arms, clumsy in their steel, the battle was quickly ended and exactly one fourth of the men who had been so laughingly confident lay dead. Ten thousand of the eager, undefeated young lay quiet on the field of Agincourt, neither defeated nor victorious, only quiet, but when they were searched for jewelry, valuable armor, and valuable prisoners, Charles of Orleans, that most valuable of prisoners, was discovered to be still alive.

He had been taken in a cart to Calais, along with Bourbon, Vendôme, and a few of the others who had escaped death but who would have preferred dying to being Henry's prisoner, forced to listen to his pious sermons and moralizing.

They sat at King Henry's banquet table, respectfully
served and carefully watched, and they pushed food about
on their plates with small pieces of bread and seemed absorbed in that occupation, scarcely looking up unless a
question or remark was directly addressed to them by the
king. In all their minds, under the nagging annoyance of
humiliation and regret, was the single thought: How soon
would they be ransomed and freed? The English king was
not at all eager to discuss those matters but assured them all
how much benefit they would gather from the experience
of being his guests in a country like England. He went
further than that; he even seemed to expect some gratitude
from them that he had delivered them from the wickedness
of France.

Charles's philosophic and intelligent mind was amused as
he completely abandoned his effort to look as though he
were eating and gave himself up to contemplation of the
king, whose hard and calculating eyes did not seem to recognize the devout homilies that were coming from the over-
full, sensuous lips. It was easy enough to see that he was
enjoying himself, but Charles thought with a smile that this
was a situation any human must enjoy—his enemies pinned
down before him and forced to listen.

"Abstinence," the king was saying as well as he could
between huge mouthfuls of meat, "abstinence is something
you Frenchmen know nothing of. Drinking, whoring, ca-
rousing even on saint's days, there's no wonder God shows
you His displeasure!" He looked about for applause and
received it from the nodding heads of his bishops.

Wonderful! thought Charles, looking at the king intently
for some smallest sign of mockery or self-knowledge. Surely
he could not have so quickly forgotten his early days, when
he was Prince Hal and had staggered drunkenly from one
low tavern to another, supposedly incognito but roaring his
identity to anyone who would listen. Charles looked about
the table and saw that memory in every face but that of the
king, and smiled at the sulky, contemptuous look on Bourbon's face.

"Surely not on saint's days," Charles murmured, and met
startled, amused recognition in some strange Englishman's
eyes.

They had remained for a few weeks in Calais, mending
their wounds, alternately listening to the king and repenting

of their defeat, if not their morals. Then in the middle of November Charles and the other important prisoners set sail for Dover on the same ship with King Henry. It was a dim nightmare, Charles thought, watching the shores of France dissolve into the horizon; surely he would waken in his home at Blois in the morning beside his young wife, Bonne. He thought of her bewitching dark beauty, her audacious charm, and he thought of his home deep in the heart of his province of Orleans. A paradise it had been, leisurely and luxurious, with his beautiful bride, his poetry, his books, and his estates to care for. Such a life could not be over, he told himself; there was no doubt but that it was only a nightmare and he would be back in Blois when he awoke. But it was twenty-five years before he saw his home again, and he never saw his dark, laughing Bonne, for she died when he had been away only a few years.

One by one the other prisoners had been ransomed and freed, and said good-by to him, half ashamed of their good fortune and his lack of it; but he was too important a hostage to be released, since he was next in line to the throne of France after the king and the sickly dauphin. He was moved about from one prison to another, from the Tower of London, where he was closely confined, to Windsor Castle, where he had a suite of rooms and all the luxuries, then to Pontefract, where he was closely kept again and which he hated because of its climate.

"This country!" he complained almost daily to his attendants. "Even the sun comes to it as little as possible! That people who are not imprisoned continue to stay in it is what bewilders me. I would rather be a dog in France than a king in England!"

"If you are cold," they suggested to him, "may we bring you some of the English or Scotch wools, to keep you warmer?"

"It is not a matter of clothing," Charles assured them in sincerity, "it is a chill that comes from within and it cannot be defeated with wool. I have worn some of the hideous things and I know." And so he clung to his light, elegant silks and shivered.

The years were very strange to him; they continued to be a nightmare from which he must someday awaken. Hope kept him alive and detachment kept him from bitterness. It was not the actual fact of being a prisoner that he minded

so much, especially after his wife died, for he was a man
with a taste for solitude and meditation, but when he looked
up and saw, instead of the bright warmth of France, the
cold gray skies of England, a nostalgia swept over him that
was like a surge of deadly sickness. The hills and the lakes
and the sun and the laughter of France were the nourish-
ment that his life demanded, and as his youth slipped away
and the continued war between the two countries kept him
prisoner, he spent his time hoping and praying for peace.
War was an anathema to him, since he had learned in his
first and only great battle that it was not the colorful, splendid thing he had made it in his poems, but in truth a muddy,
bloody horror. His poetry came to mean more and more to
him, and his days were passed in composing the delicate,
fragile verses that lived for so many years.

When England, still claiming the French throne, invaded
France again and bored its way as far as Orleans, burning
the crops and the villages, battering the towns, Charles sat
alone in his room. It was intolerable for him to hear the
exultation of the English, whose confidence that the end of
a war, victorious for them, was in sight seemed to be justified by the events. The old King of France had died, and
the sickly dauphin, huddled fearfully behind the stout walls
of Orleans, had not so much chance as the strong King Hal
to be crowned King of France. But Charles's half brother,
the Bastard of Orleans, who proudly carried that title
throughout his life, and the peasant girl who came to be
known as the Maid of Orleans raised the siege of Orleans
and marched the quaking dauphin to Rheims, where they
anointed him with the sacred coronation oil and made him
King of France.

Charles had sent what support he could, which was little
beside his prayers and a suit of armor for the peasant girl,
Jeanne d'Arc. While he waited the outcome he wrote:

> Pray for peace, sweet Virgin Mary,
> Queen of the heavens and mistress of the world,
> Bid to pray, out of your gentle mercy,
> All the Saints and take your petition to
> Your son—— ——
> Pray for peace, that priceless jewel.

Peace did not come, although the tide of battle was turned

by the enthusiasm the Maid brought the soldiers, by the desperate soldiery of the Bastard of Orleans, and by the all-important fact that the dauphin had been made a king by the sacred oil and the coronation ceremony. England withdrew its soldiers, for a while at least, although it did not relinquish its claims to the throne, and Charles was able to breathe again.

The seasons changed, the years walked by, and then at last negotiations were begun for his release. The King of France had children and would no doubt have more, so Charles was no longer a priceless hostage. He had his price, and though it was a ruinous one for him, he gladly accepted his freedom. His half brother sighed when he heard the amount, looked sadly about the depleted provinces, straightened his broad shoulders that were used to bearing Orleans's burdens, and strained together the first payment. Charles was free at last to return to Blois in the year 1440, twenty-five years after he had left it.

He sank back into France as a weary child sinks into its mother's arms. Content that he was at home again, he stayed at Blois in quiet peace, riding through the estates with the young steward, the Sire de Mornac, who was undertaking the reconstruction of the province in such a capable way, using the funds the new king had granted out of gratitude to Orleans for the support and coronation it had given him. In the evenings Charles read and wrote, and the life would have sufficed but for the fact that it would never give him an heir. So he thought of another marriage. When he had come back home from England he had looked into his mirror and said sighingly, "I have played tennis with time, and now my score is forty-five!"

When his score had been over fifty he had finally found a bride who pleased him, fourteen-year-old Mary of Cleves, sweet and blond and timid.

"A gleam of sunlight in a country garden!" he had exclaimed when he saw her for the first time, and he watched her with smiling pleasure. If a man could not have youth himself, it was good, at least, to touch it in a young wife. Bonne had been dead so many years that his memory of her did not deter him from loving his new bride, but he ruefully found that youth, once passed, cannot be recaptured just by embracing it.

Little Mary of Cleves had never questioned the marriage.

She had not been brought up to question things her parents planned for her, and when her mother had come in flurried excitement to touch her hair and tighten her waistband before she should be submitted to the approval of the Duke of Orleans, Mary had obediently made herself as pretty as possible, holding her breath for a moment before she went into the room so that her cheeks would be pink with color. She had thought he seemed a very pleasant gentleman, and there had been no desperate unhappiness in her heart when she stood beside her elderly groom before the bishop, nor later in the marriage bed.

"Odd!" she had said to herself; still it was not so dreadful as she had heard it whispered, and surely women should be willing to suffer a little inconvenience to have children. Charles was gentle and undemanding, and it was exciting being Mistress of Orleans in the enormous château at Blois with its exquisitely decorated rooms and its beautiful parks and gardens.

The Orleans Château stood high on a green wooded hill above the Loire River, overlooking the town of Blois. The stately stone towers, the strong high walls, the graceful arches had been built to withstand siege and time. Already two hundred years old when Mary came to it as a bride, it was famous all over France for the strength and beauty of its design. Inside there were the superbly paneled and painted rooms, the shining inlaid floors, the high-vaulted ceilings glittering with intricately patterned gold designs, the chiseled stone hearths with exquisite bronze fire tools, the deep-piled Persian carpets, the carved desks and chairs from Italy, the canopied beds padded with soft velvets and draped with brocaded satins, the tapestries from Brittany and Flanders, their rich deep color brightening the walls and hanging over the few windows, the gold-framed family portraits of the dukes and duchesses of Orleans in the great candlelit gallery, the wrought-iron gates from Spain, the gold- and silver-embossed plates from Milan and Florence, the jeweled goblets from Venice—everything Europe offered for comfort and luxury was there.

The main body of the château was four stories high, built about a stone courtyard, and from the towers and upper windows the view over the river, the town, and the small farms of the countryside had a great and peaceful beauty.

Dark green poplars and oaks surrounded the summit of

the hill; hawthorn, chestnut, apple, and cherry trees grew wild down the slope to the Loire, where the big willows drooped low over the water.

The formal parks and gardens of the château were overgrown and neglected because of the war with England, but Mary looked forward to overseeing the work of bringing them back to their former beauty.

There were so many things to look forward to: happy years at Blois, and also many children—especially sons, for Orleans, Blois, and the whole province would revert to the Crown if there were no son to inherit.

First she would have three boys, Mary had decided, and then it would be safe to have a girl. But months had gone by, and then, more and more apprehensively, the years had gone by and she was still waiting. She had become frightened and spent all her days at her altar, her clear, earnest voice intoning the litanies, praying for a son, until one day Charles had come to her room and found her, a weeping little bundle, at the foot of her prie-dieu. He had lifted her in his arms and sat with her in a big tapestried armchair, alarmed at her trembling frailness, and reproached himself that he had not seen her serious condition before.

He spoke very sternly to her. "It evidently hasn't occurred to you that you're making me ridiculous with your constant supplications to Heaven for a son."

Mary looked at him in bewilderment, but he avoided her eyes and continued, "Heaven, you know, is not entirely responsible for the birth of children. A woman generally requires some assistance from her husband."

Mary's face was averted and flushed. The details of confinement were not strange to her, but the odd act of procreation was laid away in the darkness of silence.

"I'm not a young man, as you know, Mary. I'm—what is it now?—almost sixty, and some people are laughing and saying it is not Heaven's help you need but a younger husband."

Mary's anger swept her embarrassment away and she sprang from her husband's arms to confront him in fury at this insult to his virility.

"Who dares to say such a thing? It is my fault! I am silly and wicked—I have such *wicked* thoughts, Charles, and it is my punishment that I can't give you a son. But if they would only see"—she had gestured toward the altar as though all the unreasonable saints were there—"if they would only see it is not fair to *you!* I have prayed to have a son, and then, for my punishment, I would be glad to die!"

Charles had reached out and pulled her back into his arms. He had known what her wicked thoughts were: only a half-formed, instinctive longing for youth and eagerness to match her own. She had been trained to obedience, but no matter how obedient her mind tried to be, her heart and body knew what they needed—love, and the excited look she saw in the eyes of people in love. She did not formulate it to herself; she was only half conscious of a lack in her life, vaguely disturbed by something everyone else seemed to know about but which must have passed her by.

Still it was pleasant enough. She loved Charles as she had never been able to love her own father, and Charles, growing always more remote from life, loved her with kind affection and asked no more from her. She reproached herself that she couldn't give him more, and her conscience, always overstern with her faults, knew all too well what should be due a husband. But reproach and instruct as much as she would, her stubborn emotions refused to yield. Charles knew all this and, remembering his own youth and its many loves, he saw he had been wrong to think he had anything to offer Mary of Cleves. He had thought wryly if he had it to do over, he would forget her sunlit beauty and marry a widow of his own age, or, for that matter, no one at all if he couldn't have children. He had sighed and recalled himself. He could regret his mistakes another time.

"I must have failed to show you my love if you think a son could compensate to me for your loss. Because we have been disappointed is no reason to embitter our lives. We must return to more pleasant ways."

Mary had started to protest, then her voice trailed off into an awed silence as her mind looked ahead and thought how wonderful it would be to return to life with a conscience at rest. To know it was not her fault!

Charles had watched her realization, his face, always gentle, grave and sympathetic. It was all he could do for her: take away her load of worry and return her pleasures, although they held no appeal for him any longer. His books and poetry were all that he needed, but she was restless because, never having known love, unconsciously she still looked for it. Charles's lips had smiled a little in his light brown beard as he saw how easily he had relieved her mind. She was so in awe of his wisdom it would never have occurred to her to disobey him. She pinned her faith to the Virgin Mary, the saints, and Charles, and it was one of her "wicked thoughts" that Charles usually seemed more reasonable than the saints.

This reverence seemed all the more touching to him because nowhere else in the world did he inspire respect. Long forgotten while he was in his English prison, he was for the most part thought unimportant and even ridiculous at court. He didn't like to leave his province, and the empty formality of the court bored him. However, he went, because of his position and its duties, sometimes to Tours, in the king's province of Berry, where King Charles VII lived most of the time, and sometime to Versailles and Paris, or wherever the States-General convened. He always took Mary so that she might have the social life she loved.

She had thought of it as she rested against him. That year at court would be perfect; she would have the finest of new clothing, she would dance and coquette—nothing serious, of course, but perhaps there would be some dark young man with burning eyes who would love her hopelessly and publicly. And there would be no galling reproach this year in the sight of the queen with her son and the other mothers with their sons.

It is not my fault, Charles says it is not my fault! Her thoughts sang inside her, and she had shuddered with relief.

"What is it?" Charles had been startled to find her shivering against him.

"You are so good to me," she had said fervently, feeling she could never do enough for this man to show her gratitude.

"Am I, my dear?" he murmured thoughtfully, but he was thinking ruefully that the best thing he could do for her would be to die and leave her a young widow.

And leave this land of Orleans to the Crown! said that persistent voice that was constantly in his mind, that woke him often at night and drove him to his chamber window to look out across the moonlit land he had loved more lastingly than he had ever loved women, the land that would pass away from his family forever when he died and belong to the king because there was no Orleans son.

Often he had stood there at the window until dawn, won-

dering why it meant so much to him that when he died
there would be no one of his name to live at Blois. He had
looked at the dark green hills; they sloped down softly and
ended in the generous Loire River that would be a shining
black mirror in the moonlight. What would it matter to
these century-old hills if other than Orleans feet were upon
them? Land was untouchable; if his son would never love
the great trees his fathers had planted nor drink the wine
they had laid down, some other man's son would. And so
he tried to console himself for a grief he didn't understand,
to reason with an instinct that had nothing to do with
reason.

Resigning himself to the fact that Orleans must return to
the Crown at his death, still Charles had other smaller
properties that could be willed at his desire, and having no
young relatives of his own, he had ridden one day to see his
good neighbor and friend, the Duke of Bourbon.

Bourbon was older than Charles, but his marriage had
been too fruitful, producing ten sons, eight more than he
could provide for. When he had heard Charles's difficulties,
he whistled and shouted until all of his sons had gathered
and offered up any one of them, except his first and second
born, to Charles for adoption.

"A likely litter!" he commented to Charles, his arms
about his two eldest as he surveyed the others, and Charles
felt a stab of envy while he smilingly agreed. "Which of the
pups would you have? René, there"—pointing to one of the
youngest, a dark, grinning, impish face on an agile little
body—"is just the one if you wish to live in constant
anxiety. He falls from the highest branches of the tallest
trees, he is thrown and kicked by the strongest horses, but
he comes rolling and scrambling to his feet and before you
have recovered your breath he is smiling again—like that.
But one day"—Bourbon shook his finger warningly at the
laughing boy—"you will not bounce!"

Charles laughed too, liking the boy, and yet for his purposes he preferred someone who was not so suicidally in-
clined. Bourbon saw that and was glad, for after Louis, his
eldest, René was his favorite.

He went on to describe some of the others. "Armand,
there, I do not recommend"—he smiled at the boy to take
any possible hurt from his words—"for he inclines toward
the church, and it would please his mother to see him there.

I think your choice might better be between Denis and Pierre." Pierre was the fifth son, a boy of twelve, and Denis was the seventh, six years old.

Charles looked at them both, embarrassed by the solemn gaze of waiting eyes, and decided quickly on Pierre, for there was the slightest resemblance, of color mostly, between the boy and Mary, and he was strong and sturdily built.

"If I may," Charles said, going to Pierre and putting his hand on the boy's shoulder, "I should like Pierre."

His decision had pleased everyone, although it surprised Bourbon, for he had always considered Pierre amiable and willing but very slow. Still it was all most satisfactory, and the two men went into the house to celebrate the new addition to the Orleans family. When Pierre was ready to go with Charles they set off in a merry and mellow mood, Charles already beginning to feel the pride of a father as he noted the boy's strong hands with the horse, his excellent carriage and his sturdy physique.

Pierre was pleased with the decision too, for his prospects had changed very suddenly from those of a much younger brother in a house with too many of them to those of a foster son of a powerful family with an excellent future.

He had soon become devoted to his new father and mother, especially to Mary. She was not so very much older than he, and sometimes they played games together like children. Mary was delighted with life these days, and after the release from her accusing conscience almost everything aroused her high, clear laughter. The more sedate persons among their circle of friends began to think her a shade too lighthearted and gay, almost—well, loose, they finally decided. But she knew how completely Charles trusted her and she paid no attention to appearances, flirting with this gentleman and that, wondering if the sudden confusions and embarrassments she felt were love.

In what she felt was a very cunning manner she had encouraged Charles to talk of love.

"How did you feel when you first loved me?" she asked, and Charles obligingly told her. In retrospect he loved romantically and desperately, collecting together all the great and ennobling emotions he had ever felt or read or written about and presented them to her as love.

When he had finished he could see her mentally compar-

ing her little set of symptoms with this wonderful thing that
he described. She would sit in thought for a moment, her
blond head set reflectively on one side, and then she would
shake it gravely, "No," and sigh ruefully. She never
dreamed he could see what she was thinking, and he would
regard her amusedly, marking his place in the book with
his finger, ready to answer her questions in the way that
would do most good. What he would do if she nodded her
head "Yes" he didn't know.

While Charles had sat comfortably in his chair, his book
on his knee, lecturing on love to his wife, France and
England were drawing to a close the exhausting struggle
that had lasted more or less continuously for one hundred
years, and in the early spring of 1453 the winter ice and the
winter truce had cracked again. Little rivulets of water
trickled in the roads, broadening and deepening as other
rivulets joined them, just as small groups of men trickled
out of the small towns, laughing and waving good-by, their
ranks broadening as they joined other small groups at crossroads. They followed the dukes who were their leaders and
walked northward, until one misty morning near Calais the
French Army fought and completely reversed the decision
of Agincourt. The English lost every piece of ground they
had taken throughout the entire war, and the Hundred
Years' War was over.

The lands of Orleans had suffered badly; Charles had
only a small remnant of the wealth he had once possessed.
The price of his ransom alone had been ruinous, and it was
only a grant of money from the grateful king that enabled
him to begin the work of rebuilding his towns and repairing
his countryside. The new young steward, the Sire de Mornac, worked hard and long to build up the properties,
regardless of the fact that Orleans would revert to the
Crown and the rest of the lands to Pierre, another man's
son.

A day in December 1457 changed some of these plans,
for Charles found himself the amazed father of a baby
daughter, Marie-Louise. He was sixty-three; everyone, including himself, was astonished.

Bourbon was bedridden, but he hoisted himself onto a
horse and came riding to Blois to celebrate with his friend.

In the dining hall, before a big fire that roared defiance at
the dim, chilly corners of the room, the men warmed their

backs at the blaze while they toasted Mary and the baby and the king and themselves in good red wine imported from Spain. They both knew they would pay for their recklessness the next day.

"But a girl!" Bourbon finally mourned. "It is very like you to have had the luxury before you achieved the necessity. Still"—he brightened—"if you can have one, you can have the other. Next time it will be a boy." And they drank a toast to next time, preferring to forget, in the glow the wine brought them, that there probably wasn't time for a next time.

"This will make no difference to Pierre's prospects," Charles had assured Bourbon. "He and my daughter Marie-Louise shall marry." And the two friends smiled together over the most agreeable prospect of their friendship being perpetuated in their children's marriage. So the fourteen-year-old boy had been betrothed to the week-old baby and he had only to wait twelve years or so for his bride.

Charles's parental pride in his pretty baby daughter had been so exaggerated as to be ludicrous. He tiptoed in and out of the busy nursery a dozen times a day, exasperating the nurses with his whispered questions and commands. Fearful that the supply of milk might be exhausted, he had hired so many wet nurses that the west wing of the servants' quarters was crowded with them and their babies.

When Marie-Louise opened wide her little toothless mouth and screamed, Charles was in a panic for fear she was ill. When she slept in motionless quiet in her carved-oak and satin-padded cradle, he was sure her breathing had stopped and she was dead. To reassure himself, he would gently touch the baby's warm, moist cheek, feel the faint breath on his hands, then stand in silent awe, searching for poetic words to express his feelings, finding all words inadequate before the exquisite purity of the sleeping child.

When Marie-Louise was three, his pride in her had made him long to show her to all his world, and he planned a state procession throughout the province of Orleans, stopping at the principal towns and, as a royal gesture, releasing and pardoning prisoners in the jails.

Mary was uneasy about this procession; not that her pride in the child was less than his—for Marie-Louise was an adorable baby; her smooth pink cheeks, her big blue eyes, golden curls, gentle smile and disposition all made her the perfect picture of an angel child—but processions like this were for sons, not daughters, and it was still a constant wound in Mary's heart that she had given Charles no son, only a daughter, no matter how sweet that daughter might be.

But Charles couldn't be dissuaded. Since the child's birthday was in December, too cold a month for parading on horseback, Charles selected Mary's birthday, in the spring, and on a soft April day a colorful cavalcade clattered into the narrow cobblestoned streets of Blois. The townspeople crowded out into the streets and leaned out to wave from the small glassless windows of their houses, and the peasant farmers and their wives had neglected their fields for the day to come in and cheer their duke and his daughter.

Charles rode a brown satin-skinned mare, chosen for her gentleness, so that in the excitement of the parade she wouldn't rear up and startle the small white horse beside her, on which Marie-Louise was mounted, carefully tied into a padded velvet and gold saddle shaped like a chair seat.

Her big blue eyes, under her tall white satin hat embroidered with gold thread, looked out in childish interest over the shouting crowds that lined the streets. She didn't understand their excitement, nor why they were shouting her name or her faher's, and once, when the noise grew too loud and the crowds threatened to press too close, her lower lip pushed out, preparatory to tears, and her pink little chin began to quiver. Charles, watching anxiously, leaned over and patted her hand reassuringly, calling to his guards to keep the enthusiastic crowds back.

The peasant women in their gray wool dresses and best white caps, and the burghers' wives in wool or velvet, depending on their husbands' incomes, all caught their breath in maternal feeling. "A-a-ah," they exclaimed, in a long-drawn-out sigh, "the poor little one is frightened! The little darling——" And nothing that the child could have done could possibly have endeared her to them more, for her small pouting mouth, her round eyes filling with fright, suddenly changed her from a remote Princess of Orleans, aloof and above them, into a small child in need of comfort like their own François or Françoise.

The women reached out and sternly hushed their shouting menfolk. "Stop it, you idiots!" they commanded. "You scare the baby with your silly noise!"

The shouting died down abruptly, and a hush fell while they all looked up anxiously to see whether the child would cry. When Marie-Louise, reassured by her father's touch, smiled and waved her hand, waggling her plump little fingers as she had been taught to do, a shout of spontaneous laughter went up from the crowd. Something about the sound of it must have tickled Marie-Louise, for she put her head back and laughed aloud too, her little white teeth glistening in her pink mouth. The crowd went wild with delight in her; their cheers reverberated against the tall stone houses of the narrow street, and Charles felt his pride expanding until it too must express itself in a shout of triumph.

The procession, the hundred Orleans horsemen preceding the duke and his daughter, and the hundred horsemen following them, drew up in the town square before the big stone buildings that housed the town council and, off to one side, the grim, graystone building that was the jail. The horsemen, their chain-mail armor, their spurs rattling, galloped to the stairs of the council building, then spread out in formation, allowing the duke and his daughter to ride through the ranks, halting, too, at the steps of the building where the town council nervously waited to render their homage. A little seven-year-old girl, the mayor's daughter, dressed in the Orleans colors, desperately clutched an armful of roses for Orleans, lilies for France, which she was to present to Marie-Louise with a little speech at the proper moment in the ceremonies. The poor child forgot her speech, dropped the flowers at the horse's feet, and butted her head in an agony of embarrassment into her father's robe. Otherwise the affair went off smoothly enough, and for the climax Marie-Louise was presented with the gold key to open the jail and release the prisoners.

Marie-Louise didn't want the big, glittering piece of metal, so Charles accepted it for her, then handed it back to the councilman, who handed it to the main official of the prison, who handed it to his first assistant, who, after a deep bow, walked over to the big iron-hinged door and acted as though he were unlocking it.

The key was only a dramatic gesture, of course. It had

been made for occasions like this. Sometimes it was the symbolic key to the town gates, to be loyally presented to the duke of the province whenever he came through; sometimes it was the key to their hearts, to their hospitality—at any rate, it was a very nice-looking gold key.

No key at all was really needed for the outer door to the jail—the keys to the inner cells had all been used an hour ago, and the prisoners were ready and waiting behind the front door, waiting for the moment when it would be opened and they could walk out to the freedom that Marie-Louise's third birthday had unexpectedly brought them.

The door creaked slowly and dramatically opened, and out they came, almost two hundred of them. (About sixty of them had been arrested just the night before, so that the day's performance might be a more impressive one.) They were an assorted lot as they crowded out of the door and then, once outside, more slowly trickled down the steps toward their duke, who was waiting for their gratitude. About a fourth of them were women, a ragged, blowzy lot, jailed for petty thievery mostly, with a few locked up for murder or, more important, throwing garbage or emptying pots out the window, a habit the town fathers were trying to discourage. Most of the men were in for robbery, murder, or treason, which was a popular charge and covered a lot of uncertain ground. Altogether they were a very disagreeable-looking bunch as they knelt on the hard stones around the duke and his daughter.

Charles motioned to the guards not to let them kneel too close; their gratitude had too strong a stench of prison life about it, and as the last one came out the April sun went behind a cloud as though to shield its face from the unpleasant aroma. It was just as well the sun did hide itself; it enabled some of the prisoners to open their eyes a little more to the brightness of the day after their days, or months, or, in some cases, years, in the windowless darkness of a cellar jail.

The din was appalling as they all shouted their protestations of gratitude and the ones who were jailed for treason all vowed renewed loyalty to the Duke of Orleans at the tops of their lungs. The women cried and tried to force their way through the crowds to kiss the duke's hands, while Marie-Louise looked on, too scared to cry.

Finally the pandemonium calmed down, and the prisoners dispersed to celebrate their freedom.

The next year, 1461, Charles VII of France came to his pitiful end, practically starving himself to death because of his constant fear that his son was trying to poison him. Whether Louis XI actively plotted his father's death was impossible to know—certainly he made no secret of the fact that he was eager for his father to die. When the king was finally frightened into his grave, Louis XI greedily took the throne, wild with impatience to feel the crown firmly on his head and to put his thousands of plans into operation.

The coronation that began the "Spider King's" long, intricate reign was a great, glittering pageant and a parade through the towns of France—the first move in his deliberate advertising campaign to gain popularity in the towns by spending money freely there.

Charles of Orleans had gone to Paris to see his cousin's entry into that city. King Louis was cordial and affectionate to his land-rich relative, whose lands he hoped soon to inherit. The king looked searchingly at the aging Charles and was pleased, as he had been pleased to see death's approaching shadow on his father's face, to see that Charles's health was failing. It had seemed perfectly safe to let him return to his wife at Blois, so the king released Charles from his duties at court, letting him return home. The king said a polite farewell, expecting never to see or hear of Charles again, except for the welcome news of his death.

But it had been in June of the next year that Charles, in awe and wonder, had stood looking down at the face of his newborn son. His age-dimmed eyes were tear-dimmed too, and his throat was aching with a joy almost too large to contain.

"My son, Louis!" he had whispered, so that he should not shout it aloud.

He had turned and looked at the bed; he wanted to see his wife's eyes. She had been watching him across the confusion of hurrying women who attended her, and she was not smiling. This was a thing too wonderful to smile about. It had been a long and painful birth, for it was five years since her daughter had been born and she was not so strong or so young as she had been then. On the satin sheets she had writhed and moaned, while the king's witnesses, and all those who were privileged to attend at the birth of a prince of the blood, intently watched. She had screamed only once, just as the child was born, and it was a scream of such sharp and tearing agony that Charles covered his ears against the pain of it; but she had forgotten it as she lay back against the fresh, smooth pillows her women arranged for her.

That was the moment she had wished for during all the years of their life together, and time stopped for her while she looked into her husband's eyes. That was the moment she had been willing to give her life for. Now it was hers and it was as wonderful as she had ever thought it would be. Her body was so exhausted that she had lost consciousness of it completely, but she was wildly grateful to it for giving Charles what he had so long wanted. Throughout the anxious months of her pregnancy she had done everything she could imagine to insure that it would be a boy. She had performed strange rituals, she had starved herself, she had eaten only sour foods until her mouth and throat had felt puckered and dry. Nothing that had ever been suggested had been too repugnant for her to do, and she had her reward in Charles's eyes.

So that now, the christening over, the baby's future already richly planned, Charles could look down at the red wrinkled face of his newborn son—"My son, Louis!"— and then past the baby's face out into the summer day where the sunlit lands of Orleans, not to be lost now through lack of a son to bear the ancient Orleans name, lay as still and tranquil as they had during his nights of despair.

The king looked at these same hills and cursed as he jolted back along the road to Tours in the big swaying carriage.

Carriages were bumpy instruments of torture, since most of the country roads were mud half the year and hard, sun-baked ridges the rest of the time. No one who could get upon a horse's back ever used a carriage, but since a recent trip through another duke's province, when a sudden arrow from a longbow had come winging toward him out of nowhere and, just missing him, had killed his horse, the king thought travel by well-padded carriage was sometimes wise, if not more comfortable; at least the many bruises weren't fatal.

It was a hot June day and the king simmered and boiled in a heat of his own. He had expected to possess all this rich land, marked off in neat green farms, that slid so bumpily past his carriage window when that old fool Charles of Orleans should die in a few years.

The sun-browned peasants, who gathered in little groups at the edges of the fields to salute and call out as the king's carriage passed, would have been his personal subjects. King Louis had gloated over the map and wiped out the boundary line that separated his own province of Berry from the province of Orleans and smiled to see how large and strong it looked. Now he would have to put back the line, forget the rich fertile fields, the strongly fortified towns, and all because the duchess had borne a son!

His secretary, Oliver le Daim, seeing the king's disposition, withdrew as far into the corner of the rocking carriage as his plump figure would allow. His ever-increasing weight bothered him today; his full face was red and perspiring with heat; his tights were uncomfortable and damp with sweat. He was hungry—he was always hungry—and melancholy because it was his fortieth birthday and he would have liked to have been in a cool, dim inn somewhere, celebrating with wine and a stuffed boar's head, or maybe a roast fowl. Instead his short, round figure was being bounced from one carriage wall to another, and his master was glaring at him as though he would like to strike him.

The king stirred and released some of his furious irritation by striking Oliver a sharp blow across the shins with his cane. "Wake up, Oliver! You frighten the horses with your hideous snoring."

Oliver hadn't, of course, been asleep, much less snoring, but he was used to apologizing for things he hadn't done. He apologized thoroughly but made the mistake of sighing.

The king heard the sigh, said sharply: "I seem to be wearying you today, Oliver. Perhaps you would prefer to get out of the carriage and walk for a way?"

Oliver looked at the broiling sun and shivered. "Thank you, Monseigneur, but unless you wish me to, I had rather stay where I am. My sigh was not from ennui; I was sharing in a small way your disappointment over this child's unfortunate birth."

"It does us no good to dwell on it, since we can't prove which side of the blanket he was born on—but I shall never forget he has no right to the land at all. If he were not heir presumptive to the throne," the king muttered darkly, "he'd never see his second birthday, but as it is——"

"He won't be heir presumptive for very long," Oliver consoled him. "And when your son is born, then it will be a good time for little Louis of Orleans to have the colic and die."

"And if I never have a son?" asked the king, with a menacing glance that seemed to indicate Oliver would be blamed if such a thing should happen.

"Oh, but you will," Oliver said hastily. "You already have a daughter."

Yes, he already had a little baby daughter, Anne, and his wife was pregnant again. He planned to keep her that way for many years to come. That was all wives were good for; scornfully he thought of the two wives he had possessed. His first, Margaret of Scotland, had been given to him by his father, and like everything else his father had given him, he had hated her. Frivolous, extravagant, barren, and consumptive, she had died at twenty-one of some sudden unexplained malady—his enemies had said poison, of course.

His second wife, Charlotte of Savoy, he had chosen himself. She was a tepid, colorless fool, but at least not a barren one. He thought of her with contempt—her young timidity, her feeble attempts at friendliness, her resigned, trembling body submitted patiently to his marital rights and then, her head turned into her pillow, crying her lonely heart out for Savoy. Such an endless fool! Crying her nights away for Savoy when she was Queen of France! *Of France!* But even if she drowned herself in tears, she understood thoroughly the necessity for producing children, and that was all that could be expected of a woman.

"Women are all fools," he told Oliver. "No wits, no logic, no pride, no honor, no strength! It surprises me sometimes that God should have made such a creature, with so little to recommend it but a breeding place for children."

Oliver agreed quickly. "A world without women would be a happier place."

The King pondered that soberly, then rallied loyally to

God's defense. "But that would make a Heaven unnecessary, and God required a Heaven."

The king was a very religious man; his clothes, his shabby black hat were sprinkled with religious medals, and he talked over all his plans for France with God and the angels, taking great pains sometimes to explain the necessity that had called for some particularly devious act. But since God was, after all, only a greater king, He would understand that scruples were expensive and did not often go with a throne. Once, having resorted to a particularly evil poison-murder of an uncle who had opposed a plan of his, the king spent several hours in the church telling the Virgin Mary, with emphasis, that it should not be entered against him in the heavenly records since he had done it for the good of France, which was a religion in itself. For all his sharp wit, he saw no humor in this explanation.

Only thirty-nine, he thought often and fearfully of death. His thin spare figure was usually clothed in black; his stern, dark face, shadowed by large black eyebrows that extended across his nose and met in one continuous dark frown, was further shadowed by the black straight-visored hat, plain and shabby, decorated with tokens of the saints. His hair hung long and unkempt, a reproach to the courtiers who were more vain and wore theirs curled, bewigged, or more trimly cut.

"Yes, I have a daughter," he sighed, and returned to the subject that gnawed his mind, "and I made use of her today. I betrothed her to the Orleans brat!" With some amusement he watched Oliver's round red face stiffen in amazement, and then after a moment he exclaimed impatiently, "Well, Oliver, when you were my barber, it seemed to me your wits were as sharp as your knives. Have I made a mistake in making you my secretary—shall I return you to your soap and your razors?"

"Oh no, Monseigneur," Oliver protested hurriedly. "I was taken by surprise—I didn't see the meaning in your plan."

He didn't see it yet, but he didn't want to admit it or lose his valuable post, probably the most peculiar position ever held by a man born to be a barber and ending as confidant to a king. In the whole kingdom Oliver was the only person admitted to the secrets of King Louis XI. On the king's good days Oliver was happy, proud of the king's trust, flattered to have the princes and lords beg for his influence with the king. On the king's bad days—and there were plenty, because Louis XI was sharp, sarcastic, uncomfortable to be with—Oliver wished the king had never laid eyes on him. Now he squirmed under the king's sardonic eyes.

"I am sure you see now, Oliver, that if I never have a son to be King of France, then at least I may have a daughter who will be its queen. If I take pains to train her correctly, even though she is only a woman, it would be better than having no blood of mine near the throne."

Oliver was nodding hastily. "I see all that, Monseigneur. What I didn't understand was that you had changed your plan to betroth the Princes Anne to Jean of Calabria."

The king answered impatiently: "No plans are changed —she is promised to Calabria. Also to Savoy. Perhaps also to Aquitaine—and now today"—his tight, bloodless lips tightened—"to Orleans!"

"But—Monseigneur——" Oliver floundered, yearning for an intelligent question to ask or comment to make.

"But nothing, barber. Promises are seeds—not all of them grow very tall. Calabria comes of sickly stock—he'll never live to have a wife. Savoy, I may take another way. Orleans I hope will die in his cradle! It would make me ill with disgust to marry my daughter to that bastard brat, but if he married elsewhere and had sons, Orleans would never come to the Crown. And I must have Orleans." His eyes looked greedily out at the fertile fields. "Orleans—yes, and Bourbon, Anjou, and Maine, Picardy and Brittany," he muttered, looking into the future.

"Burgundy too," said Oliver, and could have torn out his tongue in the next second, for if there was another tender subject with the king, that was it. Burgundy was the strongest province in France, very nearly equaling in concentrated power, if not in land, the strength of the throne, and Charles the Bold, of Burgundy, was all his name implied and more.

The king exploded, shook his fist in Oliver's face, and his voice was hoarse with anger. "Burgundy! That blustering fool! Hell is eager for his soul—and I am eager hell should not be made to wait! All of them—all the dukes like him who hold their lands as private to their names—and make their greedy private wars, caring nothing for the way they weaken France! Making it an easy victim for England! All those names—Burgundy—Orleans—all must die out that France may live—and I am the one sent by God to stamp them out—one by one!"

There was urgent purpose in his implacable voice, and Oliver was impressed and convinced. In the short year since the king had come to the throne he had already done much to accomplish his one desire—to nationalize France, strengthen the power of the throne by weakening the power of the feudal lords. It was already a well-worn struggle, and the king's popularity was at a very low ebb with the great duchies of his kingdom, for naturally they fought for their ancient privileges without appreciating his larger ideal for France.

To achieve this ideal he schemed and angled, inciting one province against another, then striking both himself when they had sufficiently weakened each other; bribing where he dared not strike, buying land he wasn't strong enough to take, his knifelike mind approaching obstacles sharply, its razor edge whittling, carving, cautiously shaving away with infinite patience and finesse, until they were obstacles no longer, only a pile of shavings, wood curls, and sawdust to be blown away with one strong breath.

And if his brilliant mind failed and fell short of being a great and wise one, it was because he saw and understood only one half of the human character. A bitter cynic, in all his plans he allowed for treachery, betrayal, and weakness, but he never expected honesty or strength of purpose. Integrity was a hypocrisy to him, a dignified haggling over price, for he was willing to stake his soul there wasn't a man in the world who could not be bought at some price or other, and his soul was very dear to him.

"Burgundy!" he said again, and deliberately kicked Oliver on the anklebone. "A curse on Burgundy and all of them! And must you take up all the room in the carriage with your monstrous fat legs?"

Oliver winced, longed to bend and rub his ankle but didn't dare, and they rode back the rest of the way to the bleak, unfriendly fortress of Tours in complete venomous silence.

2

There was no other place so satisfactory for playing tennis alone, young Louis of Orleans decided, as a moat—with the water drained out, of course. This moat had never had water in it at all; the brick and stone floor was fairly smooth under his soft leather boots, the stone side walls were high enough so the ball didn't bounce out and close enough so that one hard, well-driven stroke of the gut-stringed racquet would send the ball rebounding back and forth from each wall several times. He kept count, trying for a record, and so far he had made the ball touch each wall three times. Of course this was just the narrow little moat at Amboise, where the court was in summer residence. In the big moat at Plessis-les-Tours his record was only one bounce off each wall.

Although Louis wasn't nine yet, he could already beat most of the older boys and his foster brother Pierre too. Once he had actually tied the champion, René de Bourbon, and he trained ceaselessly, dreaming about the day when he would beat René.

Louis was tall for his age, and judging from his strongly modeled head, his wide shoulders, well developed from riding and hunting, and his long hands, the fingers powerful from clenching the reins of a horse, a sword at dueling practice, and a tennis racquet, he showed every indication of being an unusually tall man. His hair was almost black, cut short, the ends baked crisp and dry, bleached to golden highlights by the sun.

His eyes, over the high-bridged long nose, were almost black too, with flecks of yellow in the dark brown around the black pupil. He always held them wide open, as though eager to see everything at once. His full dark eyebrows arched high, one higher than the other because he had had the pox when he was three (the king had prayed for his

death, but the illness had left only two small scars in his left
eyebrow, which had thinned out the hair and arched it
higher than the right). It gave his eyes, intelligent and
quick to laughter, a slightly quizzical expression. Another
small scar had been flatteringly placed by chance—and a
fall off his horse when he was five. He had cut his cheek
open on a stirrup guard, but the wound had healed quickly,
leaving only a small indentation at the corner of his mouth,
accentuating the redness of his lips like a small white com-
ma against his clear, dark skin. In the summer he was very
brown; in the winter he faded to a creamy tan and he was
restless until the spring came and warmth was in the sun
again. All his life he was to disdain the face masks that
most of the courtiers wore to protect their skin when they
went out into the hot glare or rode horseback in a biting
wind. Louis always seemed to draw renewed vitality from
the elements—the sun exhilarated him, the buffeting winds
roused his warm blood to vigorous protests.

He loved water, too, and when he was home at Blois
sometimes he would go swimming in the Loire. He would
dive off the high bank, sometimes clear to the shallow,
sandy bottom, and come up slowly, holding his breath, his
dark eyes wide open, looking up through the disturbed
churning water and the bubbles in it toward the glittering
surface and the shining blue sky above the willow tops. His
mother couldn't see the charm of swimming at all. No one
she had ever known went swimming unless he fell over-
board, and since the Loire wasn't the cleanest river in
France, Mary hated him to go in it, but he didn't see how
the Loire could be as filthy as she said and still leave him
feeling so fresh and clean.

The only sport Louis didn't care for, if it could be called
a sport, was dancing. There seemed to be no objective to it,
no records to be made, and the formal patterned steps were
a strain on legs that were used to running and leaping. Still
his mother insisted he should practice with her and his
tutor, and because he had the quick co-ordination of an
athlete, he was a good dancer.

But of all the sports, tennis was his favorite, and doggedly he practiced his hard driving forehand, his whirling back-
hand until his doublet was ripped at the seams, two strings
of his racquet were broken, and his dripping perspiration
threatened to fill the moat. Then, his breath whistling

through his teeth, his heart thudding against his ribs, he climbed the jagged steps out of the moat, crossed the courtyard, took a short cut through the stables, through several gates and down a path, into the cool wooded gardens of the king's château.

He flopped down on his stomach beside a pretty little pool with a trickling fountain in the center and, disregarding the red and gold fish which darted around in the green shaded water, Louis cupped his hands, filled them with the cool liquid, and bathed his hot head and face.

Far down the grassy slope, on the next terrace of the beautifully landscaped gardens, ladies and gentlemen of the king's court made a gay picture in their brightly colored costumes as they sat on the white marble benches in the shade of the patterned silk awning over the summer pavilion. Their leisurely laughter drifted up the slope, mingling with the music of the ballad singers who performed for them in the smaller music pavilion. The king wasn't among his attendants—he rarely was if he could help it. He thought his dukes and duchesses, his counts and their ladies were a silly bunch of fools, and since he made no attempt to hide his opinion, his absence was always appreciated.

Queen Charlotte wasn't in the pavilion either, so the laughter was louder, the gossip more impudent on this bright May afternoon at the court's favorite summer residence. Everyone preferred the beautiful château at Amboise on the Loire to the chilly fortress at Tours, except the king, who felt safer behind the high, windowless walls of Plessis-les-Tours, but the queen's pregnant condition had caused him to be unusually indulgent and yield to her preference for once.

Louis liked Amboise too, almost as well as his own home at Blois, and as the king had insisted, Louis was frequently at court, as familiar with the king's château as he was with his own.

Cooled now by the water and the shade, Louis idly took up his broken racquet and, using it as a net, tried to scoop up some of the goldfish.

A shadow fell across the water and a girl's warning voice said: "Louis, my father will see you fishing in his pond." It was the Princess Anne of France speaking.

Louis looked up, smiled welcomingly when he saw it was Anne, then went on fishing as she settled herself carefully on the grass beside him, her back against the trunk of the large willow tree, her dark eyes, under the straight dark brows, watching him interestedly. Anne was not a pretty girl yet, but she had an attractive, interesting face. It was heart-shaped; her one really beautiful feature was her lovely curved mouth, the upper lip full and fresh. She had been taught to take good care of her skin; it was pale ivory and very clear. Her rounded nose was a little too large for her small face, but it was proud and imperious like the sharp little chin held high by a slim throat.

She, like Louis, loved bold, bright colors, and they were both particularly fond of scarlets, greens, and yellows. Today his doublet was a deep red, her gown was green. Her hair was hidden so that only the dark peak that grew down onto her forehead could be seen under the high green conical hat draped with a silver-and-white veil. Since royal children's clothes were miniature copies of an adult's, Louis wore man's boots, tights, doublets or fur-trimmed jackets, and his hats were turbans or wide-brimmed felts trimmed with plumes, and no concession to childhood was made in Anne's tight velvet bodices, the gold-brocaded stomachers, the full, long, fur-banded skirts. On her small feet she wore satin slippers, and to protect them when she went outside she slipped into flat wooden pattens which were held on each foot by a strap over the instep. There could be no childish skipping in these, even if the child could ignore the constricting stomacher and the tall hennin perched precariously on her head. The clothes themselves had a sobering and maturing effect on the royal children, and their costumes were the least important causes of maturity way beyond their years. From their cradles they were conscious of their own importance; it was constantly emphasized that they were a necessary link between the past and future greatness of their respective houses and, as such, they must be guarded from the many frightening plots against their safety. A sense of fear, of caution, is an aging emotion; it stole many hours of their childhood. And the boring hours standing beside the king's throne through endless state ceremonies, riding in the king's processions through his "good towns," listening to the long, repetitive speeches of welcome —there was no concession to childish weariness there!

Then the constant adult talk of marriage, stressing again and again the need for sons to carry on the name and

property of the house, put old thoughts in their young
minds and left no room for childish innocence.

The ground around a throne was a hotbed, a forcing
frame, ripening their youth to quick, full-blown maturity,
but even in the lower classes a girl of twelve was a young
woman, ready in body and mind for marriage. A boy of
fourteen was a young man, equal to war's responsibilities
and the adventures of sex. Of course their life span was
different—they matured early and aged more quickly. The
average woman was old at forty, sick and dying at fifty.
Even as they rose earlier in the morning with the light and
went to bed soon after the sun went down because they
lacked an easy, artificial light, so did their lives rise and
fall, maturing earlier and declining sooner, thus Louis and
Anne at nine were a mixture of youth and maturity.

"You know those fish aren't to be caught," Anne was saying. She was always telling Louis he shouldn't do something
and then curiously watching while he went on doing it.
"They were a present from Italy. Anyway, what would you
do with one if you did catch it?"

Louis didn't expect to catch any, but he answered carelessly, "Maybe I'll have one cooked and eat it!"

Anne laughed. "They'd poison you. They've got poison
in a little sac under their gills—it's there purposely so big
fish won't eat them."

Louis stared at the shimmering red-gold fish that darted
about in the clear green water. Anne knew too much and
didn't mind showing it. Outside of that, though, she was
perfect, and he valued her good opinion. So he said shortly,
"Of course I know they're poison!" Then to clinch the matter
he added, "I'm taller than you are!"

"But I'm older," she said smugly, and she was, by a matter of a few months. She was nine; he would be nine next
month.

He had a good answer for that, though. "You're a girl!"
he told her.

She couldn't deny it. Not any more, although she used
to. She always used to tell him she was dressed as a girl
only to fool people because her father had enemies who
would kill her if they knew she was going to grow up to be
king.

Louis had half believed her and had been miserable about
it, for if she was a boy, he wouldn't be able to marry her,

and, next in importance, he'd never be king. But King Louis XI's court was not a place where innocence lived very long; as the Orleans boy grew a little older he found out a few salient facts, and one day when Anne said she was a boy Louis demanded visual proof.

It had seemed a perfectly fair request to him. If she was a boy, what did she have to be so shocked about? If she was a girl, then all she had to do was admit it and that was that.

Anne had refused proof but still insisted she was a boy, so Louis had set out to investigate for himself. It had been a remarkable battle. The king's daughter had fought like a cat and screamed like a falcon, bringing to her aid some horrified witnesses.

Louis had been switched by the king himself and lectured by the bishop, who called him an immoral and depraved young monster. Louis hadn't minded the switching or the lecture. He had found out what he wanted to know and consequently found the world a better place.

So now when he said, "You're a girl!" there was no denial. But when he saw the resigned way she accepted the fact, he added, "I'm glad you are. How could we marry if you were a boy too?"

Anne was consoled because she looked forward to their being married as much as he did. To them, at their age, it simply meant a continued companionship that would never be interrupted, as their friendship was sometimes interrupted now, when he had to return to his home at Blois or when she had to travel with her father's court. They longed for the time when there would be no authority over them and they could be together every sleeping as well as waking hour.

As the king had ordered when he had betrothed them at Louis's birth, Louis had spent most of his young life at court, with Anne his constant playmate. They had teethed together, bawled and fought together, and practically the first thing they had learned was that someday they would be king and queen together.

It suited them wonderfully well. They liked almost everything about each other. Although Anne hadn't as much respect for his brains as he had for hers, still his constant wit and mischief, his laughing black eyes made him the most important person in her life. Her father and Louis—

Louis and her father, both terribly important in different ways, and it was hard to tell which meant more.

Anne spent two hours a day alone with her father in his study. He would talk to her, always as an adult, and question her, expecting adult answers. She studied with tutors too, carefully picked by the king, so it wasn't strange that sometimes she found Louis's ignorance quite a contrast.

For Louis, also with tutors carefully picked by the king, was studying nothing but the fine art of being a careless gentleman. If Louis's father had been alive, he would have been amazed and angry that nothing seemed to be offered the boy's eager young mind but pleasures and sports. The king might have had trouble concealing from Charles of Orleans that his son was deliberately being taught to be careless and impatient, so that if he ever came to the throne he would never be an adequate king but only too grateful to hand over the irksome job to a mind like Anne's which was being prepared for the work.

But Charles was dead and Mary was easily deceived. She saw Louis growing healthy and tall, his eyes bright in his sun-tanned face; she saw that he rode, hunted, wrestled, and danced well. She saw that he was polite enough and everyone was attracted to him, and when he had laughingly said that work and books were for priests, Mary had amiably agreed. She herself couldn't read and had never missed the knowledge.

Now Louis tossed the racquet away, no longer interested in the fishing, and rolled over on his back, his arms under his head, and his voice, lazily animated, began one of their favorite conversations.

"Anne, what shall we do when I'm king and you're queen?"

"When I'm queen," Anne answered promptly, "I shall exile Madame de Champion the first thing!"

Pretty, silly Louise de Champion was her father's present mistress, and Anne hated her as she hated every woman the king liked.

"Or," continued Anne, vindictiveness in her voice, "I could have her imprisoned—or beheaded—or maybe both!"

"Exile is enough," Louis suggested idly. "Send her to that country the traveler was speaking of—Russia—they have a bear for a king there. He can eat her, and she'll poison him like the fish do."

As usual Anne corrected him. "Not really a bear, Louis. That's just the sign on their coat of arms—like you have a porcupine."

Louis knew perfectly well the Russian king wasn't really a bear. He just liked to daydream about a faraway snowy country, full of sleighs and wolves with a big white bear for a king, but Anne would never pretend. He shrugged: Oh well, Anne was Anne.

"What else will you do?" he asked.

"I shall send Madame my mother back to Savoy!" Her voice held formal mockery. "She's dying to go, and I'll certainly not miss her."

There was always scorn in her voice when she spoke of her mother, that unhappy woman who had done nothing that had been expected of her, although she was finally pregnant after this long time and might still redeem herself by giving her husband an heir.

Louis thought of his mother, her sweet girlish ways, and he felt almost ashamed that he loved her as he did. If Anne thought so little of her mother, he didn't want to admit to a difference she wouldn't understand, so he just nodded as though he agreed.

"And I shall send the Countess de Lande back to her estates and all her silly friends with her!" But now it was Louis's turn, according to custom. "What will you do when you're king?"

"I'll conquer England, Spain, Italy, Milan, Savoy, and Austria." His ambitious plan sometimes included Russia, but Russia was terribly far away.

Anne nodded in agreement. He wouldn't conquer them all, she was sure. Some of them would have to be allies, but whatever he conquered she'd be queen of, and that was good.

"My father says we're going to be formally betrothed this fall. A big ceremony at Tours. He's going to send for your mother soon to sign all the papers."

Louis nodded enthusiastically, although he had heard about it before. "It should have been done long ago," he pointed out a bit crossly, then he cheered up. "And now we haven't got much longer to wait, only about four years."

"Perhaps less," Anne corrected him. "He said we'd probably marry when we're eleven. He says we're quite old for our years, especially me," Anne said complacently.

"Me too!" Louis insisted, and she nodded agreement.

"What's the matter with your sister? She's almost fifteen —and she isn't married yet. She'll be an old maid——"

Louis interrupted quickly. "She's going to be married this fall."

"Was your mother looking for a better marriage for her?"

"Oh no! Mother is very pleased with Pierre. Marie-Louise had the fever and they were waiting till she was strong again."

Anne was scornful. "Pierre de Beaujeu! Why do they make her marry him? He's nobody!"

"Well," said Louis apologetically, "they love each other."

He knew Anne's contemptuous opinion of love. It had been handed to her by her father. Louis's mother had taught him that love was a very valuable thing, and as usual, on every subject on which there could possibly be two points of view, Louis's mother and Anne's father could be trusted to be at the opposite poles.

"How," asked Anne flatly, "could anybody be in love with Pierre?"

She had him there. Louis had often wondered himself how his beautiful sister could love Pierre. Pierre was in his twenties now, agreeable enough to look at with his light brown curly hair, his gray-blue eyes in a fresh rosy face, his sturdy, thickset body—but so stupid and heavy of mind that Louis, whose mind was quicksilver, could not tolerate him.

"Maybe," Louis said slowly, remembering what his mother had tried to explain to him, "maybe she sees something in him that we don't."

"Doesn't she see that he's stupid? I see that, and I'm not in love with him."

"Of course she sees he's stupid," Louis answered hotly, defending his sister. "Do you think she's blind?"

"Well, does she like him that way?"

"Oh, how do I know? How do I know anything about it?" Louis sat up crossly. "My mother says we'll understand— later."

"My father says it's all nonsense. He doesn't believe in love."

"He loves your mother, doesn't he?" asked Louis, but he had his doubts.

"He said she's a fool and he dislikes her." Anne spoke coldly, and it was evident that she agreed with her father.

"Well, he loves Madame de Champion, then."

"He does not!" Anne cried furiously. "I heard him say she sickens him."

"Then why does he sleep with her?" Louis demanded triumphantly. "He doesn't have to. They're not married—her children couldn't inherit anything!"

Now Anne was stopped. That was truly the question. Why, if her father thought love was nonsense and women all fools, did he sleep with women whose children would be valueless to him?

They were not ignorant of the physical deed, but the emotions behind it were of course unknown to them. As far as they understood it, learning from a court notorious for its frankness, it was a thing, if done correctly, that would result in children who were valuable for political marriages. And yet—there must be more to it than that.

"I don't know, Louis," Anne sighed. "The whole thing is certainly strange!"

Anne's mother, Charlotte of Savoy, was thinking the same thing. Heavy and dispirited, she sat at her bedroom window, trying to adjust herself so she would be less uncomfortable. The end to her bulky awkwardness was a month or so away, and she longed for it. It seemed to her that she was the most miserable woman in the world as she looked out across the wide lawn toward the bright figures in the summer garden.

When she had married at twelve, she had looked forward happily enough to being Queen of France. She had pictured herself presiding in dignity over the king's household, mothering her children, being known and loved all over France for her charity and kindness. That picture had been viciously smeared by her husband's bony hand. He preferred to control his household himself, even to the smallest details. He kept Anne away from her mother, and the little crippled daughter, Jeanne, a year or so younger than Anne, he had sent away to be raised where the sight of her pitiably malformed body would not constantly assault his pride. He derisively refused his wife's attempts at friendliness and stingily refused her the opportunity to be charitable.

Then, naturally, the child that was soon to be born hardly interested Charlotte. It would be taken from her as the others had been, and she would be left with nothing again.

At the edge of the pond she could see her elder daughter Anne, with the Orleans boy she was soon to marry. Charlotte sighed and wished she could be back at that age herself with the knowledge she had now, to prevent her from making such mistakes. She would not allow herself to be fascinated into being Queen of France again. No. She would stay in Savoy and enter some quiet convent where the cruel bodies of men would not touch her.

The same summer day surrounded Blois, in Orleans, with its warmth, and the last light of the sun laid the pattern of the mullioned windows on the shining inlaid floors of Mary's luxurious sitting room. It was almost twilight, and very quiet in the room, for the two women who sat there sewing had sewed and talked all day and their fingertips and their tongues were tired.

Mary and her daughter Marie-Louise, as they sat together, their heads bent over their work, their eyes intent on their stitching, looked more like sisters than mother and daughter.

Marie-Louise, at fifteen, was taller, larger boned than her mother, with a look of common-sense maturity that made Mary seem childish by comparison. Marie-Louise had wheat-colored hair, wound about her head in thick braids under the draped wimple, and her pink-and-white fairness, her sky-blue eyes were inherited from her mother, who had come from Cleves and brought the light coloring of that country with her. Even now Mary's hair was not much darker than her daughter's, and at night when Mary took off her matron's coif and let her long yellow hair fall down her back, when she stood in her white chemise with its embroidered yoke, she looked no older than when she had come, a fourteen-year-old bride, to her elderly husband.

Marie-Louise had been engaged all her life, but now that the marriage was only a few months off, she was in a fever of excited impatience to have the most beautiful trousseau a bride ever had. As her fingers deftly stitched she made an ecstatic mental inventory of her wardrobe. There was the black cut velvet that had been made for her at Lyons, the blue watered silk with the bouffant skirt, the white satin wedding dress with the gold embroidery that glittered in the sun, the sable cloak with the crimson hood—and then, with luminous eyes, she thought of the boxes that would come by coach from Lyons. The boxes would contain the cloth of silver, the brocaded satins, seven of them, the furs, the slippers, silver ones, satin ones, and painted Turkish chopines, on high platforms. And the hats—hennins of all colors, trimmed hats with swaying ostrich plumes —enameled fans, and jewel boxes, violet-perfumed gloves and sunshades. What a glittering day when the boxes came from Lyons!

Although most of their clothing was made for them, some in Paris, some by seamstresses who lived in the château, still Mary and Marie-Louise preferred to do some of the intricate embroidery themselves. Garments of linen and smooth cambric and white soft batiste lay in neat piles beside the china silk. They did their sewing in Mary's apartments, on the second floor of the large château, in the light and prettily furnished sitting room that adjoined Mary's bedroom. Each morning they would look over the work they had accomplished, rejoicing over the growing pile of finished pieces. But they still had a good deal left to do, and they felt they would probably be working on the very morning of the wedding day.

There were millions and millions of precise stitches in the immaculate cloth, and for every stitch Mary thought her daughter must have mentioned Pierre twice. It was "Pierre —this" and "Pierre—that." Mary enjoyed the enthusiastic monotony, though, for it made her very happy to see how much Marie-Louise cared for the man she was going to marry. Love was a luxury that rarely came into marriage— it was wonderful that her daughter should possess this rarity. Her adopted son was very dear to Mary too, and although now that he was a man Pierre spent a good deal of time either at court or at Bourbonnais, his home was still Blois.

Marie-Louise spoke suddenly, as though she were announcing a very surprising bit of wonderful news. "Pierre sent me word from Amboise that he'd be here Friday."

Mary had heard this only twenty times, so she could still manage to sound quite receptively surprised. "Oh—that's wonderful, dear."

"That's three days—not counting today!" Then Marie-Louise hesitated worriedly. "Or do you think I should count today?"

Marie considered, then gave a fair verdict. "Today is almost over. I think you could ignore it."

Marie-Louise nodded. She intended to. "Pierre said to tell you that the king is already planning the ceremony for Louis's betrothal. Pierre says it will be at Tours." This was said proudly, as though Pierre had arranged the whole thing and had thought about all the places where the ceremony could be held and then had hit on Tours, the perfect place for it. "But Pierre says that he and I may not be able to be present."

Mary exclaimed, in the distress that was expected of her, "That would be most disappointing for us all."

Marie-Louise nodded reassuringly. "But Pierre said to rest assured he'd make every effort."

Mary sighed with great relief. Then there was a moment's silence.

"Pierre says the king will send Louis home to you shortly to prepare for the betrothal, and he said to tell you that Louis is very well liked—everyone at Amboise speaks highly of him."

Mary smiled fondly. "Everyone everywhere likes Louis."

"Yes," said Marie-Louise carefully, "but I think perhaps it might be wise for Pierre to have a long talk with Louis. Pierre says that Louis is sometimes lacking in respect."

Mary looked up in surprise. "Respect for whom?"

"Well . . ." Marie-Louise thought awhile. "Respect for Pierre, for one." She added incredulously, "Sometimes he acts as if he didn't like Pierre."

Mary looked down and kept her smile in her eyes only, then the smile died out as she thought ruefully of Louis's opinion of Pierre, which she knew too well.

"I will have a talk with Louis," Mary promised, and then lied. "The trouble probably is that he's jealous. He wants to be the only man in the family since his father is gone."

Her sigh was deep this time, as she thought of Charles, who had been dead for five years now. She thought she would never stop missing him. She had loved him so much —gently, as a father, a very dear brother, and a very good friend. Sometimes even now, when she sat alone and lonely, she would look toward his chair and speak before she thought.

"Charles, what do you think—" she would start, and then

stop, because she would see that the chair was empty and remember he was dead.

Loneliness was only a part of missing him. Pierre had no mind for management of the estates, and Louis was still too young, so the final decisions fell to her to make. What she would have done without de Mornac she hated to think.

Rebuilding Orleans was a tremendous job, especially since King Louis XI had stopped the allowance that had been granted the Orleans family by the dead King Charles. The present king saw no reason to spend money on territory that wouldn't be his. What if the Orleans family had been ruined protecting their king and country? The war was over now—gratitude was too expensive.

Nevertheless, the work went on somehow, guided by de Mornac's strong capable hands, and although Mary was a little uneasy sometimes about his staying on in such full control now that her husband was gone, she was forced to rely on his competence for her children's welfare.

She was uneasy at his presence because she knew very well what had been said about him at her son's birth. Every good friend had felt it her duty to tell Mary the gossip. She and Charles had discussed it. Charles had considered dismissing de Mornac and then decided that would make it look as though he believed the lies. It had been a disturbing problem. Charles couldn't go around shouting, "Louis is really my son!" to people who hadn't disputed it to his face, anyway, and who wouldn't believe it if he said it. So finally they had just pretended they had never heard a word of the slander.

Mary was uneasy at de Mornac's presence in another way too—in a way that made her ashamed of herself. The plain truth was that she thought of him too often.

While Charles had been alive Mary had flirted a bit with de Mornac, very mildly to be sure, and she had always felt perfectly safe even when she had provoked his dark eyes to that intent look that always made her blush and look around for Charles. After Louis's birth she had been more careful, because she realized that she was, in a small part, to blame for the jests about Louis's parentage. And after Charles had died Mary withdrew abruptly from any contact with de Mornac, seeing him only on unavoidable business matters.

She met him now and then by accident, because he lived in the château—not in the servants' quarters and not in the guest suites, but in an apartment half separated from both. He breakfasted early and lunched in his offices or out on the estates, so she didn't see him then, but he was generally at the long dinner table among her guests and attendants.

If Mary had been asked how many people lived under the Gothic arched roof of Blois, she couldn't have answered. It was a very quiet court compared to some of the other dukes' more sociable châteaux. Charles had never cared for brilliant parties and entertainments; a few of his literary friends gathered around the bookshelves in his library, a fire and good talk—that was what he liked, and somehow, since his death, Mary had felt no inclination to change the quiet routine. Even if she had had the inclination, she wouldn't have had the money to sustain a glittering court.

As it was, it was a drain on the whole depleted province to maintain the château at Blois in a suitably luxurious way, for well over a hundred people were permanent residents there, depending on the Orleans purse for their food, clothing, and livelihood.

First, of course, there was the Orleans family: Mary, Marie-Louise, Louis, and Pierre. Each one had his own small retinue, from secretaries, maids, and valets to hairdressers and stableboys.

About a dozen lesser members and relatives of the family lived there too. One of them was Count André Visconti, Charles's cousin on the maternal side. He was almost seventy, and every morning for the forty years he had lived at Blois he had bemoaned the fact that he had ever left his native city of Milan. About twice a year he would have all his belongings packed and carried down to the courtyard, but once there, the monumental task of getting them all packed on mules' and horses' backs must have dismayed him. He would look up at the sky and remark that the weather looked too treacherous for traveling—it was too cold or too hot, it might rain—so back up to his comfortable wing he would go, postponing his trip till better weather came along. He had been named executor of Charles's will, and legally, till Louis was of age, Count André was head of the house, but everyone knew that his signature wasn't as important as de Mornac's word. It was de Mornac's office that was busy from morning till night with Orleans peasants, come to beg protection, loans, or favors, to request more time to pay their back taxes, or, now and then, to pay taxes on time. The business of the State of Orleans was administered in its capital city of Blois by a group of councilmen, but the final word on important things had to come from the château on the hill.

Another relative, Count François d'Armagnac, lived quarrelsomely with his wife, Hermione, in the rooms next to Count André. The d'Armagnacs were relatives who dated back to Charles's first marriage to their sister, Bonne. They were elderly, too, and hadn't many more years to live at Blois.

Cécile de Brissan was a widowed cousin of Mary's from Cleves. She and her invalid daughter lived contentedly in their comfortable suite overlooking the garden. Mary had had a little balcony built off one window so that the invalid could be carried out into the sun on pleasant days, and Cécile was so grateful that she almost never went out of her rooms for fear they might be gone when she returned.

The Beauvais family weren't relatives, just very old friends, but when their home near Orleans had been razed to the ground during the war they had naturally come to Blois and had been welcomed.

There were a few assorted relations, too, not so welcome, who had come for a month and stayed for years, and there were the remains of Charles's literary group, although the best of them, without Charles's intelligent mind to attract them, had moved on to other courts and other dukes. But several hungry young poets had stayed, also some who were hungry only for Charles's extraordinary collection of books.

As the visiting poets haunted the library, there were also visiting painters always in the picture gallery: Maurice Coselli, whom Charles had brought from Italy, two dark, argumentative Spaniards, and a Flemish painter whom Mary disliked because he had painted such unflattering portraits of her children. Still she couldn't ask him to leave, because the Court of Orleans needed its portraits painted, miniatures of the children at different ages to keep alive sentimental memories, likenesses of relatives of marriageable ages to be sent to other countries to lure a prospective bride or bridegroom into a marriage contract—yes, portrait painters, particularly flattering painters, were a necessity.

A group of musicians and ballad singers were a permanent part of the household too. In the winter they entertained in the big dining hall, during meals and after them.

In the summer they practiced and played outside on the terraced gardens, in the vined and latticed summerhouse.

Orleans needed the sciences as well as the arts. There was a bearded astrologer in a tall, star-trimmed hat, and a necromancer, a fortuneteller, a herb doctor, a perfumer, leeches, midwives, and nurses.

Then too the people of Orleans needed the beautiful chapel where Mass was chanted hour after hour. The Bishop of Orleans didn't live at Blois although he visited there with his purple-liveried retinue for weeks at a time. The aging Cardinal of Rouen, also a relative, had retired to Blois and was Mary's confessor. Monseigneur de la Craix listened to Marie-Louise, Pierre and Louis; Father Paul watched over the other members of the household with his younger monks and choirboys to assist him.

Travelers of every rank, passing Blois, found it hospitable enough to warrant climbing the slope, and they usually stayed longer to rest their horses than they had planned. Mary's best friends, her neighbors, the Bourbon family, frequently interchanged visits. The Duke of Bourbon and his wife, Henriette, would ride over with their two daughters-in-law for five or six days' visit. The Angoulême branch of the family was often at Blois, also young Dunois, who wore the Orleans bar sinister as proudly as his father before him, Count Eugène de Chamfort and his beautiful, maliciously witty wife, Diane, and now and then the Duke of Mayenne, with his nervous wife, Gabrielle, who wanted to do nothing else but play cards from morning till night.

It took a small army of valets, maids, seamstresses, laundresses, cooks, grooms, and stableboys, under the stern leadership of Edouard Grévin, master of the household, and Mistress Jeanne Ledu, to serve all these people. Every straw pallet in the servants' wings, the attics, the cellars, and the stables was taken. Serving the House of Orleans was a proud and lucrative position, much sought after in spite of the fact that it was such a quiet, almost deserted court.

But among all those people who filled the candle-and-torch-illumined dining hall at supper, Mary could never prevent herself from looking for just one—de Mornac. She carefully pretended not to be looking for him, and when she saw him laughing and talking with easy assurance to Father Paul on one side of him and Madame Beauvais on the other, Mary didn't know if she was glad or sorry he was there.

Sometimes he would look up and across the table at her, and although she would turn her face abruptly away, she could feel his sardonic, knowing eyes on her.

And right now, when she should be listening to Marie-Louise talking about Pierre, she was raising her head to look out the window down into the courtyard, because she thought she had heard horses, and de Mornac might have returned from his three-day ride around the estates. She could picture him striding across the courtyard with his long steps that pressed the ground triumphantly down. She thought he walked like a calmly conquering army of one, marching to his own music.

It wasn't he, and she wondered if he would be back to-night later. Or perhaps he was home already. She hadn't gone downstairs to dinner. There had been no guests, so she and Marie-Louise had had an early meal upstairs in her room, preferring to continue the sewing as long as the light would let them. The artificial light of flickering candles was not a reliable illumination for such fine embroidery.

"Are you expecting someone?" asked Marie-Louise, surprised at her mother's expectant gaze. She was even more surprised when she saw Mary's face blush into embarrassment.

"No," Mary said quickly. "I must have been thinking of Louis's home-coming, and I—forgot how much longer there was to wait. I almost expected to see him ride into the courtyard."

It was a floundering explanation and didn't explain the blush, but Marie-Louise accepted it, leaning back in her chair and stetching out her slim young arms, tired and cramped from sewing.

"It's beginning to get dark." She rose, folding her work and laying it aside on the long carved-oak window seat. She plunged her needle into the red heart-shaped pincushion. "You'd better stop too."

Mary shook her head determinedly. "No, I'll finish this piece tonight, so it won't be waiting for me in the morning. And then—would you like to play cards with me?"

Marie-Louise hesitated. "I'm very sleepy," she said, and offered up a large and artificial yawn to prove it. "I think I'll go to bed almost at once."

Mary hid her smile and didn't protest. She knew very well Marie-Louise wouldn't sleep till midnight. No, she would lock her door, dismiss her maids, and then she would try on all her new clothes, imagining Pierre's admiring looks and comments when he saw her in them.

"Then good night, my dear," Mary said lightly, "and sleep well."

Marie-Louise kissed her good night and hastily left for her rendezvous with her trousseau, and Mary's smile lingered as she thought of her children, who were such an appealing mixture of the best of Charles and herself. Marie-Louise had her mother's fair beauty, with Charles's quiet calm and sweet disposition; while Louis, although he was not a beauty like Marie-Louise, had Charles's nicely chiseled dark features, Charles's humor and intelligence brightened by her own eager liveliness. She sighed with maternal sentiment as she thought they were certainly a pair to make a mother very proud—and sighed again with replete contentment as she thought that in a few months they would both be given their hearts' desires.

She hurried on with her sewing, knowing there were thousands of things to be done for the wedding and the betrothal. Embroidery for herself when Marie-Louise's clothes were finished, clothing to be ordered for Louis, who was growing so fast he needed a complete new wardrobe every six months; the whole château needed to be replenished and cleaned from cellars to turrets. There would be a grand reception here for Marie-Louise and Pierre, and everything must be perfect. Her mind went busily from one room to the next, critically inspecting. Many of the mattresses needed restuffing, and every single chair in the tapestry salon required new needlepoint. There was not enough time—and there never was enough money. That wretched endless war! And that stingy ungrateful king!

Deeply absorbed, her eyes straining over her sewing as the last light was draining away, she hardly heard the knock on the door, but only answered it automatically, not looking up from the last few stitches of sewing.

The door opened and closed. There was a pause and then, instead of one of her maid's speaking, an unmistakable Gascon voice said lightly, "You look like a spring primrose just emerging from a snowbank."

Mary pricked her finger on the needle, dropped her work,

put her finger instinctively to her mouth, and looked up all in one moment, to see the Sire de Mornac in the room, looking down at her in amusement and admiration. She stood up hastily. The cloth, disregarded, tumbled all around her feet.

"What is it?" she asked in great alarm. "Something's happened?"

Something dreadful must have happened, she thought, her heart pounding, for him to have hurried to her up here in her rooms, instead of sending a request for her to receive him in a more impersonal place.

"Yes," he nodded gravely, "something serious has happened." But a thin edge of his white teeth showed through in a smile behind the full red of his lips.

"What?" cried Mary, her thoughts flying immediately to Louis. "Tell me——"

"You have hurt yourself," he said calmly, and he walked quickly across the room and took her hand before she could think. "And that is very serious."

He examined the tip of her finger, where the new little drop of blood had formed, and he was as intent as though it might turn into a fatal wound at any second. He looked down into her wide, amazed eyes and, incredibly, he put her finger between his lips, and she could feel his tongue against it.

She felt five emotions all at once. She was unbelieving. This couldn't really be happening! She was horrified! If someone should see them—he in her rooms, her hand to his lips! Where were her maids? Blanche sometimes came in without being sent for! She was terrified. He was too close—and so huge a man. She was fascinated. She wanted him to continue! And she felt something else—some enormous emotion she hadn't time to name because she had never felt it before.

Fright and horror reacted first. She jerked her hand away from him and put it under her chin, her fist clenched and her arm rigid, feeling that she must protect it from him. But he made no move to take it. He made no move at all, only watched her. Then she thought of the contaminated finger in the middle of her fist and it didn't seem right that she should be cherishing it so close to her—so she flung her arm down and held it out away from her in a stiff, uncomfortable position.

And her voice, when it finally came to rebuke him, disgusted her with its high shakiness.

"If you had something important to tell me, why didn't you send someone to ask for an interview?"

"Because," he said coolly, "it wasn't an interview with you that I wanted. I merely wanted to see you—alone."

Well, she congratulated herself, you've brought this on yourself! The wretched man knows he's attractive, knows how indispensable he is to us, and he's taking advantage of it. She cast about rapidly for a way to rebuke and dismiss him from her rooms, without dismissing him from his position.

"I don't know what strange idea has prompted you to affront me this way." Her voice was gathering dignity, she was glad to see. "But if you'll go away now, I'll try to forgive and forget this mistake you've made. Will you go now, please?"

She started to turn her back haughtily on him, but she was too tangled in the white cloth around her feet to accomplish this gesture with dignity, so she stood still and watched him.

"Of course I'll go, whenever you tell me, but it wasn't my intention to—affront you." He underlined the word with the faintest of mockery. "May I explain my strange idea?"

Her first unbearable excitement had diminished a little, and she nodded permission, because she was very curious to hear it. He stood in a characteristic position, his hands clasped behind his back as though to secure them against temptation, his dark head, the hair short-cut and crisp-looking, bent to look down at her smallness.

"It's really a very simple idea—and I thought a pleasant one. I think you're very lonely. I'm lonely too—and it seemed to me it would do no one any harm if we were to spend an evening together now and then. In other times you were kind enough to let me see that my presence wasn't unattractive to you——"

She gasped, and her mouth fell a little bit open that he would dare to be so frank. There was no way out of it now; he would have to be dismissed.

He went on, ignoring the warning in her eyes. "I've admired your reserve and discretion when your family is around you—and when you have guests—but tonight I knew you were alone, and I came carefully so that no one should know I was with you. Although"—intimate laughter brimmed up into his eyes—"it would probably surprise no one, since everyone in France thinks we are lovers already."

Mary stood frozen and thought she was losing her mind. She must surely be imagining that this man—a steward— had so forgotten his position that he could walk into the bedroom—or practically the bedroom—of the Duchess of Orleans and talk about their being lovers! Lovers! And then that other word he'd said—already. Already—as though they were surely going to be!

Were they?

The question pounded at her, and she stared questioningly at him as though she would find the answer in his eyes; she looked into the dark brown of the pupils and there was one gleam of light in each that seemed to be the reflection of her white, frightened face. While she looked, his body seemed to have come close to her, almost to touch her, although he had not moved at all. She felt his closeness with a throbbing apprehension and a longing.

Charles! She thought, and turned to escape, but she tangled her feet awkwardly in the white linen, and she would have fallen if de Mornac had not quickly caught her. His arms came out in swift response from behind his back, caught her up, and lifted her clear of the fabric as easily as a child would lift a doll, holding her against him, her toes just barely touching the floor.

She pushed her hands against his unyielding chest and raised her head to demand that he release her, but as she raised her head her lips came up too—and when he leaned to meet them, although she still tried to struggle, she knew she was utterly lost. The question was answered; they would be lovers. There was no stopping now; under his warm, lingering, imperative lips she was helpless as a tired swimmer in an ocean tide.

He carried her into her bedroom and laid her down, and as he unloosened the clothes she wore, which were many and complicated, she recovered enough from the wildness of her emotion to wish in a hazy, half-conscious way that something would stop him. She resisted instinctively, with hands in which there was no strength, nor did she really want the strength—but her mind, from many, many miles away, called dimly to her to stop him. He was an enemy, her mind said, an enemy to be halted at the frontier, for once having passed, he would be all-powerful, irrevocably conquering territories that could never be retrieved. But her mind was so very far away—and her body said he wasn't an enemy besieging a starving city, but a rescuer bringing it food for which it had so long hungered.

After a timeless period she learned that there is a moment when the body, with its overpowering will, is life itself and the mind is only a supercilious lodger in its house of flesh and blood. The mind rents a room, on the top floor, a very good room with a view, but it doesn't own the property, although it would like to.

While Mary learned these things for the first time, de Mornac reviewed familiar but pleasant knowledge. The world the body lived in was the complete world to him. That was why he had been born: for good food, sound sleep, comfortable things to see and hear, hard work, and the fierce pleasures of love. He felt no contempt, as some men did, for women who could be lightly taken. That was why they had been born, too. Women had their lives and men theirs; only one thing they must do together, and that should be done joyfully, for mutual pleasure.

He had wanted Mary for a long time, and with an assurance that came from much knowledge of women he knew that when she and the time were ripe he would have her. He loved her—as he loved women, one at a time and not the same one for very long. He knew that she wanted love too. What woman didn't? What man didn't? He also knew that she had never known it with Charles. It had seemed such a crying waste that Mary, who was so beautifully made for love, should never have had it.

She had it now, he thought as he cautiously left her dark, silent room and made his way to his rooms in the far wing of the house. If he knew anything about women—and he modestly agreed with himself that he was something of an authority on the subject—she certainly had it now. He took off his boots and his coat again when he reached his room and was asleep in five minutes in his shirt and trousers.

Mary was asleep too. She had floated effortlessly toward a limitless horizon, drifting imperceptibly from languorous exhaustion into deep sleep.

She woke in the dawn, because of the sparrows squeaking in the trees, and when she saw the disordered room she sat up in bed in one swift, gasping movement, remembering. In hurried, rushing swoops she gathered up her clothes, wondering if her maids had come to put her to bed last evening and had seen this evidence. If Blanche, who had a pious quotation for every occasion, a sharp reproach for every slightest lapse in morals, had come in, how could she ever try to explain it? And if Blanche and the others hadn't come, how could she explain her not ringing for them at the usual time? Then, still agonizing over that question, she swiftly let down her tangled hair, brushed and rebraided it, found a fresh chemise and put it on, then folded back the velvet spread that had been sadly crumpled and quickly slipped into bed.

She had just begun to control her flurried breathing when another thought struck her. She flung back the covers and darted out into the sitting room, straight to the frothy white linen that had prevented her escape. It had been twisted and pulled up into a peak, like meringue on a pie, and she gathered it up, folding and smoothing it, grateful that she had thought of it before Marie-Louise had seen it. Chilled by the early-morning coolness on her bare feet, she went back into the bedroom, sliding into the comfortable warmth of the bed, while her conscience and several of the sterner saints came and sat on the footboard of the bed and regarded her with disgusted eyes.

Well, she finally told them in her own defense, it isn't as if I had been unfaithful to my husband.

Haven't you? they asked. What would Charles think of last night? He would never object to a suitable marriage for you—but to have an affair with a—servant—like the vile old Countess de Guiset, who slept with all her coachmen.

Mary squirmed. I couldn't help it, she told them, he——

Oh no, they interrupted. That won't do. You could have stopped him. You could have screamed. But you didn't want to, did you?

No, Mary finally admitted. I didn't.

I wonder what he thinks of you now, they mused. The fine Duchess of Orleans, who has never even been kissed by a man other than her husband, and he walks into your room and takes you as easily as he would have tumbled a country maid in a hayfield.

Oh, moaned Mary, shaking her head from side to side, as if she could shake herself loose from the galling, humiliating thoughts.

A very easy conquest, they repeated contemptuously. All you forgot to do was thank him.

And my body did that for me, Mary whispered to herself in shame.

Quiet as her thought had been, they heard it and gasped. And when a shiver of remembered ecstasy went through her, they got up and hurried out, washing their hands of her, leaving her to her shameless memory.

She had always known there must be more than she had experienced with Charles, and now, although her pride was anguished, still she was a complete woman, the possessor of sweet knowledge.

The whole day was like that—alternate anguish and delight, and a frightening apprehension of the moment when she must see him. What would she say? What would she do? Dismiss him? Of course. Then what would Orleans do without him? No, she couldn't possibly dismiss him. Say nothing, that would be best. Ignore it, and him. Treat him with absent-minded contempt—as though he had never really touched her. Oh, if only it had been that way—that she had hated it and him, and it was his pride, not hers, that was suffering.

She argued with herself all day, trying to be natural with her curious maids and with Marie-Louise, and then she noticed that the day was gone and she hadn't seen him at all, either to dismiss him or not to dismiss him. She ordered her dinner to be served in the dining hall, although there were no guests. But he didn't appear. She sat alone for a little while downstairs in the small salon. He still didn't appear. Her tongue absolutely refused to ask where he had gone, and she wondered if he had been afraid to face her and had ridden out from Blois.

When it grew dark and Marie-Louise went to her room to try on some new clothes that had come during the day, Mary went to her own sitting room. Probably, she told herself, that was what he was waiting for, to see her alone. Avoiding Blanche's glances of surprise, she dismissed her maids for the night and sat alone, considering what she would say to him when he came. She passed quickly over the thought of locking her door against him. That, she said sternly to her conscience, would solve nothing. Her conscience gave her a long, dubious look but couldn't actually deny it.

She finally decided what she would do when he came. She would rise and walk to the bell rope. With her hand on it, she would tell him he must go immediately and never dare to come back or she would arouse the house and have him sent away in disgrace. It would be a scandal, but she couldn't let him think that just because once he had taken her she would tolerate an affair with him.

And then, she would say, there is the loyalty you owe your dead master. She would stress that word master, to remind him of his own position. Then she would touch lightly on the chivalry he certainly owed a helpless young widow with two children. Or perhaps she had better not say "young"; he might smile that knowing smile of his. Thirties were far from young, although everyone did tell her she looked barely sixteen.

Well, where was he? She would forget everything she had to say if he didn't hurry. She walked restlessly back and forth, her eyes on the door, waiting for him. But he didn't come at all!

She didn't see him for several days, and when the moment came, Pierre and Marie-Louise were there, and de Mornac strolled casually up to them in the garden and asked some questions about horses to be sent to Amboise to bring Louis home. She answered as calmly as she could, but she wasn't able to meet his eyes. He spoke to Pierre and Marie-Louise in his usual laughing way and then went away. Mary was terribly disappointed that she hadn't been able to show him how revolting she found him.

It was so maddeningly incomplete. She never saw him alone, and although she spoke short impersonal remarks to him in the dining hall, never by the smallest look of comprehension in his eyes could she see any remembrance. It might have been some dream she had dreamed all alone—except that she knew it wasn't.

It was probably better, she told herself, that it should end this way. She didn't want to lose him as steward, and he was probably sorry for his rashness by now and worried about his position—and certainly it would accomplish no good to send for him and reproach him for what he didn't even seem to remember—but it left her with a strange feeling of flatness.

It was not, she said to her conscience again and again, that she had wanted it to happen again, but an added thorn

in her pride was the rankling thought that he hadn't cared
enough for the experience to attempt a repetition.

Her conscience didn't even answer. It wasn't on speaking
terms with her.

Mary looked forward eagerly to Louis's home-coming.
Thinking of him, enjoying his companionship, she would
forget her humiliation.

Louis came and they were all warmed in the glowing sun
of his enthusiasm, interested in his prolific news of the
court. Louis knew how his mother longed for court gossip,
and what he couldn't remember he made up for her amusement. De Goncourt had lost one of his eyebrows in a duel
over La Fontaine. The Duchesses of Mayenne and Lorraine had pulled each other's hair over a card game at
which they had both cheated. Madame Ainault had lost her
cranky, senile husband and was trying to look sad for three
weeks at least, while she coyly picked out his successor.
The English gentleman with the horrible name had killed
the king's tame bear and the king had almost hung him.

And all through his narratives ran the figure of Anne.
"Anne said this——" "Anne thinks——" "I told Anne
about——" There was no doubt that Anne was the final
court of opinion for Louis.

He had been home a week or two when exciting news
spread through France and a messenger brought it to Blois.
The expected child had been born to Charlotte of Savoy
and Louis XI of France; it was a son at last, an heir to the
throne!

Cannons boomed all over the country; guns saluted. The
towns got drunk, the villages got drunker, and they all
cheered the Dauphin Charles.

The province of Orleans got drunk because there was no
sense in passing up a good occasion and the free wine the
king's agents were passing out, but they didn't cheer so
loudly as the rest of the country, for now Louis of Orleans
was no longer heir presumptive. Pierre was very much annoyed, and Marie-Louise, because Pierre was annoyed,
showed annoyance too, although she really didn't care.

Louis himself was disappointed, naturally. He had counted
on being king, mostly because Anne wanted to be queen,
but he wasn't inconsolable. Being Duke of Orleans was
power and glory enough and he and Anne would rule Or-

leans as though it were the Court of France, and they would conquer Milan and Savoy just the same.

Mary was sorry for her son but glad for the queen, knowing what it meant to be without a son when one was so necessary, and she talked cheerfully to Louis, hoping his disappointment wasn't too great. She had really never depended on his being king someday, feeling certain that the king's marriage, already fruitful with two daughters, would bear sons too, so she concentrated on talking about Anne's coming betrothal to Louis, and that cheered him up.

At midnight they tired of listening to the chiming bells and the explosions, and they all went to bed. But not one of them realized that, from this moment on, their lives would be completely changed.

3

As soon as Queen Charlotte was able to rise from her bed after the birth of the Dauphin Charles, the whole court moved from Amboise to Tours for the christening, and it was to Tours that Mary was summoned in the fall, for the haggling and bargaining that would precede the marriage papers and the formal betrothal ceremony.

Mary took Louis with her, of course, and they went merrily and in high style on superb horses, brightly caparisoned, and with new livery for the attendants. Of course they had new clothing for themselves and a purseful of gold coins to scatter about at court to prove that the House of Orleans was not so hard up as it was whispered. Altogether it was an expensive journey, and Mary was worried about it, for money was growing increasingly scarce and since the fields and farms were just beginning to recover from the depredations of war, resources had been strained to the limit to provide for Marie-Louise's dowry. Although Princess Anne of France would bring a magnificent dowry with her when she came to Louis, still that wouldn't be for many years yet and it had already been borrowed against. The expenses of both weddings would be enormous, and Louis must always be supplied with the luxuries suitable to his position.

Mary sighed and hoped de Mornac would manage somehow. She was glad she had decided not to dismiss him, or rather that no decision had ever been forced upon her, for he never came to her with his reports and questions when she was alone, and not one word had ever been said between them concerning that one night.

He had touched her just once since then—when he had helped her into the saddle. He had motioned her groom aside and helped her himself. She had stiffened as she felt the warmth of his hand through her light doeskin glove, and she

had withdrawn her own as soon as she was barely into the
saddle, ignoring his look of open admiration that told her
how lovely she looked in her riding costume of dark blue
velvet, with a cloak of the same color, its hood lined with
ermine. She ignored his look—and yet she thought of it
all the way. The whole trip was exciting. She hadn't been
away from home for a long time, and being with Louis was
always nice.

There were about fifteen travelers in the group which
surrounded Mary and Louis, a personal bodyguard of ten
soldiers, well armed against any possible attack on the
road, Louis's valet, Mary's maid, and several grooms who
followed with the extra horses and luggage—a procession
noisy in the metallic sounds of iron hoofs on the hard road,
spurs clinking, swords rattling, and shields jangling against
glittering chain armor.

It was a clear blue October day, and the cool wind
brought the blood tingling to the surface of Mary's sensi-
tive skin. She pulled her cloak up around her shoulders and
reached for her face mask to protect her complexion. Her
mask was black velvet, lined with white satin, and it was
fastened on by a silver button which was held between the
teeth. Before she silenced herself with this impediment, she
cautioned Louis, riding behind her, to put on his mask too,
but he just smiled and shook his head, raising his face to
the warm sun, welcoming the cool wind that blew through
his uncovered hair.

With the mask on, there wasn't even an eighth of an inch
of Mary's skin visible. She was completely covered from
top to leather-shod feet. So was her maid, Blanche, riding
behind her, looking like a stout, swaying bundle of cloth on
top of the strong, trotting mare. The women didn't wear tall
hennins when they rode horseback for long trips; they generally wore a more practical small pillbox hat with a band
under the chin to hold it on, and then perhaps a wimple
over the whole thing for added protection.

The distance from Blois to Tours was about forty miles.
They left home shortly after six in the morning, and traveling at a steady but comfortable pace, stopping now and
then to rest their horses, stopping for lunch and rest at an
inn, the sun was going down when the horses clattered
noisily into the courtyard of the dreary stone fortress of

Plessis-les-Tours. Mary and Louis dismounted from their saddles eagerly, their hearts pounding with excitement.

Guards saluted them and pushed open the big doors; torches and candles were being lit in the halls as they were shown directly to their rooms. They hurried to dress, and later, when Mary descended the long stairs to the big dining hall, she walked proudly, her son at her side, Blanche and Louis's servant walking just as proudly behind them. There were all kinds of curious glances upon her, Mary knew, appraising the provincial Duchess of Orleans, who rarely came to court and whose virtue was the subject of some of the wittiest of the palace jokes. Her legs felt weak, but she held her head very high, and her face was proud to the point of haughtiness.

She took her seat at the table just one degree lower than the dais on which the king's small table stood, but before she sat she curtsied to the ground in sincere obeisance to the queen, who sat there alone, her face gray and fat and sad.

Charlotte answered Mary's greeting in listless friendliness. "It's quite a time since we have seen you here. You've not been ill—I'm sure of that. You look too fresh and young."

"Thank you, Your Majesty," Mary smiled, pleased at the compliment. "No, I've not been ill, but a woman alone has many things to keep her busy."

The queen sighed and nodded, turned back to her dinner, and Mary rose from her bow and took her place at the table, her maids standing behind her chair to serve her. Mary looked around the noisy room, crowded with lords and ladies of the court, and servants coming and going with platters and bowls, and the attendants taking the food from the servants and preparing it for their masters.

Louis was at another table with some of the Bourbon litter, his cousin Eugène of Angoulême, and the young Count of Dunois, a cousin too.

The king hadn't come to dinner, and no one seemed to expect him. Probably another of his fast days. Anne wasn't there either, and Louis was busy asking where she was. The queen ate alone, speaking to her attendants now and then and to the Cardinal de Rohan, who sat near her, but she seemed not to see the others in the crowded room. When she rose to leave, it was some time before quiet fell, and everyone stood, but she wasn't used to sincere deference and its forms meant nothing to her anyway. She wouldn't have minded if no one had noticed her going.

The court followed, drifting across the hall into the large salon, where music began, and dancing, and prearranged groups made quickly for the card tables. Mary sat with the Duchess of Angoulême and they took turns admiring each other's clothes and talking about their children.

Upstairs, out of sound of the music, in the musty little room he reserved for his work, the king sat close to the hearth, where an economical little fire was struggling, and his hands fingered his rosary, while his mind fingered his plans for the evening. He looked across at Oliver, who was writing at the big desk littered with papers, his red face made more rosy by the candlelight from the six-branched candelabra. The years hadn't changed either of the men very much; the king was thinner and Oliver was stouter.

"Cold!" the king grumbled, hunching his chair a little closer to the fire, although his bony knees were almost in it already. "Cold as my wife's feet!"

Oliver hastily rose and came to mend the fire. "I beg your pardon, Monseigneur—I hadn't noticed the fire was dying. I'll add more logs, and that will give you ease."

"My needs would certainly be small if only that would give me ease," the king said irritably, and with his cane knocked a twisted little log out of Oliver's hands. "Wastrel! Save it—I am cold no matter how the fire blazes—and get up! You look like a chimney sweep, and all my letters will be gray with filth! The letter to Milan should go at once— the duke will be glad to hear that Burgundy's latest revolt has come to such a pleasant end"—His tone was savage— "and all the rebels are suddenly my friends—clothed in that gaudy loyalty that's only worn by men whose coats are quickly turned."

Oliver looked dubious. "The price for friends like that was too high."

The king shook his head decisively. He didn't regret the size of the bribe it had taken to undermine Burgundy's last revolt. "If I could end every uprising with just my purse, I'd be a very happy man! The price was high, I admit, but this time only gold was spent—no valuable French blood was lost." His tone was more quiet; his absent gaze traveled unseeingly past Oliver into the shadowy corners of the room. "A stingy king, the people call me—and that I may

be. I know there's one thing that I hoard—fiercely with a
stingy thrift they wouldn't understand—the blood of
France! I count it carefully—every royal drop, every
peasant ounce—and I don't spend it unless I have to—to
staunch a bigger flow." He was quiet a moment, then he
shrugged. "Anyway, blood buys only enemies, and gold
buys friends. I've just bought a dozen lifelong friends. Lifelong!" He laughed shortly. "Then life's even shorter than I
thought!"

"Too much!" Oliver repeated regretfully. "They cost too
much!"

"I weighed it out, my Oliver. It was just enough to fill
their greedy hands and occupy their minds—so they'd have
no time—for a while—to cluster in the dark, like rats, and
gnaw at the corners of my kingdom! Burgundy will be quiet
for a few years now—digesting what I've given him to swal-
low." His fingers jerked at his rosary viciously. "They
scream about freedom and their rights—they say they want
nothing for themselves—but offer them a piece of my rich
black earth—one of my strong cities—and see them snap it
up and fight for it like starving curs—while they drop their
fine talk of freedom in the nearest muddy hole."

"Yes," Oliver agreed, "for dukes who said they were
fighting only for freedom and the right, they asked for
enough when we drew up the treaty at Conflans."

The king winced. Conflans and its treaty still was a sore
subject after five years. That Burgundian revolt five years
past had been waged more successfully by the army of
Charles the Bold and other dukes dissatisfied, among other
things, with the king's practice of not allowing the States-
General to convene.

The States-General was the approximate French equiva-
lent to the English House of Lords, and a check on a king's
power which the present king refused to acknowledge.

Charles the Bold of Burgundy had led his triumphant
army as far as Paris, where the king had stood siege until
forced to yield. Under the peace treaty Louis XI had lost
his good towns along the Somme River as well as the control of Normandy. Other minor disasters were included,
and the king had been required to pay the cost of the revolt.

"Treaties!" the king said heavily. "Treaties! Signed conditions no one means to obey! Give—and take back. And
the one who leaves the treaty table with the heaviest purse

—the one who sows the most seeds for future weeds of war—that one man is called the winner. Treaties have given a crippled view of all men—and yet treaties will help me to mold this divided land into one nation—under one will —and that will shall be mine!"

"You'll succeed," Oliver said soothingly. "I know you will!"

"For France's sake, I can't allow myself to fail. I can't allow these stupid selfish dukes—Burgundy—Brittany—Orleans—Bourbon—to wage their selfish little wars that weaken our country and make us an easy victim for some alien greed. England is always eager to pounce—thanks to God, she's too weak still, but she won't always be! Spain is a dark question—and we must be strong and ready to answer questions—not divided by our own petty quarrels! I must unify the fools—mold all their provinces into one land!"

"You've done much, Monseigneur." Oliver spoke hastily, nervously sorting some of the papers on the desk, anxious to divert the king's rising anger. This subject, Oliver knew from long experience, led through furious loquaciousness and seething silence to one unvarying result—Oliver's legs got soundly rapped with the cane.

Oliver was relieved to see that the king was calming. He leaned back in his chair and even smiled a little.

"Yes, I've done much," he admitted, "but there's still more to do. Do you remember the last letter from my friend in Milan? At least," he added sardonically, "the Duke of Milan is my friend at the moment, and will be until it's no longer profitable to me. At any rate, a phrase in his letter lingered in my mind, although the thought itself is not so very new. He wrote that it was impossible for me to break a sheaf of arrows with my hands, but if I separated them and took them one by one, they'd snap easily between my fingers."

He looked down at his hands and flexed the fingers slowly, thinking how good it would feel to break arrows dangerous to France, to feel them resist, hear them creak protestingly as they began to yield, then finally to feel them snap and toss them aside broken. He would break them all, all the dukes who were his enemies, and their lands would come to him and strengthen the power of the Crown.

He frowned as he encountered another sore spot in his

mind. One of the most important provinces should be his by
now; he still shouldn't be plotting and hoping for Orleans;
it should have come to him years ago when that old cuckold
Charles had died. Instead the young duke's healthy body
stood between the desirable lands of Orleans and the
Crown. The king sighed heavily when he thought how
sturdy young Louis's body was. His hopes for the boy's
death were dimming, although the time the child had been
so ill with the pox, and the time he had been thrown by
the vicious horse the king had given him, had excited the
king to enthusiastic prayers of thanksgiving. He had even
given the cathedral at Bourges a new altar, out of the
depths of his gratitude, and then the wretched boy had recovered and seemed to grow taller and sturdier by the
moment. Well, at least he hadn't paid for the altar yet, and
probably never would.

There was something insolent in a bastard's being so
flauntingly healthy, when a legal son, like his own infant
Charles, was such a puny, wizened thing. And his daughter
Jeanne—his mind turned hastily away from that mortal
blow to his masculine pride, and hastily he pushed the
blame toward his wife. Evidently a woman's body dreamed
of other things beside inheritance; evidently there was no
female response to the needs of property and power.

He spoke aloud, continuing the conversation from the
other side of the bridge of thoughts his mind had passed
over. "Has the Duchess of Orleans arrived?"

Oliver seemed to follow the connection. He nodded,
"Yes, Your Majesty. She arrived in high spirits. I saw them
enter—herself and her son. Will you see her this evening?"

"Presently—presently! In high spirits, you say? She likes
this marriage!"

There was something strange in his tone that made Oliver
look at him in surprise. "Of course. It's the most advan-
tageous marriage in France!"

"Indeed?"

Oliver was puzzled. He defended a statement that surely
needed no defense. "The Princess Anne might have had a
throne. There was Spain—Italy—maybe even England—"

The king looked amused. "The Princess Anne?" he repeated in the same questioning tones.

"Why, yes—as you know, sire. The King of Rome asked
for her——" Oliver was baffled at the king's manner.

The king suddenly seemed to be in the best of spirits; he laid down his rosary, hitched his chair around so that he could give Oliver his complete attention, and smiled complacently.

"I do recall that incident—although I know you think I'm growing old and forgetful. Still—what's the connection between my daughter Anne and the young Duke Louis of Orleans?"

Now Oliver began to grow cautious. He could tell, from the king's manner, that something was in the wind. "I thought," he said carefully, "I *thought* you had sent for the duchess to arrange the marriage between her son and your daughter."

"You thought, Oliver, you thought exactly right. That's what I've done." He stopped and watched Oliver's puzzled face in amusement.

Oliver gave up. "Well, sire——" he stared, and then stopped because he didn't know what to say next.

"Well, Sire Oliver," the king mocked, "and have I only one daughter?"

His face suddenly became intent with something more in it than amusement as he watched Oliver's blank stout face change awkwardly into unbelieving amazement and then horrified comprehension.

"You have found the answer?" the king asked sharply.

Oliver stammered painfully, his face red with embarrassment. "No, Your Majesty," he lied. "I am too stupid to see what you mean."

The king rapped his cane on the floor, and if Oliver's legs had been within reach, they would have ached. "No! You're not too stupid. You're too cowardly to say you see my plan. But I'm no coward. I'll say it. I have two daughters, and it isn't Anne I'll give to the Orleans brat."

Oliver's hands were wet with perspiration, and he tried to keep the horror he felt from showing. "You mean—the Princess Jeanne?"

"I mean the Princess Jeanne!"

Oliver said nothing.

"She might have had the King of Rome, too!" the king said mockingly.

"But—not if he had seen her." Oliver wondered at his own temerity, then he faltered on. "Do you think, sire, that she is capable of being married?"

The king laughed shortly. "I have had the doctor's word that she can bed—but she cannot breed."

The brutal words were shocking to Oliver in a room that was well used to coarse and brutal plans. He looked quickly away from the king, and before his eyes was the picture of Jeanne as he had seen her last, some months ago, when he and the king had traveled to the château at Linières, where Jeanne had lived almost since the day of her birth with Dame de Linières, her foster mother.

The king sighed suddenly. "Your eyes remind me of that day at Linières when she walked to meet us——" He stopped abruptly, then his voice went harshly on. "Walked, did I say? She dragged herself across the room to us——"

Oliver could see her now, although his eyes were closed. Her rolling, shambling gait—her left shoulder high, her right sagging low, her back humped, her childish face ugly and bitter with the pain of knowing how ugly she was. He remembered the king's sharp, indrawn breath, his horrified whisper: "God! to think that's mine—my child!"

The king was thinking of that now, and trying to push the memory away. He told himself brusquely that he had no time to dwell on thoughts like that. He had to work for France with what God had granted him. God had sent him three children—instruments for France—and he must use them well. Anne was his best tool, firm and sound, with a sharp, cutting edge to her mind that he had carefully honed. Jeanne was so weak as to be almost no tool at all— yet evidently God had planned her weakness so that it could serve France too. Out of her ruin grew his two-edged plan. Charles, his son—well, it was too soon to tell what the child might be, but he must guard the doors of every chance.

Oliver, still thinking of Jeanne, was speaking pityingly. "Sire——" He hesitated. What comfort was there? "Small comfort, I know, and yet if the Princess Jeanne, in her infancy, was wracked with fevers that left her twisted and weak—God's purpose is in it somewhere——"

"Your lies are in it, too," the king said shortly. "There was no fever in her infancy—the weakness came with her at birth." His tone changed; he was thoughtful and detached. "Was it God's judgment on me for my fault—that I loathed the mother? Yet—my hate was just as strong when Anne was born, and she's well made. Charles, my infant son, he's half between the two—not bad, not good." He shrugged, giving up the question that he couldn't answer. "Well, blame it where you will—it leaves Jeanne lame, but, lame or whole, it doesn't change my plans—even twisted royal bones are too good for Louis of Orleans."

Oliver squirmed uneasily. To think of Jeanne's wracked body being taken in marriage sickened Oliver, who had weathered many ghastly plans of the king's. "But, sire," he protested, "I don't see, even if Orleans would accept her— which they won't—that you'll gain enough to make it worth your while. I see, of course," he said hastily, "that Orleans will come to the Crown if Louis has no chil-dren——"

"And he'd have no children with Jeanne; of that I've been assured."

"But it's so far away—I still don't see its worth."

The king rose from his chair and kicked it back from him, in excellent humor again, looking forward to Oliver's comprehension of the scheme that had been growing within the king and that he could bring forth now, a round ripe plan for Oliver to marvel at.

"You don't see," he said. "Of course you don't see. You're only a barber! You lather me with tact and com-pliments—help me scrape the bristles from my plans—yet you're too intent on just that one plan's face—now there's your fault——" He laughed heartily. "*You* can't shave two customers at once! *I* can—so that makes me King Barber!" He sobered a little in order to explain. "You remember the June day we rode to Blois to baptize a bastard?"

Oliver nodded; even his shins remembered that day.

"You remember we promised him my daughter for a wife—so that if I had no son, then at least my daughter would be Queen of France? Well, I have a son, now—and he'll be king—when I die, which is not very far away——"

Oliver crossed himself, said hastily, "You've many years to live."

The king made a rude sound. "Save your lather, Oliver, for those who can't see through scented soap! When I die, there'll be a regency until Charles is old enough to rule. And who, my fat barber, would be regent according to law and custom?"

"The queen mother and the heir presumptive," Oliver said sulkily, resenting this obvious catechism.

"Yes. My sweet wife Charlotte, and . . . ?"

"Louis of Orleans," answered Oliver quickly, losing his sulkiness in his growing interest.

"Yes—Louis of Orleans would be regent! Charlotte amounts to nothing. Then, if Louis were married to my daughter, think what a powerful regency that would be! Louis's name—the Orleans popularity—Anne's character— both of them royal blood—why, they'd take the throne from my son as easily as the nurse takes the rattle from his hands now! It would be treason in me to leave him such a strong regency."

Oliver nodded thoughtfully; he could see the danger there. If Louis, as regent, wanted the throne, it would be his for the taking. Of course it was all in the future, and he murmured consolingly, "God will spare you to bring your son safe to the throne."

"I'll be dead in five years," the king asserted angrily. "But I'll bring my son safe to his throne—I'll do it through my daughter Anne. And as for Orleans—Jeanne will see that it comes to the Crown."

Two daughters and a plan for each. Anne's strength of mind, directed by his teaching, should watch over her brother till he was king. Jeanne's deformity had always been a bitter insult to his pride—now her very ruin and sterility, married to the Orleans name, would bring the line to an end and bring the land into the hands of the king where it belonged.

Oliver dared to find objections to the plan. "Orleans will never accept Jeanne!"

"Yes, they will," the king contradicted. "They'll have to!"

"There'll be talk at court against it——"

"Oh, talk!" the king said contemptuously.

"More than talk. Orleans will appeal for help."

"Let them! I've heard dukes squeal before."

"They'll more than squeal," Oliver warned. "They'll fight."

That didn't worry the king. "They're too weak to fight— they're poor as river rats. I've seen to that."

"But they'll have help."

"Who? Not Angoulême—nor Dunois—although they'd like to help. They're too young—and they're wards of mine."

"But Bourbon is their friend!" Oliver claimed triumphantly, "Bourbon is spoiling for a fight with you. Orleans and Bourbon together—their strength is more than you can meet!"

The king smiled complacently. He was about to reveal the final loveliness of his plan. "Bourbon," he said slowly, drawing out the amusement, "Bourbon will stand with me —against Orleans!"

Oliver didn't say a thing, just looked at the king with open skepticism. The idea of Bourbon and Orleans being on opposite sides of any fight was so ridiculous it required no words.

"My fat barber doubts me!" the king complained. "Today he is doubtful—questions my mind—thinks I've gone mad—while yesterday he was only curious. Yesterday he wondered why I sent for the young Bourbon, Pierre de Beaujeu, and yesterday my barber eavesdropped at the door, trying to hear what Pierre and I discussed. But you couldn't hear a word, could you, my poor Oliver?"

Oliver's face had gone red; he couldn't answer.

The king laughed delightedly. He hadn't had such an amusing time in weeks. "Well, I'll tell you today what you couldn't hear yesterday. I betrothed my daughter Anne to Pierre de Beaujeu!" He paused, then nodded. "Yes, his mouth fell open much as yours hangs now. He gasped and stuttered—thought I was joking at first—mumbled something about being betrothed to Marie-Louise of Orleans, but when I gave him the marriage papers to sign he grabbed for them as though he feared I might change my mind."

Oliver was aghast. "Pierre de Beaujeu! Why—he has only the coat on his back—and even that was given him by the Orleans house."

"Oh—come now, Oliver, he has more than that! Or at least he gives me more than that. He gives me his Bourbon blood——"

"What—what?"

"Well, have you thought of this—how could the Bourbons help the Orleans house fight for a bride that they possess themselves?"

"Oh!" exclaimed Oliver, enlightened. "You separate the friends—make them enemies by giving to one what was promised to the other!"

"I separate the arrows—one by one." His clawlike hands turned and rested on his knees, palms upward, and Oliver could almost see the fate of the House of Orleans lying in one palm, the House of Bourbon in the other. The hands themselves weren't physically strong—the skin was gray and wrinkled, the corded blue veins showing through—but when he thought of the tremendous royal power those hands could wield, the lives and deaths that hung on a signature scrawled in that handwriting, Oliver felt an involuntary shiver of pity for anyone at the mercy of those cold, bony fingers.

"A happy plan, isn't it?" the king said with satisfaction. "And now I'm ready to write another letter, if you've recovered enough to hold a pen." Impatiently he waited for Oliver to nod his readiness, and then he began to dictate: "Write to my godfather, the Sire de Dammartin, and say to him—'Monseigneur, I have seen your letters, and in so far as your affairs are concerned, I will not forget them, and do you not forget mine! It has occurred to me to make a marriage between my daughter—my little daughter Jeanne —and the Duke of Orleans, because it seems to me the children they may have together will cost them but little to nourish!' "

The king's voice paused, and in the increasing heavy silence of the room Oliver looked up to meet his master's eyes. There was no laughter in them now; there was cruelty, revenge, madness, all merging into iron determination, and his voice was metallic with it as he continued the letter: " 'I advise you that I intend to make the said marriage and any who stand out against it will never be assured of their lives in my kingdom!' "

Oliver finished the letter; it was signed—but not sealed. The king stood reading it over while Oliver was sent to bring the Duchess of Orleans. At the thought of the coming interview the smile began to creep back into the king's eyes. He would extract the utmost enjoyment from it to revenge himself for the day when he had had to promise his daughter to Mary's bastard.

There was an anticipatory smile on Mary's face, too, as she followed Oliver up the stairs and through the long echoing hall to the king's room. To settle the details of the marriage was a happy thing for Louis and herself, although she always hated seeing the king. She knew only too well the king's opinion of her, and she wished, as she often did, that Charles were alive to attend to these important matters.

Her heart was beating heavily as Oliver opened the door for her and stood back to let her pass into the king's room. As she bowed she hoped she didn't seem too nervous. She would have been surprised if she could have read the king's mind. He thought her insultingly calm and poised—an adulterous woman of brass—and looking ridiculously young, as she knelt, raising her full blue skirt of stiff satin so that the petticoat flounces of white ruching decorated with the rose-colored velvet bows could be seen as she swooped backward and then down. Her low-cut bodice was edged with the same white ruching; her face and neck were smooth and pink above it. He made a sign for her to rise; she did, and waited quietly for him to speak. He took his time, surveying her with cold eyes.

"Well, madame, you have been very prompt," he commended her. "You had a good journey, I hope."

"A very happy journey. I hope Your Majesty is well."

"Well enough. And you——" He seated himself at his desk and his eyes wandered over her standing figure with leisurely insult. "I can see you bloom with health."

"Thank you," she said primly. "I am indeed very well."

He enjoyed her resentment a moment, then proceeded to the business of her coming. "You and your son are happy about this marriage, I am glad to hear."

"We all are happy—but Louis is wild with delight." She laughed indulgently. "I think he has loved your daughter ever since he was weaned."

The king considered that thought politely. "That's very pleasant—even if I find it a little unusual. I suppose a father is sometimes blind to his daughter's attractions—I confess it never occurred to me that Jeanne could ever inspire such a passion."

Mary looked at the king questioningly but felt no uneasiness. It was a slip of the tongue.

But he continued. "Your son must be a very discriminating boy—he evidently sees past the—the not-so-beautiful body of my daughter Jeanne—into the excellent mind and disposition of the girl."

Mary repeated, "Jeanne," almost under her breath, her large blue eyes intent on the king. Was he playing one of his malicious jokes?

But he seemed quite serious, and she listened again to his voice that had gone on while her thoughts had kept her from listening. "No doubt he even sees past those things to the royal name—and the large dowry. He's very sensible, and I know he and Jeanne will be content—not that happiness is an essential part of a state marriage——"

But Mary interrupted, feeling the time had come to end the joke, which wasn't even remotely amusing. "Your Majesty, you are either jesting with me or your tongue jests with your memory. It is your daughter Anne whom my son is to marry."

The king was the picture of incredulity. He said in thunderstruck surprise, "The Princess Anne?"

Mary flung annoyed words at his preposterous surprise. "But of course, Your Majesty, you remember you promised her to him the day you stood as his godfather. You remember now, of course?"

"I remember, of course, your son's baptismal ceremony —and I remember very well that after it was over I told your husband I intended to give my daughter to Louis— and that promise I am ready to keep," he said virtuously.

"But, Your Majesty," Mary cried out triumphantly, "your daughter Jeanne was not even born then! You spoke of your daughter—your only daughter was Anne!"

He was not shaken from his calmness. "My dear, I think I know my daughters' birthdays and their names as well as you. I'm perfectly aware that Jeanne had not yet been born, but"—he smiled sardonically—"that shows the faith I had in my fruitful wife! I'm sorry if you are disappointed."

"Disappointed! Louis's heart will be broken!"

He looked at her in scornful derision at such an extravagant statement. "I'm sorry if you have misled him. It was never my intention—and I don't understand how you could have thought he could reach so high."

Mary returned his scorn. "Are there any heights to which an Orleans may not aspire?"

The king's straight eyebrows raised a little in interrogation. "Orleans, madame?"

She looked at him, hating him.

"Orleans, sire!" she said stanchly, and faced him squarely across the desk, looking down into his skeptical eyes, trying to force the truth into them. "You make no secret of your shameful doubt, do you, Your Majesty? And you encourage jests at court—ah yes, I've heard the silly tongues repeat your doubts—I hate to think my son must hear them too—because they're lies!"

The king smiled wearily and again raised his eyebrows a fraction of an inch, but he didn't speak, and Mary wanted to take the truth, like a sharp dagger, and stab him with it, again and again.

"Lies!" she repeated, her voice shaking with the effort to control her fury. "My husband was never the kind of man who could even think of trading his wife's fidelity for the hope of a son! Not that it was Charles's fault no heir was born to us in all those years." She forced herself on to say these humiliating things, loathing the man who was making her blush with shame. "It was my fault—punishment for my vanity and my sins—but when God forgave me and sent us the child, Charles knew that Louis was his son—and that's the truth! I swear to Jesus and His Mother that it is!"

Absolute truth was in every ringing syllable of her words, and the king, whose trained mind was quick to detect lies, recognized the truth when he heard it too. Of course a part of his mind had always known it was true, possibly even before the day Charles had spoken to him and denied the false gossip that was spreading about his son's birth. Charles had spoken briefly, with quiet sincerity, but even more convincing than his words, the essence of the man's character had belied the scandal. It was as Mary had said, Charles wasn't the kind of man who would stoop to sordid trickery, no matter how he longed for a son. Nor would Mary's character, her strong religious conscience, her reverent obedience to her husband have ever allowed her to be a faithless wife, no matter if the end would seem to justify the means.

No, the truth was that Louis was an Orleans, and in a way the king had known it all along. He had simply chosen to believe the circumstantial evidence, and he would go on believing it because he chose. It was a useful weapon. He could wield it amusingly to insult the people he hated and it helped to justify the stern measures he took against them. He would never, never admit to anyone, even to himself, that Louis had a legal right to Orleans. He had helped label the boy a bastard—with the king's assistance Louis would always carry that title!

He smiled at Mary, a slow widening grimace of his thin lips, but his eyes didn't change their sardonic expression.

"Very loyally said," he congratulated her. "You must almost convince yourself sometimes!"

Mary's breath caught; she saw it was no use. She raised her eyes to a point well over his head and spoke with as much insolent courtesy as she dared.

"Since it is obvious my coming here to Tours was due to a grave misunderstanding, may I have your permission to withdraw?"

She could see argument would do no good. She couldn't make him give Anne to Louis, and she knew how thoroughly he was lying when he said it had never been his intention. He had changed his mind at the birth of his son, and that was that. When she thought of Louis's disappointment, she wanted to strike this cold, greedy man to whom promises meant nothing, scratch his stiff face and hurt his bony body in which there wasn't an honest breath. She half turned to make her final bow and leave.

But he was far from done with her. "There's a misunderstanding here indeed! I sent for you to make the wedding plans. I think it's strange that you expect a choice—king's daughters aren't offered every family."

Mary looked at him without comprehension; she was still far from understanding that his full purpose was to force Louis into a marriage with Jeanne.

"No more pretense is needed, sire," she assured him coldly. "You wish to act as though you'd kept your word to us—you offer a daughter you know we will decline—you keep the one you know was ours. No arguments of mine will make you change your will. I see that—so I ask to leave. I may?"

The king shook his head. "You miss my purpose. I give you Jeanne."

"And we refuse."

"Oh no! There is no choice. I give you Jeanne!"

Mary's voice shook with fury. "Indeed there's a choice! And it's an insult for you to speak of such an impossible marriage!"

"I'm not accustomed to have my authority so questioned!" the king said sharply. "It's a sovereign's right to arrange his lord's marriages!"

"I submit myself to that right! Any reasonable marriage we'll accept—although we don't disguise our resentment that you have taken Anne from us—but a marriage with the

Princess Jeanne would be a shameful farce—shameful to her as well as us!"

"I'm sorry you regard it in that light, but your opinion of it doesn't change my decision."

Mary took a deep breath and counted ten. She knew she had already been ruder to a king than it was wise to be. "You've been an enemy to us since Louis's birth. What did we do to make you one?"

"His birth," the king answered with truthful brevity.

Even though she knew it was useless, still for Louis's sake Mary made another appeal. "Is there nothing I could say to make you know that he was fairly born of Orleans blood?"

"Nothing."

Mary faltered. It was a bitter thing to take such an insult from a man—and be so helpless to answer it. She fought against her anger, but it was rising. "Have kings no gratitude that you deny a debt which in all honor you should own? You owe your very crown to Orleans help! It was Orleans walls that sheltered your father against his English enemies—Dunois and the Maid of Orleans claimed your throne for you—Orleans itself was ruined—your crown was saved, and now you use its powers against us! You took back from us the money—and privileges—and rights that once were ours—you make us need a brilliant match for Louis—your daughter would be one, but if Jeanne's dowry were ten—a hundred times the sum it is, yet we would still refuse!" Mary was started now; she couldn't stop although she knew she had gone too far. She went further. "I tell you now—I'd sell my last chemise before I'd sell my son into a match like that!"

"Too bold!" the king shouted, and crashed his fist down on the desk before him, rising abruptly to his feet.

Mary caught her breath sharply, frightened now. Kings were not human beings to be held to account for their sins; God had put them on the throne to be obeyed. Tears came stinging to her eyes, and she bent her head to hide them, waiting for her punishment.

"I see you know you've gone too far!" he said acidly.

Mary rallied a little. "Yes, sire, I have been bold—but it matters little what becomes of me. What becomes of Louis is my thought." Wearily she asked, "If I may go now?"

"Not yet, madame, not yet. If you're so tired," he added graciously, "you may sit down—and I'll sit too."

Mary watched him sit down again, but instead of accepting his permission, she remained stiffly standing. "As there is nothing more to say, I'll stand—with your permission."

"With my permission," the king roared, "you'll sit down! There's much more to say—and papers to sign—the wedding date to be fixed——"

She stared at him in amazed horror. Could he really mean that he expected to marry his wreck of a child to her strong, healthy Louis? She shuddered. Impossible! She couldn't find words to answer, shook her head and kept shaking it.

The king watched her a moment. "I thought I could rely on you to see the wisdom of this marriage to your house. I hoped I wouldn't have to threaten you—or mention imprisonment for you—and for Louis a life in a monastery cell."

A cold numb horror began spreading over her, up the backs of her legs, weakening them. He meant it—every word. She finally answered, showing a quiet courage that she didn't feel, "If we were friendless, I might fear your words."

"And have you many friends who'd come when you called—and thank you for the danger?"

"Not many, true," Mary answered, her thoughts flying to the Bourbon family. Angoulême and Dunois were cousins and would be loyal, but not much help, being too young. "But one, I know, would come no matter what the danger."

The king smiled, amused again. This would be very entertaining. "One?" he repeated thoughtfully. "Now let me see if I can guess. Not Orleans' nephews, no—they're wards of mine—not Guise, nor Maine, they're too busy with quarrels of their own—and not Bourbon, no—not with Pierre so soon—so very soon to call my daughter Anne his wife."

Nightmare on nightmare! It couldn't be true! This was too much. Mary's face was a portrait of bewilderment and shock. She drew on her very last remnants of courage to disbelieve him.

"I don't understand—you're mistaken—misinformed! Pierre is my foster son; he is betrothed to my daughter as you very well know——"

"Perhaps I knew—perhaps I forgot. It's over now, no matter which it was."

"I know you're wrong—misinformed——"

He smiled. "I'm rarely misinformed, and in this case I feel quite sure—it was in this room Pierre de Bourbon signed just yesterday—— What is it, are you taken ill, madame?" he asked hastily, in mock solicitude, for Mary had almost fallen. At his final words her knees had bent forward, as though someone had pushed her, and she had quickly grasped at the back of a chair for support. Her stunned eyes gazed at him in incredulous fear.

"Anne for the Bourbons—while Jeanne's for my son!" she whispered. Both her children's lives slashed with just one stroke—and for additional agony, Pierre's betrayal stabbed her. Marie-Louise was the worst of it! Louis would be furious to lose his Anne, but after all, he was a boy, and he would forget! But no—Louis was the worst—think of his being married to a horror like Jeanne! Oh God, she thought, and whispered it aloud. "Oh God—God's mercy——"

"God's will," the king corrected her, "and mine! Both wills are to be obeyed. Disobedience will bring imprisonment for you and your son and Orleans forfeit to the Crown! And that would be merciful of me, for it would save me a good deal of trouble if I had Louis sewed into a sack and cast into the Loire!"

Mary implicitly believed that he would do that, too, if he had to. She knew he must have considered it more than once, and now she was helpless, for without Bourbon support—and they could scarcely give it if they had Louis's bride for themselves—she was all alone!

The king had moved to the desk and taken up the unsealed letter to his godfather. "I wish you to hear this, so that you'll realize my determination." He read aloud the letter he had dictated to Oliver. When he came to the words "because it seems to me the children they may have together will cost them but little to nourish," a moan of anguish escaped from Mary and tears rolled down her cheeks. How cruel he was, and how sure of his purpose, that he would read the insulting inner purpose of his plan so coldly to her. Her mind moaned in impotent anger as his voice came, hard and goading. "I advise you that I intend to make the said marriage and any who stand out against it will never be assured of their lives in my kingdom!"

She begged and wept, willing to make any promise, willing to humiliate her pride to any extent if he would only release her children—but all the while she knew it was useless. He just stood and smiled at her, and finally she stopped and wearily begged to be allowed to return immediately to her home where she could prepare both her children for their coming disappointment. Weary or not, he wouldn't let her leave the room until her signature was on some papers accepting the betrothal terms for Louis.

Then she went in nervous haste to her room, sending a servant for Louis to come to her. To all his bewildered questions she made no answer, only said something had happened that required her to be with Marie-Louise at once and that he should prepare for the trip quickly, they would leave within the hour. He was angry and confused at being dragged away when they had just come—he had hardly had any time to see Anne, but he could tell from his mother's trembling eagerness to be gone, her red tear-swollen eyes, that something disturbing had happened and he obediently hurried to get ready.

Mary knew it would be wiser to wait till morning to leave. The roads were bad enough by day without adding the hazards of the dark, but she couldn't stand the thought of the long hours under the king's roof. She felt she must be doing something active, if it was only jolting along the road toward home. Feeling certain that she wouldn't be able to stay on a horse's back because of her trembling weakness and the strange mental nausea that blurred her eyes and made her head feel light and dizzy, she had sent one of her servants to the stable to arrange for a borrowed carriage to take them home to Blois.

Louis wanted to ride his own horse beside the carriage, but Mary, needing the comfort of his presence and hoping he might be able to sleep a little, persuaded him to ride inside the dusty-smelling carriage with her. As they rattled along the dark roads, moist and cool with night mist, lit only by the flares of the horsemen who rode ahead of the carriage and other soldiers behind it, Mary protected Louis from the jolting as much as possible. After a while he dozed off with his head in her lap. Gently she stroked his hair, her throat burning with tears. As she looked down at his profile outlined whitely against the dark cloak she wore, she could see his black arched eyebrow, smooth and shining a little in the tossing light from the flares, the mobile mouth that was calm in sleep, the bony planes of the cheek that had lost its childish softness, the hair that grew thick and dark from his unlined forehead. If she could only protect him from what was coming. If she could only protect Marie-Louise! It was the age-old desire of the mother when she sees danger approaching her children—and always a desire that must be unfulfilled.

The entire journey was unreal to her. Sometimes she would doze, and then start awake as the wheels jolted against the rocks in the road. Mary looked out of the black windows that gradually turned gray, then pink with the dawn and blue with the day. They stopped for food and to change horses; the rear wheel broke twice and it took hours both times to fix it, but the road ahead, with Blois at the end of it, was all she was conscious of.

They reached it toward early evening. Marie-Louise and de Mornac came hurrying to meet them, the girl in great surprise and de Mornac in searching apprehension, for he could see something was wrong. Mary sent Louis immediately to bed, and he didn't object because he was tired. Then she walked upstairs with Marie-Louise to her daughter's room, leaving de Mornac to watch them thoughtfully up the stairs. He watched them out of sight and then went to talk to the grooms.

Walking into her daughter's suite, closing the door very quietly behind her as though it were a sickroom, Mary thought that this was the worst thing that could happen to a mother, to force her to bring such painful news to her children. She took a last look at her happy daughter, another look around the peaceful room, still warmed by the light from the windows that faced the western sun. On the small Persian rug beside the bed an open box spilled out its colorful contents, and two new gowns were spread out on the rose satin bedspread. A new box of clothes for the trousseau must have come today and Marie-Louise had just been unpacking it. The big carved doors of the wardrobe were open, and hanging inside Mary could see the other lovely gowns and hats, all planned to delight Pierre's eyes. She wished for the first time that her daughter's marriage had been planned only for its suitability with no heart involved.

But Marie-Louise was questioning her curiously, and the awful moment could no longer be postponed.

"What happened, Mother?" Marie-Louise was asking worriedly. "Didn't you see the king?"

"I saw the king," Mary answered heavily. "I wish I hadn't. He was terrible—terrible!" Tears sprang to her eyes at the memory.

"But—about what? The terms of Louis's betrothal? I hope you thought to send for Pierre! He'd have been firm —it takes a man to understand those dreadful contracts."

"I sent for Pierre," Mary admitted miserably, "but they said he wasn't at Tours."

Marie-Louise looked bewildered. "But of course he is! I had a message from him day before yesterday." She smiled a little as she recalled the message with its words of love.

Mary saw the smile, recognized its meaning, and went cold with anger at Pierre, who could send messages of love just before he turned his back in betrayal. She wished she could have talked to him so she could better understand what had happened. She knew he loved Marie-Louise. She could only think he had been so dazzled by the strange stroke of fortune that he had snatched before he thought. Of course it would have been difficult for him to refuse, but if he had, and if he had brought the Bourbon family's aid to back his objections, Orleans and Bourbon would have stood together and fought the whole thing. Still—perhaps it was too much to expect Pierre, a younger son and dependent on the love and charity of his adopted family, to decline a king's daughter and her magnificent dowry. He had been at Blois only last week, amiable and as fond of Marie-Louise as ever, but very likely the suddenness of the thing had bewildered his slow mind and the king's persuasiveness had worked upon Pierre's easily influenced character.

"Well, at any rate, I didn't see Pierre. I thought perhaps he might be on his way here—to tell you——" Mary took a deep breath, walked closer to her daughter, and reached gently for her hand. "Marie-Louise—the king is a very cruel and changeable man—he has changed his mind about Louis's marriage—and yours!"

"Mine!" Marie-Louise echoed in surprise. "Why mine—

and what is it to the king whom I marry? I'm no ward of his!"

"No," Mary said unhappily. "He doesn't insist you marry anyone. It's Pierre he has plans for. Pierre is to—he wishes Pierre to marry someone else." Mary floundered, conscious of her daughter's startled withdrawal, her widening eyes. "To marry his daughter—Anne."

Marie-Louise laughed, a short, puzzled laugh. "Ridiculous! I never heard anything so foolish. Even if Pierre were free—and wanted to—why should the king think Pierre was suitable—and what about Louis?"

"Oh, I don't understand most of it," Mary admitted wearily. "I talked—and argued—and begged—but in the end I had to agree."

"Agree!" Marie-Louise exclaimed in amazement. "But you can't answer for Pierre—and he'll refuse, of course."

"But—Pierre has agreed already. Had already promised before I arrived!"

Marie-Louise looked furious at her mother for this treason against her beloved. "I don't believe it!" she said flatly, her usual politeness forgotten.

"I didn't either," Mary sighed, "until I saw his signature on the marriage contract."

"Mother! You didn't! You couldn't have!"

"My dear," Mary said gently, "I did. It was there—in his handwriting." And what she had felt, when she saw the familiar rounded, careful letters, was only a thousandth part of the shock Marie-Louise was feeling now. Her face was a youthful pink mask of amazement—too soon yet for her to feel the full pain that would come flooding over her when she realized the extent of Pierre's betrayal.

"But why?"

"I don't know," Mary repeated. "I don't know what the king's planning—except I know it must be evil."

"Pierre must have been forced into it!" Marie-Louise spoke vehemently. "The king must have threatened me— and you—if he didn't obey!"

Mary started to protest, then stopped herself. If it would make Marie-Louise better able to bear the blow, let her believe Pierre had yielded out of fear for her. It could be true.

So she nodded slowly. "Yes, I think Pierre was forced to agree." Whether he was or wasn't, he had committed himself and them all now, and although Mary said all the comforting things she could find to say, they were as hollow as echoes. Marie-Louise listened to them in a dull silence, not even seeming to hear them. Finally Mary's voice ran down and they both sat in silence, Mary thinking tiredly that this was only the beginning. Tomorrow she would have to tell Louis of the horror in store for him.

Mary had seen Jeanne only once, but to think of that deformity as her son's wife—oh, it was unthinkable! It must be stopped somehow. Somehow. She stirred restlessly, and Marie-Louise, who was standing at the window, spoke to her mother without turning.

"Mother—go to bed now. There's no use going over and over it—we'll talk tomorrow!"

Mary looked at her daughter's figure silhouetted in the window and sighed. She looked so young, so vulnerable. Her blond hair, parted in the middle to reveal the clean pink scalp in a straight line from the center of her forehead to the nape of her neck, was plaited in two thick braids that hung down past her slim waist. She wore a pale pink brocaded robe over the linen chemise she would wear to bed. The robe was well-worn and a little faded—Marie-Louise was wearing out her older clothes, planning to give them to her maids when she married, so that for Pierre everything would be fresh and new. But now Pierre would never see the lovely things, chosen so carefully for his pleasure.

Mary hated to leave her daughter, but she knew that Marie-Louise wanted to be alone with her pain. Well—there was nothing else Mary could say that would make it more bearable. Time would help, she knew, and she wished she had handfuls of it to give.

She walked wearily to her own room and dismissed her maids as she prepared for bed. She wanted to be alone too, and she was exhausted. She lay in desperate weariness, every bone aching as though she had been beaten, but she couldn't sleep. Last night she had been stunned and anesthetized with shock; tonight her pain was real, without mercy. Her mind whirled dizzily from Louis to Marie-Louise, to Pierre, to Anne and Jeanne and back again, finding new horrors in details of the future until she couldn't endure lying motionless in the dark any longer.

She put on a warm robe and walked out into the sitting room, toward the window seat and the chairs, close together, where they had sat embroidering the trousseau. Marie-Louise had been sewing there today; there was a new piece that had been started before Mary had left for Tours. She picked it up, looked at the dainty stitches, and in her memory she could hear her daughter's clear, loving voice "Pierre—Pierre——" Her whole life was Pierre. Mary couldn't stand it; she dropped the white cloth, covered her face with her hands, and painful, hiccoughing sobs came uncontrollably from her. They wrenched her whole body, and she was glad of their pain.

She was so isolated in her grief that she didn't hear the door open and close, nor the steps across the room. The first she knew of de Mornac's presence was his hands, gently turning her about and firmly holding her against him. She tried at first, in startled rejection, to draw away, but he held her quietly, saying nothing. His supporting strength was so comforting, after being alone and helpless, that she couldn't repudiate it, even for her pride. She leaned against him, shaken with grief.

After a while, when her sobs were wearing out, de Mornac picked Mary up as he had once before and carried her to her bed. He laid her down there, but she struggled to sit up, pushing him away with frightened hands. It absolutely must not happen again! He smiled at her furious determination and spoke soothingly, to calm her.

"Please—don't be alarmed—I only came because I wanted to help you. Now lie down and tell me what's happened, and then you can sleep."

He pressed her gently back on the pillow, and she was glad she hadn't the strength to resist him. He sat on the bed, holding her hand in one of his and massaging the back of it with his large thumb. She told him about the terrible events at Tours, and it comforted her to see how calmly he took them.

"It doesn't matter so much about Pierre," he said reflectively, "although I know his lack of gratitude hurts you. But he's stupid—even your affection for him couldn't hide that from you. Marie-Louise hasn't lost much in him—there's other game in the forest and she'll forget him. She'll be sad for a while, and then she'll be glad it happened. You'll see."

Mary certainly hoped so, although she had her doubts.

De Mornac continued more gravely. "Louis's problem is

more serious. He'll give you a bad time—he's a stubborn
boy, and he'll be furious about losing his Anne. But the
really bad thing is his betrothal to Jeanne."

Mary twisted and cried out, "He can't marry her. He
shan't!"

De Mornac shrugged and said quickly, "It's a fuss about
nothing. It's all in the future—Louis has three years in
which to wriggle out of it one way or another. And so many
things may happen in three years, my sweet, you distress
yourself too much. Look, the king may die, the dauphin
may die—we all may die! A catastrophe that is three years
off isn't a catastrophe at all!"

De Mornac laughed in the darkness, and Mary almost
smiled herself, it was such a comforting sound. And—"my
sweet," he had called her, as though there was a deep understanding between them, and it had sounded beautiful in his
deep, smooth, Gascon voice.

It was good not to be alone. It was good to have someone
with a strong, courageous mind to comfort her fears. She
had been too long alone, and no one knew so well as she
did that there was no woman in all France less suited to a
lonely life and responsibilities. She was so grateful to de
Mornac for the comparative peace he was bringing her that
she did not protest, although her breath caught in her throat,
when he lay down beside her and gathered her into his arms.
She was ready to push him away, but he made no move to
possess her, only held her to him and continued to talk
quietly.

"The king's no fool; he doesn't bite anything he can't
chew. It'll take all our wits to get out of this. There's nothing to do now—you've signed the papers, but we can always say you signed them under protest——"

"Which is certainly the truth!"

"Yes. We'll get no help from Bourbon—but later there'll
be other dukes who'll resent this insult with us. There's
nothing for it but to wait—your hardest task will be to
make Louis see that. He'll want to start fighting the entire
world right away, of course."

He laughed again; she could feel the laughter in his arm
under her head, and it was companionable to feel mirth so
close. There was one pleasant thing, at least, about being
so exhausted—her conscience seemed to have died of it, and
it didn't nag at her for lying so acquiescently in his arms.

The shock of the disappointment had closed her mind to any hopeful aspects of the situation, and now, though she still knew there was immediate sorrow and grief to be faced, if she could cling to the longer view, she would be able to get herself and her children through the worst of it.

De Mornac was talking again in a lowered voice, and she heard it only intermittently as she sank into sleep under its comforting assurance.

"—Marie-Louise will forget—to England perhaps for a visit—glad someday—Louis rash—temper his boldness—but three years—much can happen in three years——"

Mary didn't know how long she slept, but she woke in the darkness, her first exhaustion satisfied, and her waking thought was relief that de Mornac was still beside her, sleeping too. She was still in his arms, as she had been when she had fallen asleep, and his face was close to hers, although she could only dimly see it. She could hear his regular breathing and feel the warmth of his body moving with his breath. She felt a content she had never known before, and she realized the simple and direct truth—that she never wanted to be without him. The peace that enveloped her seemed as tangible as his arms. Then she wanted more than peace—she was conscious of their bodies' closeness, and she moved a little, hoping it would waken him. She put her arms around his neck and drew herself up to his lips. Desire woke him—he murmured her name into her soft warm mouth.

Some of the calmness he had given her lasted even through the stormy scene with Louis, for he, as de Mornac had predicted, was eager to fight the world singlehanded. Anne had been promised to him. She counted on marrying him. They had plans for when they were married. Anne had been promised to him and he intended to see that promise was kept! The substitute was ridiculous and insulting and horrible! That must be made clear to the king immediately! If the king sent an army to Blois to enforce his will, that was all right too. The army would be met. If Louis died—and if Blois was burned to the ground—that was also all right. It was much better than meekly accepting the hideous Jeanne!

It was amazing to Mary to look at her son, hear him, and realize he was still only a boy, not able to decide his own destiny. He was so furiously determined; he stated his case so definitely. He wouldn't see that it was not his decision that counted but his mother's. When he heard that she had actually signed the papers he looked at her with glaringly scornful eyes.

"You'd let the king do that to me—without any objection?" His voice cracked with angry incredulity. He couldn't believe it of the mother he had always adored and who had seemed to adore him.

"Louis, there's nothing else for us to do!" Mary was almost crying again. She couldn't blame him for his fury, and yet it was so painful to see him hating her as he did. "How would it have helped if I had refused? We would have been separated immediately, and punished, you'd be taken to prison—and Orleans would have been confiscated——"

Louis interrupted vehemently: "I'd rather be in prison. I'd rather be dead than married to that hunchback!"

She hastily quoted de Mornac. "But we have three or four years, perhaps, to wriggle out of it. The king may die, the dauphin may die—we all may die! A catastrophe that's three years off isn't a catastrophe at all!"

But Louis was not to be calmed as she had been. It was too near, too personal, to be viewed that way. After all, it wasn't happening to her—she could afford to be calm.

"He won't ever die, he's too mean! And the dauphin won't die either. I know it. Nothing will change—we'll have consented and we won't be able to escape. We've got to fight now! *Now!*"

She assumed as much authority as she could. "I'm bitterly sorry, Louis, that we disagree, but I must do what I have to do. When you're older you'll see I did the only possible thing."

"You think I'll be a coward when I'm older, then!" he said reproachfully, folding his arms and staring straight into her eyes that were on a level with his own.

Mary looked at him miserably. He was a mixture of man and boy, and Mary wished he were a complete man so he could make his own decision. As it was, she had to make it for him, and how could she know whether it was right or not? It was certainly the wisest, the most prudent, the only sensible course to take, and yet, if Louis matured in the direction he was now growing, the prudent would never appeal to him. In any situation, if there were only one chance in a million, he would take that chance. But how could she take such a chance for him? She couldn't. It would only result in open war with the king, a hopeless war, ending in his death or imprisonment. Was ever a poor woman in such a dilemma? she asked herself, and then, as soothing unguents to a burn, came de Mornac's words: "Three years is a long time—anything can happen!"

She tried to cling to that thought, tried not to hear Louis's furious words: "Go away! I hate you! Go away!"

She went to Marie-Louise's room. Pierre had sent word that he was coming, and Marie-Louise was dressing for this last meeting. He was coming to explain why they couldn't marry, for he had no way of knowing that she already knew. Marie-Louise was very quiet, but she seemed calm, and for the first time in her life she didn't want to talk to her mother about Pierre.

When Marie-Louise was ready she went down alone to wait for Pierre in the large salon. They weren't accustomed to meeting there. This was his home as well as hers, and they usually used the smaller, informal rooms. Today Marie-Louise thought this large, impersonal salon, which had never seen their happier times, might help them through a painful one. She walked about the room, looking at it as though she were a stranger in the house. She critically surveyed the elaborate draperies, the valuable tapestries, the great fireplaces at each end of the room with their heavily carved mantels, the formally posed portraits that looked down at her, small and alone, in the quiet, empty room.

She heard her steps on the polished, shining floor, and the whisperings of her moire gown that was to have been a part of her trousseau. No need to save it now. She heard other steps, too, in the hall outside. Pierre's they must be! She turned and stood watching the door, looking calm and serene, a welcoming smile on her face. Pierre must be suffeing as she was; she would make it as painless as she could.

It was not Pierre who came in, but his older brother Charles, now Duke of Bourbon. He was a good deal older than Pierre, almost fifty, a short, dark, stocky little man, smiling nervously and distressingly embarrassed in the face of her astonishment. They did manage a greeting, and he smiled something about her growing more beautiful every day and then they came to a dead stop. Marie-Louise waited

for him to speak, but when he grew redder and unhappier
by the minute, she helped him.

"Your brother wasn't able to come?" she began, and the
words, in spite of her, were heavy with disappointment.
Even if he had come to tell her they couldn't be married,
at least she could have seen and touched him while he said
it.

"My brother Pierre," Bourbon said, as though he were
introducing someone he didn't like, "my brother Pierre has
asked me to come in his place, to explain to you a new
situation which has just been—created. He thought his coming would only give you unnecessary pain, so it has become
my duty to bring you very unpleasant news." He looked at
her wistfully, hoping she would guess so he wouldn't have
to tell her. She came to his rescue again.

"My mother has just returned from the king. He told her
then, I think, what you have come to tell me now. The king
has arranged a marriage for Pierre; he is to marry the Princess Anne." Although she had said it to herself often enough
through the nights, to hear the words spoken aloud was a
shock to her. The duke saw her grief and looked away from
it.

"My dear, I know what a surprise it must have been to
you; it was to us all. We had never had any inkling of the
king's intentions, and I may say I was most displeased with
Pierre's hastiness. I think, and I told him so, that he shouldn't
have signed the papers until he had consulted me—and until
he had talked with you."

"I'm sure he had no alternative," Marie-Louise said
quickly. She couldn't let herself think it had been a matter
of choice for Pierre. Losing him because of circumstances
they couldn't control was horrible enough, but to feel that
Pierre had been weak in his love for her couldn't be borne.

The duke understood that feeling. "The king is very
strong, and of course it would be impossible for Pierre to
refuse if the king insists, but still it is a sudden and disgraceful thing and I am sorry for it."

Bourbon hated the position he was in. This brilliant marriage suddenly thrust upon his house was really unwelcome,
but Pierre had accepted and it couldn't be refused now.
Bourbon's hands were tied, but the great advantages of the
marriage didn't console him for his uneasy sense of treachery toward his dear friend, Charles of Orleans, and toward

his own dead father who had left him the heritage of friendliness. If Pierre hadn't been so weak, both in his love for Marie-Louise and his love for position, Bourbon would have offered his support in the battle to see that Orleans was given what it had been promised. He would have preferred to teach this king, who had grown entirely too insolent and strong, what he owed to the nobles of France. But now Bourbon straddled a most uncomfortable fence. Although he must support the king, since their families were soon to be joined, he thought Louis was being inhumanly treated.

After a ludicrous attempt to console Marie-Louise, the duke left her. Then, in the outer hall, he encountered Mary and had the same thing to go through again. Injudiciously, he said enough to let her see that he considered it a great shame, and she took hope and begged for his help. Then Bourbon was forced to retreat and hide behind the king's wishes, seeing himself a mean figure in her eyes and his own as he did so. She gave him a cold farewell, and he left her, torn between his family, the king, his friends, and the right. The king would have smiled to see the Duke of Bourbon crawling heavily and unhappily back onto his horse for his miserable ride home, cursing his younger brother almost all the way.

Mary ached with longing to console her daughter, but Marie-Louise was nowhere to be found; evidently she wanted solitude. Louis was invisible too. Mary thought, with one of her very rare moments of detached humor, that life with her children was going to be a game of hide-and-seek from now on. Determinedly she marched back downstairs to the little salon, a warm, comfortable room with the sun in it, and sent a servant to tell de Mornac she wished to see him. He, at least, could be summoned, and must obey.

He came very quickly, and when she saw him she wondered what she was going to say. There was a good deal that might be said, but had she better say it?

He began to speak before she could worry for very long. "I saw the duke as he was leaving," he said. "He couldn't have enjoyed his visit. He looked as though he were about to cry."

"I asked him to help us, but he only talked about the king's will! I'm disappointed in my friends!"

"You're too hard on him. It's that stupid Pierre who has

made all the trouble. He wasn't even brave enough to come and tell her himself. A sickly love his must have been!" De Mornac was contemptuous.

She plunged in with no idea of where she would come out. "Evidently that's not the way love would affect *you?*"

He smiled as though he wondered, too, where this would lead them. "No, it isn't," he said.

"I suppose even the king and his armies couldn't take someone you wanted from you?" She was arch and inviting, in spite of herself.

"It would be difficult," he admitted, smiling.

"You've loved often, I suppose?" It wasn't a thought that gave her much pleasure.

"An agreeable number of times."

"But you've never loved enough to marry?" That was what interested Mary.

"I've been strangely situated for marriage," he explained, walking about the room, encircling her so that to see him she was forced to revolve slowly, like a Maypole pulled by ribbons.

"In what way?" she asked, trying to look as though it were a purely impersonal discussion in which she had only a polite interest.

"Well, I left home when I was very young—and much too poor to think of marriage—unless it were with some aging, wealthy widow." He smiled to see how she compressed her lips and looked displeased at this possibly distant description of herself. "Unfortunately, I'm a romantic man with a taste for beauty—and wealthy widows—with only one exception—are always very plain. Then, when I came here, still very young, there were plenty of pretty serving girls to be loved, but hardly to be married, my birth and family being above that level—and the many lovely ladies visiting or living here could be—admired, but not married, since their level was above my own. I'm a very sad case," he admitted, laughter in his eyes. "I'm not fit to be married to the fish that swim about the lower levels of this château nor the fowl that flutter so elegantly through the salons. I'm neither fish nor fowl; I'm flesh!" He turned and looked directly at her.

She devoted all her energy to the amazingly pink blush that she could feel all over her. She thought even her elbows were blushing. Yes, he was flesh. Strong, smooth flesh.

He went on walking. "I've never met anyone else in the same position, so I think I must resign myself to going wifeless to my grave."

"But," she protested, "if you married a nice country girl, you could raise her to your level." She didn't know why she suggested that; she certainly didn't want him to marry a nice country girl.

He must have known that, because he didn't seem to take her suggestion very seriously. "Because if I married a fish, I'd become one myself."

"And if you married one of the elegant fowl?" she asked, trying to say it lightly, as if she had just thought of it. "Then you would raise yourself to her level."

He laughed. "No, it wouldn't do. I'd still be flesh."

That word—she wished he wouldn't say it. It sounded so naked.

Mary said in irritation, "That's certainly a very pessimistic view to take!" Certainly, she thought haughtily, she had no intention of marrying him; it wasn't necessary for him to refuse in advance. "I've seen many such marriages"—she couldn't think of one, really—"that have turned out very well."

"Your acquaintance is, of course, wider than mine," he admitted. The subject didn't seem to interest him and he didn't continue it, to her great annoyance.

"You're very disagreeable this morning," she said sharply.

"Disagreeable?" he echoed, looking amused. "If that was being disagreeable, then I am nearly always so."

"You weren't disagreeable last night!" It took all her courage to say it, and it came in a whisper. The room became very still suddenly, and she was trembling in its listening expectancy. De Mornac's amusement immediately disappeared and he walked swiftly to her, took her in his arms.

"I'm glad you think so," he murmured and kissed her.

When the sound of the blood pounding in her ears had diminished enough so that she could hear him again, he was saying, "—never meant to be disagreeable to you—ever! Watched you—wanted you—for years—I knew you well—that's why I took you so suddenly. If you were given time to think—and a choice—I knew your conscience would refuse—your saints would hound you and keep you in eternal hell—so it seemed to me the least I could do was to carry the blame upon my shoulders, which, God knows, will never feel it."

"Having so much weight there now, they'll not notice one more burden," she thought, but pushed the thought from her, for he was continuing and she preferred to listen to his caressing voice.

"You've wanted love all your life—I have it to give you. You're bound to no husband and I have no wife. If we were in other circumstances, we'd marry——"

"Why shouldn't we?" she asked recklessly. "Why shouldn't we anyway?"

"You're sweet," he said gently, "very sweet, to say it, but it isn't worth the trouble—the scandal and the embarrassment to us all. We will be as good as married—or better!"

Her saints, who believed only in a marriage blessed by the church, were not convinced, but after all, it wasn't her saints who were being kissed breathless. Mary wished it was night and she and de Mornac were alone in her room. He wished so too, but they parted, discreetly, Mary to resume her search for the children, and de Mornac to his never-ending task of wringing money out of unlikely places. He walked more triumphantly than ever, pleased with his new love, and Mary walked in a dream, ecstatic because she had found love at last.

How could she know their definitions of love were not quite the same?

4

Louis couldn't understand it! Relentlessly he was being dragged toward his wedding day like a bawling calf is dragged at the end of a rope to its disaster, and nobody lifted a hand to help him! Nobody even seemed to care very much. Count André Visconti, to whom Louis went for advice, was aging, his memory wandering so that he couldn't keep his mind on the subject and could only suggest that Louis pack and move to Milan, which was the one civilized city in Europe. Count André offered to travel with Louis when the weather was better.

De Mornac only smiled encouragingly and said not to give up hope till the last boar was skinned. Marie-Louise sat at her window and stared out, thinking of Pierre, and although the cardinal and Monseigneur de la Craix prayed for Louis, counseling patience and fortitude of spirit, and his other relatives were voluble with outraged sympathy, nothing definite enough to suit Louis was being done.

His mother cried over him at times, but that didn't help either, and she was quite as likely to be found laughing with de Mornac in the next moment. Mary was often ashamed of her own happiness when she thought how her children were suffering, but de Mornac found an answer that soothed her conscience—as he always did.

"It's not in the nature of things," he told her, "for children and their parents to be happy at the same time. Their turn will come and they won't throw it away because you're old and miserable!"

So she enjoyed their love. They were together as often as they dared to be, and her dependence upon him grew so strong that she thought almost continuously about marrying him.

But it was no time for her marriage plans. Although Louis thought she did little or nothing to aid him, in the

four years that slowly passed, the Orleans family squirmed
and twisted and sometimes almost thought they had wrig-
gled out of the coming marriage of Louis to Jeanne. Mary
appealed again and again to the king, which was less than
useless. She hoped he would die; he stubbornly refused. She
appealed to the guardians of her young cousins, Angoulême
and Dunois, but, as the king had foreseen, those wise councilors refused to have anything to do with the quarrel.

Young Duke Eugène of Angoulême was having his own
troubles. He wanted to marry the beautiful Mary of Burgundy, daughter of Charles the Bold, but the king had
decided he would be happier with Princess Louise of Savoy.

Dunois had no marriage plans at all, and wished he had.
But he was a son of the illegitimate branch of Orleans, and
although they had been given the county of Dunois and its
title by the late king, still the young count couldn't aspire
to the brilliant marriage his advisors wished for him.

Both of Louis's cousins wanted to help him—especially
Dunois—but they had no strength to offer, only their
wishes and promises for the future.

Marie-Louise was very miserable too, but in a more listless way. Pierre had never once ridden to Blois to see her.
She had had one awkward letter from him, and that was
all. He thought it best for them not to meet for a while—it
would be too painful, he wrote. The implication, that after
a while it might not be so painful, that the sting of their
separation would disappear with time, was a thought that
rubbed sand on her wounds. She fought against her humiliating doubts of him.

Another marriage had been considered for her, but she
had looked so stricken that her mother had said no more
about it. Marie-Louise spoke of entering a convent, and
although Mary resisted the idea, sometimes she thought
helplessly that it might be the answer.

Inexorably the time passed, the date and the place for
the weddings were agreed upon, for it was the king's charming whim that his daughters should have a double wedding,
and it was arranged that on September 8, 1476, at the
Château Montrichard, Anne should be married to Pierre at
the same time that Jeanne was being married to Louis.

Montrichard was another of the king's castles on the
Loire, a smaller château, and only the king's immediate
household, not the whole court, was in temporary residence

there. Perhaps the king thought a quieter place, without too large a group of spectators, would be a wiser choice for such strange weddings.

In his room with his mother and de Mornac, on the eve of the day on which they were to leave for Montrichard, Louis's exterior of sullen obedience exploded like a barrel of fireworks into which a match had been tossed. He called his mother and de Mornac everything he could think of, and his vocabulary, along with the rest of him, had matured.

He wasn't going to Montrichard to marry that humpback. He'd be eternally goddamned if he would! Because other people were yellow cowards didn't mean he was too. If the king wanted him, he could come and get him, but, dead or alive, he was not going to marry anybody but Anne!

Mary left Louis and de Mornac to fight it out. They stood up to each other, fairly evenly matched, for Louis was in his teens now, as tall as de Mornac, and although he was slighter and less experienced, he had the fire of his hot convictions.

"I know you think we've done nothing to save you——" de Mornac began.

Louis interrupted, "And have you?"

"We've done our best—and if we'd done a thousand times more it will still have been useless. We're all alone! We've got nobody to fight with us!"

"Because you haven't fought!" Louis yelled furiously. "You've whined and appealed and signed everything you were told to! How can anybody come help us if we lie down and allow ourselves to be walked on? Why should they help cowards like that? If we'd refused in the first place——"

Mary found courage to speak. "He'd have put you in prison."

Louis whirled on her contemptuously. "What's so terrible about prison? It would have been the best thing for us! Every duke would have rallied to us, simply to protect his own rights! Brittany—Burgundy—even Bourbon would have come at that! But that's in the past—now is the problem!" He turned and faced de Mornac again. "I'm not going to Montrichard!"

De Mornac was silent for a moment and then he nodded

his head toward the window. "Do you know what's down there in the courtyard?"

"Oh yes," Louis answered contemptuously. "I know the king's sent a pack of soldiers he calls an escort of honor to see me to Montrichard. What of it? There's only two hundred men or so. We have almost that many—well, almost," he added, in answer to de Mornac's look of derision. "And more would come if we called!"

"But not in time," de Mornac answered. "Do you know what's down in the village?"

Louis looked at him questioningly, a worried furrow between his dark brows, his eyes very wide open in the way he always held them, measuring de Mornac with intent annoyance. He pushed back the ruffled cuff of his riding coat and, holding his left wrist in his right hand, revolved it with a massaging movement—an unconscious gesture he often used when he was worried. He had broken his left wrist some years ago in a bad fall from a beautiful horse the king had given him. The bones had taken a while to heal, and they still ached a little sometimes when he was tired. He had massaged the wrist to quiet its throbbing and the gesture had become an unconscious habit. He did it now because he was furious with worry. In spite of everything de Mornac had said about the dreadful day being so far off, it was here at last, and de Mornac was still advising him not to resist.

De Mornac was answering his question. "A portion of the king's army just happens to be passing through—it's a nice coincidence. Perhaps the king thought you'd be feeling a little reluctant about coming—in need of urging." Then he dropped his light, sarcastic tone and said gravely, "Louis, you've got to marry. Your mother's as wretched about it as you are—but the odds are too heavy. You can fight if you insist—anybody can fight—but you won't win. If you refuse to go to Montrichard tonight—then tomorrow this room——" He looked around Louis's big, shabby, well-loved room, its wall hung with trophies of the hunt, the mantel above the fireplace cluttered with medals and prizes Louis had won at tennis and broad-jumping, at which he was a champion. The beautiful carved paneling of the walls was decorated with brightly colored pennants and banners, souvenirs of different tournaments in which Louis had excelled in horsemanship and jousting. A complete record of Louis's life was visible in the room, from the broken tennis racquet tossed carelessly into the corner beside the scarred dueling swords, the big hunting dog stretched out in sleep before the fire, the miniature of his mother, his sister, and Anne standing in gold frames on his little-used desk, to the sketched caricature of the king nailed to the inside of the wardrobe door, along with ribald doggerel that didn't try to escape treason.

"This room," de Mornac repeated, "will be as charred and ruined as every acre of Orleans land. Your mother will be dead. Your sister will be dead. You will be dead. The king will have won even more by your death than he will by your marriage. The last Orleans will have been executed for treason, and his lands confiscated to the Crown. If that's what you want, then stand and fight!"

He drew Mary along with him out of the room and left Louis to think.

When he came back in a half hour he didn't have to ask what the decision was. Louis was standing in the center of the room, slowly pulling on his leather riding gauntlets, his gaze absent and thoughtful as he reached for his riding cloak and his felt sugar-loaf hat.

De Mornac sighed with relief. He hadn't been at all sure. He spoke comfortingly. "It won't be so bad. You'll hardly know you're married—you'll rarely have to see her—only to visit her now and again is all the king insists upon." For it had been conceded, after long hagglings, that Jeanne should return immediately after the wedding to Linières and stay there. Since she was in no way capable of managing an establishment of her own, she had begged to be allowed to go back to her home and the king had grudgingly given them that relief at least.

De Mornac went on, enlarging on the pleasant aspects of the marriage. "Her dowry will enable you to live in luxury——"

Louis interrupted as he looked up and shook his head. "I'll never touch a penny of her dowry!"

"But why not, in God's name?"

"I've a plan," Louis said soberly. "There's more than one way to kill a boar. I'd rather have done it in one thrust—but if I have no support," he sighed, "I will have to corner it and starve it to death."

De Mornac was looking at him worriedly, and Louis smiled a little.

"Don't worry," he said grimly. "It'll be a very quiet battle in which nobody'll get hurt."

"What——" began de Mornac, but Louis shook his head.

"I can't tell you," he said. "It'll be a long battle—but I'll win." He spoke with the conviction that stayed with him all his life. "I'll win!"

Jeanne's wedding gown was cloth of gold, and when she was dressed and ready she looked at herself in the mirror and laughed.

Anne, also dressed in cloth of gold, came hurrying toward her sister, saw the shining dress that made a mockery of the twisted body in it, the tortured look on the ugly face, and she tried to turn Jeanne away from the mirror. But Jeanne resisted, and shoulder to shoulder, they stood and were so reflected in the glass. It was a pitiful contrast. Anne wished for once that she didn't look so freshly beautiful, her hair and eyes gleaming dark against skin that was ivory pink and smooth. Beside Anne, Jeanne's ugliness was even more unlovely, with the long nose in the heavy sallow face with its self-deriding smile. Worst of all was the comparison between Anne's slim young body and the ruined shell Jeanne lived in.

This was exquisite torture for Jeanne, to be taken from her quiet retreat at Linières, where people didn't start and shrink at the sight of her, and brought to this cruel castle, where everyone was beautiful except herself, to be dressed in shining gold and set upon a stage, the central figure in a public ceremony, to be gaped at and discussed, laughed at and pitied.

She had begged to be spared from this marriage; she had never expected nor wanted any marriage for herself, and the news had come into her quiet life, changing it overnight. She had cried until her sallow face was blotched and red, but it hadn't done her any good. She was here, and in a few hours she would be married to a young man who turned away his head in disgust at the sight of her. She didn't blame him for that; sometimes she turned away in disgust at the thought of herself, but it was especial torture to see it in him, for he had all the things she loved in other people, including a bright alertness of mind that co-ordinated with the quick gracefulness of his body. His hair and his eyes and his tongue all sparkled, and she would have given her soul to have been a fit bride for him.

Anne was finding a different kind of mockery in the beauty of her dress and herself. It was all to be given to the wrong person! There would have been so much joy in her wedding day if she were to be married to Louis. Marriage with Pierre was more than distasteful to her—it was hideous; but she was a realist by birth and by training, and when her father had completely outlined his plan to her, she had been forced to see, as he had known she would, what a thoroughly practical thing it was, although she regretted what it required of her. If her father said it was inevitable, they must all adjust themselves to it, although to exchange her beloved childhood companion for the dull Pierre was hard. She cried sometimes when she suddenly thought of Louis and what they had planned together, all of it impossible now.

Jeanne turned abruptly from the mirror and was laughing in a frenzied hysteria of ugly sounds, tearing at her golden dress with weak, bony fingers.

"It's too cruel, too cruel! Oh, Anne," she cried imploringly, "send for our father, explain to him that it's too cruel. I can't do it! I'll go into a convent, I'll die—anything, oh, anything but hobbling down that long aisle with people laughing and looking at me. It's too far!"

Anne tried to comfort her sister, but Jeanne's panic was too deep for words to have any effect. She continued to cry and claw at her dress until she actually tore it at the throat and down into the shoulder. Anne was frightened and ran for Madame de Linières. Together they came running back, and the older woman's sweet, lined face was pitying when she saw the bitterly crying girl. Madame de Linières had raised Jeanne from a small baby and she had taken the girl's agony to herself, as she now took Jeanne in her arms. She said the things she always said when self-horror became too strong for Jeanne to bear quietly. In the familiar arms, listening to the familiar words, the girl's cries subsided and she sank into exhausted quiet. Madame de Linières motioned to Anne to leave them alone, and Anne went sadly from the depressing scene.

According to custom, the two brides and bridegrooms were expected to meditate alone for an hour upon the seriousness of the step they were about to take and must answer to the bishop at the end of that time as to whether they had decided of their own free will to marry. It was a farce, of course; in this case, as in many others, it was only a form that wasn't too seriously regarded, so that Jeanne would probably spend her hour "alone" with Madame de Linières; Louis probably with his mother; Anne would be alone if her father were busy; and Pierre, the only one of the lot who was sure he desired the marriage, would probably spend his time alone, conscientiously meditating.

Anne went down into the little waiting room near the chapel that had been allotted to her for her meditations and looked curiously around the dark, musty room that smelled of dust and incense. She used a corner of a draped tapestry to brush the dust from the hard bench that stood against the wall, arranged her skirts carefully, and sat down wondering what to do with her hour. As to meditating on the seriousness of marriage—that was something she felt she would be happier not to think about. She started to wonder what Louis was thinking and then decided not to wonder about him either; her father would be far from pleased if she arrived at the altar with tear-swollen eyes.

Louis was certainly not meditating; he was searching for Anne with an urgency that allowed only for physical activity. He had been trying to find her alone for a moment, but he hadn't seen her since he had arrived at Montrichard the night before. Now he knew she would be in one of the rooms near the chapel, and he burst in and out of them in a hurry, looking for her. Some of the king's soldiers, who had been warned to arrest Louis if he tried to leave the castle, uneasily watched him dart past them and considered stopping him, but he was well out of their reach before they had decided, and since he very obviously wasn't trying to leave the château, they let him go on his urgent way.

In one of the rooms he found Anne, sitting primly upright on the bench, her glittering dress spread carefully around her, her astonished eyes large and beautiful. He closed the door quickly behind him and went to her breathlessly.

"Anne, I've a wonderful plan! We can be married after all!"

She was startled and didn't understand what he said. "What are you doing here, Louis?" she asked uneasily. "My father may be here at any moment. He'll be furious if he finds you here. Go back to your room."

"And meditate?" Louis laughed. "I've been meditating. I know what I intend to do—and then suddenly I thought, Why shouldn't you do the same thing, and then someday when we're older and stronger we can marry as we planned."

Anne looked at him incredulously but with some hope. "What does that mean, Louis?"

He spoke hastily, with excited warmth. "I decided never to touch Jeanne's dowry, nor ever live with her—as if anybody could—and then someday I'll divorce her! You could do the same—refuse to live with Pierre, divorce him when you can, and we'll marry as we were promised in the beginning," Louis finished triumphantly.

Anne looked at him intently. "You mean you intend to divorce Jeanne—you think of it now, even before you've married her?"

Louis nodded emphatically. "I can't help marrying her, but nobody can make me live with her." They were both thoroughly conversant with the grounds of divorce; if a marriage wasn't consummated, divorce was practically certain to be granted. "You must refuse to live with Pierre, Anne, so you can divorce him too!"

Anne's realism slowly spoke. "It might be possible for you—I mean with Jeanne—but how could I avoid it?"

They had always spoken frankly and unblushingly about sex; but now suddenly the words meant something different, and they were both embarrassed. Four years had matured them and put meaning into the words. Marriage now meant more than a continuation of their childish friendship; they had a glimpse of the emotions involved. Anne was virgin, of course, but Louis had had a few slight encounters with sex. It was part of a young duke's education to frolic with pretty young serving girls and pretty, mature maids-in-waiting. Looking at Anne now, the thought of her married to Pierre made him furious and he forced himself on. It was too important to let embarrassment stop him.

"Tell Pierre you hate him." Then he burst out, "Tell him I'll kill him if he kisses you!"

Anne looked away from him. She didn't answer, just shook her head.

"Tell him you're much too young."

"But he knows I'm not!"

Louis caught his breath. "You don't like him, do you? Do you, Anne? Have you forgotten me—all we planned?"

Then she turned and looked into his anxious eyes, the familiar dark eyes, eager and warm. She looked at his full fresh lips, the dark patches around his mouth and cheeks where his beard was beginning to grow, and his slim, still growing body. She compared him to Pierre and her own eyes were moist with tears of regret.

"I hate him," she said. "And I haven't forgotten anything!"

He smiled with relief. "Then it's all right. Tell him anything—you'll think of something—only don't let him near you. It won't be for long." He didn't say what he was thinking—that it would only be till her father died and Louis was regent. "You can do it, Anne. Promise me. Promise!"

Anne looked down at the stiffly embroidered dress that formed a hill of gold around her. She thought of her father, and the important plan of which she and Louis were only a part. She had been so continuously drilled in the ideals of the king that she couldn't separate herself from his opinions. Pierre was odious and she loved Louis. But she loved her father and France also. And could it be done as Louis thought? She didn't know. Louis's ideas were always so daring—— She took a deep breath and was about to shake her head regretfully, when she felt Louis taking her hands and drawing her to her feet. One of his arms went about her tightly bodiced waist, his other hand turned her face to his, and he kissed her, awkwardly, at first, his mouth grazing the corner of her lips, and then, gaining confidence, both arms around her now, he kissed her fully.

France and her father were forgotten in the amazing emotions that were released in her. She did think of her dress for a swift moment. She thought: "Oh, this waist is too tight, I can't breathe, I can't—it will rip. How terrible to be married in a torn dress." And then she didn't think of anything for a second till he let her go.

"Anne," he begged her, "you must do it. We were promised! We've a right to see that promise is kept any way we can!"

Yes, she nodded, that seemed reasonable to her now. They had been promised; it wouldn't be right for them not to be together.

"I'll do it, Louis," she promised, not quite seeing how, but for him she would try. "I will! I promise."

Louis sighed in exquisite relief. He had known she would see what a wonderful idea it was. Now they would outwit the king, they would toss away the dreadful marriages he was so sure he had forced them into, and they would regain their companionship—and the jokes—and their pleasure in each other, gilded by this bright new excitement that had suddenly grown in them—and then maybe one day, with luck, the throne too.

"It may be hard," he warned her sternly. "It will be hard —for both of us—but if we're absolutely firm, they can't force us. Remember that."

Anne was firm in her resolve now, firm enough to defy her father. "I'll remember. Nothing will make me yield—I promise!"

They smiled at each other in optimistic triumph, feeling as though the difficulties had already been conquered and it was their own wedding day already. And then the door opened and the king walked in!

He stopped sharply, surveyed them both in surpised displeasure, and their maturity and triumph melted. Anne sank down into her mountain of skirts, her head bent so low that her jeweled headdress touched her knee, while she wished she could stay there and never have to look up. Louis bowed too, but then he met the king's eyes defiantly.

"I see, my obedient godson," said the king, "that you know very well you shouldn't be here!"

Louis bowed again. Yes, he knew.

"But you have a ready explanation, I have no doubt," the king continued maliciously. "I imagine it was lovers' talk that brought you here."

Louis looked startled and Anne blushed red; both things the king noted. "You were thinking of your bride, weren't you, and your happiness was so great you felt you must talk of it to someone? That was it, wasn't it?"

This little grating piece of cruelty applied to a wound already painful goaded Louis into equally malicious speech. He looked directly at the king and fury tightened his jaw.

"Yes, monseigneur, that was it! It isn't every groom who has so beautiful a bride! There should be no difficulty in being always true to her. And when I thought what an excellent mother she'd be, teaching my children the honesty and courage she must surely have inherited from her father, I wanted to share my joy with my bride's sister."

Louis waited for the king to call out the guards to seize him, but in his present mood it would have suited him very well if they had.

There wasn't a single indication in the king's face to show that Louis's words had touched a vulnerable spot, only a heavier accent of malice in his voice as he struck back. "You forget, my young cousin, in your cataloguing of your bride's virtues, to mention that she is the daughter of a mother whose chastity has never been questioned, and that will be a rarity in the Orleans family!"

Louis knew the talk about his mother, but he had never had it thrown at him so brutally before, in a situation where he was so completely helpless. He looked at the king and wished he could kill him. It would be worth being hanged, drawn, and quartered if he could get his hands on that skinny throat and squeeze the cruel words out of it.

The king spoke more calmly now, having inflicted the deeper wound. "Go to your room, Louis! The bishop will be coming for you at any moment." Louis was moving toward the door when another thought struck the king and he spoke emphatically. "You understand I want no scenes, nor scandals, at this wedding, and no tears, either—you hear me, Anne? There is no need for all of you to look like scalded cats. I want smiles and pleasant looks from three of you at least. I expect nothing from Jeanne. Now go, Louis, but remember what I have said."

Louis flung a meaning look at Anne and resentfully returned to his small room. He found the bishop already there, distressed at Louis's lapse from custom. Louis flung himself into a chair and listened glumly while the bishop gave him the customary, pious advice on marriage. Then he asked the formal question that required only one answer. Had he considered the seriousness of marriage, consenting to this one with a free will?

Louis shrugged his shoulders impatiently and answered, not to the bishop's satisfaction: "My friend, what else can I do? I cannot resist. I might as well be dead as to do so; you know with whom I am to deal."

He said this deliberately, hoping that at some time in the future these words, submitting, yet withholding free consent, would help him to his coveted freedom. The bishop tried again, hoping for a more enthusiastic answer, but that was all Louis would say. Time was growing short and the bishop was forced to be satisfied with Louis's noncommittal submission. He accepted it, blessed Louis and conducted him to the chapel.

In spite of the fact that two princesses of France were being married at the same time in the same chapel, the weddings were conducted with a quite remarkable speed and economy. The king wasn't present, although those who knew him felt that he was surveying the ceremony with grim approval from some hidden corner. Frugal by nature, and having no foreign power to impress, he saw no need to make a costly, impressive occasion out of what was purely a family affair.

If he was watching with approval, certainly he was one of the very few who felt that emotion. Anne's marriage to Pierre was strange enough, the court thought. If her father had planned a domestic marriage for her, surely he could have found someone more fitting than a fifth son, but it was upon the other pair that the eyes of the king's household rested in a shocked silence. There was resentment that such a thing should be done to a great lord of France and fear that the king's power had grown to this degree. If such an affront to natural decency could be forced upon an Orleans, what might fall upon themselves? If there had been one strong hand to gather up this anger and use it as a weapon against the king, Louis might have been rescued, but there was no one.

The organ sent out its sonorous tones and the elder daughter of France walked down the aisle and stood beside Pierre at the altar. Anne looked down at the floor, glancing neither at her husband-to-be nor at Louis, who waited for his bride with a white face. Then the younger daughter of France came to the altar, Madame de Linières close beside her and other attendants grouped about her so it should not be apparent how deformed she was. At her destination the others dropped back, and she took her place beside Louis.

The small chapel was closely crowded with people who seemed to hold their breath for an instant as they watched this twisted figure, with one shoulder and hip drawn up, completely out of line with the rest of the body, the other leg dragging limply along after her as she walked. Mary felt so horror-stricken that she almost fell. It was as though the whole marriage had come to her as a complete surprise, as if she had never heard of it before. Seeing it, realizing the fullness of its wickedness, pain and self-reproach hammered at her. Louis was right. Everyone had been wrong! No one had realized but Louis; they should never have submitted! Better if he had been dead and they had all been killed and Blois a smoldering ruin than to have this repugnance forced upon them. An insult to their pride and their honor that could never be erased, to stand here in the sight of God and man and accept this evil. Mary had thought she was being wise, but Louis had known its name —cowardice. She sank to her knees on the prayer rail and sobbed into her hands.

The Duke of Bourbon, in the midst of his happily beaming family, felt heavily depressed. He tried to reassure himself as he watched the bishop say the words that made his brother a member of the royal family. He looked contemptuously at Pierre and wished he hadn't been so easily bought. Across the church Bourbon saw Mary slip to her knees, and he felt more at home with her grief than with his own joyous household.

Marie-Louise hadn't come, but Louis's two young cousins, Eugène of Angoulême and Dunois, were there. Eugène watched somberly, thinking that soon it must be his turn to stand unwillingly before an altar with Louise of Savoy, while the one he loved, Mary of Burgundy, was married to Maximilian, Holy Roman Emperor.

Dunois was very angry with himself for not being able to stop it. Beside Dunois sat George d'Amboise, another friend of Louis's, and he was angry, too, but told himself more comfortingly that there would come a day when they were not all too young and helpless, and it would tell a different story.

The ceremony was almost over, their control had worn away, and what the principals in this heartless wedding thought about it was not hard to see. Contrary to the king's instructions not to look like scalded cats, two out of the four were crying. Jeanne was sobbing horribly, embarrassing everyone; Anne was crying more quietly, and Louis, ashamed, couldn't control his trembling fury. But whatever Pierre may have thought—if he remembered Marie-Louise at all—at least he smiled, a wide, silly, vacuous smile.

5

Back at Blois after the wedding, Louis surprised everyone
with his cheerfulness. Their surprise amused him; they
didn't know of his secret war with the king. Someday they
would find out that this resigned submission was only an
enforced wait. Now only Anne knew, and she was fighting
on his side.

Louis wrote a long, explanatory letter to the Pope and,
with a clarity and frankness that the king would consider
treason, stated his opinion of the disgusting marriage he had
been forced into and his request for its annulment. He knew
well that the Pope, friendly to the French king, would refuse in pious terms and forward a copy of his letter to the
king, but still his objections and his request would be on
record, paving the way for more drastic action later.
Dunois set off for Rome with the letter, and Louis looked
forward to the next spring as the time of his and Anne's
deliverance.

The Burgundians were rising in revolt again—so were
Brittany and many of the other duchies, who fiercely re-
sented the king's absolute disregard of their rights. The
winter truce would hold, but in the spring the struggle
would begin and the king must surely be forced to see that
his policy of supreme power could not be maintained.
There was a limit to loyal endurance, a point at which a
sovereign became a tyrant, and the king, no matter how he
tried to justify it by his ideals for France, had passed that
point.

The peasants fully agreed. When the king's taxes were increased thirty percent, when the king's soldiers rode through
the farms, taking a larger portion of the cattle and crops
than they usually claimed, when every road was a toll road
and every bridge over which the farmer had to pass with
his produce as he went into the town's market place charged

111

not only the farmer but also levied a toll on the estimated weight of the foodstuff in the baskets on his mule's back and on each head of livestock—then the peasants felt, their exhausted resentment irritated by perspiration, that the king's sole purpose was to starve them to death. Taxes like these could be endured in wartime, when a foreign enemy threatened their shores, but now their sacrifices would be used against their own dukes and themselves, for when the inescapable moment of open revolt came, the peasants would be fighting in the battle line. They were beginning to look forward to that moment; no matter how bad it was, it couldn't be much worse than what they had!

The only people in France who didn't violently hate the king were the townspeople and the king's soldiers, whom he paid well and who scattered his money over the towns in which they were quartered. The king was building up a large army; his uniform could be seen everywhere, a popular uniform, because where it was stationed profits automatically followed. The merchants and the middle classes liked the king—nobody loved him—and if they grumbled a little about a tax on leather and window glass and haircuts and bread, still there was brisk enough trade so the taxes could be absorbed and still leave a good profit.

So the army and the towns, as the king had planned it, were his stout allies—for he knew as well as the dukes and farmers that he had engaged in a struggle to the death. The only knowledge on which they didn't agree was the outcome. The dukes expected ultimately to win—so did the king.

Louis was confident of the result—both the solution to the other dukes' problems and of his own personal victory. He had now to wait till he received the Pope's answer or till spring, when some of the power would be pried loose from the king's hands or, an even more cheerful thought, the miser might be dead by then.

Louis sent messages of encouragement to Anne at Tours and Amboise and Paris, as the court moved around. They were always carefully worded so the meanings were evasive to anyone but her. Somewhere in the message he would write, "Do you remember that day at Montrichard?" or "Do you still remember?" and her careful notes would come back by messenger, not so frequent, nor so long as his, because she mistrusted the messenger and she knew the king was closely watching herself and Pierre, wondering about Pierre's sulky, baffled look. But proud of her difficult success so far in holding her husband off, she could answer, "Yes—I still remember Montrichard!" And Louis, adoring her loyalty, would carry the notes with him and read them over hundreds of times. Louis never gave a thought to Jeanne. She wasn't a person to him at all, only an unsightly obstacle, now far away at Linières. De Mornac was sufficient to the estates; Louis's mother and Jeanne Ledu administered the household, so he was completely free. With Georges d'Amboise, Dunois, and Eugène he hunted and rode, gambled and danced, passing the time as pleasantly as he could while he waited for the coming battle.

The four friends were a strange assortment. Georges was the oldest and soberest. Plump, good-natured, his serious blue eyes were thoughtfully turned to his future in the Church. He intended to be Pope someday. Dunois was a soldier; he planned to march through many battlefields toward a marshal's baton and enjoyed every moment. Built like a Percheron, strong, direct, still there was a gentleness in the steady gray eyes above his long, straight nose. Eugène was more like Louis; he had more wits and humor and was darkly handsome, yet he lacked strength and decision, and of the three Dunois was Louis's best friend.

He liked them all, though, and they visited back and forth, from one family château to another, leaving a trail of noise and laughter, love ballads and strong oaths, boots to be cleaned, shirts to be washed, and tunics to be mended.

When the four were at Blois, Mary made up large house parties, entertaining them with picnics and balls. Of course such generous hospitality required money, and de Mornac began to speak of drawing on the dowry Jeanne had brought them. Two installments had already been paid, but Louis had not touched them. In the meantime it was de Mornac's responsibility to see that there was elaborate food for the guests, food for the servants, food for the guests' and servants' horses, linens for the beds and plate for the table, music and entertainment, food, beds, linens for the entertainers—there seemed no end to it.

Mary reveled in the gaiety till she saw how it worried de Mornac, then she knew she ought to put a stop to it, but she hated to disappoint Louis. She felt she owed him much after that moment in the chapel. The king had granted her an income of eleven thousand francs yearly, but that was a very small drop in the bucket.

De Mornac finally protested that Louis must be told, since they were in debt everywhere, and lands and jewels would have to be pledged unless Louis used Jeanne's dowry.

When they mentioned it they were surprised to see him turn from a smiling young man, lounging in his chair and playing with his greyhound, into a tense figure of determination.

"No!" he said shortly. "I can't touch the dowry. It doesn't belong to me!"

Mary said in bewilderment, "But your wife brought it to you——"

He stood up abruptly. "I have no wife!"

De Mornac and Mary exchanged a look.

Louis realized he owed them some explanation. "I don't consider myself married to her. I'll never touch her, nor her dowry, and when the king—damn his soul to eternal hell —dies, I'll throw both Jeanne and her money back where they came from!"

Mary gasped, "Divorce her!"

De Mornac started to smile. It was very fanciful, a duke divorcing a princess of France.

"I'll be regent when the king is dead—which will be any day now, I hope," Louis said. "With a regent's power, it won't be so difficult."

De Mornac stopped smiling and looked at Louis with a new respect. The regent's power might make it possible. De Mornac didn't like the plan, because he needed the dowry, yet he admired Louis's determination.

Mary was alarmed. "That's an impossible hope—and it will only make trouble for you. Naturally you don't want Jeanne, but you may as well have something out of the wretched marriage. Take the dowry—and if we're careful, perhaps the king will never insist on her coming to live here."

Louis shook his head decisively. "I'd never let her come here. She isn't my wife—that wasn't a marriage, and some-day I'll make everyone acknowledge it. I must have her dowry intact, to return with her. If I take her dowry, I admit she is my wife. She isn't my wife. I have no wife!"

"But, Louis," Mary wailed, "what are we to do? We need the money. We're in debt everywhere!"

Louis was surprised. He had never been trained to know the value of money. "You never told me."

"Well, where did you think it all came from?"

"I thought it was your grant from the king."

Mary laughed stiffly. "Eleven thousand francs! We spend that in a month! If it weren't for Alain's worrying himself crazy, we couldn't live as we do!"

Louis repeated, puzzled, "Alain? Who is Alain?"

Mary's tongue had slipped. She was usually so careful to speak distantly to de Mornac in front of the children. She stammered a little. "I mean the Sire de Mornac, of course." She smiled at de Mornac with uncertain dignity, then said quickly to Louis, "Sometimes I call him by his Christian name—I've known him for such a long time."

"Yes," said Louis reflectively, "yes, you have."

He had never worried about the gossip that said de Mornac was her lover and her son's father. There was so much loose talk at court, especially about a young, beautiful woman with an elderly husband. It had often hurt his pride but never touched his feeling for his mother. Now, as he looked from one to the other, he wondered for the first time whether there could be anything in the rumor. Certainly his mother looked embarrassed enough. Hating himself for the doubt, he wrenched his mind back to the financial problem and listened while de Mornac explained the situation.

While de Mornac talked, Louis absorbed enough to know approximately how matters stood, and the rest of the time he gave to studying the face of the man who had been a part of the Orleans household for more than twenty years and was said by the king to be Louis's own father.

Louis looked sidewise under his lashes at de Mornac's face, and it was apparent, even to his now prejudiced eyes, that de Mornac possessed much that would attract a woman. There was certainly strength in the large, strongly modeled nose, the strong jaw with the flat planes across the front, the tanned leather of his cheeks with the bristles showing blackly through, and there was humor in the wrinkles around the bright dark eyes and in the deep laughter creases that slanted from his nose down toward his jaw. He wore a mustache in the Gascon fashion; it was almost black, darker than the hair on his head, and his lips were unusually red. He must be forty-five or fifty, Louis thought, and yet his teeth are white and strong and he looks hard enough to lift a horse.

"So you see," de Mornac was saying, as Louis tried to complete a mental picture accurate enough to measure himself against later, "why we must have some money."

"Don't you think," Louis criticized, "you should have told me before you let us get in so deep?"

De Mornac sardonically raised his eyebrows and politely looked over Louis's head. "I may have hinted as much to your mother, but she felt you should enjoy yourself, especially since she didn't doubt the dowry would be open to her to repair the damage."

Louis flushed at the rebuke but felt it was deserved. "I shouldn't have been so careless," he admitted. "I'll be more economical in the future, but as to the dowry, I've no intention of touching it."

De Mornac regarded him, rubbing his face with his hard brown hand so that Louis could hear the bristles scrape against it. "Does this plan of yours really seem possible enough to sacrifice the money? We'll very likely have to sell a good piece of land if we can't have the dowry."

Louis said with emphasis, "I'm sorry about the land— but it will have to be sold."

De Mornac said with feeling, "So am I sorry about the land, very sorry."

All three sighed in a communal sorrow for the land and then they parted. Louis went quickly to his room before he should have forgotten every detail of de Mornac's face. There, before the mirror, he stood and compared his own face with the face of the father gossip had given him.

There were some similarities—their coloring was about the same, their noses were alike, and their mouths had the same full, unusually red lips. Louis was taller now than the older man but much slighter, and when he had finished his inventory he knew as much as he had before. There was no striking similarity. As far as looks were concerned, he could have been de Mornac's son.

Louis then went to the heavy drawers of his massive clothes chest and, searching in one of them, found a little miniature of his mother she had had painted for him and given to him on one of his birthdays. With it in his hand, he went down to the large salon where a portrait of his father hung upon the wall. He looked at the tiny features of his mother, painted so delicately on the ivory in dainty pastels, and then at the blues and browns of his father's picture and tried to imagine what combination of features would be the result of that union. In the portrait his father wore a beard, a medium-brown beard, and it was hard to decide what the contour of his face really was. His eyes were blue and his body seemed very slight. In his mother's painted face Louis couldn't find a resemblance to his own. In fact, when he really looked at it, it hadn't much resemblance to his mother's real face either. It was just a picture, prettily smiling, with rose-pink lips and cornflower-blue eyes. In the intensity of his eagerness he had forgotten he was doing a far from loyal thing and he had also forgotten to close the door. It was with a start of surprise that he heard Mary's voice.

"What are you doing?" she asked curiously. She had been passing the door and had glanced in and seen him, staring so intently up at Charles and then at something in his hand. She had no idea what he was thinking.

Louis's hand closed quickly over the miniature as he turned to answer her. "I was looking at my father's portrait," he said as calmly as he could. "I never knew him so I sometimes wonder about him."

"Oh," said Mary, "haven't I told you often about him? I used to, when you were smaller, but I imagine you've forgotten."

"I was wondering if that was a good portrait."

Mary found that hard to answer. It was a picture painted by a popular court artist, Jean Fouquet; it had cost a fortune, it should be a good portrait. "I always thought it was very nice. I like the colors."

Louis smiled. "My father didn't always wear a beard, did he? I imagine he looked very different without it."

Mary's forehead was corrugated with the effort to remember. "He looked just like that, only without the beard," she offered.

Louis laughed. "You aren't telling me much about him."

"But you ask such odd questions!"

Elaborately casual, he asked: "Did he look very much like me?"

"Well," she considered, "not so very much. Perhaps you looked more like him when he was very young, but you see I never knew him then. You're darker than he was; all your coloring is brighter than his. Your nose is about the same, but your mouth is nothing like his, it is more like——" She stopped in a dead stillness, and her eyes went from his red mouth, which she was going to say was very like Alain's, to his intent eyes, and dreadful comprehension of his thoughts came to her. She stood staring at him, her face rigid and her eyes growing so large they were not focused on him at all. His face had flamed with distress, and he was rigid too, unable to think of words to pass it off, to pretend he didn't know what she was thinking.

Mary tried to turn and go away, where she could be alone and as ill as she liked, but pity for her had released his rigidity and he hurried to her. She couldn't look again into his eyes and she didn't even like his touch. She drew away from him, tried to push his hands from her, but he wouldn't let her go.

His words came to her unevenly. One moment they screamed into her ears, the next they came from many years away.

"Mother, please! Please listen." Louis was pleading, ashamed of himself for his cynical thoughts. "It wasn't exactly what you thought. I was only thinking about him, wondering what he was like and how much I resembled him—and if for just a minute I wondered—something else —well, I can't help but hear other people's words—although I've never believed it—never!"

"I saw," she barely whispered, "I saw what you were thinking!"

"No. Not what I was thinking," he defended himself and her. "I've been told that the earth is round, and I think about it sometimes, but that doesn't mean I believe it. I think about you too, and things that have been said, but I don't believe them either."

Mary was crying in his arms and most of her pain was gone, but this moment added a strained carefulness to the relationship which had already suffered under the long dispute about Louis's marriage.

The winter passed quickly, except for the long, rainy month of March. Every single day the gray skies opened at dawn and poured a steady torrent till nightfall. The rivers were oceans, the roads were rivers, and the defiantly budding trees swayed sodden, heavy branches in the wind. Day after day Louis moved about from one window to another, looking hopefully out through the misted, rain-washed panes, but the sky never showed any signs of clearing. Instead it seemed to threaten it would stay that way forever. Fires in every one of the big hearths smoked as they fought the chill in the damp, moldy air, and when the sudden vicious gusts of wind blew water hissingly down the hot chimneys, it almost seemed as if the castle were under water.

Then Louis, irritated by the lack of physical activity, would snatch up a cloak and, climbing the spiral stairs of the tower, would emerge onto the roof, impatient for a breath of air. He would pull the cloak about him, the big hood over his head, and, standing half in the shelter of the round tower, let the rain spatter across his face and the wind blow out of his lungs the stale air of the château with its musty odors of acrid candle and torch smoke, damp stone floors that never seemed to dry, the strange odor of the dogs' wet fur when they came in from exercise, the strong odor of horseflesh, too, that the grooms brought in from the stable, and wet leather. From the dining hall came the accumulating smell of roasting meat, from the kitchens the steamy odors of baking and washing. Louis's nostrils longed for spring and the moment when all the doors and windows could be flung open to the freshening breeze.

But spring seemed so far away!

It came suddenly one afternoon when it was least expected. It had been drizzling all day, and Louis was on the rooftop, his spirits low and heavy as the gray sky. He hadn't heard from Anne in weeks—messengers didn't travel the flooded roads unless the news they carried was exceedingly important. He was worried about her and depressed. His plan for their release, scrutinized in this dreary light, seemed impossible, if not ridiculous. How could he hope to oppose this powerful king on such an important matter? He would only end up with his silly head on the block and the black-robed executioner breathing on his bare neck. Then Anne would be in trouble with her father, whose paternal affection, Louis thought, wouldn't help much. And his mother and sister—what would happen to them if he persisted? Maybe his plan was just a childish daydream that would lead them all to disaster. Maybe he had better accept the bad bargain and make the best of it. Sometimes the dowry was a strong temptation, it was so badly needed.

Maybe he should try to forget Anne and all his hopes of a wife and children. What great difference would it make to the world if he led a purposeless life and died without a son? Not much.

He could admit his marriage, take the dowry which would repair the Orleans shabbiness like a coat of glittering paint. He could live luxuriously, giving himself up to pleasure . . . He sighed heavily. Yes, that would probably be the wisest thing to do, and since it was probably what he would be forced to do in the end, then he might as well yield now. He sighed again and turned to go in, then he swung back sharply, looking up. Absorbed in his dark thoughts, he hadn't noticed that the rain had stopped. Gray clouds were still spread in an uninterrupted layer over the sky, but they were translucent now and brightness was behind them. A strange gray-green light lay over the drenched lands; the muddy waters of the flooded fields gleamed with it and everything was very still, waiting tensely with hushed expectancy. Far off in the stillness Louis heard a few clear notes of a lark's excited announcement, then toward the west, low on the horizon, the misty clouds were torn and the sun came through. It poured through vigorously, melting the jagged edges of the clouds and showing a great patch of bright blue sky. It turned the leaden, dripping trees to glistening silver, and under its gentle alchemy the river and the muddy fields were liquid gold. On a moment like this, years ago, Louis's father had written:

> The season has put off his mantle
> Of wind, of coldness, and of rain
> And wears the bright embroidery of the sun . . .

Louis pushed back his hood, feeling the faint warmth on his face, and watched the sky eagerly. Far below him he could hear the grooms and stableboys come running out onto the slippery stones of the courtyard to look up at the rapidly clearing sky. A horse in the open stables neighed and a mastiff hound barked in deep, baying tones. They could smell the first moment of spring in the moist air, feel it in the growing warmth of the sun. Excitement spread through the castle. Louis could hear doors and windows opening and voices exclaiming over the beauty of the afternoon sky.

He took a deep breath—another—and all his winter lassi-
tude and dejection dropped away. He laughed at himself for
his mood of cowardly submission. True, it made little difference to the world what he did, but this was the only life
he would have—it meant something to him—and he would
make of it what his courage would let him, not be a
whipping boy for some idiot king. Yield now—before the
battle had begun? No, by God! He would fight for Anne
and for his own name, and if he were as sensible and persistent as he thought he could be, he would bring Anne and
his family and himself through to ultimate victory.

And it was spring at last! In a few days the roads would
be almost safe to travel, but whether they were or if he had
to swim all the way, he would go to Amboise and see his
Anne!

April in Amboise set the court poets into a frenzied
search for new similes to describe its beauty, new rhymes to
go with drifting breeze and fleecy clouds and flowering
trees and dewy violets and, of course, love. Fortunately for
love, *"toujours"* always went well with *"amour,"* and if
pronounced with a little poetic license, *"du cœur"* could be
relied upon to finish a couplet satisfactorily if not originally.
But spring didn't have so many rhymes, and all their flowery
words fell far short of the reality. There were no similes
good enough for Amboise in the spring. In one of the love-
liest parts of France, twelve miles east of Tours, its magnificent castle had always been a favorite residence of its
kings; the town might have been the nation's capital, except
that the Loire wasn't navigable at that point. The river was
shallow there, with shifting sandbanks, and could be used
only for light pleasure gondolas and flat fishermen's craft.

The castle was built on the river, and its gardens stretched
down in colorful slopes and terraces to the yellow sandy
beach. Where the water flowed more deeply past the garden,
and there was no beach, white marble steps led down into
the green current and the small pleasure boats anchored
there, bumping gently against the steps while gallant gentlemen got their feet and their clothes wet, holding the swaying gondola steady for the ladies' hesitant satin slippers.

Gardeners worked miracles with the rich soil, helped by
the moist cool night, the warm daytime sun, and the tem-
perate climate. They were constantly busy in their leather

hose and their earth-colored smocks, carving the plump
green hedges into fantastic shapes around high-springing
fountains, pruning the twisting shady maze in which lovers
liked to lose themselves from sight of the world, spraying
and worrying rose trees into exquisite color and form so that
careless beauties might scatter the petals heedlessly to the
lover's litany, "He loves me, he loves me not." Thick
green vines climbed white marble walls, yellow and purple
trumpet-shaped flowers blossomed in the vines, and in their
season poppies of every shade, from deepest scarlet through
the oranges and yellows to the purest white, rippled their way
down the slope. French and Spanish lilies stood in their proud
formality, and the humbler flowers added their brilliant
colors to the whole.

Over it all were the great trees, some of them centuries
old. The giant oak trees brought from England laid the dark
green of their shade on the yellow green of the sunny grass;
the low boughs of the willow trailed over the riverbanks;
the straight tall poplars stood like sentinels guarding the
formal avenues and paths. From the strong boughs of the
oak, beribboned swings hung down, and on summer after-
noons laughing ladies of the court swung idly back and
forth.

Around the castle the forests were rich in game. In the
mornings the hunters would set out, shouting and eager for
the chase, returning later in the day with the wild boars
that made such succulent pink roasts. There were picnics
in the forests, too, the ladies gay in their elaborate riding
clothes, their hair caught up in snoods of gold net knotted
with pearls, turbans tilted becomingly over their sophisticated eyes.

And in the evenings there was gambling and dancing,
scandals and complicated love affairs in the glittering rooms
and torchlit gardens.

All this beauty and springtime gaiety contrasted sharply
to the ache in Anne's heart. She hadn't written to Louis in
weeks. She knew she must send him a message soon, but
she dreaded it because she could no longer write, "I still
remember Montrichard."

It had been a few weeks ago that she had found her father very much annoyed when she had gone to his study for
instruction, as she still did every day. He had met her with
the blackest look she had ever had from him.

"What *is* this ridiculous nonsense I hear about you from Pierre?" he had asked, and there was no doubt but that he wanted an answer very quickly.

She hadn't had a reasonable one to give him; she had been completely unprepared. But then, she had thought contemptuously, she might have known Pierre would run to her father with his troubles! It had been stupid of her to rely on his being decently silent! She prepared to defend herself, and she answered with some spirit. After all, she was married now and should not still be answerable to her father for everything.

"Anything at all that Pierre says is likely to be ridiculous nonsense."

His eyes went stabbing directly to the very back of her mind. "I want none of that, my girl, none at all! You have a clever enough brain when it's acting as I have directed it, but if someone has made you think you can provoke Pierre to divorce you by refusing to live with him, you have miscalculated. I would never allow it! We'll have no divorce in our family, neither you nor Jeanne! I've taken pains with you, Anne; your life will be powerful and necessary to France. I won't have you endanger your usefulness!"

"I married Pierre as you said I must! I realize you wouldn't permit a divorce, even if Pierre considered he had sufficient grounds. He'd never be able to obtain one; how does it matter, except to myself, if I refuse to be his wife? It wouldn't even matter to him; he doesn't really care."

"Why do you refuse? It seems to me he is a personable young man." As dull as ditchwater, too, he thought, but didn't say. "You would have healthy, handsome sons." And that, to his mind, was the only reason for women's presence on earth.

Anne spoke frigidly. "I detest him!"

The king laughed sourly. "An excellent reason if you were a burgher's daughter."

"I wish I were, then I could marry someone I loved," Anne muttered resentfully, but her father heard her.

"Someone you loved?" he repeated sharply. "Is it possible that Orleans bastard is still in your thoughts?"

Anne could not meet his eyes; she became occupied with some rings on her fingers. His glance became more intent as she did not answer.

"I have asked you a question," he said.

Her mind darted about to find an answer that would not betray her. "Because I don't care for Pierre doesn't mean I love Louis."

"It doesn't necessarily follow, I suppose." But his suspicions were in no way quieted. He spoke suddenly. "Is this some trick of Orleans'?"

She was startled at the shrewdness of his guess, but she denied it valiantly. "Of Louis'? How could it interest Louis?"

"How could it interest Louis?" he mimicked unpleasantly. "A very sensible question, I'm sure! I'll only tell you, so that I may get on to more urgent business, that both as your father and as your king I absolutely order you to abide by your duty with Pierre."

His voice was imperative and he turned away from her to his desk, ready to get on with the problems of state he was already sharing with her, and it was with surprise he heard her still protest.

"No!" Anne said firmly. "I won't!"

It was the first time she had ever defied him. He whirled from the desk, papers clutched in his hand, and glared at her.

"You what?" he asked ominously, and tilted his head a little to listen, as though he couldn't have heard right.

She was trembling, but she steadied herself against a corner of the desk and raised her chin defiantly. What could he do about it if she disobeyed him? Nothing she couldn't live through. Of course, if she weren't a king's daughter, he could imprison or execute her for treason. As it was, the worst punishment would be confinement in a convent till she changed her mind—which she wouldn't! And she even doubted if he would do that to her. He wouldn't want to proclaim her disobedience to all France, nor would he wish her to be absent from her duties to her small brother. It was terrible to have him angry at her—his look of betrayal hurt her more than she had thought—but it would be terrible, too, to betray Louis and be really married to that stupid Pierre.

So she repeated, "I won't! You can't make me!"

No one could force her to accept Pierre, she reassured herself, no one! All she had to do was to stand firm and let her father do what he would, and there wasn't much he could do without hurting himself. But her knees shook and her gaze faltered under his terrible eyes.

"So," he said slowly, "you defy me. You fling all my care and confidence back into my face. All my work for nothing——"

"No!" she exclaimed miserably, but he went inexorably on:

"How mistaken I was to think I ever saw a brain in a woman's head!" he said contemptuously. "To think I counted on a woman's loyalty and trusted the future to your silly hands! I deserve to be betrayed—but does France?"

"Oh no," Anne said wretchedly, "and it won't be! I promise you, all our plans—all you've taught me, I'll remember, but in just this one thing—this one thing——" She faltered and reached blindly out to touch him, but he drew back sharply from her. She couldn't bear his gesture of distaste, and his contempt was a crushing weight that was breaking her resistance. "But how does this one thing matter, except to me? You wouldn't permit Pierre to divorce me —he wouldn't even try! He doesn't really care; it is only what he thinks he should do."

Her father laid his papers down upon the desk and leaned over it toward her, speaking quickly and harshly. "You're right—I wouldn't permit Pierre to divorce you, but I won't be here always, and when I go I leave you with only one thought in your mind, to safeguard Charles on the throne and continue my policies for France. If some silly infatuation makes you waver in your duty, you may be sure I'll see the object is removed, no matter what it costs me!"

"No, Monseigneur, no, please!" Anne whispered it, but by the urgency of her whisper he gauged the depth of her feeling for Louis. Then she calmed a little. Louis was safe, unless he defied her father openly—or at least he was as safe as he had always been. Her father was frank enough about his hopes for Louis's death.

He admitted it. "I've considered it often enough as it is, weighing the benefits against the storm, and it wouldn't take very much more to decide me it was for the good of France that Louis of Orleans vanished from it."

But Anne knew he couldn't take the chance. Not now.

With so much trouble coming in Burgundy, he couldn't handle the Orleanists too.

"It depends entirely upon your attitude in this matter, Anne. I won't leave you swaying between your work and some silly sentiment. I won't die and know that you've left yourself a loophole through which you might climb and abandon Charles—and have all my work go for nothing! You should have known I'd never have left you a choice!"

Yes, but she did have a choice, Anne thought, sighing— a wretched choice. She could continue to defy her father, suffer his biting anger, and lose contact with his stimulating intellect and the bold vistas of power he showed her. The whole exciting world of France was in this room and, circling round it, the complicated world of Europe. Never to be admitted to the secrets of his desk again would be a million times worse than having a wonderful book snatched away, half read.

"I've taken great care with you, Anne; and I thought you were growing to be the least foolish woman in France, steady and reliable, with a mind of your own, not one to be persuaded into impossible stupidities by the love braying of some calf."

Out of all his household, Anne was the only one who gave him affection. From her childhood he had been impressed with the clarity and soundness of her mind. He had recognized that here, among his children, was one with an unusual mind. The others were useful in the barter and trade of marriage, Jeanne's sterility serving a very good use, and Charles was an heir, if not a very impressive one, but Anne had talents which were worthy of care. In his respectful treatment of her, she reflected a respect and affection for him he had never inspired anywhere else.

But if she stayed, Anne was thinking, and recovered his esteem, so essential to her now, Louis would be forever lost to her. Was he lost to her anyway, she wondered, even if they did resist? Would the purpose that had seemed possible of achievement in his excited telling be stanch enough to oppose the king's power? Here in this room she had seen many another duke's most cherished plans vanish before her father's strength like a morning mist before the sun. Her father's triumph had always seemed inevitable to her —wasn't it equally so this time? If it was, then she would lose both Louis and her father too.

She weighed the chances—the odds against Louis were too great—and made her decision.

"Monseigneur," Anne said, "I had no intention of abandoning Charles and your plans—our plans. I am one with you in everything, but in this matter it did seem to me it was only important to myself."

"But you see now that it is important to our plans?"

She twisted her fingers in a way she had, and one of her joints cracked so suddenly that she was startled. She looked at him appealingly, knowing she and Louis had lost. Yet she made one more small attempt.

"Must it be, Monseigneur? I—I dislike him so much!"

Even he was touched. She was so pretty, fresh, and inexperienced. He went to her and put his arm about her shoulders, something he almost never did.

"I'm sorry you dislike him so much, my child, because he's your husband. I would rather have given you what you wanted—if I could have—but Pierre will not be a great bother to you. You can make what arrangements you will with him, but you must live with him! It cannot be avoided. Now," he said more briskly, giving her shoulder two stiff pats, relieved to be finished with this unpleasant business, "that is all settled. Let us get to work."

He returned to his desk and plunged into questions connected with her studies. Anne answered as well as she could with a divided mind. She was terribly relieved to be back on friendly terms with her father. His approval was necessary to her, but to have been defeated so easily in Louis's battle was ignominious. And now, instead of the hope that someday she would share her life with Louis's smiling charm, Pierre would be always beside her, lumpy and thick of mind as an overcooked, understirred pudding.

She had sighed when the lesson was over, received her father's reminder docilely, and left him.

Her own advanced lessons having been heard, she had gone to her little brother to hear his. The Dauphin Charles had a tutor and all the attendants that belonged to his importance, but Anne saw to him almost completely, for her father wished Charles to be as much under Anne's influence as she was under the king's.

Charles was seven, an undersized boy with a large head, prominent eyes and ears, and an incomplete mind. How incomplete they had not realized, but learning to read was proving to be an almost impossible task for him. It was irritating work trying to teach him, and Anne's patience sometimes wore thin. When it disappeared and she snapped at him in the course of the lessons, his eyes brimmed over with tears and he crouched away from her, "Like a dog, waiting to be struck," she thought contemptuously.

On that particular day he had seemed incapable of remembering anything, and, irritated by the thought of the coming submission to Pierre, Anne had been exceptionally cross with him.

"You haven't remembered a thing I told you yesterday! I never knew anyone could be so stupid!" she said, and the frightened tears oozed from Charles's eyes.

"I tried, Anne. I tried to remember!" he wailed, shrinking away and annoying her still further. She had never treated him cruelly so that he had to fear her—only a slap on his hands when he was really naughty.

"Well," she said in exasperation, "there's no need to be a baby about it. We'll have to go over it again. Now start here and say the words as I point to them."

Stammering and stuttering, taking what seemed hours to her over each one, he identified two out of the ten words. She went painstakingly over them all, explaining how they sounded, how they looked, and what they meant, and when she asked him again, out of the same ten, he managed, hesitatingly, to get one right. She was almost in tears herself with nervous exasperation, and he was in a literal fever of exhaustion.

Anne gave up. "We won't do any more today, Charles; it's no use. Study them again and perhaps tomorrow you will do better."

Pity overtook her when she looked at the sobbing boy, and she reached out and took him on her lap. He lay against her shoulder, in an ecstasy of weary relief, his legs dangling awkwardly down. She talked consolingly to him, patting and soothing him so that soon he was quieted and almost sleeping in her ams.

She looked down at his swollen, unprepossessing face and thought bitterly that she would give much to be Charles, stupid as he was. He was male and heir to France; without any effort on his part he would be given what she, with all her brains and effort, could not have. If she were a man, she wouldn't have to submit to hateful marriage. But she wasn't a man. She was a woman—evening was coming, and with it would come Pierre!

Pierre, too, had felt an uneasiness with the knowledge that night was coming. He knew the king had spoken to Anne and he knew she was ready now to be his wife. He hadn't enjoyed telling the king his marital troubles. He had been discomfited by the contemptuous way they had been received. It was all very well for the king to say Pierre should be able to handle his wife without help. Anne wasn't the kind of wife her father would know much about. He knew Anne was an unusual woman, but that wasn't a virtue to his mind. He had tried to make her like him, had been very gentle and understanding, he thought. He had occupied his separate rooms, never seeing her except when a flock of giggling maids clung to her as though they had been ordered not to leave her side. Over six months married and he had never been alone with her! At first he had supposed she was frightened and shy and he had had no inclination to hurry the actual marriage. The ceremony had made it legal; time would make it intimate. But time had passed, and on one pretext or another she had evaded him. Then finally she had said frankly that she thought this marriage ought to continue as it was, simply a formal alliance of two houses. Empty marriages of convenience were common enough, but Pierre, like any other man of title, wanted children to his name.

Anne had refused, and he had retreated when she threatened a screaming hysteria that would bring all her maids to her side and a scandal of ridicule on him. That was something no man should be called on to fight.

It wasn't that he yearned so terribly to embrace her, either. The marriage wasn't particularly of his making, although he had agreed to it eagerly enough, stunned with the high position it would give him and the great wealth. But it wouldn't be a fair exchange if he gave up his previous plans to be discarded on the grounds that his marriage hadn't been consummated. He refused to take that chance—Anne was his wife; she would have to live as such. When she had refused, he had gone in a sensible manner to the king and now it was all settled.

He should have been happy, but he wasn't. Wealth beyond any of his hopes he had, and a princess for a wife, but his life limped along aimlessly. He missed Marie-Louise more than he had thought he would, and his foster family too. Louis wouldn't speak to him; neither Mary nor Marie-Louise ever answered his letters. He was lonely. It was easy to see the king thought him a nonentity. Anne disliked him, his elder brother thought he had behaved badly, and a large part of the court seemed to agree, saying nothing direct, but indicating by the polite way in which they avoided him where their sympathies lay. There were a few who were his friends, but even to his unanalytic mind they were only parasites, clinging to him for the favors they could extract. He was very lonely, but he tried to console himself, thinking of course it was all new to him and sooner or later he and Anne would settle down into a settled, more friendly routine and former friends would return.

Evening had come and night. Pierre had secured his wealth, his wife, and his position against future divorce; bitterly Anne had lost her hopes of Louis and now she could no longer proudly write: "I still remember Montrichard."

6

Anne put off writing, using the flooded roads as an excuse, and when the weather cleared she continued to procrastinate.

But the day came when her conscience firmly pushed her to her rosewood desk and forced her to pick up her gaudy peacock-feather pen. She was sitting there an hour later, absently stroking her cheeks with the soft feather, her eyes fixed on the blank page before her, trying to decide whether she should tell him the shaming news by leaving out the code sentence entirely or being so frankly brutal as to write, "No, I no longer remember Montrichard."

She winced when she thought of how he would look when he received the shock. He would crush the thick crackling paper in the long brown fingers that were so warm and strong to the touch. He would stride to the hearth and, kicking the fire shield aside, hurl her note into the heart of the flames. He would stand and watch it disappear, wishing the vulgar news in it could disappear too. Maybe he would take his left wrist in his other hand and rub it hard and viciously, as she remembered he sometimes did when he was terribly disturbed. Maybe he would hate her for her failure to keep her promise——

Her head jerked up sharply at that thought, and she stared blindly at the tapestry hanging over the desk. She couldn't stand the thought of his hating her. She was still studying the tapestry intently, as though she planned to copy each stitch in its elaborate pattern by memory, when, after a discreet tap on the door, her most intimate lady-in-waiting, Denise de Vernier, hurriedly and excitedly entered with the news that the Duke of Orleans had just ridden in, was going to stay for two or three days, had retired to the guest suite reserved for the Orleans family to change his travel-stained clothes—he had been absolutely drenched from head to foot—he had passed Pierre in the halls and pointedly ig-

131

nored his greeting, so Pierre was sulking in the cardroom—
he would be singing or crying in a little while—and the
Duke of Orleans had come down again in a most unusual
jacket—maybe it was a new style from Milan, but wherever
it was from, it was stunning—crimson velvet—the body of
the jacket snug to here—and then from his waist it fell in
straight lines halfway to his knees—his tights were either
very dark green or black, it was hard to tell in that light—
but it wasn't the cut of the jacket so much—it was just
that it was so different—absolutely no trimming—not brocaded—no pattern—no embroidery—no scallops that
everybody's getting so tired of—just a beautiful scarlet velvet, tight up to his throat—and then right up here, high on
his right shoulder, there's an enormous golden porcupine—
it's painted—*painted* in thick gold paint—a beautiful design
—the animal's eye is a big diamond—and when the duke
walks, the sharp little quills—or what do you call them?—
twinkle and move, just as if the porcupine was moving and
stretching—it was very stunning, and the duke was wearing
a new mustache that made him look even more handsome,
and he had been asking how Princess Anne was and if he
could look forward to seeing her in the dining hall—or
would she be present for dancing afterward?

Denise, finally out of breath, paused and waited expectantly for a flow of eager questions from Anne. But
Anne sat there, rigid, her eyes still on the tapestry.

Louis was here! Instead of a difficult letter, she had the
more difficult task of telling him, and no way out of it.
But she couldn't face him tonight. Tomorrow, when she
was more prepared.

She put the pen down and pushed the chair back, hearing it squeak on the bare, polished floor. She stood up,
avoiding Denise's curious eyes. Denise was too curious.
Anne had never confided in her, but Denise could make
a passionate love affair out of two innocent words and
one careless glance. Love affairs, including her own—too
numerous for even her indifferent husband to remember—
were the breath of life to her. She could scent now that
there was trouble between her mistress and the duke.
Something had gone wrong.

"I'm sorry I won't see him tonight," Anne said in
carefully indifferent tones. "I'd like to see his beautiful
jacket, but I'd planned to stay in my own apartments this

evening and retire early. I have a headache—I think I may have caught a chill." And disregarding Denise's solicitous offers of help, Anne dismissed her and went into her bedroom.

But later, after the candles had been blown out and her maids had left her, she rose and dressed again. She hesitated over which gown to wear. Far back in her wardrobe, wrapped in thin paper to protect it from the tarnishing air, was her wedding dress of gold tissue. Although it was exquisite and very costly, she hated it and had never worn it since that day at Montrichard. Impulsively she reached for it, tearing the paper away. She would wear it tonight and let it tell Louis, with its significance, what she dreaded to put into words. Or if there had to be words too, they would be fewer.

"That's your wedding dress," he would exclaim in disapproval, and she would nod and say, "Because I am married now."

It was difficult to dress herself in the stiff, very tight low bodice, the long tight sleeves that fit like gloves down to a point on the back of each hand, but she didn't want maids chattering around her. She tried on a tall hennin and then discarded it, pulling the jeweled pins hastily out so that her long dark hair fell loosely over her shoulders down to her waist. She caught it back at the nape of her neck, turned her head for different views of herself in the mirror, and decided she would wear it a new way tonight— a way that would make her look older, more experienced, like the married woman that she was.

She parted it down the middle, allowing it to fall in soft waves back from her face, then she rolled it into a gleaming chignon, low on her neck, almost between her shoulders. She held it there with a gold net, securing it in place with four little gold combs. She decided against any jewels. The brilliant material of the dress was enough, and with a sense of being suitably gowned for disaster, she walked out through the quiet halls of the castle, where the rustle of her full skirts was heard in the stillness and where the silent guards stationed along the empty corridors raised their swords in salute as she passed.

She walked down the wide staircase to the next floor where the court gathered nightly for music and dancing, gambling and any theatrical entertainment that was pro-

vided: jugglers, the low comedy of court fools, charades
or pageants in which the courtiers themselves sometimes
acted. The laughter and music, high voices and the metallic
clatter of gold pieces at the gaming table met Anne in the
halls long before she reached the door of the main salon.
She walked steadily in, feeling no excitement now, just
numb and chilly and conscious that the gold cloth scratched
her arms. She nodded greetings and answered polite inquiries as to her health, then she stood beside Pierre's chair
at the card table. He was silly with wine, and losing heavily.
Then she looked around for Louis.

He was standing across the room, only half facing her,
talking to René de Bourbon—probably about tennis, because
that was all René ever talked about. René was still champion and had just returned from a trip to England, where
tennis was popular too, and he was pleased to report he
had beaten the English champion.

Anne watched Louis, glad he hadn't yet seen her. She
decided she didn't like his mustache; it changed his face,
made him look older, or maybe she didn't like it because
Denise had. Anyway, he had too nice a mouth to hide,
and she would tell him to shave it off. He wasn't as brown
as she remembered him—of course the last time she had
seen him it had been September, the end of the summer.
His hair was different too, shorter, brushed back from his
face, revealing the dark peak on his forehead. He didn't
look interested in what René was saying—he answered
absently and gazed restlessly around the room, probably
disappointed that she wasn't going to be present and
wondering how ill she was.

She willed him to turn and see her, and in a moment he
did. He stopped in the middle of what he was saying to
René, excused himself to his friend, and started toward her,
smiling. Her numbness dropped away and her heart began
to pound, but they were both carefully formal in the greeting and Anne still remained near Pierre, her back touching
the back of his chair.

Louis's eyes were not formal, though, as they wandered
over her face. He thought she had changed a little too. She
seemed older—well, of course they both were, but only
seven months. As children together he had often teased
her and told her it was lucky she had been born with wit,
because she would never be pretty. She wasn't pretty now—

she was beautiful in a most unusual provocative way, and he cursed the king again for having taken her away from him.

"I don't like your mustache, Louis," she was saying.

He laughed aloud. She hadn't changed so much; she was still the same direct Anne. "It will be gone in the morning," he assured her, "or shall I take a sword and cut it off now?"

"The morning will be better. But I do admire your coat."

"Thank you. I like it myself. My cousin Dunois brought it to me from Florence."

As a consolation prize, Dunois had wryly said, for the disappointing answer he had brought from the Pope. He had traveled home from Rome by way of Florence and had ordered the coat with Louis's own personal crest and the porcupine painted on it. When Louis had enthusiastically admired the superb workmanship of the golden porcupine and had asked the name of the artist who had painted it, Dunois had said carelessly, "Oh, he was called Bonnicelli, or Botticelli, some long name like that. His price was more for this one little animal," Dunois had said aggrievedly, "than he asked of a friend of mine for a whole wall full of nymphs, but he promised the gold paint wouldn't flake off and it wouldn't tarnish. It had better not!" Dunois had ominously hunched his big shoulders.

So far it hadn't, and the scarlet coat with the golden porcupine on it had been a great success. It was certainly very becoming to Louis's slim, tall figure.

Louis was, in turn, admiring Anne's gown, and then suddenly realizing when he had seen it before, a curious look swept over his face.

Anne stiffened and leaned back against Pierre's chair. He was paying no attention to her as he fought to regain his losses from the noisy group around the table.

"Anne," Louis said in a very low tone, "that's the gown you wore at Montrichard."

"Yes," she answered, the monosyllable flat and distinct.

He looked wonderingly into her eyes, and then amazingly she saw relief and happiness leap into his. He drew a long, contented breath and then leaned a little closer, anxious not to be overheard. But they were safe; in the middle of the crowded, noisy room they were isolated.

"You wore it to tell me something!" he exclaimed, admiring her subtlety. "You wore it to say that you still remember Montrichard!"

She caught her breath in dismay that he had so misinterpreted her costume. She saw now that the subtlety was too subtle; it was ambiguous. Then, in surprise, she heard her own voice speaking, without her will, giving him the answer his loving eyes expected.

"Yes," Anne lied, "yes, I still remember Montrichard!"

The next morning Louis woke early, anxious not to miss the chance of a few moments with Anne. She might be breakfasting now in the dining hall, she might be strolling in the gardens, she might be riding in the forest, and he could be with her. Hastily he sprang out of bed and pulled open the door to the antechamber where his personal servant slept. Léon was a squat, ugly man of forty who had quick, deft hands and never spoke unless he had to.

"Léon," Louis called, "get hot water quickly and come shave this mustache off. I'm sick of it——" Then he stopped short in annoyance as his voice echoed in the empty room. Where the devil was the man? Louis walked to the bell rope and pulled it vigorously, cursing just as strongly. It would take forever for someone to come from the servants' hall downstairs and bring him a barber. Very dubiously he considered trying to shave himself with the cold water left in the pitcher, but just then there was a knock at the door and, hoping it was Léon, Louis shouted: "Come in!"

The door opened and a tall slim man, with olive-colored skin and dark melancholy eyes, dressed in valet's livery and carrying a pitcher of steaming water, entered and spoke deferentially. "Good morning, Your Grace. I hope you slept well. I took the liberty of coming——"

Louis interrupted crossly, "Where's my man? Léon Clouet?"

"I'm sorry, Your Grace, he's dead. I'm very sorry." But the sorrow in the melancholy eyes was obviously for the inconvenience to the duke and not for the dead man.

"Dead!" Louis exclaimed, startled.

It was a shock, although he hadn't been especially fond of his servant. Léon had been too silent and negative a man either to be liked or disliked.

"How did he die? What happened?"

"There was a quarrel—some of the servants were gambling in the stables late last night, and Your Grace's servant was stabbed."

"But he was right here when I went to bed, and that was very late!" Louis said in bewilderment.

"I beg your pardon for the suggestion, but he may have waited until Your Grace was asleep and then slipped out." The man's voice was full of the disapproval he felt for such a neglectful servant. "It was almost dawn when he died."

"Where's the man who did it?" Louis said angrily. "Bring him here!"

"I'm sorry, Your Grace"—the sad eyes were even sadder with new regret that the duke's command could not be obeyed—"but he is dead too. They killed each other."

"Well," said Louis slowly, "they had an exciting night in the stables, didn't they?"

"Yes, Your Grace. A very terrible night. Two other men were hurt trying to separate them."

"I'm sorry about them too. Was the quarrel of Léon's making?" It seemed so strange that the quiet, pudgy man could end in such tragic violence. There must have been a dark side to his life that Louis had never seen.

"It is difficult to tell, Your Grace. The grooms all talk, and they all tell different stories."

"I'd better go down to the stables and question them later. If it was my man's fault the two others were injured, I must see they're compensated. Find out if Léon had any family—I never heard him mention any—but if he has, I must send them a purse—and you will need something to bury him——"

"You're very generous, Your Grace." He took a short step forward, looking down at the pitcher of water he carried. "May I assist you this morning?"

"If you're a barber."

"Oh yes, Your Grace. Perhaps while you're here I might take Léon's place?" And when Louis nodded he cleared his throat and went on very timidly, "Perhaps even longer, if I should prove satisfactory?"

Louis, anxious to get the offending mustache off, had started into his bedroom and the shaving chair, but now he turned and regarded the man critically. He looked exceedingly neat; his sallow skin was clear, his hair, dark and hanging to his shoulders, looked clean, his big dark eyes expressed an eagerness to serve, and his speech and bearing had a pleasant refinement.

"What is your name?" Louis asked.

"Paul Capporetti, Your Grace."

"Italian?"

"Born in Venice, thirty-two years ago—but of French parents and I have lived in France for a good many years."

Not quite long enough, Louis thought, to lose a very faint Venetian accent. "Why would you want to leave the king's service and enter mine?"

Paul's long-fringed eyelashes flickered and he looked hesitant.

"You may speak freely," Louis told him. "Nothing you say will reach any other ears than mine."

"You misunderstand, Your Grace. There's no treason in my wish to leave. It—I am not liked here!" He stated the fact without self-pity, so Louis felt sorry for him.

"Why not?"

Paul hesitated, then sighed. "You would find it out if you chose, anyway, Your Grace, so I will tell you myself. It's my fault—I made a mistake. There was an incident with a young lady—another barber's wife . . ." He paused, and Louis's imagination filled it in. "So I would like to leave here and start again where people won't all know—where it can be forgotten." Humiliated at what he had confessed, he looked at Louis beseechingly. "I am an excellent servant —an expert barber—I can read and write—and your clothes would be well cared for——" He stopped short, for fear he had said too much.

Well, thought Louis, with Léon gone, I'll need someone, and at least this man's honest. He could have spun a tale about having always yearned to serve the glorious House of Orleans and the chances are I would never have found out about his past.

"We'll see," he said, and Paul's melancholy eyes looked almost happy. "Now let's see how good you are with a razor, and I hope to heaven you justify the good reference you've given yourself."

Louis had to admit, when he left his rooms a half hour later, that Paul was an expert barber and had a neat knowing way with clothes, so he had told him to arrange to leave for Blois in a day or so.

Louis had to admit, too, as he felt his smooth-shaven, lotioned face, that Anne was right about the mustache. It hadn't suited his kind of face, and he felt better without it. He looked forward to Anne's smile when she saw it gone.

But she wasn't to be found, not in the gardens, the dining hall, or the forest. Louis supposed she must be with the king, and he waited for a long time in the hallway, within sight of the study door, but Anne didn't come out. Then when he did find her, late in the afternoon, she was surrounded by the queen's ladies and they were all embroidering tapestries and talking. She didn't see him or his signals for a long time, she was so engrossed in her work, and that was strange enough, for Anne had always detested any form of needlework. She had always preferred to read. When she finally did meet his eye and obeyed his signals to join him, one of her ladies, the Countess de Vernier, came with her, and no matter how politely he hinted, she didn't leave them alone.

He was terribly disappointed. He wanted to tell Anne that Dunois had been to Rome and that Louis planned to go to Rome himself early this summer and see the Pope. But he couldn't say any of those things with Denise de Vernier flirting with him and begging him to wear the red coat with the golden porcupine again tonight.

The next day was the same—if he approached Anne and stood beside her chair, one of her ladies was certain to interrupt. He realized it was a deliberate plan not to leave them alone. Evidently the king's watchful eye had ordered that Anne should be constantly chaperoned. It was done so cleverly that Anne didn't even seem to suspect it, or if she did, she thought it wiser to seem unaware. In that case there was little he could do, but he would have given a great deal for one moment with her and one kiss.

Denise watched him curiously and wondered what he would think if he knew the plan was Anne's. Denise had been puzzled enough when Anne had ordered her to remain close at hand and to interrupt any tête-à-tête. She didn't know just what Anne was afraid of—but evidently she was terrified of being left alone to talk intimately with the duke. Denise had looked a question Anne had ignored, and Denise had shrugged her slim, frivolous shoulders and obeyed, but it was very baffling. For a long time she had

had orders never to leave Anne alone with her husband (not but what that wasn't an excellent idea for any wife), but then that order had been withdrawn and a ban on Louis substituted. All very baffling—but interesting.

Louis didn't find it interesting. Here it was, his last afternoon at Amboise, and instead of holding Anne's hand in some secluded corner of the gardens he was holding a tennis racket and running around on the newly paved tennis court; instead of lovers' talk and kisses he was shouting in the jargon of the game and hurling balls as hard as he could across the high net at René de Bourbon. Tennis was all right when he had nothing more important on his mind, but now he couldn't keep his attention on the game.

Now and then, out of the corner of his eye, he would see Anne, sitting with the many other spectators in the crowded pavilion. Her face looked white in the sunlight, her eyes seemed tired, and she must have lost a little weight, because the point of her little chin looked more pointed. But she watched him intently—only him, not René. Her head didn't swing back and forth to watch the play, as the others did; she kept her eyes on him.

With his mind divided as it was, he didn't realize how exciting he was to watch or how superbly he was playing. Not even thinking about the game or caring how badly he was beaten, his body was relaxed and effortless as he gathered up and returned shots that seemed impossible to recover. The sun was hot on his head and his tanned face was peeling a little from yesterday's burn, but the heat that was wilting René's energy was pouring strength through Louis's whole body. His hair was tousled, curling a little from the dampness of his perspiration, his strong forearms and the base of his throat were very brown against the white linen of his full shirt, and his black hose outlined the strong curves of his legs and his slim hips.

He heard the score, knew he was winning, but it meant nothing to him. That was strange, after the many years he had dreamed about beating René, the months and months he had spent practicing, the hours he had spent massaging his broken wrist so it would heal as strong as his right and he could play left-handed if he needed to.

The game went on; Louis was everywhere at once. Excited shouts followed his brilliant serves, gasps applauded him when he leaped incredibly high into the air, and the people who had bet on René—most of them had—saw they were about to lose their wagers. When the game was over, René fell to the ground in laughing exhaustion, vowing he was too old now for this game—he was twenty-seven—and the bets were paid, large wagers some of them, of jewels and horses and purses of gold.

Louis accepted the riotous applause smilingly, but his one idea was to escape the men and women crowding around him and follow Anne, because he could see her, walking alone toward the castle, and Denise was very busy consoling René with a kiss. Quickly he pleaded exhaustion and the need to change his clothes before he should catch a chill, but he didn't look exhausted as he snatched up his doublet and ran across the green lawn of the garden after Anne.

As he rounded the hedge he saw that she wasn't alone; her brother Charles was beside her, but that wasn't so bad. The boy was only seven; he wouldn't understand what they said.

"Anne!" he called, and she stopped and turned.

Her gown was white, reflecting the sun, and she had stopped to pick some of the Flemish tulips. Their deep colors, reds and purples, bloomed in her arms and added to her beauty. Louis caught up with her and, oblivious to everything but his desire for her, reached out to take her in his arms.

Anne saw his intention; she wanted his kiss, but she was conscious that Charles was beside her and that other people might see. It would be reported to the king, and he would be furious with her. Quickly she put out her hand and held it up restrainingly, so that it stopped Louis as he walked into it. She could feel the warmth of his shirt, and under it the pounding of his heart, and a shiver ran through her that ended in a sigh. He looked into her warning eyes, and then at her lips that were so close but that he could not touch, and he felt a terrible, yearning incompletion. And then, for a moment, he felt a flash of anger at her eternal caution. It wouldn't have brought about a state of war if she had let him have the kiss he had wanted so badly. A little talk, a scandal at most, what would it have mattered in comparison with the lovely moment they might have had? Sometimes the price of caution was too high.

Anne saw she must break the silence quickly. Charles was watching with inquisitive eyes. She smiled at Louis appealingly, begging him with her eyes not to believe she had stopped him because of disinclination, and she said, with every ounce of love she could put into her voice: "You played wonderfully well, Louis. I was so proud of you!"

Her tone consoled him and she went on, purposely calling his attention to Charles. "Charles screamed himself hoarse calling your name!"

Charles nodded excited corroboration with his large head, and they walked on toward the castle, the three of them, the boy between them, happy to be with his exciting cousin whom he called "Uncle" out of deference to Louis's great age. Charles admired Louis tremendously and asked eager questions about tennis and hunting and war. Louis answered indulgently, exchanging amused glances with Anne over the boy's head. But he was thinking how he could induce the child to leave them after they entered the château.

Anne knew he was thinking that, and it terrified her. He would speak of their plans for the future, and then she would have to go on lying or telling him that she had lied. Either way he would hate her.

But when they reached the stairs of the château one of the king's guards hurried up to Louis and breathlessly delivered a message from the king. The Duke of Orleans was requested to undertake an urgent errand for the king. His Grace was to present himself in the king's study within the hour, prepared for a trip. It was most important.

Louis curtly accepted the message. The guard bowed and left Anne and Louis to look wonderingly at each other.

"Now what does he plan?" Louis asked thoughtfully.

"I don't know, Louis, but you must obey him—promise me you will!"

Louis shrugged ruefully. "There isn't much else to do—now! But very soon it will be different. Be firm a little bit longer, Anne."

Anne broke in hastily. "We can't stand here talking—if you're late, he'll be angry." She hurried up the stairs and he had to follow.

"I'll send a message to you as often as I can," he was promising when he saw her shaking her head worriedly. "Why not?"

"He'll read them before I do," she explained unhappily. "I think it better for us not to write, Louis; it only makes him suspicious." Which was certainly underestimating by a great deal.

"You don't understand how dangerous your plan is. If you go too far, he'll say treason and then you'll be lost. I think you'd be wise to forget the whole impossible plan!"

He was aghast for a moment, and then he laughed. Anne was always the same, cautious, warning him not to do something, then walking along beside him while he did it. Naturally she was worried for his safety, but he couldn't turn back now. He smiled at her reassuringly. "There's nothing impossible about it—we'll continue as firm as we have been. I won't write, if it worries you. I'll be careful—I promise— and I promise you it won't be much longer. Good-by till then, Anne."

"Good-by——"

He took the stairs two at a time, while she stood half-way up the broad flight and watched him go. At the turn he looked back and waved. "Remember Montrichard!" he said, not as an injunction, but as a confident rallying cry.

"Yes, I will," she answered.

When the Duke of Orleans, prepared for a trip, presented himself in the king's study within the hour, the king greeted him brusquely and proceeded immediately to the discussion of the errand as though not a moment must be lost.

"You will ride out from Amboise at once," he said, "and deliver a most urgent message to my daughter Jeanne at Linières! Then you may return to your home, where you will undoubtedly wish to rest for some time and not return to Amboise till I send for you!"

Louis looked at the king suspiciously. "And what is the very urgent message, Your Majesty?" he asked grimly.

The king's false air of haste dropped away. He leaned leisurely back in his chair, rubbed his bony nose thoughtfully with his bony finger, and studied the ceiling. Then he smiled blandly at Louis. "I will think of one in a moment," he said.

Louis went cold with fury but was determined not to give the king the satisfaction of seeing it. He waited deferentially a moment, then he offered helpfully, "If I may suggest one?" He waited with an exaggerated air of suspense for the king's permission.

"Of course," the king said pleasantly, but he wasn't having as much enjoyment out of his joke as he had hoped.

"You could request your daughter to pray for your soul, which might benefit from her pious intercession—you could ask her to pray for your health—its condition looks urgent enough to warrant my hasty trip. I'll ride as fast as I can, and only hope I'll reach her in time."

The king was livid. He was a dying man and he knew it. He feared death, and after it he was afraid he might find himself in hell. Louis had hit both painful targets.

The king stood up and walked toward the door. He could think of nothing cutting enough to say, and his amusement in the joke was gone. "Tell the Princess Jeanne —I mean your wife, of course—tell the Duchess of Orleans that I hope she is well, that I think of her—and that——" He hesitated. There was something in what Louis had said, although he had meant it mockingly. Jeanne was a good, pious girl; her intercession might help at that awful moment when he stood before God and God measured him for heaven or hell. "And tell her she may pray for me!" He avoided Louis's sardonic look and flung open the door. "Now I'll see you on a horse's back and wish you Godspeed myself!"

When Louis rode into the courtyard of the ancient stone heap that was the castle of Linières, he thought ironically that the ugly, humped fortress was a suitable home for the king's ugly daughter. It had been built almost five hundred years before, when a castle's primary function had been that of a fortress, capable of withstanding indefinite siege successfully. It proclaimed its invulnerability in every one of its unsightly belligerent lines. The high blank walls had jagged stones and iron spikes cemented in around the top to prevent the enemy from climbing over. The narrow slits of windows weren't placed to admit air and light, but were only big enough to allow the defenders of the castle to shoot arrows out and to hurl down heavy stones, boiling water, crushing iron weights, and flaming torches onto the heads of the attackers. Louis contrasted it in his mind with his own beautiful, more civilized château and was glad he hadn't lived in those savage times when war lords had roamed the country and made their daily bread by pillaging any vulnerable town or isolated castle, when every man's hand had been raised greedily against his neighbor. Now, in these modern, civilized times, there were a few decent rules in war. You could travel the roads with only a dozen guards and still feel safe, and—he smiled ruefully to himself—only every other man's hand was raised against you.

He ordered his retinue to halt at the courtyard gates and rode in alone. The big door of the castle stood open, and one of the guards came down the steps, bowing deeply when he saw who it was. Grooms came running, quarreling among themselves for the privilege of helping him dismount. He tossed them some coins, but he remained on his horse.

He addressed the guard. "I bring a message from the king to his daughter—the Princess Jeanne. Is she here?"

The bewildered guard nodded and started back toward the house to inform his master, Count de Linières, that the Duke of Orleans was in the courtyard but for some reason didn't seem to wish to enter or even dismount.

Louis stopped the guard quickly. "I am on the king's very urgent business!" he said with loud distinctness, so his words could be clearly heard, well remembered, and reported to the king. "So I can't delay to see your master. Just answer quickly—the Princess Jeanne is here?"

The guard nodded violently.

"Then you will take this urgent message to her from her father!" Louis stressed its great importance by the exaggerated impressiveness of his voice. The guard and the grooms within hearing distance listened tensely. What had happened? they wondered. Was the king or his son dying—was it war?

Louis ended their suspense. "Tell her the king hopes she is well—that he thinks of her—and that she may pray for him."

The guard waited for more. Surely that was just the formal prelude of the message, but the Duke of Orleans was already reining up his horse and turning to ride away.

"Is that all, Your Grace?" the guard asked awkwardly, awed with his own importance. He was actually addressing the great Duke of Orleans.

"Yes," said Louis crisply, "that's the message. Take it

to the lady without an instant's delay—and take her my regret I was in such urgent haste I could not deliver the words myself."

Turning his horse, he rode at the most leisurely pace toward the gates of the courtyard, stopping once to rearrange the short cape around his shoulders, adjusting each fold as though he had all the time in the world. Then, walking his horse past his waiting guard, they all proceeded out of the gates at a snail's pace, their saddles squeaking, the horses' hoofs loudly slow on the cobblestones.

Louis was smiling to himself as he thought of the king's face when he heard how the duke had delivered the message. Louis knew he himself was intended to be the message; he had been meant to visit with Jeanne—the first step in the king's campaign to make him accept Jeanne as his wife and ultimately to force her to live at Blois with him.

Well, the king would see, from this small incident, how little chance there was of that.

Louis whistled cheerfully. He felt wonderfully happy on this sunny April day. Although he had been dismissed from court without seeing Anne alone, still he had been reassured as to her success at keeping her marriage with Pierre only a formal alliance, and the battle was progressing slowly but well. He had shown the king the path he meant to follow, both by his letter to the Pope and this insolent visit to Linières, and with Anne's wonderful loyalty to encourage him he would follow that path with stubborn, unrelenting persistence until it ended at the chapel altar at Montrichard with Anne beside him—yes, in that same wedding dress, to show she had planned it for him from the first and that she had never been married to anyone but himself!

Once out of sight of Linières, he touched his spur to his horse's flank and raced for home.

7

Marie-Louise helped settle some of the Orleans financial difficulties and relieved them from selling too much land. She felt, in a dull and listless way, that her life had really ended when Pierre had married. She had tried to forget him, because she didn't enjoy suffering, but when she woke in the mornings and couldn't think of a reason for rising, not one moment in the day that she could look forward to, and not one person who would be desolate without her, she became disgusted with such an aimless life and decided a change must be made. She had always had strong religious feelings, and in May she packed away her trousseau in a deep oak chest and traveled to the Abbey of Foualt, where she put on novice's robes and prepared to take holy vows.

Mary had felt her daughter inclining toward convent life and had tried to dissuade her, but Mary was pious enough herself to see that some kind of happiness might be found in service.

So Marie-Louise left them for an existence which included the satisfaction of some accomplishment, although there was little joy in it. Her departure left them with the dowry they had put aside for her and of which they had touched only a small part when the need became too great; now it was theirs to use, clearing the more pressing debts. It was not so enormous that they could continue at an extravagant rate of living, but since Louis had understood the need he had economized readily and cheerfully.

Louis and Dunois had planned to leave for Rome in April, but their cousin Eugène of Angoulême promised to go with them if they would wait till the middle of May. Eugène had his own reasons for wanting to see the Pope: to protest against his betrothal to the infant Louise of

Savoy, but, unlike Louis, Eugène had only a weak, flickering hope that the marriage could be avoided.

The three of them argued over maps of the road, planning their itinerary. Dunois had recently been to Rome, so he could speak knowingly of which roads were safer and which inns were best. Georges d'Amboise was already in Rome, establishing himself in the Church, and eager to see them. They planned to keep it a small party, about twelve in all: Louis, Dunois, Eugène, with their respective valets, three guards, and three grooms with extra horses.

Louis wasn't enthusiastic about taking his new valet, Paul Capporetti, with him. Louis didn't like the man, although Paul was certainly the best servant he had ever had. He took excellent care of Louis's clothes, saw that his food was served exactly to his liking, handled Louis's scanty correspondence with dispatch, was always at hand when he was wanted, always respectful and humbly eager to please. But still Louis was uncomfortable with him because he was used to Léon's silent, negative presence. Paul, when he was in the room with Louis, seemed to be everywhere at once. Wherever Louis turned his eyes, somehow he met Paul's melancholy gaze.

And the man talked too much, entirely too much. At first, trying to put him at his ease and feeling sorry for him, Louis had talked to him expansively, encouraging response. Now he found that unless he constantly checked Paul with severity, he couldn't stop the valet's low-toned flow of words. His favorite topic was women, and no matter how the conversation began, whether it was a discussion about which coat Louis should wear or if his hair needed cutting, it always ended up with one of Paul's experiences with a woman. Louis liked women too, liked discussing them with Dunois, Eugène, or even Georges, although Georges's churchly robes implied a lack of experience, but the way Paul spoke was strangely distasteful. That was difficult for Louis to explain too, because Paul never used coarse terms nor went into too intimate details; still there was something unctuous and disagreeably sensuous in his low, smooth voice that skillfully created an amorous atmosphere, sketched in the beginning of the incident, then stopped on a key word of voluptuous suggestion and waited for Louis's imagination to unlock a door with it and explore the erotic meanings within. Louis listened uneasily, fascinated in spite of himself, and because he was young and warm-blooded, and because it was fragrant spring, his thoughts and his dreams were sometimes troubled by the pictures Paul's voice conjured up.

Paul seemed to think, too, that Louis's life was crammed with romantic experiences. He never helped Louis on with a jacket or smoothed the tight-fitting hose around Louis's ankles without some flattering comment about the lucky lady who was about to receive the Duke of Orleans. When Louis laughingly protested that his life these days was very scantily furnished with lucky ladies, Paul would smile too, gentle skepticism in his sad eyes, and he would meaningly sprinkle a little powdered scent over the plumes on Louis's hat before he would deferentially present the hat to Louis. Such a firm belief in his nonexistent amours was irritating, but flattering, since no one really dislikes being considered experienced in love. Louis, although he was a married man, wasn't expected to be faithful to his wife, even if she was really his wife; being a great duke, he was expected to be as constantly unfaithful as opportunity offered, and opportunity was very generous to the Duke of Orleans. Lovely ladies of the queen's retinue flirted with him and let him know with intimate looks how much they would welcome a light romance, and at home, among his mother's small court, there were several attractive girls who invited him with their eyes. But, appetizing as they all were, Louis was afraid of an attachment to someone at court. That was too close to Anne; she would know of it and be hurt. And then a liaison with someone in his own class might divide his attention and complicate his divorce. No, it was better to assuage his needs with the willing serving girls at inns, or the pretty ladies of the town, who could be generously paid and rapidly forgotten. No complications there, either to divorce or to his emotions, and Anne could never be hurt by such trivial moments of pleasure. Naturally she wouldn't expect him to be an inexperienced milksop.

Even these unimportant amours were seldom, though, because, while his desire was strong, it was for Anne, and his constant thoughts of her made it difficult to feel the inclination for a substitute. But since he had been listening to Paul's never-ending experiences, which he told, Louis thought, like memorized stories planned to inflame the hearer's mind, Louis's thoughts strayed more often to pro-

vocative eyes, red lips, and white shoulders. He decided he
would use his trip to Italy as a good excuse to get rid of
the man, but Paul precipitated an immediate dismissal one
morning when, in just a few words, he went altogether too
far.

He was deftly shaving Louis with the long, very sharp,
very bright blade of Spanish steel. The brown of Louis's
skin showed in even strips through the white lather, like
miniature paths shoveled through snow, and Louis leaned
back in the shaving chair, irritably trying not to listen and
thanking God he would be rid of this fellow in a couple
of weeks. Today he would speak to Grévin, master of the
household servants, and see what valet would be suitable
for his trip south. Too bad about this Paul—he was so
good in so many ways, but just too uncomfortable to have
around. When his tongue wasn't talking, his brown velvet
eyes were. Well, Grévin could find some other post for him,
wish him onto old d'Armagnac, who was deaf and wouldn't
be bothered by his sibilant voice.

Then Louis began to hear what Paul was saying. Encouraged by what he had thought was Louis's interested
silence, he was discussing in more intimate detail than usual
his exciting adventure with a malformed, hunchbacked girl
who had looked, begging His Grace's pardon, a little like
the Princess Jeanne, but who had more than made up for
physical limitations with a furious ardor——

Louis sprang out of the low barber chair, snatched the
razor from Paul's hand, and shouted savagely at the
startled man:

"Get out! Get out of here!" And, shaking with disgust,
Louis stalked to the door, yanked it open so hard it flew
out of his hand and banged against the wall. "Get out and
don't ever come back!"

Paul's sallow face was drawn with fear, his eyes were
piteous with it. "But, Your Grace——"

Louis couldn't stand to be in the same room with a man
who could suggest such a horror, and he strode out through
the ante-chamber and flung that door crashingly open too.
Paul had followed and had dropped to his knees on the patterned floor.

"Your Grace—forgive me—I don't understand how I've
offended you—but forgive me."

He reached out for Louis's shoe, to touch it appealingly,

but Louis jerked his foot forward and barely restrained himself from kicking the groveling man. He might have, except he couldn't bear to touch Paul. His hand involuntarily clenched on the razor handle and he thought he ought to slit the Venetian's throat, just to cleanse the world of a foul spy who had been sent by a foul king to watch Louis, to try and turn his mind so rancid that the thought of consummating the marriage with Jeanne could be considered, without retching, as an interesting experience.

Paul saw the murderous hate in Louis's face, saw the strong hand tighten on the razor handle, and he scrambled up hastily, half on his hands and knees till he reached the door.

"Get out of this house!" Louis shouted after him. "And don't ever let me see your slimy face again!"

Louis stood in the doorway, shaking with fury, watching Paul stumble down the corridor and out of sight. He thought grimly back to the morning Paul had come into his service, substituting for Léon, and he wondered whether the king had used the opportunity of Léon's death to plant a spy so conveniently close to Louis, or had Léon been deliberately killed to create that opportunity? Louis remembered Léon's body, lying on a hard marble bench in a little room off the chapel, seeming no more silent in death than he had been in life. Two of the fatal stabs were in his back, and the other dead man had similar wounds. None of the grooms were certain just what had happened. They had heard shouts and sounds of a scuffle. When they rushed into the stables the two men were sprawled together, bleeding and dead. They could have killed each other, as it was claimed, but Louis had a sick feeling that two absolutely unoffending men had died to give the king his chance to send Paul to Louis. It was impossible now to prove how it had been; too late to do anything about it but regret their deaths, get rid of Paul, and hate the king a little more, if that were possible.

And, right this minute, nothing to do but get another valet, because the small patches of lather were drying on his face, and even if he were experienced at shaving himself, a thing no duke ever did, in his present mood of tenseness he might scrape his chin off. He was about to close the door when he saw a manservant in valet's livery coming down the hall, carrying a man's cloak over his arm and going toward Monsieur Beauvais's suite.

"You!" Louis called. "Come here!"

The valet, startled, came hurriedly toward him, and as he came closer the angry lines of Louis's face began to relax and he smiled a little. The servant—a young man—had such a cheerfully absurd face, like a small woods animal, Louis thought, a hare, or a good-natured squirrel, with the same high round cheeks, like little pouches for storage; the small, shiny gray eyes, already creased with laugh lines at the corner, and, completing his similarity to a rabbit, his two front teeth, big and square and white, with a little space between them, slightly overlapped his upcurved lower lip. His skin was red from the sun and blistered; he looked like the kind who never tanned, and his thick shock of hair, a strange color somewhere between the red of an apple and the orange of a tangerine, had been cut to the pattern of a kitchen bowl and shaved up on all sides to where the bowl began. He was short and slight, and his valet's livery seemed to have been made for his father; it wrinkled profusely and the shoulders dropped down over his arms. He was looking at Louis eagerly, his small, bright eyes taking in every detail of Louis's clothing. Louis smilingly motioned him in and closed the door.

"What's your name?"

The young man squared himself off and, as though he were announcing a titled stranger, said clearly, "Maximilien Armand Edouard Marie Poquelin, Your Grace."

"Max Poquelin will do," Louis said, smiling.

"Yes, Your Grace. Max Poquelin." Anything to please you, his cheerful manner said; call me what you like, it shall be my name!

"Are you Monsieur Beauvais' valet? Is he expecting you?"

"Oh no, sire, Your Grace. I was just taking up his cloak left in the hall by mistake."

"Whose valet are you?"

"Nobody's, Your Grace. Just anyone's who needs me, Your Grace."

Everyone in the family had his own valet, but an additional staff was kept to substitute when a regular valet was ill or off duty, and to assist guests who might have traveled without one. Max Poquelin was evidently one of these.

"Is there something you would like me to do, Your Grace?" Max asked hopefully.

"Perhaps," said Louis, considering Max thoughtfully. He was so wonderfully different from Paul, which was almost all the reference he needed at the moment. He was as eager to serve as Paul had been, but without Paul's embarrassing humbleness. He was so cheerful, so open; he stood proudly in his wrinkled livery, and behind his ridiculous face there might be coarse and ribald thoughts, but nothing dark and perverted. If he were any kind of a valet at all—and if Grévin had trained him, he must be fairly good—it might be pleasant to have his amusing face along on the trip to Italy.

"Are you a good valet?"

"Yes, Your Grace!" Max stood, if possible, a little straighter in his wrinkles.

"A good barber?"

"Yes, Your Grace."

"Are you honest? Hard-working?"

"Oh yes, Your Grace!" Max was answering eagerly, even before Louis's questions were fully ended. He had sensed that the questions led, if they could be answered satisfactorily, to a wonderful position—permanent valet to somebody—maybe even to the duke himself!

"Do you drink?"

"Oh yes—oh no, sir, Your Grace. Only a little ale now and then."

"Can you read? Write letters?"

Max didn't falter for a moment, although his shiny gray eyes flickered. "Yes, Your Grace."

"Are you a good traveler?"

"Of course, Your Grace." His confident tones indicated travels all over the continent and a competent handling of the many details, but he had been born in the nearby town of Blois, and up the hill to the château was as far as he had ever gone.

"Would you like to go to Italy with me as my valet?"

"Oh! Your Grace!" Max swallowed ecstatically and grinned, showing the rest of his square white teeth with the little spaces between each of them. It was such an infectious smile that Louis laughed. What a refreshing contrast to Paul's lonely, wistful eyes, his pale smile.

"Have you any ties that should keep you here at home? A wife—children?"

"Oh no, Your Grace!" Max exclaimed in horror.

"I may be gone a year or more," Louis warned him.

"Yes, Your Grace. Certainly." Max's shining eyes said a year with Louis in Italy was what he had always wanted.

"Well . . ." Louis turned and walked back through the sitting room toward his bedroom and the shaving chair. "If you're suitable—and I imagine you're a good valet, or Grévin wouldn't have you here—we'll be leaving within the month."

But when he had settled himself back in the shaving chair and Max bent eagerly over him to moisten the lather and finish the shave, Louis's eyes widened and his nostrils distended as he smelled the heavy aroma of horseflesh that surrounded Max. He smelled like a ripe stableboy. Louis looked at Max's hand; the fingers were calloused, the nails broken off and stained with saddle oil. He was no valet!

"Max Poquelin!" Louis said sharply, sitting up in his chair.

"Yes, Your Grace?"

"You're a stableboy, aren't you?"

Max hesitated a moment, then he sighed. "Yes, Your Grace."

"You're a liar too, aren't you?"

"Yes, Your Grace," Max admitted heavily.

Louis snickered in spite of himself, then he spoke sternly. "You took some valet's livery, didn't you?"

"Yes, Your. Grace. Just borrowed it, Your Grace, from Henri Duval."

"You know what I ought to do with you, don't you?"

"Oh yes, Your Grace. You ought to have me flogged and fined."

"But you know I won't, don't you?—and stop saying 'Yes, Your Grace'—just answer with the truth. Why did you take the valet's livery?"

"Because I like it," Max said slowly. "I think it's the most"—he was going to say beautiful but substituted—"nicest coat I ever saw—and I always wanted to wear it someday—but I knew I never would, because I haven't any training or anything—but now and then—I couldn't help it, I borrowed one to wear——"

He looked lovingly down at the wine-colored coat decorated with silver buckles bearing the Orleans crest. The dark hose were sizes too big for him—they bagged ludicrously around his ankles—and the wine-colored coat fought with the orange red of his hair, but still Max had felt himself an elegant figure in Henri's livery, and for one exciting moment he had thought perhaps he could brazen his way into a position where he would proudly wear the duke's own personal crest, the golden porcupine, in addition to the Orleans coat of arms. But he had been caught in his lie, and now he would be lucky if he would even be allowed to wear a stableboy's livery, which was no livery at all, really, but just castoffs from the grooms.

He laid down the razor and slowly, with trembling fingers, began to untie the barber's towel he had carefully wrapped around his waist to protect Henri's livery.

"I'm very sorry, Your Grace."

Louis watched Max's downcast face and his thoughts were mixed. It was hard for him, raised in luxury all his life, to put himself in the mind of a man whose highest ambition was to be a valet. But Louis had an unusually sympathetic imagination, inherited from his poet father, and for a moment he saw just a thousandth part of what Max's life must have been.

He couldn't know the details, of course. Max's illegitimate birth to a mother who abandoned him when he was three—his stray existence, like a wandering dog, fed here and there by a moment's kindness from strange people—sleeping in halls and doorways—living in a convent orphanage till he ran away at six to his first job helping on a fishing boat and cleaning the fish in the market—then to a less odorous job in a bakery, watching and tending the fires till one night his childish weariness put him to sleep and he burned up the whole oven's baking. The baker had thrown a heavy flour bag at him and told him to get out—since then he had done all kinds of things, in the tanneries, working in the summer on a farm for his room and board, and going cold and hungry through the towns in winter, looking for work.

He had been working in the town stables, feeding and currying the horses, when he had first seen his first hero,

Henri Duval, a real valet to Count Visconti at the Orleans castle. Henri had been amused by Max's face, favorably impressed by his cheerful willingness, and had told Max that if he wanted to come up and see the head groom at the castle, Henri would speak in his behalf. Max had come breathlessly—he had been about seventeen then, he had thought—and he thought he was about twenty or twenty-one now. He had been a stableboy for three years; in five more he might be a groom, but if he was at Blois all his life, he would never be a valet, because that required refinement and training he didn't have. But now and then, dressed in borrowed glory, he would enjoy a few moments of stealthy pleasure in the upper corridors and back stairs where Grévin's sharp eye wouldn't catch him; elegantly he would walk through the halls in his wonderful livery, pretending he was that luckiest of men, an Orleans valet!

And now he wasn't even lucky enough to be an Orleans stableboy.

But Louis was speaking impulsively. "If you like the livery so well, order a suit to your own measure, not Henri's, only see that the tailor has it ready in time—because we leave for Italy in two weeks!"

The look of incredulous delight that flooded Max's face was so overwhelming that Louis turned away, embarrassed by so much gratitude. What a shabby life the poor little rabbit must have had, Louis thought—and then thought wryly how much trouble he would probably be in the future. He would make a sorry mess of Louis's clothes; Louis would have to tend to his own letters, and he hated letter writing. Just because he had liked a stableboy's face he had wished all this nuisance on himself. He sighed, already annoyed at his own decision, but, still with no impulse to change it, and cutting short Max's stumbling thanks, motioned to him to take up the razor again.

"Stop calling me Your Grace every other word, and get this lather off before my skin stretches tighter than a drum——" Then apprehensively, as he saw the razor gleam in Max's hand that was shaking with excitement, "And, for God's sake, remember I'm not a horse!"

Later, his skin burning but without any visible scars, Louis went down to Grévin's office to tell him that he had a new valet who would require some hasty training and some new livery—Grévin's correct face would blanch with horror when he heard who it was—and that he had also an ex-valet who would require dismissal wages and travel money to Amboise.

But before he saw Grévin he met de Mornac, who was on his way to Louis's room.

"I thought I'd better tell you," de Mornac explained, "that if it's agreeable to you, I'll keep Paul Capporetti on as my valet and secretary. He said you'd dismissed him——"

Louis flushed angrily. "Did he say why?"

"He told a very sad story about your not liking him— that nobody liked him. I know I don't like him either, but" —de Mornac shrugged his broad shoulders—"he writes an unusually good hand, and I need that kind of help."

"I won't have him under this roof!"

"Why not?" De Mornac was surprised.

"For one thing, he's disgusting," Louis said shortly, "and for another, he's a king's spy."

"Oh!" exclaimed de Mornac. "When did you find that out!"

"Today—although I should have known sooner. The thought had crossed my mind——"

"Yes, mine too. I thought of it when you brought him from Amboise."

"I have an idea Léon was killed so I'd take Paul into my service."

"That's very possible," de Mornac admitted gravely. "Does he know you've found him out?"

"No. What he knows isn't important—I know I want him out of here at once!"

"But"—de Mornac said slowly—"the king will only slide someone else into the house. Isn't it better for you if you know who that man is?"

Louis didn't like the idea, but he had to admit its wisdom.

De Mornac nodded and a grim smile spread over his face. "I can work him day and night, abuse him roundly, and still he'll have to stay. And best of all"—de Mornac sighed happily—"the king will have to pay his wages, because I'll forget to!"

Louis nodded agreement and it was arranged for Paul to stay, but Louis had an uneasy feeling that wasn't the end of it. Paul, being a king's man, would make all the trouble he could.

He did—the very next day, when he walked into the servants' dining hall for noon dinner.

A strict caste system was used to determine the seating of the household staff, and even as in the court dining room, where etiquette said the king's table should be on a raised dais, the dukes a few steps down, seated in order of their importance and their kinship with royal blood, and then at separate tables the lesser counts and sires, so here in the kitchen hall the same system of separate tables was used. The lowest table, set in the draftiest place near the door and some distance away from the other tables, was the exclusive property of the stableboys and grooms, and no one envied them their lowly place. The next table accommodated the miscellaneous groups of scullery maids, cooks, laundresses, and pot boys. A more elegant table was composed of the chambermaids, apprentice valets, nurses, midwives, and if there were any artisans in the house, bricklayers, or cabinetmakers, they sat there too. An even more refined table accommodated the clergy's servants and secretaries, and then, at the highest table of all, sat the royalty of the Orleans staff.

King Edouard Grévin and Queen Jeanne Ledu sat at the head and foot of the table, respectively, and along its two sides ranged the personal valets and maids to the immediate members of the Orleans family. Max Poquelin, hardly daring to eat lest he spill on his beautiful livery—still borrowed, but closer to his own size, and only borrowed till his own should be ready—sat in a dream of ecstasy next to Blanche, who was Mary's prim maid, then came Henri Duval, valet to André Visconti, then Suzanne and Pauline, maids to Mary's cousins from Cleves, then Armand and Henriette, valet and maid to the d'Armagnacs. There were empty places, reserved for the maids and valets of visiting titles, and one special empty seat that had been reserved for Pierre Roget, valet to the late Duke Charles of Orleans. Pierre was dead now too, presumably serving his master in heaven, but no one had usurped his place until this noon, when Paul Capporetti walked smoothly in and sat down in that empty chair next to Jeanne Ledu, who dropped her bread in her soup with a splash and gaped at him.

A hush fell over the whole noisy room, and the grooms and cooks at the far-off tables stood up to see what had happened. When they saw what it was, the hush was swept away by the noisy whispering that followed. They passed the news from one to the other. De Mornac's valet was sitting in the chair that belonged to the old duke's servant! And by this bold act proclaiming that since his master was also master of the duchess, he, Paul Capporetti, had the right to Pierre Roget's place at the table!

By right of etiquette, since his demotion from Louis's service, de Mornac's valet belonged at the second table with the clergy's servants, but Paul's bold manner, his calm ignoring of their excitement, dared them to try and send him there.

Grévin tried. He rose majestically in his place and looked down the table at Paul, who was busily serving himself steaming soup out of a tureen on the center of the table.

"Monsieur Capporetti," Grévin said sharply, "you have made a mistake. You must not take that chair!"

Paul's dark eyes looked over the room slowly, with insolence. He finished spooning soup out of the tureen and put the cover carefully back on before he said, "Why? You think it too good for me? Well, I am like my master. Nothing in this house is too good for the Sire de Mornac! He takes what he likes!"

Gasps and angry exclamations protested his insult. Of course a good many of them knew of the affair between their duchess and de Mornac, but to have it announced like this was shocking. Jeanne Ledu was crying into her apron; Blanche looked straight ahead with a flaming face. It was like having her own shame revealed to all of France, and in a way it was worse than if it was herself. Her pride in her mistress, her sweet, pretty mistress, was mortally wounded.

Grévin's hands were shaking, and he thought if he were a younger man he would like to throttle Paul—but yet there must be no fighting, or the scandal would spread.

Max was one of the few puzzled ones. The scandal had been loyally protected as far as possible, and it hadn't proceeded out to the stables yet.

Grévin's voice said shakily, "You're a coward, and a lying one——" But he faltered and stopped as Paul laughed.

"A coward and a liar, Monsieur Grévin, for saying what you all know? Well—in that case"—he rose abruptly—"perhaps we had better take this discussion to the Duke of Orleans—and he can settle where the Sire de Mornac's valet should sit!" He pushed his chair back as though he were anxious to go right away.

Grévin was aghast. Take this ugly incident, which must lead to the ugly truth, to Duke Louis, from whom it had been so carefully kept? No! He tried desperately to think of what could be done, and nothing came to his mind. He was helpless to defend his duchess against the consequences of her own sin.

He sank slowly down in his chair. "Such a trivial thing isn't worth the duke's attention," he said gruffly. "Sit where you choose!" He stared down at his plate and tried not to hear Paul's insulting laughter as Paul too sat down again and with heartiness began to eat his soup.

Max was still half bewildered but furious. This Venetian, whom his master disliked, had insulted the duchess and nobody was doing anything about it. Well, Duke Louis should know about it! He got up hastily and hurried out of the buzzing room. Paul watched him go with smiling eyes that clouded when Blanche rose, too, and ran after Max. She caught up with him in the lower hall.

"Wait!" she called. "You mustn't tell the duke about this!"

"Why not?" He stared in amazement. "Let that liar spread his stories all over France?"

"But," Blanche protested, her cheeks scorched with humiliation, "but—you see—if it isn't a lie, it will only be made worse by trying to deny it!"

"Isn't a lie!" Max exclaimed angrily, and then stopped short. If anyone knew the truth, Blanche would be that one. Her devotion to the duchess was absolute, and she wouldn't be in such misery now unless it were true.

"Isn't a lie?" Max repeated weakly. And she shook her head, keeping her eyes averted.

"So if her son knew," Blanche said painfully, "he would have to kill the Sire de Mornac."

"Well?" asked Max sharply, meaning that it might be an excellent idea. He already completely idolized Louis and so identified himself with his master that he was furious at de Mornac for touching Louis's name with scandal.

"But my mistress loves him," Blanche said appealingly, thinking of Mary's happiness these last few years. Blanche knew it was a black sin, this affair; she condemned it in her mind and prayed for Mary's soul to be cleansed of it, but sometimes she wondered. How could sin have made a good woman so much kinder? Mary was so considerate and appreciative—more than she had been before she had fallen in love. Warmed by her own happiness, her eyes were open to the needs of others less happy, and from the moment in the morning when she woke with a smile and a pleasant word for Blanche till she retired with a warm good night, Blanche was willing to swear that Mary never had an unkind thought. If it was sin, and of course it was, it wore a strange disguise.

But Max naturally didn't have that view of the situation, and he was frowning. Louis's mother, according to Max, should love Louis and that was all.

Blanche saw Max's frown and tried to convince him on more practical grounds. "If he kills the Sire de Mornac, the scandal will travel even farther than the boundaries of France, and the House of Orleans will never find another steward like him!"

That was true, Max knew, and he hesitated. There didn't seem much to be gained by telling Louis, and a great deal to be lost if he did. Still it was impossible to let that Capporetti sit there gloating.

Blanche denied his thoughts. "And it's just what the Venetian wants you to do—tell the duke and stir up trouble. He hopes it will end with both the duke and the Sire de Mornac dead, and my mistress out of her mind with grief!"

Max nodded slowly. Yes—that would suit the slinky Venetian. Well, then, there was nothing to be done but keep it from his master—and try and find Capporetti alone some night in the darkness of the stables. But he didn't want any lunch now. He went thoughtfully up to Henri Duval's room for his lessons. Henri was trying to compress years of valet training into the weeks before Max was to leave for Italy.

Some of the repercussions of the servants' hall scandal leaked upward and reached Mary's ears, in a very expurgated form, not through Blanche but one of her younger, slightly malicious ladies-in-waiting. It formed a decision toward which she had been drifting. Since Marie-Louise was gone and Louis was a grown man who was home less and less, she was lonely. In her room one night, talking and resting with de Mornac beside her, as they were used to doing as often as they could, she told him of it.

"Alain, I think we were very foolish not to have married a long time ago. We've wasted so many happy, peaceful evenings like this."

"Not so very many," he said, feeling no huge regret. They were well enough as they were, as married as they would ever be, priest or no priest.

"But it's getting more dangerous all the time. So many guests in the house—Louis grown up, and his friends prowling through the halls at all hours. Think what would happen if Louis were to see you leaving my room some night!" It made her breath stop to think of it.

De Mornac smiled in the darkness. "He'd probably provoke a large scandal and make no one any happier by trying to kill me."

Mary was very serious. "He's heard so much talk, if he saw you, he'd believe what was said of me."

De Mornac's smile deepened. "It would be difficult not to!" he admitted.

"And it's not easy to know how much the servants guess."

"Except you may be sure it's more than you think." Everyone was perfectly aware of the liaison, of that he was certain. He could see it in the discreet entrances and withdrawals of her attendants; he could hear it in the servants' talk that stopped at his approach; he could sense it in her friends' curious looks; but if she chose to think it was only faintly suspected, he saw no point in disillusioning her.

"And so I think the best thing for us to do is to get married. I think we could be very happy together," Mary said primly.

De Mornac was always amused at her sweet seriousness, and it further tickled his sardonic sense of humor that after having lived together for eight years she could wish to have their union tardily blessed by the church and live happily ever after.

"I think we could be very happy too," he answered with a shade of prim mockery in his voice. "But I think it's a happiness we'd better deny ourselves. Think how it would please the gossips—the king would encourage them to enjoy it."

"Why? If we're married it would stop the talk."

He shook his head at her density. "No, my dear, it would prove to them that what they'd been saying is true, that we've been lovers for years and years—that Louis is my son."

"How can it prove what isn't true?" Mary asked as indignantly as though none of it had any foundation.

De Mornac was glad it was dark. She would have been offended if she had seen his smile now.

"I think some of it is true. We've loved for some time, and we have no hourglass to show at what precise moment our attachment began. How are your friends to know?"

"My friends know me," she said proudly, "and they know I was a faithful wife to my husband."

"And the king's friends?" he asked.

"The king's friends will say what they've been saying since Louis's birth. It was false then; it's false now."

De Mornac spoke more seriously, seeing how serious she was. "Mary, they think they know the truth already; if they should see us married they'll think it a further proof of their knowledge. It'll be harder for you to stand above their words if you've admitted before them all that you love me enough to marry me. And think of Louis's position."

But Mary's interest in his argument had lapsed before he came to the end of it. She knew what she wanted—Alain beside her for the rest of her days, with the approval of the Church and her conscience, so that she was not always worried for fear they might be discovered or, more menacingly, that Alain might leave her. She knew his interest in her was less than it had been. She had lost much of her youth and beauty in the last years, for while her quiet days and nights with Charles, untouched by strong emotions, had kept her young and unlined, the years with Alain had aged her much more than their actual time. Passions and shame, arguments with her conscience, fear that her children might know, sometimes fear of physical consequences, all those things had laid heavy fingers of time on her beauty. She looked into the mirror more and more apprehensively, searching for the face and figure that Alain had first called a "spring primrose emerging from a snowbank." She feared she would lose him entirely someday, and she expected marriage would help keep him with her.

So she didn't listen to the reason in his voice but only to the note of reluctance, and she asked with asperity: "You don't wish to marry me?"

"Of course I want to. I told you long ago that if we were

situated otherwise we'd marry. I'm only thinking of your good."

Mary answered with severe imperiousness; the Duchess of Orleans in a temper, using a tone she never employed with him. "I think I may be allowed to judge for myself what's for my good. I think we will be married!"

De Mornac shrugged his shoulders. It made little difference to him one way or the other. Marriage with Mary would have its advantages, of course: a more secure future, a more comfortable present. His affection for her was stronger and longer than he had ever felt for any woman before, and the years weren't standing still for him either. Sometimes, walking stealthily through the cold halls of the château in the dark hours of the early morning, he thought approvingly of the warmth and comfort of marriage. Whether the pleasure of sleeping and waking leisurely in the same bed would be enough to offset the disadvantage of being faithful to that one bed, he didn't know, but that disadvantage had been solved by other husbands. He thought, too, with a smile of rueful reminiscence for the many beds he had visited, even that pleasure was becoming not so important to him as it had been. Perhaps the faithful life would be easier and more comfortable than he thought.

"Do you love me?" Mary was asking. "Do you love me as much as you did then?"

She asked that question much too often to please de Mornac, but fortunately, from force of long habit, his answer was very convincing.

De Mornac knew that Louis would hate the news of their intended marriage, and he asked Mary to let him tell her son, feeling that a calm, unemotional explanation to Louis of his mother's need for friendship and advice in the coming years would meet with a better reception than if Mary deluged him with a story of undying love. It would seem ridiculous to Louis, and he would be tormented with doubts as to whether this love had been born about nine months before he had. Mary, however, felt she could explain the marriage with more delicacy.

But before either of them could tell him an imperative message came from the king, ordering Louis to visit his wife in Linières immediately. This time the king wasn't in a humorous mood and his command left no room for evasion.

He wrote plainly that Louis was to stay at Linières overnight and since Jeanne was fifteen now, the marriage might safely be consummated.

Fury at the king's tone and intention mingled with an uneasy eagerness to enter the battleground and declare his intentions; that first little skirmish didn't really count, but now the actual war had begun. An Orleans told to go and mate with a humpbacked monstrosity and be grateful into the bargain! By every God there was in heaven, that king would soon find out that this Orleans wouldn't dance to his filthy tune. Louis went up the great staircase to his room three steps at a time, the riding stick he carried whistling in the air with vicious strokes. He hesitated over the clothes he should wear. Should he go as he was, carelessly clothed in hunting shirt and breeches, showing his bride and her family how little he thought of the honor they felt they had done him, or should he go elegantly attired, the Duke of Orleans, haughty and superior, contemptuously refusing their insulting gift? He stood in the center of the room and contemplated both courses, then quickly flung out of his clothes and into his best. He was afraid if he went carelessly dressed, they might miss his subtle point and think him only poverty-stricken.

Dunois had been with him when the summons had come, and Dunois rode part of the way with him toward Linières, in the king's province of Berry. They rode some little distance ahead of the group of attendants that followed.

It was a beautiful day for such a disagreeable errand. Their way followed the course of the Loire River, and everywhere about them in the freshly green valley beauty and life ripened under the May sun. In the forests it was cool and dim, and green streams turned to foaming white and leaped high over the stones to touch the trailing boughs of the great willow trees, sometimes carrying away a long, slim leaf to take to the river. Blackbirds, their bright yellow eyes unseen among the leaves, whistled their shrill-noted song, and at the edge of the forests the fields were heavy with the scent of blooming roses and the spring wheatfields were rippling yellow waters. The province of Orleans was a prosperous land, rich in its growth of grapes for wines and wheat for life. Sheep and cattle thrived in its abundance, and it was no wonder the king eyed it so greedily.

Sun and shadow alternately fell on Louis and Dunois as

they walked their horses side by side and talked of the coming visit to Jeanne. Dunois was one of the few—Georges and Eugène were the others—who approved Louis's plan for the future, and he, too, was glad the time had come for the first important encounter, although he was worried for Louis's safety.

"How long must you stay at Linières?" Dunois asked.

"Overnight, at least," Louis said, his young face set and grim, his brown hands clenched tightly on the reins of his horse.

"Overnight," repeated Dunois reflectively. "What will you do, Louis?"

"I'll demand a separate room, of course. I won't stay in the same room with that creature."

"No, you mustn't do that," Dunois agreed worriedly. "The king would say you'd slept with her."

"I'll have to wait and see how my request is answered before I know how to proceed. I'll sleep out in the stables if I have to."

"I think I should go with you, Louis, you might need me."

"No." Louis shook his head. "If he has me arrested and imprisoned, I want you safely at a distance, so you can try to convene the States-General and protest to the Pope."

"Do you think he'll dare arrest you?"

Louis hesitated. "I don't think he will, no—but I'm not sure. If he does——"

"I'll get an army together and march against him!"

"Only as a last resort. If my arrest could rouse the dukes to call a meeting of the States-General and re-establish its power, then I'd consider a few months in prison well spent."

The present lords of France had good reason to regret the result of their fathers' patriotic unselfishness when, during the last war, they had proclaimed a state of emergency, dissolved the States-General, and voluntarily renounced its right of collecting the national tax, in favor of the Crown. They were too busy fighting and dying to meet for business as usual, and while they were away at war the king, whom they trusted, could more efficiently collect the tax and make the necessary new laws. Of course this was only to last for the duration, but finally, when the last echoes of war had died away, the last medal awarded, the last dramatic speech made, the king, a new king now, and one not to be trusted, refused to return the power to them.

The tax remained in his hands, and he was able, with the money they had given him the right to collect, to maintain a large standing army to enforce his laws against them. The States-General had been accustomed to an annual meeting, at which grievances were discussed and settled, at which laws were passed, subject to the king's veto, and the king was voted funds for his requests. If his vetoes were too frequent and annoying, the funds voted him were less, and in that very practical monetary way a king's power was kept within reason.

This House of Lords could also be convened to consider any emergency, but since it had been dissolved during the war, the king had never allowed it to reorganize. So, in their patriotic eagerness to win a war, the past dukes had signed a death warrant for their own States-General and left their sons no weapons to fight a tyrant king.

It was Louis's purpose to see this House of Lords reorganized, and if the injustice done to him was the focal point, the emergency for which the dukes defied the king and reconvened the States-General, then whatever he suffered would be well worth it.

Louis and Dunois stopped at a crossroads to finish their plans. Dunois was to return to Blois and wait there. If Louis hadn't returned by tomorrow night, or the following morning at the very latest, and if he hadn't sent a message, although he would try to send Max with one to let Dunois know just what had happened—then Dunois was to begin his campaign to rouse the dukes and reconvene the States-General. Louis's would be an excellent test case, its cruelty was so apparent.

Then Louis and Dunois said good-by and they parted. Dunois set out at a trot, turning to wave at his cousin, and Louis took the left fork of the road, bending low over his horse and riding rapidly, his followers spurring their horses on to follow his pace. The wind blew the white plumes in his hat, billowed his bright blue coat out behind him, and he and his cavalcade were a brilliant spot of color on the hot, deserted road. He wasn't anxious to get to Jeanne, but he was eager for the world to know, the world being the king, that the Duke of Orleans had not been sulking in subservient defeat but had been biding his time, the time that was coming closer with every swinging stride of the horse's powerful legs.

At the Château de Linières, that great ugly tower of rock, he was met in the most friendly manner by the Sire de Linières, a soldier well known for his loyalty to the king, and his wife, a small woman with pitying eyes. They were so very pleasant to him, and showed him in such a civil manner to a room that showed no traces of Jeanne, that he began to feel less belligerent. His natural courtesy took possession of him. After all, these people could only do as they were told, there was no use in being unpleasant to them. When he was summoned to the dining hall, having neither seen nor heard Jeanne mentioned, he went cheerfully, as if he had come on the friendliest of errands. Nor was Jeanne at the long and elaborate table, so that the dinner, shared with his host and hostess, their large family group and assorted guests, was entirely to his liking.

The food was excellent—hot, spicy, well cooked—and the wines were delicious. He was hungry. He always had a good appetite, but after his ride he was exceptionally so, and he ate a good deal, too, and became very animated and gay. They lingered at the table for two hours, and by that time Louis was enjoying himself so well with one of Madame Linières's nieces, who showed an equal amount of enjoyment in his attentions, that he rose very reluctantly when his hostess came to his side and asked him to come with her for a few minutes' visit to Jeanne, whom she said had not been well and had preferred to dine in her room.

He followed Madame de Linières up the long, circular staircase, the stairs of heavy gray stone returning the sound of their footsteps to them, then down the dark hall that was chill even in the heat of July. By the light of the torch pinned to the wall behind them, their shadows went ahead, long black caricatures that ran around and followed behind as they approached the torch at the end of the hall. All of the doors along the way were closed, so that the hallway echoed with the sounds of their progress: Madame de Linières's light brisk walk, the jingling of some keys in her belt, the somber swish of heavy clothing, and Louis's longer stride that thumped out an accompaniment to every third step of hers. As they walked he felt more uneasy at every step. He felt that loose, disintegrating sensation in his stomach that always came to him at the thought of seeing Jeanne. His hostess had forgotten her easy friendly manner and was strained and silent. Almost at the far end of the hall she stopped at a door, then hesitated before opening it and turned to face him in the flickering torchlight.

"Your Grace," she said, and she reached out and gently touched his arm as though she could change something in him with her touch, "be kind to my little Madame Jeanne. She suffers so much."

Louis stiffened with surprise and resentment and looked down at the hand on his arm. Be kind to the thing that had been thrown into his life, changing it beyond recognition. Why? She was probably just as evil as her father. He didn't answer, but Madame de Linières sensed his feelings and sighed, withdrawing her hand, turning from him sadly, and opening the door. He followed her, thinking scornfully of her ridiculous request.

The room was very dark, lit by a few candles that fought to lighten the blackness of the chamber that was filled with massive, dark furniture. Louis looked toward the bed, a large tapestry-hung shadow, but Jeanne was not there. Following the direction of Madame de Linières's eyes, he saw, huddling in the shelter of a large wing chair, the patch of light that was Jeanne's face. She was dressed in the black she always wore, with an added black shawl about her shoulders for concealment, and she must have been suffocating in the hot stuffiness of the room that seemed almost unbearable to Louis after the musty coolness of the hall; but she pulled the shawl even closer about her and huddled deeper into her chair as they came toward her.

Madame de Linières asked a few solicitous questions, and Jeanne answered in a patient, tired voice. Then the elder woman murmured something about leaving them alone for a few moments and walked quickly out of the room. Being alone for any length of time was something Louis planned to avoid, and he settled quickly into the few questions he must ask for formality's sake so he might call it a visit and leave.

He asked after her health, and when she answered him her voice was almost inaudible.

"Thank you, I'm very well. Your mother and sister are in good health, I hope?"

"Excellent health," Louis said, not liking to speak of his

mother and sister to Jeanne, who was one reason for their unhappiness. "Your mother and sister also?" He had no interest at all in the queen's health, and Anne he knew was well, but there was little else to talk about.

Jeanne only nodded and he went on. "Your brother, I hope, has entirely recovered from his illness?"

"He wasn't so very ill, only uncomfortable with the rash. He's quite well now, thank you."

"I'm glad to hear it."

Now there was only her father's health that hadn't been discussed, but Louis refused to do that. He considered that the king's order to visit Jeanne had been obeyed; and if there was to be some remonstrance from the Sire de Linières later, on the shortness of the visit, he looked forward to stating his intentions never to live with or acknowledge Jeanne as his wife, and he stood ready to take the consequences. So he rose and prepared to leave her.

"Madame de Linières tells me you have been ill; I think it would be better for you if I leave you now so you may rest."

He waited for her answer, but there was none, only a sudden sound of hoarse, agitated breathing. He stood irresolute for a second and then he told her good night and expressed the false hope that he would see her perhaps in the morning before he left. Still she didn't answer, and he turned to go. His steps were loud in the silent room and he hastened them, eager to leave this uncomfortable place. But his bewilderment changed suddenly to a murderous fury when he came to the door, for it was firmly locked against him. He crashed his fists against it and then, turning, came blazing across the room to her.

"Whose filthy trick is this?" he cried, although he knew. "Only one man in France, your thieving father, and only one thing that's called a woman would be evil enough to help him. You think I can be caged with you and then you'd say you've been my wife! My wife!" His tone was scathing, and she bent her head under it. "Give me that key or call someone to let me out! And tell your cowardly father to kill me if he must have my land, for I'll never acknowledge his humpbacked daughter as my wife!"

He raved, in fury at her father and at her for being a willing part of the king's plan. Then, enraged at no response to his demands for release, he reached out and took hold of her shoulders, shrinking with repulsion as he did so, and pinned her back into her chair, facing him. He glared down into her tear-swollen face and spoke through teeth that anger had clenched.

"Now, give me the key!"

She shook her head weakly. "Oh, please," she moaned, "please! I haven't a key and no one will come if I call. I didn't want this—I didn't plan it. I begged—I couldn't help it."

Her abject misery convinced him, and he took his hands from her quickly. He felt a fleeting moment's sympathy for the sobbing girl who hadn't wished to be locked in with him, and his hatred for the king deepened with contempt for a man who had so little paternal feeling that he could expose his pitiful daughter to this disgusting situation. Seeing her misery, realizing now that she was just as helpless to oppose the marriage as he had been, Louis wished he had been less cruel, but there was no time for polite regrets now—he must think only of how he could escape. He looked at the window, but it was too high and too small, and furthermore too far from the ground. Pounding on the door would do no good, he knew, although he did go to it and pound noisily. If he were meant to stay, noise wouldn't release him, but if worst came to worst and he had to stay, he could say with truth that he had protested vigorously. Exhausted at last by his unanswered pounding and his rage, he came back into the room and sat as far from Jeanne as he could manage, looking at her with embarrassed dismay and thinking he had never seen anything so ugly as she was. Jeanne was exhausted too. She sat limply in her chair, her head leaned back and her drowned eyes staring up at the ceiling.

Louis surveyed his situation and blushed with shame for himself. He thought of his excited eagerness earlier in the day when he had been glad the time had come to draw his sword and fight in the open. If this was how he fought, perhaps it would be wiser to leave his sword undrawn! The king hadn't stopped to wonder which costume would be the more becoming; he had used his time to better advantage. Louis pondered gloomily on the effect this night would have on his freedom, and even more gloomily on the faces of his friends when he would have to tell them. Dunois would be furious, Eugène appalled, and Georges, he was sure, would counsel him to give up all his hopes. And Georges's judgment was the one in which Louis placed the most of his reliance. He shook his head and sighed when he thought of Georges's face.

And then a reaction began to creep over him. The long day, with its tiring emotions, had worn him out; he was drained and empty of feeling, indifferent now as to his situation. He had behaved like a careless young fool; to-morrow he would have to start to undo the damage. There was nothing for him to do now but sit. He leaned back and arranged himself as comfortably as he could in the straight wooden chair with the high carved back and the armrests that ended in lions' heads. Sleep laid a thin surface of protection over him. He slept uneasily, turning his head and mumbling, his dark hair falling over his forehead, his tanned face, that had been flushed and angry, relaxed in a half-smile. Jeanne watched him with eyes that moved tenderly over him, smoothing back his hair, touching the black lashes that lay on his cheek, and his red lips, thinking she would gladly give her soul and her hopes of heaven if she could have strength and beauty such as he had. Or if she could have been Anne and loved by him!

He was dreaming of Anne, and Madame de Linières's pretty niece, and a blithe young maid at an inn, who had been delighted with his caresses, and then, for some reason, his thin veil of sleep was torn and he slipped through it into consciousness. But his dreams came with him. He remained very still in his chair, his position unchanged, only his eyes awake, as though listening for something in the dead quiet of the room, waiting for his dreams and the feeling of desire they had aroused to leave him. But his longing persisted. His blood and his heart pounded, and his whole body was persistent. He couldn't understand it. Alone in the night with almost any other woman in the world but Jeanne, it would have been pleasant and understandable, but to feel a desire for Jeanne was degrading and dangerous. He struggled to control a longing that was so unwelcome, but it was stronger than he was. He remembered something Paul Capporetti had said, and, almost nauseated with his own depravity, he looked consideringly at Jeanne. With a shock he met her eyes, fastened on him with an expectant, fascinated horror. The depth of her strained expectancy told him something. She knew how he felt. She expected him to feel that way. She had been waiting for that feeling with apprehension. How could she have known?

Suddenly comprehension blazed up through his taut body, like fire through a hollow tree, and flared hotly from his eyes to hers, so that she shrank back. A full understanding of the loathsome trick almost drowned him with disgust, and contempt for his own credulity choked him. What a fool they must have thought him, laughing and drinking the delicious wine the king had ordered filled with a strong aphrodisiac! It wasn't so rare a trick but that he might have thought of it and taken care. A simple and evil plan, like most of the king's. Poisoned with an appetite that had no connection with either love or passion, Louis had been led to Jeanne, like a stud horse, and locked into the same stall with her for the night.

Louis got up from his chair, trembling so with rage and screaming nerves that it was all he could do to walk over to her. He had said every cruel thing he could think of when he had discovered the locked door, and so he had no more words, but his simple intention needed none. He meant only to kill her, if he were still strong enough, before the wild confusion of his mind and body might make him do the hideous thing the king had planned. Perhaps his intention was apparent in his eyes, or perhaps Jeanne's tortured endurance couldn't stand another moment of this suspense, but as he came toward her she began to scream. She screamed and screamed, tearing at her hair and her face and her clothing in a frenzied orgy of hysteria, and then was seized with epilepsy, to which she was subject. Louis stood appalled at this writhing mass of human flesh, not knowing what to do, but a part of the king's plan came to his rescue.

A spy who had been sent to report on the success of the night and the drug, watching from another room, saw Jeanne's distressing state. Seeing that the fastidious scheme had gone awry, he ran to Madame de Linières, and it was she who opened the door and rushed across the room to help her poor little Madame Jeanne. She had known the evening would be a disastrous one. She had added her pleas to Jeanne's to avert it, but she had been forced to obey the king. She fought the struggling Jeanne to take her in her arms and calm her. This, she could see, was going to be a very bad seizure.

Louis was beyond caring what happened to Jeanne. All he could see was the door that stood open. He ran to it, then out into the hall, running, stumbling against people, tripping down the unfamiliar stairs and out of the nightmare château to grope his way in the darkness to the stables. He didn't wait to rouse his own servants; a sleepy and confused night watchman took him to his horse and hurriedly they saddled it together. Louis was still possessed by the nightmare feeling that he was being pursued—that he would be caught by clutching hands in the darkness and dragged back to the evil room and Jeanne.

He gasped with relief when at last he had mounted his horse, passed the gates of the château without being stopped, and was out on the blackness of the road. He galloped until he could feel the foam from the horse's neck and mouth on his hands, then he stopped the horse altogether and listened for sounds of pursuit. Reason would have told him there would be none, but this was no night for reason.

There was no sound at all in the night but the animal's winded gasps, the clinking of the bridle, the heavy muffled sound of his feet on the soil as he moved about in a circle, uneasily feeling some of his master's terror. Louis took a deep breath.

Then, as he began to realize some of the full loathsomeness of the evening, his tired, poisoned body, trying vainly to withstand the fearful nervous shocks it had received, completely rebelled and the first engagement in a great battle for freedom ended with a weary young man sliding awkwardly off his horse and being violently ill in the grass beside the road.

8

Mary, not knowing what had happened at Linières, unfortunately chose the next afternoon to tell Louis of her coming marriage. At no time would it have been acceptable to him, but that his mother should choose this day to babble of love and loneliness was too much to endure. Love and loneliness he could have sympathized with, but when she told him it was de Mornac she intended to marry, he simply refused to believe her.

It was incredible, it was impossible! Deliberately to bind, gag, and deliver themselves, helpless, to the mercy of the world that already doubted her chastity and his paternity was insanity he couldn't believe possible. If she was lonely, let her marry, of course let her marry, and a good thing, too; but anybody in the wide world, even a black Russian from the barbaric East, would be better than de Mornac. She declined the whole world, tearfully, and clung to her love for de Mornac. Louis refused to see how love could have anything to do with a suicidal marriage, and soon they were in a bitter and heated argument.

They could have argued endlessly without reaching any kind of agreement. Louis, like de Mornac, saw how it would appear to the court, where he knew it would verify the suspicions concerning his mother and himself. She would never be able to appear without enduring the most humiliating innuendoes, the most galling laughter from women who were not better, only more discreet. As for himself, couldn't she see what it would do to him?

"But it isn't true! You're Charles's son, and you know it," she kept saying.

"But you will be *making* it true!" He lost his temper and shouted it at her.

"How can I make you someone's son now, when you're grown up?" she asked with infuriating misunderstanding.

"What's true is true, and it can't be changed by my marrying now!"

Mary really didn't appreciate the point he was trying to make, or at best she underestimated its importance. She knew she had been faithful to Charles. She felt everyone else must know it too, and those who talked about it only did so because that attitude had been encouraged by the king. Her husband had been dead many years now; she was perfectly free to marry, and if it was a very unusual alliance, that was her business. Once married, with the sanction of the Church upon them, their honor would be secure.

Her absolute inability to see what she was doing was more irritating to Louis than if she had seen but had refused to change her intention. He shouted himself hoarse against her tearful incomprehension and then left her finally, swearing if she didn't change her mind he would never come back to Blois. She knew he didn't really mean it, but he hoped she would be impressed by his ultimatum. She persisted, however, and when the marriage plans went ahead he packed and left for Italy in such a hurry that Max's new livery was almost minus the small porcupine he had begged to have embroidered on the coat.

Surely this was a dream, Max thought as he rode out of the courtyard into the brightening dawn, bound for Italy! Was he really going to cross the high mountains, see the beautiful little Savoy lakes, the wonderful cities of Milan and Venice and Padua and Ferrara and Bologna and Parma and Florence and Sienna and Rome?

He turned in his saddle for a last backward look at the stables where he had expected to spend all his life, waved farewell to the stableboys and grooms who enviously watched the departing cavalcade, took a deep breath of the fresh morning air, thanked God he was alive and that he was Maximilien Armand Edouard Marie Poquelin, valet to the Duke of Orleans! And on the way to Italy with his master!

Outside the gates of the castle the horsemen halted and reassembled their formation. Two guards, the advance guards, trotted past Louis and set out ahead; then came Louis, Dunois, and Eugène, three abreast when the road allowed it. Max and Eugène's valet, Albert, were next, and behind them was Joseph, Dunois's man. Then, following at a little distance, came the grooms with the pack animals and the extra horses. At the very end was another guard— twelve men in all, their itinerary well in mind, their marked maps tucked in their belts. Not that the maps were very essential, because the main roads were few, and after they had dropped down to Lyons and gone eastward over the mountain pass to Savoy, every road led to Rome. They planned to reach it, traveling leisurely, stopping in other cities, by the end of summer. They would stay till Louis had a satisfactory audience with the Pope, probably remain through the winter, and start for home in the early spring.

What a man of the world he would be by then, Max thought, admiring the picture of himself returning with suave cosmopolitan manners and memories of romantic interludes with exotic foreign beauties, and how he would hold his friends' fascinated interest as he described his exciting adventures! Thinking of it, he was almost eager to be back now.

The only cloud in his happy sky was his master's face, which was stormy indeed, and Max sympathized with the cause. That the duchess should love a servant was terrible enough, but to marry him was suicide. The whole castle was shocked and disapproving. Maybe the duchess would change her mind when she thought over her son's words and recognized their truth by the chill already in the air of the château and the amazed distaste with which some of her friends had received the news.

Louis himself was hoping that as he rode down the hill away from his home, resolutely not looking back, in case his mother had risen early to watch his departure from her window. Maybe his absence would make her think and change her mind, where his many words had made no impression. He hoped so—desperately he hoped so for her sake and his too.

The thought hung over him gloomily; but gradually, with the morning sun coming up over the horizon, with the cheerful tuneless bellowing of Dunois on one side and Eugène's well-pitched voice on the other, both of them vigorously singing about a mademoiselle from Toulons, who was evidently no better than she should have been, Louis's depression slipped off the back of his horse and was left behind in the road. He lifted his voice to join in the uncertain harmony: ". . . and there was a young Countess of Tours, whom we hope is no friend of yours . . ."

The gloom never caught up with him again. It was too pleasant traveling through the springtime with his friends on his way to the hope of accomplishment at Rome. Laughter followed their trail southward through the towns of France; it stopped with them at pleasant inns where they feasted and flirted and slept well, and then it turned eastward with them and climbed the foothills up into the cool mountain air. The altitude and the increased effort of traveling quieted the laughter but didn't subdue their enjoyment of the beauty around them. The silent mountains, snow- and cloud-topped, were constant sources of changing loveliness under the varying light. The waterfalls, some of them coated with ice, and the clear cold lakes caused them to stop again and again to exclaim in pleasure. They followed the old Roman roads and stopped at hospitable monasteries on the hilltops. They crossed bridges once built by Caesar. They forded streams and rivers when they came to bridges which were no longer usable. It was amazing that any of the roads and bridges still held up after all the years of very little repair.

This was the first kind thought Louis had ever had about that long-dead Caesar, one of whose books he had finally been forced to read by Father Paul, who had been shocked by Louis's ignorance. Louis couldn't see much sense in studying such a dead language; he chanted his church Latin by heart, sometimes without knowing what the words meant, and that seemed enough Latin to him, but Father Paul had insisted it was the basis of all languages so he must learn it. He had spent most of his time under Father Paul's absentminded gaze with a copy of Caesar open in front of him to conceal the smaller book inside—a translation of one of Boccaccio's stories. He had wished then he could read it in the original Italian—there was always something left out of a translation. Eugène spoke Italian well, and he promised to teach it to them on the way. They had a rule that it should be spoken at meals, but they would forget or start laughing at their own strange pronunciations.

They took longer than they had intended on the road; there were so many places to stop and see. They stayed longer than they had intended in Savoy too, for they had relatives in almost all the main towns—Geneva, Tarentaise,

Annecy, Aosta, and Turin—so they traveled back and forth in Savoy from one welcoming castle to another, feted and entertained at each one.

Savoy was an independent duchy, although the look in the French king's eyes threatened its independence. His sister Yolande was regent there during the minority of her son, Philibert I, and it was Philibert's cousin Louise to whom Eugène was betrothed whether he liked it or not, and he definitely didn't, especially after he had gloomily surveyed his infant fiancée, who was just learning how to walk.

"Horrible-looking little brat!" he muttered unhappily to Dunois and Louis later in Louis's room in the hospitable Italian palace of the horrible brat's father, Philip.

"Well," said Dunois thoughtfully, "I was a horrible-looking brat myself as an infant, but regard my countenance now!"

Louis looked at him incredulously. "You mean you were even more homely as a child!"

Dunois threw his boot at Louis, but they sobered when they saw their foolishness wasn't amusing Eugène. He was looking at a miniature he carried of Mary of Burgundy, and Louis felt a pang of sympathy for him, because her picture was all he would ever have. The lovely girl herself was married to Maximilian of Austria.

And what would become of her now? Louis wondered. Her father, Charles the Bold, had been finally defeated in his long battle against the king. His body, hacked to pieces by the axes of the king's Swiss mercenaries, was scattered over the battlefield at Nancy, and some said his head had been triumphantly carried to the king!

What a day that must have been for the king! Louis thought grimly. How he must have gloated over his dead enemy! Louis's imagination could picture the skinny king striding excitedly around his airless study, his long black gown flapping about his legs, carried away by exultant triumph. And Louis's imagination was correct. The king had paced back and forth the day the news had come that the Duke of Burgundy was dead and defeated. He had chuckled and talked disjointedly to Oliver of the dead duke, nervously fingering his rosary, his hands almost warm for once.

"Charles the Bold!" he kept saying over and over, in

derisive mirth. "Charles the Bold!" How bold are you now, Charles, without your head? Without all your lands of Burgundy that belong to me! You were bold—I was careful!" He laughed stridently. "And you may have been very bold, but you weren't fruitful! Only a daughter! Better to have been careful, like me! I have a son and my head too!"

How wonderful it was, the king thought, to have won on both those points. The wretched Burgundy, who had been a thorn in his crown since the beginning, was dead now, dead in the midst of treason, so that everything he had had could be claimed, even his daughter! The king sobered a little, thinking about what he would do with Mary. She had escaped to her husband. Well, he could have her for the time being, and he probably wasn't so pleased with his bride now that her father was dead and she had inherited nothing, except perhaps his bold disposition.

"Charles the Bold!" the king said again. "Well, well, well!"

Burgundy's death had sobered all the dukes, and now that he had ceased to occupy most of the king's time, they wondered who would be next. This was a dangerous time for Louis to be disobedient. He knew it, but he didn't hesitate. Burgundy had lost, but Orleans would win!

Eugène felt more uneasy about his own petition to the Pope. He hadn't Louis's stamina. One moment he was excitedly sure that he would defeat the king's marriage plans and he would shout brave defiance; the next minute he was gloomily ready to admit defeat.

He was in that dejected attitude now as he put the miniature away and sighed, "I think I won't go on to Rome with you. What's the use?"

"But, Eugène," Louis protested, "what would you lose by going?"

"Nothing," Eugène said shortly, "but my head!"

"But any duke has a right to consult with the Pope about his marriage! We must have his permission before we marry, but he must have our permission to it also! And he must be made to realize that the way the king overrides us makes his permission a farce as well as ours!"

"Yes," Eugène admitted, "he certainly should know how we're pushed into these marriages."

"And you must protest now—while you're only betrothed. That's what I'd have done if I'd been older. It's easier to have a marriage prevented than annulled."

"Yes," Eugène nodded, his face clearing. "After all, I'm not married yet!"

Dunois pointed out encouragingly, "And never will be if you stand as firm as Louis."

Eugène said vehemently he would and could, but Dunois and Louis exchanged a dubious look. They could feel his courage evaporating with every step closer to Rome, but Eugène decided to continue the trip with them.

It was the middle of July when they left Aosta in Savoy and headed southeast to Milan, about a hundred miles away.

The night before they left, a rider came from Blois with a message from Louis's mother. The news it contained was over two weeks old, and in it Mary wrote that she and de Mornac were married, that she hoped Louis had relented, and it would make her happiness complete if Louis would only send word that he forgave her.

Louis stood for a long time looking down at the note, his face grave. There was no anger in it now, only sadness. Too late for anger. No use ever having been angry, because she didn't realize what she was doing to herself and to her son. He would have given anything to have prevented it, but now that it was done, he could only hope it wouldn't be so disastrous as he thought. She would have sense enough—or de Mornac would—never to go to court or invite any uncertain friends to Blois, and perhaps she could be happy alone with the very unsuitable but attractive man she had married. After all, Louis knew enough about the loneliness of being separated from love not to wish her to suffer it too, and while it was a shameful marriage according to the standards—a duchess and a country sire—still it wasn't so shameful as his own marriage to a princess of France.

What the news would mean to him he realized all too well. But then he had heard cruel jests about his parentage all his life; now there would be new fuel added to the fire, but it would have to be endured.

He sat down at the desk, scrawled out a short, hasty message to his mother telling her he hoped she would be happy, that he sent his love and would be home again in the spring, and after he had paid the messenger and sent him off he went to a gay farewell party, feeling much better.

The next morning, as they swung jarringly into their saddles, their heads throbbing and their eyes swollen slits that tried not to look into the full glare of the July sun, Louis, Dunois, and Eugène thought dully that it had been too gay a farewell party. They didn't talk much—it required too enormous an effort—but each one considered the possibility of postponing their leaving till tomorrow.

But then that would only mean another farewell party tonight.

Louis was in a foul temper. Max was missing. When Louis had returned from the party, in dire need of having someone help him off with his damned tight coat that laced up the back and someone to bring him a bubbling brew that would put his head back where it belonged, Max hadn't been there. Dunois's Flemish man, Joseph, had helped him, but then this morning again there had been no Max to bring breakfast and see to the packing. Now here they were, all ready to leave, and still no Max.

Where was the silly little rabbit, anyway? No one knew.

The men talked and considered going on without him, but Louis was getting too fond of him not to be worried at this disappearance that was so unlike Max, for he had, in spite of his comic appearance, turned out to be an excellent valet. He had no education, but his quick mind and native wit helped him to learn easily. His orderly packing was the envy of the other valets, and his extreme devotion to Louis's clothing kept Louis's wardrobe in wonderful condition, especially the scarlet coat with the golden porcupine on it. Louis thought Max would hesitate a long time if he were asked to decide which was more valuable, his master's life or his master's coat.

And now Max was lost. They were still hesitating in the courtyard, discussing where to start looking, when a uniformed guard rode in and respectfully asked for the Duke of Orleans. The guard spoke in Italian, so Louis's host, Philip, answered for him, and in a moment they were talking rapid Italian, only a little of which Louis could follow. But he did catch Max's name and the word for jail.

Max Poquelin was in jail!

And it was his adoration of Louis's clothes that had led him into disaster, for he had been picked up the previous night by the city guards for disobeying an edict forbidding a common man to wear shoes with stuffed toes longer than six inches and a long trailing tailpiece on the peak of his hood, called a liripipe, longer than one foot!

Max had been wearing an old costume of Louis's—the stuffed toes of his shoes had been two feet long, held up by a chain from the pointed tip of the toe and fastened to his ankle. This style was called a poulaine. And the liripipe attached to the hood Max wore had been so long it wound about his throat like a scarf and hung to his heels in back! Both these extreme styles were restricted to noblemen, and when the guards had seen Max's face and haircut they had stopped and questioned him.

He had answered fluently, but in French, that he was the Count Antoine de Noire, and it was a good thing they hadn't understood him, because his impersonation would have been an additional charge against him. They had taken him in for questioning.

The officer in charge spoke French, and to him Max explained he was confidential secretary, nurse, and traveling companion to the great Duke of Orleans, so he had better be gently treated and his master notified at once. The officers agreed, but their idea of "at once" was the following morning. He had been put into a damp basement cell with a hundred other petty offenders.

He was very sheepish when he was released and found his master waiting sternly for him. Louis was very angry, what with the bad news from Blois, his pounding headache, and now this idiocy of Max's. He had given Max the cloak with the long liripipe and the long-toed shoes because he had never liked them, the shoes especially, and was glad they had gone out of style in favor of plain, square-toed shoes of sturdy, soft leather with one strap over the instep. But when he had given the things to Max he had presumed the valet would sell them or have them altered so he could wear them without breaking the law.

Dunois and Eugène were very much annoyed, too, at the nuisance and the delay, and each one had a few sharp things he meant to say to that fool Max. But when the valet came downstairs in his hose, the offending shoes and cloak bundled under his arm, when they saw his scared grin, his small eyes flickering over their faces to judge how deep was his disgrace, and his shock of red hair tousled so that it looked like a straw-thatched roof with the wind blowing, when he came rapidly downstairs, his stockinged feet skimming rapidly over the hot stone steps, like a cat on hot bricks, his one big bare toe pushing through his torn hose and curling upward to retreat from the July heat of the pavement, the mirth they had tried to control, so that Max would realize the enormity of his error, broke out and they yelled with laughter that echoed in the narrow street.

When they finally stopped laughing, they found their heads and their dispositions were so much better that they forgave Max. They waited tolerantly while he dug through his pack for a legal pair of shoes. Opening one of Louis's small trunks, he suddenly turned into the accuser as he reproached everyone in general for having ruined the duke's clothes by such disorderly packing. He wanted to go back to the palace, empty the trunks, and begin again. They jeered at him and, turning their horses' heads toward the city gates, set out for Milan.

In Milan the ruling duke was Francesco Sforza, the Visconti dynasty having just died out for lack of a direct heir, and Sforza, with an army behind him, had taken Milan for himself. The Visconti family were close relatives of Louis's, so the young men were welcomed and pressed to stay at the elaborate Visconti palace on the Piazza del Duomo.

The magnificence of Milan was dazzling, and in contrast the court of France seemed shabby, poor, and very old-fashioned. In fact all the towns in Italy had been amazing. Dunois had tried to tell Louis his impressions of Italy when he had returned from his former trip, but had failed because his descriptive vocabulary had only three levels. To Dunois a thing was either "Very magnificent!", "It will pass!", or it was "God's curse!"

Milan was "very magnificent." Most of the buildings shone with their newness and the beauty of their modern design by architects who had turned their backs on the popular, elaborate Gothic and were reverting, with modifications, to Roman simplicity. Many more buildings were going up, including a great cathedral close to the Visconti and Sforza palaces. The city echoed with the sounds of many hammers, and great prosperity for the middle classes was the result of all this work. The three young men from France looked in wonder at the well-clothed crowds in the busy streets, the high prices charged in all the shops, yet everyone seeming to have the money to pay.

"But where are the poor?" Eugène asked in bewilderment.

"There they are!" Dunois smiled and pointed to a group of velvet-clad merchants lining the street, interestedly watching the work of excavation for a new building. Across the street artisans swarmed over the scaffoldings of a half-finished palace. The middle and lower classes in Milan were too busy to be poor.

And the widespread interest in the arts was another amazing thing. In France there were court poets and painters, of course, but not so much was made of them. In Italy it was all anyone ever seemed to talk about—this young painter, da Vinci; that wonderful old sculptor, Donatello, who had died and whose students didn't seem to show much promise, except possibly Andrea Mantegna. There were hot arguments as to whose designs were most suitable for the big new church to be built at Rome, fierce discussions about the new low level in books, no new outstanding writers, just imitators of Dante and Petrarch. Money and leisure being helpful godparents to the arts, Italy was breeding artists with vigorous fertility.

With chagrin Louis had to admit that Italy was far more modern and progressive than France. It was not too difficult to understand why. France's long, impoverishing war with England had left her so shabby she yearned for necessities, while Italy, although wars between the separate duchies continued spasmodically, had had a little more time to care for herself and, warm and well-fed now, she wanted the luxuries.

There was a cynicism in Italy too, a materialism after the shock of disillusionment the people had experienced when the corruption of the church government had been revealed and pointed out to them by their own churchmen who had first seen the need of reform. The long-fought schism in the Papacy, the bribery, and the selling of indulgences weakened the people's faith, and they were beginning to read the fiery articles and poems a young monk named Savonarola was writing and circulating from his cell in the monastery of St. Domenico at Bologna. This general loosening of their faith loosened their morals too, and not so sure any longer of the wonderful palace they would have in the glorious world to come, they felt they had better enjoy the glory they could find on earth.

So the sculptors stopped proclaiming the glory of God and glorified man instead, and a good many artists left their paintings of the Madonna and Child half finished for the more popular voluptuous nymphs and satyrs. As the exquisite cathedrals grew more numerous and beautiful, the hearts inside them were fewer and more worldly.

Louis and Dunois and Eugène thought they had experienced lavish hospitality in Savoy, but it in no way compared with Milan's. Something was planned for every minute in their day, and the three young Frenchmen were very popular, especially with the young ladies, many of whom fortunately spoke French. Those who didn't hastily began to learn so they could flirt with the handsome young Duke of Orleans, whose grandmother had been a Visconti.

Eleanora del Terzo already spoke French with a piquant accent that made everything she said sound provocative. Louis thought her very attractive, and evidently the feeling was mutual, because he found her sitting next to him at banquets and balls, his partner for rides and picnics in the forest, and then one evening, in the wall-enclosed garden behind the Visconti palace he found her in his arms, her dark eyes half closed, her lips reaching up toward his.

She was very lovely and close in the warm Italian moonlight—Anne was far away in France, and a light flirtation here would never hurt her. He leaned down and kissed Eleanora's soft lips, held her for a long moment, and was pleased, then startled, at her ardent response. Her returning kiss, her little pointed tongue, was inviting him to something more than a light flirtation! If she had been one of the other court ladies, more experienced, with a careless reputation, Louis would not have been so surprised, but Eleanora was young and unmarried and a girl of impeccable reputation and good family—Louis thought fleetingly of her large family of large brothers and her large, stern father and released her. But she didn't draw away from him. She leaned closer, looking up at him, half smiling, and they were both breathing rapidly.

"I love you!" she said in Italian, and then repeated it in French. She said it in both languages with the same fervor and sincerity.

This was more than Louis wanted, and he heard with relief the footsteps of other couples wandering out into the dimly lit gardens. Hastily Eleanora slipped her cool bare arms up around his neck and whispered, so close that her lips were against his ear, telling him that she was staying in the palace, telling him carefully which room was hers— that she would go there now, and if he would come in an hour, she would be waiting for him! Then she turned, before Louis could answer, and, holding up her full brocaded skirts, hurried away across the garden. Louis started after her, then hesitated and went slowly back into the palace by another path.

He knew he would go—his racing blood told him so. He thought of her small daintiness with pleasure as he bypassed the dance going on in the main salon and mounted the wide stairs to his room. She was very pretty, with soft brown hair parted in the middle in the popular Italian fashion and smooth, dusky skin. He was certainly a very lucky man to have been invited to share a night with her— only, what did she mean when she had said she loved him? He hoped it was a pleasant exaggeration, a nice formality to cover the situation. He wanted nothing more serious. From another kind of girl he would have felt sure it was nothing more, but Eleanora, with her very correct background, her three very large brothers . . .

On the landing, at the spacious curve of the stairs, he came face to face with two of those brothers and he stopped dead, feeling awkward and guilty. But Giovanni and Phillippo del Terzo greeted him with elaborate courtesy. They had looked forward to seeing him this evening, they also looked forward to his long stay in Milan, which was, in a way, his own home, and as their family had once served his family, they would like to continue serving him. In every way.

Louis thanked them, thanked them again, but still they didn't seem to think the encounter was over. The two brothers exchanged a questioning look, and then Giovanni, the elder, asked if they might continue the discussion where they could be alone.

Mystified and uneasy, Louis suggested the quiet of his apartments and curtly led the way. If it was going to be a quarrel about Eleanora, he didn't want it shouted all through the halls; if it was going to be a matter for drawn daggers, well, his was ready and sharply waiting in the jeweled sheath at his belt. With the two of them he might not last long, but one of them would come with him. And at least he would arrive in heaven, Louis thought wryly, with a clear conscience, even if her brothers didn't believe him.

He pushed open the door of his suite and saw with relief that Max was there. Evidently he had just come in, and he had been up to his old tricks again, because he was wearing the long-toed poulaines and was just taking off the hood with the long liripipe. Furthermore, he was wearing a silver chain with small silver bells attached to all its links. That was also a fashion no commoner was allowed to wear, but Max had eyed it lovingly the few times Louis had worn the foolish thing and had kept it carefully polished even though it was never used any more. Evidently he had resisted that temptation as long as he could, or Louis wondered if maybe he had been wearing it all along and had just been caught tonight because Louis had returned sooner than he had expected.

Louis thought of the tongue-lashing he would give Max tomorrow, then stopped to wonder if he would be alive to do it. He gave Max a warning look, meaning he was to stay close at hand, and then he politely ushered his callers through the antechamber into his beautifully furnished sitting room, its dark carved woods gleaming against the rich velvet draperies of maroon and gold.

Louis drew up two ornate gilt chairs and the two men sat down, arranging their long legs and arms uncomfortably on the tiny chairs. Louis stood between them with his back to the marble fireplace. It felt cool through his thin silk coat and he felt better standing looking down at them, waiting for them to begin.

Giovanni began: "We think it a great privilege to have you here in Milan."

He had said that already, out in the hall, but Louis nodded politely. "Thank you—it is a great privilege to be here in this beautiful city." He had already said that too.

"Our whole family admires you so much—my brothers —and my sister—of course you remember my sister?"

Now it really begins, Louis thought. "Yes, of course I remember her."

Phillippo took his turn. "She finds you very charming."

Louis looked modest and rubbed his left wrist absently. He hoped it wouldn't fail him tonight if this interview ended as he feared it was going to. "No one could see her and not find her charming."

Giovanni's big swarthy face wrinkled in what seemed to be a coy smile, and one of his beady black eyes flickered in a meaning wink. "It wouldn't surprise us if she is in love with you!"

Louis shook his head. "It would surprise me."

"You're too modest, Your Grace. All the ladies in Milan find you fascinating."

"But my sister"—Phillippo took up the sentence—"is not like some of the ladies. She is a virtuous girl."

"I could never doubt that," Louis said promptly.

"Where she loves," Giovanni said firmly, "she should have the blessing of the Church!"

"I agree that she should!" Louis nodded vigorously.

Phillippo and Giovanni hesitated, and another questioning look flickered between them. Giovanni nodded very slightly, stood up and faced Louis, who was tense and waiting.

"She is fifteen," Giovanni admitted, "and should be married."

Louis was bewildered now. "I'm certain such a beautiful girl would never lack for a suitable marriage."

Phillippo stood up, too, and said firmly, "There are dozens of good marriages to choose from."

"I am certain of it," Louis repeated again, now completely at sea. This wasn't going the way he had thought. If they were reproaching him for interfering with Eleanora's marriage plans, they were going at it in a strange way.

"We would like you to consider an alliance with our family," Giovanni said formally, "and a marriage to my sister, Eleanora del Terzo."

There was silence for a moment as Louis looked from one plump swarthy face to the other. They looked enough alike to be twins; they spoke alike, used the same gestures, sat and stood in the same positions. It was hard to tell their ages because they were so fat; they could have been anywhere from seventeen to thirty-seven. They wore clothes of the same cut, although Giovanni's coat was deep purple and Phillippo's was violet, and now they were watching him with the same eagerness in their black eyes.

"Legally," said Louis slowly, after a blank moment, "I am married."

Phillippo smiled and Giovanni made a scornful gesture with his big, rounded shoulders under the purple cloth. "A disgraceful marriage."

"I agree to that!" Louis said fervently.

"One that could be"—Phillippo's shoulders imitated his brother's scornful gesture—"easily dissolved."

"Not easily," Louis contradicted. "But I am on my way to Rome for an annulment."

"You will never get it!" Giovanni stated flatly. "The Pope will not defy the French king. But there is an easier way out of your difficulty."

"I will be glad to hear of it," Louis told them frankly.

The two men moved closer, and although their voices dropped only a little, Louis had the feeling that the three of them were huddled close together, whispering a plot. He could smell the sour odor of wine on Giovanni's breath, and from Phillippo the sweet scent of violets.

"The Princess Jeanne, your wife," Giovanni was saying, "is very frail and ill, we hear from friends in France who report to us about her. It would be no shock to anyone— and no loss—if she were to sicken and die. And even if the king inquired into her death, what blame could attach to you—so far away in Italy?"

Giovanni paused questioningly, but Louis didn't answer. He was looking down thoughtfully at the floor, his head turned to one side as though he were considering intently.

Phillippo went on to point out the advantages. "And with your Visconti heritage allied to our strength, we could take Milan and put you on its throne in a month's time!"

"As Duke of Milan and Orleans," Giovanni said excitedly, "your power would exceed your king's!"

"We could take Savoy!" Phillippo said greedily.

"Perhaps even France!" Giovanni added in a breathless gloating tone, and his eyes were gleaming hungrily.

Louis wasn't listening to the points of vantage; he had seen them at a glance. He was being offered freedom and a great deal of power, but not even for one moment, one fleeting instinctive moment, had he considered this short cut to freedom that would lead past the murdered body of a helpless crippled girl.

No, he would free himself, and not with poison! He raised his head slowly, not liking to look at their avaricious faces.

"Gentlemen," he said sharply, "I do not like anything about your plan and I must ask you not to consider it again. It shocks me."

They began to stammer, but he stopped them abruptly. "Let us try to forget this—and it will be as if you've never said it. I wish you never had. I will free myself legally— no other way!" Then he added, just in case they should think he declined for the sake of appearances but really wanted them to continue their plan, "I'll tell you this, so you'll know how firm I am in my denial. I am already secretly married to another lady of France, and that marriage will be legalized and blessed after I have an annulment of my forced alliance to the Princess Jeanne—who"—he decided it would be wise to go a step further—"is not my wife, but for whom I have an affection. Tell your friends in France that if any accidents should happen to her, I will know where to place the blame! I will hold you responsible!"

He looked at them contemptuously for a moment and then deliberately turned his back on them and stood looking up at the carved, metal-lined hood over the fireplace. He could feel their hate boring into his back and he knew their fingers itched for their daggers. Probably they were exchanging a questioning look, wondering whether it was wise now to let him live, but after a moment's suspense he heard them stamp noisily out of the room, leaving the door open behind them, then he heard their retreating footsteps across the antechamber, the opening and slamming of the door.

He took a deep, disgusted breath and turned away from the fireplace. The room seemed full of the sweet scent of violets and the sour scent of wine, and he crossed to the window and pushed it open. A full moon was caught in the top of an ilex tree, the warm breeze blew through the twisted cypress and the pines like the faint sound of surf, and up there, off the balcony, the flickering candlelight beckoned through Eleanora's window.

He wondered if she had known about her brothers' sordid plan and was a willing part of it, or if her brothers had seen the attraction and had taken advantage of it. He thought she must have known; he was not vain enough to believe that, without even trying, he could have captured her heart so suddenly. The moon and the wind in the trees suggested he might see her and find out, but he remembered Anne and slammed the window on the moon.

Max was standing in the room, looking at him with big, excited eyes. He had forgotten to take off the silver bells and the shoes, and the bells jingled faintly with his excitement. Louis looked at him and thought that the ridiculous fashion of poulaines certainly reached new heights of absurdity when Max wore them.

"Well," Louis said sharply, "you stand there jingling like a court fool! Take those damned bells off! Do you want to see the inside of every jail in Italy?"

Max quickly took off the bells, which rang more loudly. "I'm sorry, Your Grace, I just borrowed them—I knew you never cared to wear them."

"You take liberties, Max, no other valet dares to take!"

"Yes, Your Grace," Max agreed. "I'm wicked about clothing—I ought to be whipped," he accused himself, but his voice was vague. He didn't seem to be really thinking of his own wickedness, and he revealed his true thoughts when he looked at Louis in awe.

"Duke of Milan too!" he murmured. "Equal to the king!"

"So you were listening at the door!" Louis said in annoyance. "I thought I heard those bells jingle."

"Isn't that what you meant me to do, Your Grace? If there was trouble, I had to hear."

"Forget what you heard!" Louis ordered.

"Yes, Your Grace—but—Duke of Milan too!"

Louis looked at him in displeasure. "You liked their pretty scheme?"

Max beamed. "If you didn't like this Italian lady, you wouldn't have to marry her. Once they got you free, you're free of them too, because they could never tell anybody what they'd done for you. It'd be a good joke on them," Max grinned, "if they did it all for nothing!"

Louis shook his head in wonder at Max's knavery. "And what about the murdered princess, is she a joke too?"

Max shrugged. "Better off dead," he said with a matter-of-fact reality. If it was cruel, his manner said, a lot of things in life were cruel. It was a battle for survival, and if a hunchbacked princess was in Louis's way, she should be removed as painlessly as possible, like drowning kittens instead of letting them grow up to be starved, unwanted cats.

"You're as disgusting as they are," Louis exclaimed

angrily, and his eyes flicked over Max in distaste. His hand reached for the dagger that hung at his belt, and he drew it out, the blade reflecting the bright flames of the candles.

"Come here, you!" he said harshly.

Max lost his smile. He had never heard this tone from Louis, had never seen that look in his eyes. He was frightened, but he obeyed and walked steadily over to his master.

Louis took his arm, backed him up to a chair, and, glaring at him, forced him back into it, tilting him so his feet were off the ground, his head lay back, and his throat was bared. Louis raised the dagger in his hand and Max's eyes followed it like a hypnotized bird's. The blade gleamed menacingly as it approached him—slowly, closer and closer, and then it swooped down and hacked off the stuffed toes of Max's poulaines!

The material of the second one squeaked and softly resisted, but the blade was razor-sharp, and in a moment both the foot-long ends dangled loosely, their only connection to Max the chain fastened around his ankles.

"Now," said Louis sternly, fighting to control his mirth, "hand me the hood!"

Dazed with grief, Max got up and crossed the room to get the hood, the mortally wounded poulaines trailing their lifeless bodies after him.

"They're better off dead," Louis assured him gravely.

Sadly Max brought the hood back to Louis and miserably he watched while Louis measured and hacked off a yard of the narrow cloth liripipe, then tossed it down.

"There," he said, "I've left you six-inch toes, which is legal, and a yard-long liripipe, which is more than you deserve. Have the stumps sewed up—and get rid of those bells, because I don't want you in jail tomorrow morning when we leave for Venice!"

Venice was definitely not a success. Louis rather liked the novelty of a city with rivers for streets, but Dunois detested it. He admitted that visiting in it for a week might be amusing, but it would be God's curse to live in. To be deprived of a horse, man's natural mode of transportation, and forced to rely on a shifting little boat was also God's curse.

Venice was busy with its war against the Turks, and there was a strain in the moist hazy air over the tall bell towers

of the city. Dunois was so obviously ill at ease in this watery
element that they stayed less than a week. They rode westward, passing through Padua again, then southwest through
Ferrara and Bologna toward Florence.

Dunois was pathetically glad to be on a horse's back
again, and as they left Venice behind them he kept shaking
his head in wonder that anybody would be fool enough to
build a city like that and then fool enough to live in it.

"It's my opinion," he said, summing it up, "that if the
infidel Turks take it, it will be exactly what they deserve.
God's curse!"

Louis smiled at Dunois's vehemence. It had seemed a
charming city to him, strange and beautiful, with the many
shimmering waters reflecting the light colors of the buildings
by day, and then at night the black water tossing back the
reflections of the yellow flares and the candlelit windows of
the stately palaces. Of course he liked water and Dunois
didn't, so that made the difference in their tastes, which
were generally the same. Water was treacherous, Dunois
stated solemnly, not to be counted on like a horse that
could be trained to obedience, and Louis smilingly agreed
that there was no connection between water and horses,
except when the water was in the horse.

Eugène had no opinion of Venice, because he had stayed
in Milan. A young lady there had interested him, and his
interest in the trip to Rome had correspondingly waned.
He had argued it would do him no good anyway, so why
disturb himself? Louis could take both petitions to the Pope,
and Eugène would stay in Milan and wait for them till
they made the homeward trip.

While Dunois and Louis were sorry Eugène's purpose was
flagging, they were glad to continue without him. A little
of Eugène and his moods was enough, and on this trip they
had had more than enough. It was pleasanter with just the
two of them. Louis and Dunois could never be bored when
they were together, and they found increasing pleasure in
their friendship as their journey continued.

Florence was a larger repetition of Milan's wealth and
hospitality. It was a colorful, boisterous city, swelling to
power under the cut-throat Medici family. Lorenzo de
Medici was its leader, and his court was staggering in its
opulence, the clothes, the plate, the entertainment. Art here,
too, was all-important, and artists were showered, literally,

with gold in reward for their work. The streets weren't safe to walk after sundown. Exquisite artistry, sensual cruelty, lusty gaiety, amorous freedom, and cynical moral standards —all that and more were encompassed in the colorful boundaries of Florence.

Louis loved most of it, the beauty and the freedom, but some of the vulgar cruelties of the court disgusted him. The Medicis' idea of entertainment required a strong stomach, in many ways. Watching horses gored and mangled by bulls, seeing people crushed by stampeding cattle, and similar bloodthirsty sights didn't amuse Louis.

Max thought if he were given his choice of heaven or Florence, he would snatch at Florence. Everyone was so gorgeously dressed, their manners so elegant, the maids so pretty and willing to entertain a Frenchman and show him all the charms of Italy. In his own way, Max was a great success with the ladies of his class. At first glance they had to smile at his amusing face, topped by the strange-colored red hair. Once having smiled, it was impossible to be cold and haughty, and in less than ten minutes they would be surprised to find themselves on Max's slight knee, laughing into his twinkling eyes at something funny he had said, made funnier by his ludicrous accent. Max knew how to talk to them, too, with a cheerful boldness that never seemed coarse because of his engaging face. Since he was French, the first thing they asked about was Paris, on which he could talk lengthily, his lecture based on complete ignorance. The next question concerned Paris fashions, for that city's fame as a style center was two hundred years old. Max was well prepared for that discussion, so well that he was often the center of a large crowd of exclaiming maids, as he was now in the servants' hall of the Medici palace. The women pressed close around Max to examine the fashion doll he had cleverly brought with him.

Most of the Italian cities imported an annual fashion doll from Paris, displaying the newest styles in miniature. "Fashion babies," they were called, but they were very rare and mostly kept as a trade secret. So Max's possession aroused great interest, and the beautifully dressed wax doll was passed carefully around for the women to examine. They exclaimed over the tiny black velvet pillbox hat with the short nose veil that was wired around its edges, the wire holding it so it couldn't blow in the wind or dangle limply against the doll's face but remained always in the same graceful folds. In the doll's little pink ear lobes were dangling earrings of gold and diamonds, a new thing, since earrings had been out of style for years but were evidently going to be widely used again. The women didn't think they cared for the diamonds—diamonds were a man's jewel; ladies preferred the softer pearl. The doll's dress was gold brocade with ermine bands at the full, long sleeves and ermine around the square, low neck. The wide, trailing skirt was slit up the front to the waist, revealing the black velvet underskirt edged with white ermine. On one of the doll's tiny hands was a scented doeskin glove, dyed black, and the back of it was embroidered with gold thread and diamonds. Doeskin shoes to match were on the fashion baby's feet, and attached to her other hand was a small handbag, shaped like a tiny trunk. It was made of leather, covered with black velvet, and decorated in a manner similiar to the gloves.

The maids "ohed" and "ahed" as Max gently demonstrated that the little satchel could be opened, and inside, he showed them, was a padded case for the lady's jewels, room for cosmetics, a tiny glass mirror, comb, liquid whitenings, rouge, and scents. The fashion baby was very complete and a complete success.

There was only one maid who didn't join in with eager approval. She hardly looked at the doll and passed it on indifferently, with a blasé manner. This was Catherine, personal maid to Beatrice del Lucca, the belle of the Medici court.

Catherine shrugged and said superciliously, "It's a pretty little doll, but there's nothing very new about its costume. My mistress wore all those things last year. What I'd like to see is this year's fashion baby, with the new-style slashing and puffing my mistress has heard about."

Max was only a little deflated. He had to admit his fashion baby was a little old now, but he had a new one coming. It would be here soon—perhaps today—and it would include the startling new style as Paris interpreted it.

Catherine seemed very much interested, and later, when she saw him alone, she told him her mistress would be willing to pay him well if he would give her a private showing of the new fashion baby a day or two before the others saw it. Max said no, he didn't think he could do that, it wouldn't be fair to the other ladies, and she flounced angrily away. He laughed; he knew why she wanted it, but he didn't like her or her mistress.

Beatrice del Lucca prided herself on being first with any new thing. She led the court and took her position very seriously. There was no style so daring she wouldn't try it, because she knew her beauty could carry it off. She was tall and very slim, with a haunting fragile beauty. Her skin was white and perfect, and she guarded it jealously, bathing it in cream and sleeping in a mask saturated with lotion. Her blue eyes were held languidly half open, as though her dreams were too lovely to abandon completely. Her hair was blond, but she bleached it even blonder and wore it cut short all over her head to be different from the others with their long hair, madonna style. Hers was three inches long, curled and fluffed up like a baby's soft fuzz and then sprinkled with gold dust to make a shimmering halo around her lovely face. She wore no cosmetics on her cheeks or eyes, only deep carmine on her delicate mouth. She had her fingers and toenails painted with gold paint—she had even tried gilding her teeth once, but hadn't cared for the appearance or the taste. However, if the effect had been attractive, she wouldn't have hesitated, even for a mild case of poisoning. She had beautiful sloping shoulders and a full, high bosom, the whiteness of which she sometimes emphasized by tracing over the blue veins in her skin with a faint blue dye. She had a sweet, slow smile, a frank, childlike air, and graceful gestures, all accomplished through long hours of practice before a mirror. Her own beauty, she well knew, was the most important thing in the world.

Although every man who had ever seen her had wanted her, she was still unmarried and a virgin at seventeen, and while she never indicated it, it was her stern purpose to remain both of those things for life. She had a great deal of money in her own right, her name was one of the proudest in Florence, so marriage could in no way improve her lot, except for children, whom she secretly detested, and love, which she didn't admire because it was such a—a disheveled thing, and men were so clumsy and careless. Of course she took pains to see they didn't read her thoughts, because if they felt she was cold and critical, their admiration would drop away, and that would be unendurable. Men's adoration was her daily bread. So she smiled her sweet, virginal smile, held her breath, and blushed now and then to show the warm blood below the cool white skin, so they would know that all that was necessary to awaken her was the right man's touch, and her eyes asked each man the same wondering, half-frightened question—was he that man? Most every man was certain he was.

Louis, like every other, couldn't take his eyes off her beauty, although it was a little pallid for his taste. Most men she never saw at all, using them only as a mirror, but she looked with critical pleasure at Louis, sitting beside her, well groomed and handsome in his scarlet coat. They had danced and were resting now.

She considered ordering a coat like that, for riding, with her family crest on the shoulder, just where he wore his golden porcupine. No, she decided that would be too obvious an imitation—then she had an inspiration. She would have her name embroidered in bold script on the shoulder, and what if she wore black velvet hose, like his, that showed off his long straight legs—— Then she stopped suddenly, and a look of infinite sadness came into her eyes and made Louis want to comfort her.

It was the great sorrow of her life, a secret grief she struggled to keep hidden from the world, that she was bow-legged! It was the one terrible, heartbreaking flaw in her perfect beauty, and one that, although she would never admit it to herself, had kept her from love and marriage. The thought of anyone seeing her imperfect legs was a nightmare to her! No, she couldn't wear tights, not even with a split skirt over them!

"What is it?" Louis murmured. "You look so wistful."

She turned on her smile, and he thought how sweet she was; for all her exquisite beauty, she was as unaffected as a child.

"I was thinking of my poor maid Catherine," she confessed shyly. "You know your man is making her very unhappy."

"My man!" Louis was startled. "Now what has Max done?"

"He has a new fashion baby from Paris—I think she said it had just come—or was just coming—and he won't show it to her. Isn't that dreadful of him?" She smiled indulgently to show how nice she was to take her insignificant maid's troubles so to heart.

Louis knew what a fashion baby was, but didn't know Max had one. He shook his head and smiled at Beatrice. "My Max is an idiot for clothes. But I'll see that he takes the fashion baby to Catherine."

"Make sure he doesn't disappoint her with the old one." Beatrice touched his hand appealingly and let her hand remain softly on his. "Tell him it must be the new one that's just coming."

"I will see to it myself," he promised her.

She looked directly at him, opening her eyes fully for just a moment, acting out her favorite moment of flirtation. "Are you," her naïve, frightened eyes plainly asked, "could you possibly be the one man I've waited for—the one man, at last?" Then her lashes dropped, she swayed a little, held her breath, and the pink obediently flushed up into her cheeks.

It was a good performance, but Louis was very quick, and his experience in Milan was making him skeptical. He caught the artifice in her pose, the practiced gestures, the excellent timing, and in a flash he realized that all her attitudes of sweet timidity were false as the narrow line of her penciled eyebrows. She was a chilly little piece who enjoyed teasing.

She looked up to find him smiling at her, and it seemed to her that his eyes were more mocking than admiring. She drew back swiftly and stood up, as though her emotions were too strong for her. Louis rose politely.

She pretended to be searching for something to say to cover her sweet embarrassment. "You—you will not forget the fashion baby for Catherine?" she asked appealingly, her eyes shyly saying that she wanted to be alone now, to dream of him.

He smiled. "I will not forget the fashion baby for Catherine." He stressed the name, and it made her wonder a little, but not much. Surely he hadn't guessed she wanted the doll for herself—no, he couldn't have, not when she was using her charms so expertly. Still, she decided she didn't care for Frenchmen after all; they seemed a little too quick, too sophisticated.

Next day Louis remembered the doll when a messenger brought up a box from France and Max had to borrow against his next month's salary to pay for it.

"Bring that box in here, Max," Louis called out, and

grinned at Dunois, who was lounging on the padded window seat, looking out at the blue Italian sky. It was September now and very hot. The two men had just come in from the sun-baked streets, tossed off their coats and boots, and were trying to cool off in their sheer white cambric shirts and hose.

Max stood in the doorway, the big box in his hands, and looked uncertainly at his master. "Did you want me, Your Grace?"

"Would I have called you if I hadn't?" Louis asked reasonably, and Dunois smiled.

Dunois liked Max, too, and only occasionally protested to Louis that he let the valet take shocking liberties of informality and disrespect. Louis would agree, then they would both laugh, thinking of Max's foolishness that was so much more endearing than cold formality or excessive humility, and Max would continue as before.

"What's in that box?" Louis asked.

"Oh, Your Grace wouldn't wish to be bothered with it. It's just a trivial thing a messenger brought."

"It must be quite trivial," Louis agreed, "if he brought it all the way from Paris. Is it a fashion baby?"

"A fashion baby?" Max echoed blankly, wondering how Louis could have known.

"A fashion baby," said Dunois. "Now we've all said it, let's see it."

Uneasily, Max put the box on the floor and, using his knife, pried it open, unwrapped the straw and cloth padding, and drew out the doll, exclaiming over the costume.

"It's the new fashion—the slashings and puffs!" He thought delightedly what a stir this would create among the maids.

"It's damned extreme," Louis complained, "so much fuss —and all those feathers!"

"It's God's curse!" was Dunois's opinion.

The gown was of green velvet, and its complicated trimming was made up of slits and slashes in the velvet, with small pieces of different colored silks sewed under the slits, showing through in bright-colored patches. The style had originated on the battlefield of Nancy, where the victorious Swiss mercenaries of the king had derisively used the bright silk banners of the dead Burgundians to patch the tears and holes in their own uniforms, which had been slashed by swords and ripped during the battle. The bright patches, showing through the tears, had given their uniforms a gay new trimming, very different from the past brocades and embroideries, so the Paris dressmakers had been quick to adapt the idea to men's and women's clothing.

The full sleeves were pushed up, caught and puffed in three different places along the length of the arms. The bodice, heavily slashed with purple and violet and red silk showing through, was puffed in two places. The skirt was not slashed, but heavily puffed. The general outline was clumsy and the enormous hat, heavy with plumes, added to the cluttered effect.

Dunois muttered, "Looks like she has five waists and three sets of biceps."

"I don't think it will be popular," Louis reassured him. "It's too bulky and uncomfortable." Then he smiled thoughtfully. "But I know one woman who'll wear it!"

Dunois and Max were both nodding. They knew he meant Beatrice del Lucca, whom they both disliked.

"I promised it to her——" Louis started, and frowned as Max involuntarily groaned. He continued sharply, "I want you to take it to her, Max. Say I wanted Catherine to have just a little look at it before I take it down with me this evening to show the ladies. Wait for it and bring it right back."

"But, Your Grace," Max protested, "she has a dressmaker waiting to copy it, and she'll wear it tonight and say she ordered it long ago."

"That's exactly what she'll do," Louis agreed. "Get your razors, Max."

Max, bewildered, brought his sharp razors. When he came back Louis had clumsily taken the doll's dress off, to the accompaniment of lewd comments from Dunois.

Louis handed the dress to Max. "Rip out all the colored patches, but be careful and neat about it."

Max was puzzled, but obedient. He sat down, cross-legged, and began to rip out the varicolored silks, Dunois watching curiously. When he had a few patches ripped out and the flesh of his fingers showed through the slits, he looked up suddenly, met Louis's smiling eyes, and began to laugh. Dunois quickly saw the intention and was delighted.

"We'll show the doll with patches sewn back—but that

little piece of God's curse will come down tonight with her pink hide showing through!"

The room echoed to their hilarity, and Max's fingers flew to accomplish the purpose.

It worked out even more amusingly than they had thought. After the enormous banquet, when the court had moved on into the salons for dancing and cards, Louis let it be known that he had a new fashion baby—just arrived that day from Paris—yes, the new slashed style, and he sent for the baby while the ladies waited excitedly.

Beatrice del Lucca hadn't come down yet. She had dined in her apartments, goading her seamstresses and maids to nervous frenzy in order to get the dress finished for a late, dramatic entrance. She could taste the admiration when she would appear, see the shocked looks in the ladies' eyes—it was a bit daring—and see the tantalized looks in the men's gaze when they realized it was her white skin peering through the dark green slashes.

Her entrance was late enough to give all the ladies time to have seen the fashion baby and comment on the slashing, and her entrance was dramatic enough when they saw her. She walked boldly through the room, toward the table where the fashion baby presided, and the women's expressions were amazed and shocked as they craned their heads to look more closely.

Was that white material showing through the slits—or was that Beatrice showing through? When they ascertained that it was really Beatrice, they banded together and took a firm stand. She had led them by the nose long enough—now she had gone too far, and they told her so. The style itself was odd, but at least it was decent—her adaptation of it was a disgrace.

Completely bewildered, her eyes went from her gown to the doll on the center table, and she caught her breath.

She heard a man's voice at her elbow. "I see," Louis said, "that Catherine didn't describe the gown to you with absolute accuracy." She started and looked up at him. His dark eyes were smiling pleasantly at her, and then they wandered to the widest slash in her bodice where the beginning of a white curve could be seen. "Still, I think it is a very becoming costume, and it is a shame you will never wear it again!"

She wanted to scream and then slap him! But there was

nothing she could do except try to carry the evening off boldly. She couldn't admit to the other women the trick that had been played on her without admitting the trick she had tried to play on them.

"Annoying, isn't it?" Louis murmured questioningly, and she knew he was reading her thoughts. She gave him a look full of hate and the promise of revenge and walked away.

Dunois, shaking with suppressed laughter, came up and said: "Unless you like poison in your wine, I think we had better leave for Rome—quickly!"

The Italian countryside had never before seemed so beautiful to them as it did when they rode out on the last step of their journey. They paused at the top of the hills, exclaiming over the deep green of the tall pines, the olive groves, the clear strong blue of the little lakes that reflected the sky, and the soft haze that lay on the side of the hills, like bloom on a purple grape. From the top of this last rise they looked down at Rome and marveled. There was beauty, made by man and cupped in nature's hands.

Rome and the Pope had always had an awesome sound throughout the Christian world, and now the travelers were awed by the actuality. Louis, especially, was impressed, for upon this city and the Pope depended his future freedom.

But if Rome was the acknowledged home of the Christian faith, there was very little evidence of it. The court of the Church was as splendid as Florence or Milan. There were plenty and to spare of churchmen, cardinals, bishops, archbishops, all elegant in their full-cut, gloriously colored robes, purple and scarlet, all eager to build up the states of the Church as a powerful political unit.

Sixtus IV was Pope, and his palace was as worldly as any secular king's, thronging with beauty and riches, busy with artisans coming and going, for they were planning the great new church of St. Peter. Soldiers were everywhere too. They were necessary for the maintenance of the states of the Church, which consisted of a wide bias strip slanting across the middle of Italy, over which the Pope reigned in temporal as well as spiritual power. Also a tug of war was going on between Rome and Florence, a battle between the Pope and the Medici family, with Florence as the prize.

The Holy Roman Empire had cracked apart, and Maximilian, king of the Austrians and Holy Roman Emperor, despairingly asked his God why such an empty honor had been given him. His hands were busy in the unification of the Germanics, and it would require at least one more pair to hold onto Italy at the same time. Italy was splitting up into strong and separate duchies, some of which the church- ly states were trying to absorb, and Maximilian could only look on, helpless, and to some extent careless, for he had more than enough to keep him in a state of permanent pov- erty trying to subdue and unite Austria.

In Rome, Louis and Dunois found their friend Georges putting on weight and dignity as a son of the mother church. Their reunion was joyful, and Georges's round, placid pink face turned from one to the other, his blue eyes shining with interest as they relived their travels for his benefit.

"But where have you been?" Georges asked, in impatient affection. "I had given you up!"

"We loitered a little," Louis admitted, and he and Dunois exchanged a smile.

"Loitered! You must have come by way of England!"

"Well, Milan was very beautiful," Dunois explained, "so beautiful that Eugène stayed there with her. Louis's young lady was beautiful, too, but her brothers weren't."

"I see," Georges said, nodding pontifically, "you've come to the Holy City laden with sin. We'd better arrange con- fession for you, so if you die tonight, you'll die in grace."

"If I must die tonight," said Dunois, "I think I'd rather take sinful memories with me than a purged mind. Eternity is a long time."

Louis acted shocked. "You mustn't say such heresies be- fore our little priest. They'll either sear his soul or he'll become envious and go to Milan himself."

Georges looked insulted. "Rome has everything and more than Milan! Your sinful memories are mere babies besides those you'll find in the Holy City." And they all laughed at the absurdity.

Louis looked from one to the other as they talked, and he smiled with pleasure and amusement, for there never could have been two other men so loyal but of such dif- ferent temperaments and viewpoints. Their love for Louis was all they had in common.

Both were fairly short and stout, but it was a different kind of heaviness. Georges was plump, with the fresh pink plumpness of a man who lived a quiet, sedentary life, who ate and slept well and never had any more violent exercise than kneeling to pray, and that was getting to be difficult. Already Georges's round stomach had pushed his cassock out in front of him, so that it hung shorter in the front and drooped on the sides, a fact which annoyed him, but he did nothing more about it than to give it an impatient jerk now and then.

Dunois, in his well-fitting hunting clothes, gave the impression of powerful bulk, his face dark and weather-beaten. His waist was thick, but his shoulders were thicker, and his chest was more noticeable than his stomach. He was a column of impressive strength, planted on stocky legs a little bowed from his constant riding. His stallion power and courage were in contrast to Georges, who was like a fat, lazy, clever cat. And they found in Louis the charm that neither of them had, the leaping fire of brilliance and driving purpose they needed to excite their calmer lives.

They stayed with Georges in his elegant apartments within the papal palace, and he showed them all over Rome with the proprietary air that a resident, even a short-time resident, uses to newcomers.

"This is where the new church of St. Peter is soon to be built—I think from Rosellino's design—it will be beautiful."

Dunois considered the site and the first beginning of an excavation without enthusiasm. "Too many churches already."

Louis reproved him smilingly. "That's not a tactful remark to make to a budding cardinal. Georges doesn't think there could be too many churches."

"It gives employment to the artisans," Georges said defensively.

"Who pays them?" Dunois asked bluntly.

That wasn't a tactful question either, because the widespread sale of indulgences to make money for the church bothered the many sincere churchmen, among them Georges. They protested against it themselves, for they could see the harm it did to the people's faith. They saw the need for church reform and wanted it to start within the church as a self-cleansing action, rather than to have the need ignored till the reform was forced on them by outsiders.

So Georges hastily changed the subject. "Have you seen

the ruined temples on the hill, and the old arena by moonlight?"

"Yes, very beautiful," Louis and Dunois both answered
promptly, for old-fashioned ruins weren't to their taste, and
they went on to more modern sight-seeing.

The most important sight Louis wanted to see was the
inside of the Pope's study, and Georges arranged an audience for the following week.

Pope Sixtus IV was cordial, but a little hurried. He was
an elderly man, sixty-three, not well, and time was slipping
by with too much left to do. He talked consolingly and
rapidly, then they were interrupted by his nephew, Cardinal
Riario, and Louis was blessed and ushered out before he
had said half of what he had come to say. He wasn't dismayed, however, and he asked for and was granted another
interview in two weeks. Then he went up to Georges's apartments and told Max and Dunois to settle down for a long
siege.

Georges was not hopeful that the Pope would be able to
help. Sixtus IV had his own quarrel with the French king,
and he couldn't afford to have it complicated because the
Duke of Orleans didn't like his wife. Georges had discussed
the case with the Pope once briefly, and so had Dunois.
The churchman had said he had received a very clear letter
about it from the king, who had written that Orleans was
married without force and by his own permission, that the
marriage had been consummated, and that the princess, a
pious girl as the Pope well knew, would swear a holy oath
to the truth of this if the Pope wished a witnessed affidavit
to that effect.

Months dragged by while Louis steadily besieged the
Pope with his side of the case. The war with Florence had
begun in earnest and the Pope had other things to do, but,
weary of putting Louis off, he wrote the king and requested
the affidavit from Jeanne.

More months went by, while Louis waited in irritated
impatience, sending two messengers after the first to see
what had happened to the request. Louis was curious to see
how the king would handle this, since he couldn't believe
the pious Jeanne would deny her conscience and commit
this perjury before God.

Finally the messengers came riding back, one of them
bringing the Pope the sworn statement, signed by Jeanne

and witnessed by two unimpeachable churchmen, the Cardinal of Bourges and the Bishop of Rouen. Louis stared at it on the Pope's desk and sighed heavily.

"I can't believe they'd be a part of such a lie, Your Eminence."

"Then what do you believe, my son?" the Pope wearily asked.

"It could be a forged paper———"

The Pope raised tired, dubious eyebrows, and Louis's long-pentup impatience burst out angrily: "If God himself signed it, it's still a lie!"

Then, seeing the Pope's disapproving face, he apologized and left in such dejection he almost forgot to ask for a later interview.

He rode out alone, along the Tiber River, thinking furiously. How could he counteract this perjury? The people involved—Jeanne, the bishop, and the cardinal—he couldn't believe would kiss the Holy Cross and then lie. Or could Jeanne hate him so terribly after the night at Linières, the dreadful things he had said to her? He couldn't blame her if she did. He often winced away from the memory of himself, lashing her with words he had really meant for her father. After all, she had been as helpless as he had.

He thought of writing to her, telling her with complete honesty that he was sorry he had been so cruel, and asking her about the affidavit. She might not answer—probably she wouldn't—but he could try. He decided to write.

In a little more than a month the answer came back, a gentle, forgiving answer and very helpful. She understood his anger that night was really not against her but against their dreadful circumstances, which she regretted too. She had no blame for him, and as to an affidavit, witnessed by the Cardinal of Bourges and the Bishop of Rouen, yes, her father had sent them to witness a paper concerning a gift of money and land that was being given by him, in her name and at her request, to a convent close by. And how, she wrote curiously, had he heard about such an affidavit, and how did it interest him?

Louis exclaimed in triumph. So that was how it had been done! The king, knowing he dealt with people of integrity, and needing such people for the validity of his paper, had tricked them, securing their signatures to what they thought

was an unimportant grant of land, when perhaps underneath that, or written in later, were the lying sentences.

Hastily he took Jeanne's message to the Pope.

But his triumph didn't last. The Pope shook his head.
Because Louis's wife repudiated the affidavit later, in an
informal note that might or might not be from her, didn't
change the legality of the witnessed paper.

He was sorry, but he saw no grounds for annulment
whatsoever, and he wished this decision accepted as final.
He would always be glad to see the Duke of Orleans, but
not on this matter. He blessed Louis and dismissed him.

Louis went somberly up to his apartments and told Max
he might as well begin packing—they would start for home
in a few days. He went on into Dunois's room, to tell him
the Pope's discouraging final answer. At least it was final
for this trip. There was nothing else to do here, and a great
deal to do in France—see the Cardinal of Bourges and the
Bishop of Rouen and get a true affidavit from them.

Dunois was standing in the middle of the room in a
strange attitude. His eyes looked at Louis vaguely; his
usually ruddy face was a peculiar gray.

"What is it, Dunois?" Louis asked sharply.

Dunois shook his large head loosely from side to side.
"Don't know," he said. "Feel like God's curse!"

"You look like it too," Louis said in alarm. "You must
get to bed."

"Not bed," Dunois said scornfully. "Not that sick. It
will pass——"

And then he pitched forward, sprawling on the floor.
Louis caught his shoulder just in time to keep his head from
crashing against the marble hearth.

Louis shouted for Max and Joseph, but by the time they
came he had lifted Dunois's limp heaviness onto the bed. It
was terrifying to see Dunois, who had never been ill a day
in his life, gray and unconscious.

The doctors and leeches came and argued. It was the
fever, it was his lungs, it was his stomach, it was his heart,
but anyway, they all agreed that he was seriously ill. Louis
sat beside the bed during the anxious days and nights,
watching the doctors with dubious helplessness, watching
Dunois's sturdy pounds melting away, his steadily decreas-
ing strength, with frantic worry.

Dunois was bled almost daily, to kill the fever, till Louis

stopped it, feeling it would be better for Dunois to have a little blood left, even if it was feverish. Dunois was frequently delirious, but now and then he would have a waking rational moment, would see Louis there and smile weakly.

"Going to die?" he asked once.

"Absolutely not!" Louis told him firmly, and prayed to God he was telling the truth.

"Good!" muttered Dunois. "Hate to die in Italy."

"You'll die in France."

"Hate to die in bed."

"You're not going to die anywhere—not till you're ninety."

"Die on a horse!" Dunois insisted. "A better place."

"Not a very comfortable place to die," Louis told him.

But Dunois insisted: "Die on a horse—a big, fast horse—sword in my hand," then added vehemently, "In France—not Venice. All that water."

"Not Venice," Louis assured him. "I promise you—on a horse, in France."

"God's curse if I don't!" Dunois muttered peevishly, and slumped back into a restless, tossing doze, while Louis sat heavily on and watched him despairingly.

But finally his short, once-thick body survived the doctor's help and very slowly he began to regain his strength and pounds. It would be many weeks or months before he could travel, though, and it troubled him that he was keeping Louis from returning to resume his battle with the king, since progress had come to a halt here.

He urged Louis to return without him, but Louis wouldn't even listen. During the anxious time of Dunois's illness Louis had realized fully how much his strong, loyal cousin meant to him. Except for Anne, Dunois was his closest friend, and even if it meant delay and complication, he would wait till spring, when he was positive Dunois would be well fit for the long journey home.

"We'll wait," he told Dunois firmly, "together, till you're strong enough to let a horse carry you—and if you mention it again, we'll wait till you're strong enough to carry the horse!"

9

"Alain, do you love me?"

The Château de Blois seemed to echo constantly with Mary's whispered questions to de Mornac and her need for reassurance.

"Alain, do you still love me?"

She began asking it a month after their marriage, when she already feared she had made a mistake, for married life with de Mornac certainly wasn't as she had planned it. He was with her a little more in body; but in spirit, if he had one, which she was beginning to doubt, he gave her no more of himself than she had had before. Instead of increased companionship, she was more lonely, for he took even more interest in the estate and most of her friends had dropped her abruptly. They felt she had flown a little too high. It was all very well to have had him as a lover, but to make such a mésalliance only acknowledged that they had been lovers. The few friends who remained loyal were deafeningly so. They called her "poor dear Mary" and, proud of their loyalty, went around stirring up battles about her.

One visit to court had been enough. She had come home tingling with anger at the insults and the too-intimate laughter. Her constant chorus of "But it's not true!" when Louis's parentage was mentioned began to sound as silly to her as it had to Louis.

She cried frequently, thinking it over in the quiet of the night, the tears running over the bridge of her nose as she lay turned on her side, and then when she couldn't stand the loneliness any more she would turn to the sleeping de Mornac for comfort.

"Alain!" she would whisper, shaking his shoulder a little. "Are you asleep?"

He came slowly up from the depths of a dreamless sleep, rambling and grumbling a protest.

"Alain, are you asleep?" It was such an irritating question to meet at the surface.

"What—what?" Then, annoyed, "Of course I was asleep. What is it?"

"I had a nightmare," she would lie. "Talk to me a little so I can forget it."

Talk! In the middle of the night, when he had said all he had to say hours ago. Was there ever such a woman for talking in the night! But he relented and stretched out his arm to her so she could lie on it and forget her nightmare.

"What did you dream?" he asked, his voice slow with sleepiness.

She would make up a long tale about being dragged by runaway horses, anything at all to be talking to him and to hear his voice grunting a response. And then, as he slipped nearer and nearer to the edge of unconsciousness, she would always ask the invariable question:

"Alain, do you still love me?"

And he would give his invariable answer: "Of course, my dear, you know I do."

That being attended to, he would slip away from her, back down into his isolated oblivion, leaving her only half comforted and hours away from sleep.

This procedure occurred once or twice a week, and de Mornac's patience began to wear thin. Wakened one night after a tiring day by the same irritating question, "Alain, are you asleep?" he hauled himself awake and flung himself out of bed in one violent movement.

"By Jesus and the Holy Mother!" he roared at her. "How could I have been more asleep?"

With one furious yank he denuded the bed of its top spread and wrapped it viciously around him.

"I'm going back to my own bed, where I won't be wakened every half hour to hear some fool's dream!"

Clutching his blanket, he walked furiously out of the room, his bare feet almost stamping the floor in his usual robust stride. She called after him pleadingly, but the door crashed shut after him and she was left to call herself an idiot for having awakened him. She felt it would be comfort enough now if he were only sleeping soundly beside her.

De Mornac muttered and stamped his way back to his

old room in a far wing of the house, thinkly grimly if this was the warmth and comfort of marriage, other men could have it and welcome. Mary would have to be taught to leave his sleep alone, or he would return permanently to his bachelor bed.

Mary had learned her lesson, and his nights from then on were more peaceful. But hers weren't. Insomnia was her master. She never fell asleep till three or four in the morning. These endless nights melted what was left of her waxen prettiness. That worried her too, and she fought a losing battle to cling to her beauty, her sleep, and her husband. If she had understood him better, if she hadn't required so much of him, if she hadn't disturbed his comfort, she might have won the battle; but her continual need to be reassured, her terrible dependence on him, was pushing his patience past endurance.

"Alain, do you still love me?"

She asked that question just once too often!

He stopped short, turned, looked at her thoughtfully, then answered abruptly, "I don't know."

She looked foolish in her amazement. "You don't know?"

"You've asked that question so many times, you must really want the answer!"

"Of course I do."

"Well," he said, "I know I loved you once—maybe I still do; but we've made so much noise about it, I'm not certain."

This was nonsense to Mary. "Either you love or you don't!"

He sat down slowly and looked at her. "You know, it's more than likely our ideas of love are quite different. What's yours?"

Mary was surprised at his grave interest, but she was happy to be talking about love to him.

"I can only tell you what I think it is by telling you how I love you. I want to be with you always—I'd give up my life and my hope of heaven for you—I'd commit my soul to hell if you asked me to!" Mary's voice shook with sincerity; she meant it, exaggerated as it sounded.

De Mornac looked at her and shook his head, somewhat pityingly. "No," he said.

"No?" Mary was all eyes, bewildered and apprehensive. "What do you mean?"

He got up from his chair as though he were very tired

and walked to the fire. "If that's love—that collection of
words without meaning, and greedy possession—then I
don't and have never loved you—or anybody else!"

"Alain!" she cried. "That isn't true! You're only angry
at me for bothering you tonight!"

It would have been easier for him to admit it, assure her
that he really loved her and regain some measure of peace
for the evening, but a weary dislike for her tears and emotions made him persist. After all, he thought, if they
couldn't ever achieve any harmony, it was just as well for
her to find it out and stop straining after the impossible.

"I'm not angry at you, and I'm not hurting you because
I like to. I've tried to answer your questions truthfully—evidently you don't want the truth. But I'm everlastingly tired
of pretending we're still young and in the middle of a great
romance. If you can't be satisfied with the affection I feel
for you—then I'm afraid you'll just have to be unhappy!"

This seemed the wildest cruelty to Mary. Through tears
that had long ago ceased to move him, she implored him to
relent, thrusting her love at him, feeling he must accept and
return it. But he was driven further and further away from
her by her voluble emotions. Then she made another major
error.

"When I think," she complained, "what I gave up for
you! My son, my friends, my dignity——"

He interrupted her shortly. "Did I ask you to do any of
those things?"

"If you never loved me—why did you let me ruin myself?"

"I suppose I should have expected that," he told her
scornfully. "You prefer to forget it was you who wanted
marriage, not I! I told you then exactly what you'd lose—
but you insisted. You must always have your way, no matter
how it affects others."

"Oh," she answered hotly, "that isn't true!"

"No?" he countered sharply. "You wanted marriage and
the blessing of the Church to salve your conscience—did
you care how it affected your son?"

Mary didn't answer. She sat rigid, waiting.

"You've always pretended Louis was another of your
great loves," he continued contemptuously. "One of those
loves for which you *say* you'd give up your life and your
hopes of heaven! Words are cheap enough. But you ruined

him just the same—so that you could have the bishop's blessing on your sin. Is that a sample of your love? Is it?"

"No," she finally said in a low voice. "I was wrong, Alain, I didn't realize."

"Because you wanted what you wanted, and you wouldn't listen. Not," he added with a shrug, "that what happens to Louis makes much difference to me. I don't mind people thinking he's my son. It amuses me. But I can assure you it doesn't amuse Louis when filthy pamphlets about his birth are circulated all over Europe—and people snigger at him when he passes."

Mary caught her breath. "I'm sorry," she said helplessly, and then she stood up and said wildly, "Oh, why did you ever have to come into this room—why couldn't you have left me alone?"

He regarded her a moment in silence. "Perhaps if I had known it was going to be a *grande passion*, and not just a pleasant affair, I'd have stayed in my office that night and sent for the prettiest maid. God knows I haven't the time nor the energy for a great devotion that makes my days and nights miserable with tears and reproaches. I don't even want you to commit your soul to hell for me! All I want is peace and comfort, but evidently that's too much to ask!"

There was no answer from Mary; she had sunk down into a corner of the chair and was dissolved in tears.

"Well," he finished sarcastically, "I see you're now determined to have a great sorrow. You can enjoy it by yourself—I've had enough!"

He left her with finality and moved back into the bachelor rooms he had once occupied.

His stabbing words aroused Mary's furious pride so that she was able to leave him alone—at least for a while. She treated him with distant formality in the daytime, and at night she prayed he would come back to her. Surely he would come back, she thought, when he saw that her possessiveness had been subdued. Surely he didn't mean it about not loving her.

But as weeks went by Mary's poise began to crack and the nights grew longer and longer. Hard to bear, too, were the knowing glances of her maids. She spent more and more time alone because she didn't care to talk with her attendants, and she no longer had any friends.

One night her loneliness became too much for her. She

put on her prettiest robe and decided to go to de Mornac's room. She planned to point out very quietly that if he wished to remain separate from her, he should at least move back to one of the larger guest chambers, so that it wouldn't look so strange. However, her hope was for a more intimate move.

She walked as unobtrusively as possible to his rooms, her heart pounding with excitement at the thought of seeing him and with a fear that she might be seen and her visit laughingly discussed among the servants.

Outside his door she stopped for a moment to control her hurried breathing and adjust the revealing neckline of her robe. She was just reaching out to tap softly on his door when she heard low laughter. She whirled to see who it was. There was no one at all in the dim passageway behind her, and as the laughter came again, a woman's laughter, she realized it came from inside de Mornac's room. He was not alone! There was a woman with him!

Before her husband's door, in the quiet darkness of the hall, she tasted a bitterness that turned her sick with disgust. Here, in her own home, while she yearned for him, he was being unfaithful to her with one of her own maids! She heard his deep low laughter now, mingled with the girl's. They were laughing at her!

She turned and walked back to her room, careless now whether or not she was seen. In the precise manner of a sleepwalker, who evades obstacles without seeming to see them, she went directly to the little altar in her prayer closet. She lit two candles and knelt in the flickering light. Her body seemed to be numb, but her mind was working more clearly than ever before in her life. She wasn't looking for consolation: she was surveying her life, the qualities in herself that had brought her to this shamed moment, and what her life must be from this moment on.

She spoke steadily to herself. "Don't pity yourself because he's unfaithful to you. That's your punishment because you were unfaithful to Charles—and to Louis. Alain was right—it was always what you wanted! When you had Charles you weren't content with his kindness. You wanted romance. Well, you've had it—and when it came you didn't think of your son or your name, Charles's name or your friends. You threw it all away, and now you've nothing left—only your conscience. The conscience you thought you'd quiet with the bishop's blessing! How will you explain to it that selfishly you've given Louis shame to carry all his life? All his life he'll suffer. Always in his mind, and in the minds of everyone, will be doubt of his birth, the doubt that you changed to certainty by your marriage."

"Oh, God," she asked, in bitter amazement at her own act, "how could I have done that to my son?"

She crouched there with that one agonizing question in her mind until dawn. Then, numb and cold, she slumped down in an exhausted heap and fell asleep with her head against the carved wooden draperies of the Virgin's skirts. In the morning she could hardly walk. Her head and eyes ached with a fierce pain, and by evening she had a high fever and a parched throat.

She was very ill for several weeks, and when she was able to be up again she seemed an entirely different woman. Remote and tired now, where she had been alive and eager, frankly old and careless of her looks, indifferent to everything, even de Mornac. She continued to hear in her mind the echoes and reverberations of that question: What have I done to my son?

De Mornac was kind and considerate. She answered him with polite civility. There was no point in being angry with Alain because she had been wrong, but she made no effort to recall him from his bachelor quarters. Sometimes she was troubled with a longing for him, but the desire never really touched her mind and she accepted it as something to be conquered and forgotten, a part of her punishment.

She knew her illness had aged her, but she hardly ever looked into a mirror, and when she did she could see that the spring primrose, as de Mornac had once called her, had completely vanished.

And in a rueful way it was a relief.

10

When Louis came home he was stupefied at this change in his mother. He had returned still half angry at her, but when he came in sight of the village of Blois and saw beyond and above it the towers of his home rising above the treetops, he was eager with sudden anxiety to see her, and when he did he felt only pity. He couldn't add a single word of reproach to what he could see she was already feeling.

One of his first actions was to ride to Linières to see Jeanne. Georges, who had returned home with them, cautioned him against it. It would seem to be admitting the alliance between them, but Louis felt he must see Jeanne and, even if it made things more difficult for him, thank her for her kind help and try to erase the memory of his cruelty.

Everyone at Linières was surprised to see him—they had had no message from the king telling them that the duke had been ordered to come. When he went up to Jeanne's room and she realized this was not a forced but a friendly visit, her thin cheeks glowed with pleasure and her lips trembled. It was early evening and she had been reading, but she hastily put her book aside to talk to him.

Louis looked at her face, really looked at it for the first time, and found some traces of beauty there. Her dark eyes were wide and sad, with a lovely expression of gentle pity like the Virgin Mary in the chapel at Blois. Her hair was light brown, but most of it was concealed under an immaculate pale blue wimple, and her pale mouth was as gentle and sad as her eyes. As to her body, it was a desolate ruin that she hid as much as she could.

Louis greeted her warmly and, firmly controlling the small shiver of repulsion that touched his nerves, took her hand in his and smilingly bent and kissed it. When he felt it tremble in his and saw the sudden tears in her eyes, he swallowed to control the ache in his throat, and suddenly all the shrinking revulsion he had ever felt drained away. He felt completely at ease with her—he could think of her as a person, not simply as a terrible obstruction in his path.

He sat down in a chair across the hearth from her and began to tell her about his trip to Italy. She was especially interested in Rome, a city she had always longed to see but never would, for her infirmity made travel very difficult. He was a little surprised at her unusually intelligent comments and her quickness, for, carelessly, he had assumed her mind might match her body and that she might be as slow and stupid as her brother Charles. But instead she was well educated, thoughtful, and interesting in a direct, serious way, and in a few moments they were talking together as informally and easily as though they had been friends for years.

Suddenly she stopped herself in the middle of a sentence and turned her head sharply, as though she had heard an unexpected sound. Then all the animation and pleasure left her face and she looked at Louis in fear.

"There is something I must tell you, before you discover it for yourself—and are furious!" she said apprehensively.

He smiled at her gently. "You mean that the door has been locked again? I heard it."

She was surprised, "But——" she began, and stopped in embarrassment.

"It makes small difference," he said, lying a little to reassure her. It wouldn't do his cause much good to have to admit he had spent a night alone with her, but the affidavit stated all this anyway, and he was so ashamed of his former treatment of her that he almost welcomed the opportunity to pay for it.

"I am very comfortable here," he said, settling himself more deeply into the chair, then, on second thoughts, he jumped up, put more wood on the fire, found a small footstool which he carefully arranged under Jeanne's feet, easing her strained position as he smiled at her. "And in pleasant company. We'll have the quiet hours in which to get acquainted, and I'll tire you with talk of my travels."

Then he pulled a larger stool up to his chair, sat down and, putting his legs up, settled back as though this were the one place in the world he had longed to be. "Now where were we?" he asked. "Oh yes, in Venice——"

Jeanne lifted a shaking hand in a quieting gesture, and he stopped. Her eyes, desperate with gratitude, adored him. "Thank you," she said in a trembling voice, "thank you—you are so very kind."

He shook his head and said in a low, shamed voice, "I only hope you can forget that once I was not!" Then hastily he broke the memory of that humiliating night, made her laugh at Dunois's description of Venice, and through his vivid telling, her eager listening, she traveled with them on the road to Rome.

When he told her he had seen the Pope many times, he hesitated, and then, deciding to be absolutely honest with her, he told her why he had gone. When he said the word "divorce" she started and looked away from him. It was not a word that her God and conscience accepted.

Louis floundered unhappily. "It is not that I don't like and esteem you—but——"

How to explain his repudiation without being cruel again? There was no way, so his voice stopped, and the big, dimly lit room was very still except for the spanning sound of the wood burning in the fireplace. Jeanne looked into the glowing hearth for a long time and then looked across at Louis.

"There is no need for you to explain," she told him. "We both have eyes. I never expected nor wanted marriage." She looked into the fire again. "I'm not fit for marriage—nor any of this worldly life——"

"My dear," Louis said pityingly.

"No!" she said. "There is no reason for you to be sorry for me. I have my quiet pleasures—and my faith in God—a strong faith and consolation—but that is why I have no answer for you about a"—her voice hesitated in distaste—"a divorce, although I understand—and I sympathize with your situation. It was not right of my father—not right——"

She stopped, her face showing her inward struggle. The marriage had been wrong, yet it had been performed in church and blessed by the Pope. Surely that made it irrevocable. She looked at Louis questioningly, but he didn't answer. It was a question to which her own conscience must reply, or the answer was worthless.

"Surely," she said, "your religion does not accept divorce?"

"I should have said 'annulment,' not divorce," he an-swered slowly, "since a divorce can only be granted where there has been a marriage. Without disrespect to you, I must insist that we have never been married."

There was silence again, while Jeanne thought. She sighed. "It is too puzzling—I cannot see my way out of it. But I pity you—tied to an empty alliance."

Louis twisted miserably in his chair and rubbed his wrist that seemed to throb as Jeanne's poor humiliated heart must be throbbing with the shamed sense of her own unfit-ness. This was too terrible to discuss with her, and he tried to change the subject.

"I forgot to tell you," he said, "but in Siena we saw the famous shrine of St.——"

Jeanne interrupted firmly. "What answer did the Pope give to you?"

"My dear Jeanne"—he smiled at her—"let's leave a pain-ful subject. I only told you because I wanted you to under-stand my feeling for you is separate from my wish to defeat your father!"

"Tell me what answer the Pope gave you," she insisted. "I must know."

"He said he saw no grounds for annulment—after he had read your affidavit."

"My affidavit? You wrote about one and I didn't under-stand. What paper is this?"

"The one you signed, witnessed by the Cardinal de Lisle of Bourges and the Bishop of Rouen."

And he told her what the paper had contained. When she realized how the perjury had been accomplished, she was furious that two good and holy men had been used to cor-roborate a lie.

"I will have a true one witnessed and sent to the Pope," she said indignantly.

"It would help me to an annulment," Louis thought it only fair to point out.

That troubled her for a moment, then she took a decisive breath. "That would not be my purpose in sending it," she told him frankly, "although I—I don't regret it if it helps you. I seem to be of two minds on the subject—I know the marriage was not wise—yet we took the vows—and they are not to be broken till death."

"But if the Pope absolved you of them?"

"I must accept his decision, of course," she admitted slowly, "and he must have the true facts of the marriage. In any case," she added with spirit, "the perjury must be corrected. I will write the Cardinal de Lisle and the Bishop of Rouen and ask them to come and witness a denial."

Louis was relieved and then worried. "Your father?"

She smiled wanly. "How can he punish me? Life in a convent? That would be pleasant. I have already requested it, and he has refused."

"And the witnesses?"

"My father would never dare harm a good churchman, especially these two old men."

"I must admit I long for the Pope to have that denial— and I think you're very kind and brave."

"Brave?" She laughed. "I have so little to lose, but you— you have everything." She looked at him with admiration, at his strength, his vitality, his courage; she was proud of him even though in a sense he was using those weapons against her. And yet it seemed as if they were trying to work out a common problem together, like husband and wife. The fact that the solution to the problem would separate them and that she did not approve of that solution seemed to make no difference in the warm feeling between them.

They planned together that Louis should ride to Rouen and Bourges, see the two churchmen, and ask them to come to Jeanne at Linières. Carefully she wrote a note to each, and Louis as carefully put the notes in the leather coin purse attached to his belt.

Then they went on to talk of other things. It grew very late and the fire burned low. Louis suggested that Jeanne lie down and try to sleep, but she preferred to remain in the chair, so he brought a velvet coverlet from the bed, wrapped it around her, and brought one for himself.

They dozed a little and discomfort wakened them. They talked again and finally, toward morning, fell into a deeper sleep, although their muscles were aching. Sometime in the early dawn Louis was startled by the stealthy sound of the door being unbolted. He knew he could go now. He looked at Jeanne. She was in an exhausted sleep, huddled into a corner of the chair. He rose quietly, went over to her, and very slowly and gently slid his arms under her and picked her up, the coverlet twisted around her. She stirred but didn't waken, and he carried her over to the bed. He was

amazed at her pathetic lightness in his arms. She couldn't
have weighed ninety pounds. Gently he lowered her onto
the bed, and she relaxed gratefully into its softness. He
straightened the coverlet over her and stood there a moment
looking down at her. Poor twisted body, poor tortured mind.
He wanted to say good-by to her, but he didn't wish to
to waken her, she looked so frail and tired. He thought of
leaving her a note, but the desk was on the other side of
the room. The floor would creak, the paper would rustle.
The gleam of gold on his hand caught his eye and gave him
another idea. Swiftly he drew off the big gold ring from his
finger. It was a beautiful thing, massive and square, with
his crest and his own porcupine in heavy gold. He hesitated
a moment. It wouldn't be wise, he knew, to give this to
Jeanne. It was so distinctly his own, and so valuable, the
gift might seem to acknowledge her right, as an Orleans
wife, to wear it. Georges would be appalled—and yet Louis
wanted Jeanne to have it. She had so little—so very little—
and, in spite of his problems, he had so much: Anne's love
and loyalty, Dunois's friendship, and now Jeanne's kindness.

The ring would give her pleasure, he knew. And if the
gift were unwise, well, there were other more important
things than wisdom. He reached toward Jeanne's hand; it
lay white and bloodless against the dark spread. As he
slipped the ring on her thumb he noticed there was no flesh
on her poor bones. The big ring hung there loosely, and
carefully he closed the hand over it. Then he straightened
quickly and left the room, closing the door without a sound.
Behind him, in Jeanne's silent room, the first rays of the
morning sun came through the small window. They fell
across the bed, making the gold ring glitter on the thin hand
of the sleeping girl, and the room seemed infinitely more
bright because it was there.

The next week Louis went to Bourges. Bourges was about
eighty miles away, south and west. Dunois had wanted to
ride with him, but the long trip home from Italy had tired
him more than he would admit. He kept insisting that he
was all right, that it would pass, but Louis refused his
company with finality.

"I promised you could die on a horse, in France," Louis

said, "but I didn't say you could do it as soon as we reached home. Now go to bed and stay there till I come back."

If Dunois had obeyed that injunction, he would have been in bed a long time, for it was over two months before Louis returned to Blois. And he came home with a long, gloomy face. The Cardinal de Lisle had been very ill when they arrived, and although Louis had waited on in daily hope, the cardinal had died without Louis even having seen him.

Louis was yearning to go to Amboise, to see Anne, but sternly he turned his horse's head to the north and rode to Rouen, more than a week's ride away. This time Georges rode with him, for Georges had been appointed to a position in the great Cathedral of St. Ouen there and his future looked brilliant and secure. With calm, patient confidence he knew he would be Cardinal d'Amboise at Rouen someday, and perhaps at a later day Pope at Rome.

Rouen was a busy city on the Seine, and a chilly city, too, for it was November, and a light icy rain was falling, making the narrow stone streets slippery under their horses' hoofs as Louis and Georges, followed by their attendants, rode through the heart of the town.

It was beginning to get dark, the rain was threatening to turn to snow, something Louis rarely saw at Blois, and a cold wind blew the rain in his face. He was tired and depressed and wished he were at Amboise with Anne. His errand seemed futile and childish. He would deny and the king would maintain; for every paper he'd send the Pope, the king would send two! It was like a foolish game with no enjoyment in it, because so much time was passing by, and would Anne have faith in him forever?

They were riding single file down the darkening street, Georges ahead, and Louis was so occupied with his own thoughts that he had scarcely noticed where they were and he reined in his horse suddenly to keep from riding into Georges, who had stopped.

Louis saw then that they were directly in front of the cathedral. The massive dark shadow rose high above them, tapering into graceful towers and spires. One of the newest, lovely towers had an incongruous name: the Tower of Butter, it was called, because the money to build it had been gathered together by selling indulgences, allowing the people to eat butter during Lent. But whatever it cost, it silently promised to remain there forever, a tower of strength and beauty.

It was a saint's day and a celebration was going on in the church. The big carved doors were thrown open, and through the arches, under the high-vaulted ceiling, the altar gleamed with silver and gold and deep rich colors and hundreds of candles flamed and gave their light to the color and drama of the Mass. The purple-robed priests moved about, chanting as they walked; the gray smoke of incense and the clear voices of the altar boys drifted up and mingled together; the statues of the saints were at their stations, and near the altar the Virgin Mother, in her heaven-blue robes and pity in her eyes, looked down, and above the altar was her Son, hanging on His cross.

Outside, in the dark, cold street, Georges's eyes were lifted to the great stained-glass window, through which the light flowed like many colored waters and spilled out into the darkness. His lips were moving in the Latin words of the Mass.

Louis looked up too, toward the beautiful rose glass window, and listened to the music that was strong yet soothing, and just as it had happened once before on a first day of spring, it happened again, and the spiritual warmth, shining from the many candles, melted the cold dejection in his heart and gave him back his faith—in God, in Anne, and in his own strong purpose.

As if to justify that renewed faith, his errand in Rouen was accomplished very easily. The bishop, a white-haired man of energetic character, promised to leave for Linières within the month, take with him Archbishop Delaye, who would be the second witness, and he himself would see that the affidavit went with speed to the Pope. He would also send a sharp letter of remonstrance to the king.

With that accomplished, there was nothing more for Louis to do but wait for the Pope's answer; so hastily, without stopping at Blois, he rode to Amboise to see Anne.

He sent Dunois a message, asking him to come to Amboise. Eugène would be there too, because his wedding to the child Louise of Savoy was taking place in costly elegance despite Eugène's last-minute reluctance.

Since every marriage of a Savoyard into France tugged Savoy looser fom its allegiance to Italy, all Louise's visiting relatives must be shown how brilliant was the Court of

France. In a case like this, where there was something to be gained by it, the king was craftily and temporarily extravagant. There was lavish entertainment, the castle glittered with jeweled ladies, and the terraced gardens leading down to the river were gay with banners and torches.

In the midst of this excitement, while the women with their bare shoulders sank gracefully down in smiling curtsies and the men, colorful in brocades and velvets, with jeweled orders heavy on their breasts, bowed their knees to him, all of them seemingly delighted to welcome him home again, Louis looked for his Anne of France.

He caught his breath. There she was! There she was at last!

She was standing on the king's dais, a little raised above the sparkling, laughing crowd, and she was watching him. How beautiful! was his first thought, and then he corrected himself. No, she is beauty itself! Her big dark eyes—quick with spirit and intelligence—the dark smooth hair, darker than he remembered it, in contrast to skin that was fairer than he had remembered. A wide band of sable, dark as her own hair, lay smooth and sleek straight across her bosom, and that was about all there was to the bodice of her dress. Her white shoulders were bare, and her softly swelling breasts, half seen, looked provocatively warm and white in contrast to the sable fur. Only one ornament was about her neck—a beautiful gold chain, the locket of which hung in the round valley between her breasts.

When Louis was close enough to see what it was, he could feel his heart pounding with excitement. It was the locket he had sent her from Milan! He had sent it with no name, no message attached, since he had promised not to write, and the locket itself opened up innocently enough to reveal a picture of her patron saint. But the goldsmith's beautiful workmanship concealed another opening, the secret of which Louis had sent her separately, and underneath the saint's picture there was a tiny miniature of Louis and one word engraved so delicately it was difficult to read. "Remember!" it said.

Anne wore it constantly, and now, her eyes on Louis as he made his way toward her, her hand rose to finger the locket and he knew the answer to the question that had been harrying him. She still loved him. She still remembered Montrichard.

He reached her side, took her hand, bent over it and kissed it slowly, then looked directly at her lips, letting her know how much he wished he could kiss them too. Conscious of the crowds around them, she drew back a little and spoke with polite carefulness.

"Welcome home!" she said.

"Now I feel I'm really home," he told her meaningly.

"You've changed, Louis," she said, drawing back farther to look at him. "What did they do to you in Italy to change you so?"

He laughed. "I haven't changed—in anything!" he said with meaning.

She thought, This is happiness, this is what it feels like! And then she sighed; her life was so uneven, only one flushed moment of happiness in so many gray years. She looked at his brown, smiling face, the young skin tanned by the Italian sun, making his eyes look brighter and his teeth whiter by comparison, and his young, strong body with its supple charm enhanced by the crimson and white he wore so well. Her eyes told him she saw all that, but her tongue said, "Oh yes, you've changed. You're older, for one thing."

"I can't blame Italy for that—although I think my stay in Rome may have aged me beyond my years——"

He interrupted himself as he realized that the music was playing and people were beginning to dance. He wanted to dance with Anne, to have her hand in his, his arm about her, and, when he could manage it, a kiss. He drew her toward the dance floor, and after a few moments of dancing, of enjoying each other's closeness, Anne realized she mustn't let herself look so dreamily in love, she must make court conversation.

"Then you didn't like Rome?" She resumed where they had left off.

"Rome?" he asked vaguely, not caring.

She gave him an amused but cautioning look.

"Oh yes, Rome," he said hastily. "Well, Dunois was ill there, and the leeches bled him dry, hoping, I think, to sell his bones to that new academy of anatomy they're founding. We were glad to escape with our skin."

"But Milan—that was different, wasn't it? Anatomy was more generous there. We heard reports that you'd left with one heart too many!" She looked directly up into his eyes, and he felt exactly like a husband whose wife has caught him in some harmless flirtation. "They tell me all the Italian ladies have taken the veil since you left."

"Anne," he assured her, "I'm no saint, but——"

"I'm sure you're not," she interrupted provocatively.

"But whatever you may have heard, I've heard nothing but your voice—all the time, wherever I was, there was only you in my heart."

"Shhh!" she cautioned him, looking quickly around to see who might be listening.

He lowered his voice, but it was full of urgency. "And you? It's been so much longer than I thought—I hoped you hadn't forgot Montrichard."

"No," she said slowly, "I didn't forget——" They were near the long doors that opened out onto the darker terrace. He had deliberately danced in that direction, and now his arms pulled her closer to him, they whirled in a big swooping curve through the door, and, still dancing, he held her tightly against him and kissed her.

"Oh, Anne," he murmured. "Darling——" and kissed her again.

Another couple came through the door, their shadows preceding them and announcing their presence so that Louis had time to release Anne a little, and then he resumed the dance and they whirled through the next open doors back into the room.

Anne's mind was whirling too. She had lied again without exactly meaning to. She hadn't forgotten, but there was quite a distinction between forgetting and keeping a promise. Louis would have to be told—or would he? It was over five years now since Montrichard, and what did it really matter now whether or not she had been able to keep that childish promise? It was amazing that Louis still thought she had. He couldn't honestly still think his plan for divorce would be possible, so what did it matter except that, loving her, he didn't like to think of another man's possessing her? Well, Pierre didn't very often.

She and her husband lived in separate apartments; she had kept her own name, Anne of France, instead of calling herself de Beaujeu. There were no children, and she hoped there never would be. In public she and Pierre spoke with distant civility; everyone knew she disliked him. Everyone knew that he consoled himself with a jeweler's wife. About once every six months Pierre would come into Anne's bedroom, just to remind her that he was her husband. Sometimes she allowed him to remind her; sometimes she didn't.

Her conscience had become callous to the fact that she had lied to Louis, and she justified her continuing to lie by the reiterated question—what difference did it make? There would be no divorcing anyway; he might as well continue to be happy in the thought that she had kept her promise. Her marriage wasn't a thing she enjoyed talking about, and Louis wouldn't enjoy hearing it, so what was there to be gained by a bald statement of her inevitable failure?

"How long will you be here, Louis?" she asked as the dance ended.

"I must leave tomorrow night," he said regretfully, and intended to tell her that he was riding westward to Brittany, because he had had a message from the Duke of Brittany requesting him to come. Louis was not well acquainted with Duke Francis, but he knew the older man was an enemy to the king, and that was recommendation enough for him.

But before he could tell Anne a footman came to his side and bowingly told Louis the king would like to speak to him.

Louis looked up and across the room quickly to where the king sat alone, his steady eyes regarding them intently. Louis disliked the thought that all the time he had been talking and dancing with Anne her father had been watching them. Louis excused himself reluctantly to Anne and went toward the king.

Anne watched him go anxiously, and her eyes went to her father's impassive face, trying to read the intentions behind the bony mask. If he chose, he could imprison Louis for his disobedience in appealing to the Pope—her father had been wild with fury when he had heard from Rome— but unless Louis was too insolent, she didn't think the king would take the chance of making a public martyr out of so popular and important a duke. She wished she could hear what they were saying as she watched the two men who were so important in her life. What a contrast they made; the king's square, black-robed body seemed wizened and shrinking beside Louis's tall vitality. How splendid he looked standing there, and how splendid her own life could have been if those two men whom she loved had not been enemies! Think of having them both, sharing her father's power and the exciting affairs of France and sharing love with Louis!

The king was regarding Louis with an expressionless countenance. "You are leaving us tomorrow then, Godson?" His tone made the title an epithet.

"Reluctantly, Your Majesty," Louis politely agreed.

The king thought over this reluctance and his eyes went across the room to his daughter. Louis showed no comprehension.

"You had a pleasant journey to Italy?" the king asked.

"Very pleasant, Your Majesty."

"You were gone a long time?"

"Yes, Your Majesty, three years—but then time passes swiftly in Italy."

"Especially in Rome?"

"In Rome, especially."

"I believe you saw the Pope?"

"I did, Your Majesty."

The king looked at him for a long moment without speaking, but Louis knew his thoughts, knew he was longing to give on order for Louis's arrest, but realized he mustn't let his anger prejudice his careful thinking. Since Burgundy was out of his way, he had begun a campaign to take Brittany, and he must reserve his strength for that large struggle.

So he sighed and said acidly, "And do you think that was wise?"

Louis shrugged. "I am not certain just what wisdom is, Your Majesty. Perhaps when I am as old and near heaven as you, I will know."

The king made an involuntary and angry gesture. "Well, then, was it a cautious thing to do?"

Louis seemed to consider. "Perhaps not—but the price of caution is sometimes more than I care to pay."

"I see," the king said sharply. "You prefer to be bold— like a certain Duke of Burgundy! The price of boldness is sometimes a head!"

"We must all die someday"—Louis smiled—"and some of us may die sooner than others." Then, very solicitously, "I was sorry to hear that you had been so ill again!"

"I'm well enough," the king snapped, and turned away

from a verbal battle he was losing to another subject where he knew Louis must lose. "And how is your mother? We have not seen her at court since—well, since shortly after her happy marriage."

"She has not been well," Louis said quietly. "A long fever has drained her strength and she is happier at Blois."

"Of course she is. And your father—I should say your stepfather—how is he? Well, I hope, and able to give your mother his usual faithful care and devotion?"

"The Sire de Mornac is very well—and will be amazed that you inquired after him."

"Your lovely sister—did I hear that she was marrying soon?"

"No, Your Majesty, I think you couldn't have heard that mistaken rumor," Louis answered evenly, holding firm to his control and refusing to be angered by this favorite game of the king's. "Marie-Louise is in the Convent of Foualt—we visit her from time to time, and she seems very happy there. She hopes to be the abbess one day."

"It's strange," the king said wonderingly, "how all these young and lovely girls wish to hide themselves behind a convent wall. My daughter Jeanne speaks of it now and then, but I tell her that if she moves from Linières, she will go to Blois, where she belongs!"

Louis looked very much puzzled. "Why should she go to Blois, Your Majesty?"

The king exploded in loud anger. "Because, Godson, she is your wife!"

The dance had come to an end, and the music had stopped for a moment. The king's anger had caught the attention of the courtiers who were closest. Louis grasped the moment to make an announcement he had long wanted to say.

"My wife, sire?" Louis looked amazed and spoke very clearly, so he could be heard half across the room. "I have no wife!"

It was a good moment, worth waiting for. A hush fell around the two of them. People had heard and were waiting for the lightning to strike. Louis stood erect, waiting for it too. He felt exultant and strong. With Anne's love in one hand, her promise in another, he could fight the world, including this skinny little old king who was staring at him with sharp black eyes.

Let him stare, Louis thought. He can kill me but he can't hurt me. Louis felt clean and free of the wretched marriage for the first time, now that he could fling his defiance straight into the wizened face before him. With triumph he could see that he had caught the king off guard, who hadn't expected this—at least not so openly and so soon. Louis smiled just a little—he couldn't help it—and waited.

The king was thinking rapidly, a little confused by the cold rage that numbed him. Louis was one of the few people who could make the king furious, and he was furious now.

Orleans bastard, he was thinking, son of scum! Where does the ill-born dog get the courage to defy me? He must have strength behind him—more than I thought—to dare this. Who's with him? I wonder. Is Brittany? I could put him under arrest—see that he's killed—but Orleans would revolt—can I afford it now? Is Brittany with him? That's the important thing. If it is, I can't afford the fight. Temporize—and find out!

The music had started again. Good—he would use it as a screen. He leaned a bit toward Louis. "The music is loud," he complained. "I don't hear you. Go to my study, and we'll discuss it where my guards will see we're not disturbed."

Then he turned abruptly away before Louis might speak again so loudly that the king would have to hear.

Louis laughed aloud, a gay laugh that raised a blister in the king's mind. He bowed very low to the king's back.

"Your Majesty," he said, and then, turning, walked toward the door.

People drew back to let him pass, and a hush spread over the room as almost everyone in the room realized what had happened. Orleans had defied the king and denied his marriage.

Louis reached the door, turned very leisurely, searched the room for Anne, smiled meaningly, then his eyes found Dunois. He indicated with a jerk of his head that Dunois was to follow him, and, smiling, he winked at the court and the world in general and hurried out.

In the hall outside Dunois had to run to catch up with him.

"Where are you going?" Dunois panted. "The king's study is back there!"

"I know it," Louis laughed, "but Brittany's out there! And we'd better ride while the gate's still open!"

It was a long ride westward to Nantes, in Brittany, where the Breton court was in residence. Brittany was a large, powerful, almost entirely independent duchy. Although in theory it owed allegiance to the French king, in reality it was almost a separate country with Duke Francis as its king.

The Breton laws of succession, derived from the Normans, differed from the French: Brittany didn't require a male heir for its descent. So elderly Duke Francis, with only a daughter to inherit, had no fears that his lands would go to France at his death. Instead his eight-year-old daughter would one day be ruler of Brittany.

This was an irritating fact to the King of France, who had sent hundreds of his agents into Brittany to spread discontent among the towns and revolts along the borders. Duke Francis realized that this undermining of his subjects was the forerunner to a seizure of Brittany by force. He was aging, and it didn't help his waning health to think of leaving his daughter and her wealthy inheritance to the greedy schemes of the French king. And so he had sent a message to Louis.

The Duke of Brittany greeted Louis and Dunois warmly when they arrived and took them to their quarters himself in a dignified overflowing of courtesy. He was a tall, lean man with a carved and wrinkled face, bright blue eyes, tangled white eyebrows, a sharp, high nose, and a profusion of white hair.

When he left them with a lavish display of hospitable wishes for their comfort, they looked at one another with approval.

"He likes us," Dunois smiled. "Especially you."

"I like him," returned Louis. "He's very different from a time I remember he came to our court. He was all Breton ice and independence. Didn't care for our good king."

"Who does?" asked Dunois.

Dunois relaxed on the bed, stretching out his tired legs, weary from the days of constant riding, and his servant removed his boots. He whistled contentedly as he idly watched Max and Joseph coming in with boxes and scuttling about the room, settling the clothes for a week's visit or more, as the occasion might arise.

Louis was tired too, but he was eager to talk with Duke Francis and, when shaved and dressed, warned Max to see that Dunois was wakened in an hour and then started for the duke's study.

Louis walked slowly through the great castle. The château at Nantes was five hundred years old and had stood through many sieges. It was gloomy and dark, with few windows. What windows there were were small and barred, but the interior was warmly and colorfully furnished. Doors, woodwork, tables, and chairs were carved with magnificent Breton attention to detail. Tapestries that had taken years to complete hung on the walls and decorated the mantels on the innumerable fireplaces, for Brittany, swept as it was by its clean, energetic sea breeze, was cool most of the year and very cold for some of it.

Louis became so interested in his inspection that he entirely missed a turn he should have taken in the maze of corridors, and when he opened a door that should have been a busy office with men coming and going, he was in a small sitting room instead. It was a charming sitting room, its barred windows entirely hidden by soft velvet draperies that glowed with reflected light from the fire in the grate. A beautiful clavichord of wonderful workmanship stood invitingly open, the bench before it turned out at an angle, as though it were waiting for someone who had just been playing to come back and finish the piece, and in a large armchair of apple-green brocade, her feet on a footstool of the same embroidered green, sat a girl, her eyes fastened on him in wondering surprise. For one amazed second he thought he must have wandered straight into the past, for surely this was Anne of France when she was a child.

It was Ann, but not Anne of France. It was Ann-Marie of Brittany, and when she suddenly smiled at his frank stare of amazement, her likeness to his Anne disappeared, melted away into irregular dimples and mischievous sweetness. Her hair was dark and gleaming; it fell down her back in two fat braids that exploded into tasseled curls at the end, and her eyes were dark but they didn't have his Anne's level seriousness. They sparkled and smiled and danced and were everywhere at once. Her brows were more mobile. Their noses were alike, both high-arched and imperious, and their mouths too, until Ann-Marie laughed, which, he was to find, she did a good deal of the time. Their faces were alike, pointed chins and widow's peaks making heart shapes of them. Ann-Marie was plumper and softer than his Anne had been at eight, but she was delicately made.

While Louis stood still against the doorway and made his comparisons, Ann of Brittany was taking inventory of him. She saw a dazzling figure, for Max had insisted he wear his scarlet coat which was always in fashion because its style was so unusual and timeless. The golden porcupine painted on it told her who he was, but she would have known anyway. Her father had described Louis to her enthusiastically, and now, as she looked at him, saw his tall, straight figure, his legs long and powerful in the clinging hose, saw his thick hair that fell loosely about his face in dark waves, his brown eyes in his tanned face and his red lips that were an echo of his scarlet coat, Ann-Marie thought he was the most handsome man she had ever seen and she never changed her opinion as long as she lived.

This silent inspection couldn't go on forever. Louis found his voice and asked her pardon, explaining how his mistake had happened.

"You were looking for my father," Ann-Marie said. "I'll take you to him."

"Please don't disturb yourself; you're so comfortable in this charming room," Louis protested quickly, surprised that she would suggest so unconventional a thing, but she insisted upon accompanying him out into the halls, her little figure walking slightly ahead, the fat braids bouncing and slapping her back.

They received salutes and bows from the guards and courtiers as they came to busier halls, but Ann didn't stop, only acknowledged them with dignity. Louis smiled at her small importance, although he was careful to hide it as she turned now and then to see that he was not getting lost again.

"I've never seen you at our court," Louis said. "You must come with your father sometime."

Her braids flew around as she turned to speak vigorously. "We of Brittany have our own court; why should we need to visit France?"

"Only so we may have the pleasure of seeing you there."

That was different; her dimples came and went quickly.

"Perhaps I'll come sometime. I hope you'll like Brittany."

"There's no one in the world who wouldn't like Brittany," he said sincerely, and she thought him the nicest as well as the handsomest man in the world.

"Why is that animal on your crest?" she asked curiously.

"Don't you like porcupines?" he asked.

"Their daggers are very sharp," she said dubiously, "and they kill animals much bigger than themselves."

"Only if they're attacked," Louis reminded her. "They prefer to be friends—if you'll let them." He smiled at her. "And I hope you'll let this one!"

They came in sight of her father's suite and she left him, with a formal leave-taking, to go back to her room. He watched her walk away, smiling, thinking what an adorable girl she was, and when she looked back before she disappeared around a corner and he saw the shadowy dimples flicker over her face, he laughed aloud with pleasure.

Louis went into the duke's antechamber, was welcomed and led immediately to the duke. They enjoyed a friendly reunion as though they had come together again after years of waiting.

Duke Francis related his grievances against the king, and Louis could, in honesty, sympathize, and offered whatever help Duke Francis might need. Duke Francis, in turn, sympathized with Louis's efforts to free himself of marriage, and then the duke asked reflectively, "And when you're free, what shall you do?"

Louis hesitated to find an answer.

"I haven't looked much beyond that. When I'm free will be time enough to think of another marriage."

The duke looked down and played with the pen on his desk. "A thought occurred to me. I hope it will seem a pleasant thought to you, because it was why I requested you to come." Louis looked inquiringly at him, and Duke Francis laid down the pen and continued: "If you've made no steps toward another marriage, I'd like you to know I'd consider giving my daughter to you."

Louis was thunderstruck. This was a predicament he had never expected. He couldn't afford to offend the duke, even if he hadn't already felt so much affection for him. An alliance with Brittany would be wonderful indeed, exactly what he would have wanted, except that Anne waited for him in France. He didn't know how to answer, so he laughed and spoke lightly to cover his nervousness.

"I've met your daughter," and he explained the circumstances. "She's the most enchanting girl I've ever seen; her husband will be a very fortunate man, but she's young——"

"She won't always be." The duke was nervous too. He wanted the marriage very much. Louis was just the man for his daughter and for Brittany. "In three years she'll be ready for marriage. She's mature for her age, and she's been well educated for the position she'll have. She is very intelligent and her disposition is sunny. She's been a great consolation to me since the death of her mother. If I could leave her in a more settled condition, I wouldn't mind death at all."

The duke's wistful eyes came up from the pen and met Louis's anxiously. His own marriage had been an unusually happy one. He wanted the same thing for his daughter, and he felt if a marriage with Louis could be arranged, she would surely like, if not love, this young and charming man.

Louis was in a quandry. He had no right to tell Anne's secret and his nebulous hopes of marrying her, and it was completely impossible for him to wound the anxious eyes. He vacillated, wishing he had never come to Brittany.

"I can think of no marriage that would honor me more," he said, and meant it. "However, Ann-Marie is very young, and my plans hang on so slender a chance I wouldn't consider it honorable to ask for your daughter. When I have my freedom would be the time to discuss—ah—everything."

The duke leaned back, hoping it was settled for the time when Louis should have his divorce. Louis leaned back in his chair too, perspiring with nervousness and far from pleased with himself. To leave Duke Francis still in an impossible hope was hateful to him, yet he could have said nothing else. He could almost dread the moment of divorce, now, when Duke Francis would have to be disillusioned.

The evening went well and the whole week passed quickly. Louis spent some time with his small hostess and found her completely adorable, a merry little queen with a strong, imperious mind. The duke encouraged them to become informally friendly, for he felt no one could know his daughter and not love her.

When Louis wasn't discussing plans with her father he played with Ann-Marie, chess, games of cards, mild versions of tennis, riding, and talking. Ann-Marie was a charming companion, finding cause for laughter in the same things that amused him, and if something occurred to make her quickly and thoroughly angry, she forgot it as quickly and was gay again.

"Where do they go?" Louis asked her one evening. Their card game was finished, but they continued to sit at the table, Louis in a high-backed chair and Ann sitting on a low bench across from him.

"They?" she asked, looking up at him.

"Those." He pointed to her dimples teasingly. "Those funny little holes in your cheek—when you smile, do they make round little hills inside?"

"I'll see," she said, feeling around inside her mouth with her tongue, in obedient research, while she smiled and was solemn in turn. She looked so silly and so sweet, smiling lumpily in frowning concentration, that, unthinkingly, he reached out to her and affectionately cupped her chin in his hand, shaking it gently, so that her head, with its laughing eyes, waggled back and forth. Answering a strong impulse of her own, she slid her chin down out of his hand and pressed her lips in a warm soft kiss into his palm. Quicker than he could think to control it, sweet, sensuous delight shivered up Louis's arm to his brain and he drew back his hand and stood up.

"She's just a child!" he told himself in amazement both at her action and his response. "She's just a child!"

To Dunois, Louis confided his predicament concerning the duke's wishes. Dunois was more amused than helpful.

"You'll need a long life, Louis, to accommodate all the wives planned for you. I wish you could spare me one or two. If I can have my choice, I think I'd wait for the little Breton. And I think that's what you'd better do too!"

Louis looked at him in annoyance. "And what about Anne?"

Dunois was the only person to whom he had confided that Anne had plans for divorce too.

Dunois shrugged. "Well, I realize you won't agree with my judgment, but I'd never hesitate for a moment if I had to choose between the two."

"According to you, then, Anne is to wait for me all this time and be forgotten?"

Dunois hesitated. "No—that wouldn't be right." He sighed. "But marriages like this don't grow on trees, Louis."

When they returned home they left two fast friends at Nantes.

There was nothing else Louis could do to further the annulment until he heard from Cardinal de Lisle, who had taken the new affidavit to the Pope himself.

The Pope was very ill, perhaps dying, and Georges counseled waiting, not to try and force the annulment, till his successor was appointed, but Louis and Dunois were both scornful of waiting.

"By God and an Englishman," Dunois exclaimed, "if you wait much longer, you'll be too old to want a wife!"

Still, that was all they could do—wait impatiently for a courier from the cardinal in Rome, or for even the king's guards to arrest Louis for his disobedience in leaving Amboise and going to Brittany.

Louis suggested to his mother that she go to Cleves for a lengthy visit, so she might be in safety if he lost the coming battle. Mary suddenly came alive at the thought of returning to her childhood home and seeing the friends and relatives left to her there. She called herself a fool not to have thought of it before. Louis was surprised at her enthusiasm and reproached himself that it hadn't occurred to him before.

De Mornac remained at Blois, of course. He had never for a moment wished to relinquish his position as guardian of the house, and Louis never considered asking him to leave, although the situation was strange, and made Blois an uncomfortable place for visitors. The marriage had fallen apart; all that was left was an irrevocable scandal.

As Louis grew older it seemed to him and many others that he grew to resemble de Mornac more and his own father less. It took a concentrated effort of remembering his mother's obvious honesty to reassure him.

A courier didn't come from Rome, although many months passed, but on a Saturday, the last day of August 1483, a courier came at breakneck speed from Tours, his horse's neck and flanks a mass of foamy lather, and the man almost as winded as the horse, to give them the news that Louis XI, King of France, was dead!

Strong winds of exultation swept over Louis. Now it was

only a matter of days until Anne and he would be able to adjust their lives to each other.

Charles VIII, the new king, was thirteen, a boy completely under his sister's influence and devoted to Louis, who, as heir presumptive, would be Regent of France until the boy's majority.

"Regent!" Louis breathed. "Regent with a king's power!" Now it was only a matter of days!

11

At Tours the palace was in an uproar. The king's body lay, yellow and shrunken, between tall candles, waiting for the dukes and lords to assemble for the funeral. They came, riding rapidly from all the corners of the country to acclaim the new king.

Charles, now Charles VIII of France, was glad to stand beside his sister as his subjects presented themselves and their loyalty to him. He didn't know how to conduct himself, but kept turning his big, round, empty head toward Anne. With a furious impatience at his inadequacy in this important moment, she answered for him, speaking with competent tact.

Anne, whom her father had described, in what was for him a burst of enthusiastic praise, as "the least foolish woman in France," seemed to have grown in stature and mind since her father's death, and the lords, who had come to pay their respects to King Charles, remained to pay their sincere respect to his sister. Her father had worked hard with her to prepare her for this moment. Now that it had come, she was more than equal to it. She savored the sweet taste of power, for as they looked to her after each evidence of Charles's helplessness, she began to feel in her own mind that she was ascending the throne and these were her subjects. Capable and confident, she was ready to be King of France.

She was regally dressed, in conventional mourning colors of white and black. White had, up until recently, been the traditional mourning color; now it was black and white, and Anne's dress was stiff white satin, the full, rustling skirt banded with rows of black velvet ribbon up to the tight bodice of plain white edged with black at the low, square neck. Her long, thick hair was braided in a full coronet on top of her uncovered head; pearls were wound in through the braids, and it looked like a black-and-white crown, much more becoming than the jeweled crown on Charles's large head.

Among the leaders who had already assembled there were two groups forming in opposition to each other, for the news was being rumored about that the dead king had left his will in written words, and although the will was contrary to custom, still it had some reason in it and it was a king's reason.

He had written that there should be no regency, but that the "body and person" of the new King Charles should be "held and guarded" by Anne and Pierre de Beaujeu. That, of course, was regency by another name. By the laws of custom the regency belonged to the queen mother, Charlotte of Savoy, and the heir presumptive, Louis of Orleans. Since everyone, including themselves, knew that Pierre and the queen mother were of no account politically, Anne and Louis were left in direct opposition to one another for the regency.

Indecision and confusion swirled through the crowded hallways of the palace like a strong March wind through littered streets, sweeping groups together in agreement on one point, sending them indignantly apart over other disagreements. Cautious whisperings, angry shouting, furious gesticulations—the nobles of France were making up their minds. On the one hand was the dead king's will, appointing a person they could see was capable and whom they were accustomed to see in the middle of political affairs. On the other hand was the will of custom and the law, appointing a person of whose competency they had no way to judge but whose position entitled him to the right. Anne was undoubtedly the person to handle her brother, but there was the dangerous question of Louis's rights. If his claims weren't honored, a dangerous precedent would be established, and one day perhaps their rights might be as lightly disregarded. It was certainly a problem that required much thought and talk.

Louis knew nothing of this will. It hadn't as yet been made public, and he had come directly to Tours, happy in his confidence, quickly making his way to Anne without stopping to speak to anyone.

Anne wasn't alone when he came to her in the small chamber that her father had always used for his workroom.

It was littered with papers, maps, and letters, the same chilly, dingy room where Mary had been told of her son's coming marriage to Jeanne, the room in which Pierre had made his profitable and unhappy bargain, the same room in which Anne had abandoned her promise to Louis, a room dedicated to the good of France, no matter what came to the individual Frenchman in it.

Anne wasn't alone; the new king was with her, although he looked anything but a king, standing before her in dejected submission while she tried to instruct him in some of his duties.

Anne was thunderstruck at the sight of Louis, as he pushed open the door, his face eager and excited, and strode toward her, oblivious to everything but the fact that Anne was here, the wasted years of waiting were over, and that at last the secret need no longer be kept. He could take her in his arms and tell her he loved her in the best way love can be told, with lips and arms and tight-pressed bodies.

Anne saw his intentions, and as she had done once before in the gardens of Amboise, she looked at him warningly, indicating they weren't alone. And, as before, his mood of exultant triumph was abruptly shattered. The angry thought, that she was as cautious as her father, flashed across his mind before he could stop it. Then he swiftly reproached himself. All the time in the future was theirs now; there was no need to snatch at it with Charles and a guard looking on. She was right; they could afford to wait now till they were alone. So with good grace he gave his attention to the king, to dispose of that duty and get back to Anne—alone —as soon as possible.

Anne watched him offer his sincere allegiance to the silly little king, and Louis's happiness puzzled her. Was it possible he didn't care about the regency? No, that wasn't possible. He must not have heard yet.

Charles smilingly accepted Louis's homage. He felt almost like a real king now that Louis had come. He had always liked and admired Louis. Louis's warmth and friendliness made him feel comfortable, not silly and stupid like other people made him think he must be. Like Anne, for instance. She treated him like a baby and fool, and she did so now as she suggested he go amuse himself, since she and Louis would be busy. Peevishly the king accepted her command and left them.

The moment they were alone Anne turned hastily to Louis. "How long have you been here—at Tours?"

He laughed, surprised at the question. "I've been here about five minutes—and that's four and a half minutes too long without a kiss."

"No," she said quickly. "I mean, did you come to me directly, to this room?"

"Directly, Anne," he told her blithely, "as a released spirit goes to heaven. Where else would I go, if you were here?"

He was close to her, his hands on her shoulders; the small satin-covered hardness of them filled his palms.

She still held him away, looked up at him curiously. "Didn't you stop to light a candle for my father's spirit?"

"No," he said shortly. "He'll have to do without my prayers. All I could think of is—he's dead at last, and we're free!"

She stepped sharply back from him. His hands dropped from her shoulders and he looked shamefaced before her shocked expression. "I suppose I shouldn't say that to you, Anne, but you know what he was."

Anne looked at him steadily. "He's dead, Louis!"

Louis thought that was the best thing about him, but he said more conventionally, "I can't pretend to be sorry about that. Why should you? He was needlessly cruel to us both."

"No, not needlessly. That's what you never tried to understand about my father. He did only what he had to—for France!"

"For France!" he said scornfully. "For himself!"

"He was as willing to sacrifice himself for his ideals," she defended her father sharply, "as he was to ask a sacrifice of others!"

Louis looked at her wonderingly. "How can you say that with such sincerity in your voice, when you know as well as I that his ideals—which were nothing more than a desire to give the throne complete and unreasonable powers —those ideals only came to him suddenly, after he was on the throne himself? Before he was king——"

Anne interrupted. "A man's beliefs can grow—and change!"

"Yes—conveniently for your father, his did! Before he was king, Burgundy was his ally—he used Burgundy's strength against what he said was the tyrant power of the throne. Evidently it was only tyranny if he couldn't be the tyrant!"

"When he grew older he saw that the throne needed the power for the unity of the country." Anne had evidently questioned her father about the discrepancy between the ideals he preached and the practices of his youth, and that had been the explanation he had given her.

"Unity!" Louis exclaimed hotly. "Unity! How does it unify France to make an enemy out of every ducal state, so that there's nothing but revolt—revolt—revolt? And that's all we've had, steadily. But it will stop with my regency! One man can't rule a nation of enemies, Anne, and that's what your father made of us—enemies until he needed our support in foreign wars. A king can't rule alone—he needs us all. If it hadn't been for us, neither your father nor your grandfather would have had the throne! Was that why we fought—why my father spent twenty-five years in exile prisons—so that a king could cheat me of a wife—and an Orleans son?"

His vehemence had burst out and surprised both of them. He stopped, recovered his temper, and then his tone changed. He smiled at her in intimate reproach. "You didn't think so that day at Montrichard!"

"What a long time ago it was," she said ruefully. "I think of that chapel room sometimes—dim and dusty—and then you rushed in——"

"If I had known it was going to be so long!" he exclaimed, drawing her to him with demanding hands, and this time she didn't resist. He had the kiss he had wanted, and several more, and then he held her close, resting his cheek against her hair that smelled of Spanish musk. She relaxed against him, forgetting for a moment the complicated tangle they would soon have to unravel. She needed this moment of peace.

"But all that time, Anne," he told her softly, "there wasn't a moment of the day or night you weren't in my thoughts. The wasted years—well, they're done now! We're free!"

She stirred a little in his arms, wanting to shut out the sound of words. This was enough, to be quiet against him.

But he went on planning excitedly: "Cardinal de Lisle is in Rome, petitioning for my divorce, and I have sent a message to Georges in Rouen telling him to prepare a petition for you."

She drew back abruptly and looked at him, amazed. "A petition for me?"

"Yes—is there some other churchman you'd prefer?"

"No," she said uneasily, thinking rapidly. She hadn't expected to meet this problem today. Also she hadn't known how actively Louis had been working for an annulment. Her father had never told her much about it, although she had known why Louis had gone to Rome. But she wished he hadn't told Georges that she wanted a divorce from Pierre.

"Have you told anyone else that I want an annulment?" she asked anxiously.

"No—only Dunois and Georges."

"You should have consulted me first," she said. "You've been too hasty!"

She drew away from him and leaned back against her desk. Her peaceful moments of memory were over. The present and the future were too difficult to leave time for the past.

"Hasty!" Louis laughed incredulously. "I've been hasty? Years of patience, and she calls me hasty!" He didn't take her disapproval very seriously, but smiled down at her, eager happiness in his shining eyes.

"What if the new king opposes your freedom?" she asked carefully, and a flicker of watchful caution crossed her face and for a brief instant there was a fleeting resemblance to her father.

"Oh, Charles couldn't stop us if he would."

"You're very sure!"

"He's just a boy—and he's my friend—and anyway, what does it matter what he thinks? I'll be regent."

She walked around and sat down at her desk, instinctively wanting the official desk between them. Then she spoke without looking at him. "If you hadn't come in such a headlong rush, you'd have heard news that might have kept you from coming at all."

"News? The king was dead; that's news enough for me."

"He left a will."

Louis looked puzzled. "And if he did, what of it?"

Anne looked up at him briefly and then away uneasily. "I wish you'd heard this from some other source."

"What is it, Anne?"

"His will said there should be no regency, but——"

"No regency!" Louis interrupted sharply.

Anne continued. "Instead he appointed guardians for my brother!"

"No, I hadn't heard!" Louis said angrily. "Ridiculous! Well, we'll ignore the will, of course."

"No," Anne said.

His eyes focused on her intently. "Who's named? I'll see them and have it settled. I'm regent now!"

"It's the king's will," Anne said evasively. "It can't be fought."

"You'll see me fight—and win! Who's named?"

Still she didn't look at him. "My husband and myself," she said.

"You! Pierre and you?"

She nodded.

"But, Anne," he cried, more bewildered now than angry, "you surely see that isn't right. The position is mine by the laws of France. You'll yield, of course."

She shook her head stubbornly. "It's my father's wish. I can't yield—even to you."

Louis exploded. "His whole life long he robbed me and cheated me! Now even when he's dead he thinks he'll rob me of my rights!"

Anne looked up sharply. "You call a dead man names! He was my father too!"

"How can it change the things he's done to me, that he's dead and was your father too? I'll not be cheated, Anne, again!" he warned her. "This pilfering of Orleans rights must come to an end! I intend to convoke the States-General."

"The States-General," Anne said flatly, "dissolved by its own vote and will not be allowed to reconvene. Even if it did, it wouldn't support your claims—it would only confirm the king's will!"

Louis stamped his hard fist on the edge of her desk, so that the paperweights bounced ridiculously. "I'm not a child any more, you know, to be pushed about as it suits the king's purposes. I'm tired of tyranny—so are my friends— and they'll stand with me and demand our rights!"

Anne adjusted the paperweights back to their former positions, setting them down precisely. "I can't think you'd upset your friends' private interests for your own fortunes—especially at this time."

"Why especially at this time?" he demanded, although he guessed. It was the accepted thing for a new sovereign to make gifts, grant privileges, and make new appointments.

She looked through papers on her desk. "I've tried to remember all your friends." She found the piece she was looking for. "Here—I've promised Lorraine my support in Naples; Bourbon I've made constable and lieutenant-governor; I've granted the Duke of Orange free pardon and a return from exile, and that I know will please you all. I'll give your cousin Dunois the dauphine to govern, and I'll find something equally valuable for your cousins of Angoulême and Alençon. And you, Louis," she offered placatingly, "shall be governor of Paris and of Ile-de-France!"

"Bribes!" he said shortly. "I can hear the echo of your father's voice!"

"You're certainly grateful——" she began sarcastically.

"What's there to be grateful for? He's simply trying to buy my friends from me! He was always willing to pay for what he wanted—and he always managed to get more than he paid for. Jeanne's dowry, for instance, seems quite magnificent—but when you know that he'd get all of Orleans when I died without heirs, it's easy to see he was a bargain hunter. Well, it won't work—any of it! I've never touched Jeanne nor her dowry; there'll be no trouble getting a divorce—there'll be no scheming king to prevent it with his filthy tricks!"

Anne sprang to her feet and leaned angrily across the desk toward him, speaking imperiously. "I've warned you against speaking like that of my dead father! I'll not tolerate it again, Louis, I want that understood!"

Louis looked at her in surprise and suddenly realized that although she was the one who claimed his regency, she was also the girl who owned his love. He leaned across the desk and took her tightly clenched hand that resisted him.

He spoke gently. "How does it happen we're talking like this to each other, Anne? We're free at last; we should be happy, and instead we quarrel."

"We quarrel because you insult my father. We've yet to discuss him without getting angry."

"I should not talk about him to you, I suppose," he admitted. "It's because I can never remember you could have any connection with one so evil."

In his attempt to explain, he angered her again. She snatched her hand from his and spoke harshly, wishing to annoy him too. "Do you like it, Louis, when you hear people laugh and insult your mother's virtue?"

Louis flushed an angry red. "Not even you, Anne——" he said in ominous annoyance, and then he changed his tone, looking at her with a new idea. "Surely you don't feel that way when I speak of your father—I mean, I thought it was respect, at most, not affection, that you felt for him. You surely couldn't have liked him——"

"Why not? How could you judge? You never knew him!"

"How many times I've hurt you!" he marveled. "And you've never revenged yourself—except just this once to make me realize. Forgive me, Anne, I'll never do it again." He smiled at her disarmingly. "I'm surprised you haven't hated me."

She sighed a somber sigh. "Sometimes I've wished I didn't love, so I could hate."

"We will never quarrel again," he announced.

"No?"

"No. Not about your father, nor the regency. It's simple enough, if I'd stopped shouting long enough to see it. When we're married, I'll be Charles's regent, you'll be his guardian. Then everybody will be satisfied, including ourselves."

Anne shook her head wonderingly at his optimism and reseated herself, while Louis settled himself on the corner of the desk, negligently slapping his dangling leg with his riding gloves.

"It's all easy enough now. We can both prove we were married against our will, and we have the word of friends and servants to prove our marriages have never been—completed."

"That will scarcely be enough," Anne said, looking away from him.

"If we must," Louis hesitated, "we can demand a doctor's inquiry—for Jeanne—and you——"

The moment Anne dreaded and yet had never expected to meet was upon her, and she braced herself for it. "I have no proof," she said.

Louis didn't understand. He repeated, "No proof?"

"No, none," she answered rigidly.

"A doctor's inquiry will show——"

"Will show that I have shared my husband's bed for seven years!"

She spoke very distinctly, with something hard and cruel in her that wanted to hurt him as she had been hurt. Anne felt some degree of shock at her own vindictiveness, for his pain seemed to please her, in some twisted way. A man was suffering now for what a man had done to her. Women were too much at men's mercies. Years of regretting that she wasn't a man made her cruel toward the one man who had always been glad she was a woman.

Louis's body had jerked with the cold shock of her words; the gloves slipped from his fingers, the silver buckles striking noisily against each other and the floor. When the first current of electric surprise had passed over him, he sprang to his feet, strode around the desk to her, and pulled her up from her chair with a tight grip on her arms. He looked intently into her face and spoke with angry panic.

"You're lying to me! You want to be regent alone!"

"No——"

"You're lying—your father's greediness has poisoned you! You want to be regent alone—well, be regent! Be empress for all I care, but don't lie to me!"

Anne tried to shake herself loose from his bruising fingers. "I'm not lying! Anyone but you would have known it was only a daydream!"

"You promised——"

"I tried! But I couldn't——" She finally thrust him away with all the strength she had and stepped back, facing him in scorn. "Look at me! If you'd been my husband, would you have let a few tears and hysterical refusals keep you away? No, you wouldn't!" Scorn for him and for men was in her voice, and she was beautiful with warmth that now she rarely had. "It was easy enough for you!"

Louis thought of a night of horror at Linières. "No, it wasn't easy for me!"

A sudden unbearable vision of Anne and Pierre came to him; he felt the pain from it shooting through him. His wrist throbbed and pulsed.

"Anne, you must be lying! You told me you'd kept your promise!"

"That was when I lied!"

"Why—why? Why did you leave me to think—all that time—that you were——"

She tried to defend herself where she knew she was wrong. "I thought—it would only make you unhappy—and what did it really matter?"

"God! What treacherous reasoning! What did it really matter?" Aghast, he couldn't realize yet. The most important fact, the keystone of his plans, and then she couldn't see that it really mattered. He stared at her. "All this time?" he asked painfully.

"Yes," she answered defiantly.

All that time! Seven years of thoughts and dreams of her, a few treasured notes and kisses, and all the time Pierre had possessed her at his stupid will! The pain of his disillusionment was actually physical; he thought surely somewhere— in his head or his heart—there was a raw wound, bleeding. He hated her for a moment.

"You must have found my boyish illusions very amusing. You must have laughed—you—and Pierre—in your cozy bed." Like scratching nails, the words tore across his mind.

"Louis," she said miserably, "there wasn't—we weren't— often—and—I hate him."

Louis made a sound of exaggerated cynical laughter that hurt them both.

It roused her anger again. "You, of course, were constancy itself!"

"My little affairs of a night," he said scornfully, "didn't affect the future of our plans. Oh, what do we gain by calling each other names?" he said more quietly. "I'm sorry—I suppose it was too much to expect of you. I know you must have tried——"

"Thank you," she said icily.

Yes, he knew she had tried, and he admitted heavily to himself that it wouldn't have been an easy task. He could understand failure, but not her consistent lies. And how easily his faith in her had made him accept the lies. But all the circumstances had corroborated her lies—the formal way she treated Pierre, the way she never used her married name, the way Pierre lived at Bourbonnais most of the time and with his mistress, the rest of it. Anne's lack of children. And her lies—her steady eyes, full of love and falsehood. How could she have done that?

Then his sympathetic imagination made his anger calm

even more, and he felt he understood her lies too. It would not be an easy thing to tell the man you love.

"I think I understand, Anne," he said gently, and tried to smile reassuringly at her.

"Our plans will have to be changed, that's all. It'll be more difficult now to get you free."

This was a disappointment he would never forget, but it didn't change his desire to marry Anne. She was gazing at him in surprise as he outlined the change in plans.

"We'll have to say the marriage was consummated by force——"

"Persistence is your name!" she exclaimed in grudging admiration. "All France would laugh—the Pope himself would ask to see my bruises! I should have a rich collection in seven years!"

"Let them laugh—does it matter?" Louis paced restlessly around the room, watching Anne anxiously as he walked. "Am I mistaken in you, Anne? I had expected a sturdier love—not one that would be frightened by a few rough jokes."

Anne sat down at her desk again. It seemed to her she had done nothing but jump up and down like a jack-in-the-box.

"Louis, please sit down. You make me nervous. We must clear up this misunderstanding."

Louis walked to the window, pushed it open to let the summer afternoon sun come in, and sat down on the window seat, physically and mentally depressed. "I'll need time to think. You've blocked your path so thoroughly, I'm beginning to wonder——" A premonition had been growing with sickening force in his mind. "You don't seem eager to be free!"

She spoke more gently, but her firm decision was in her voice. "Both our paths were planned for us by the king. We must walk in them, Louis—that's unalterable. I won't say it'll be a happy journey"— she sighed—"and if I could have chosen, you know I'd rather have walked with you."

"You could have chosen! You did choose! You still can choose!"

"No!"

"Anne, you give up too easily—always! And now, when it's so simple—we're regents, the Pope will want to please us——"

"But it wouldn't please me! You refuse to see that I agree with my father's plans, and I want them carried out, no matter what it costs me!"

Louis listened to her in despair, seeing how firm she was.

She continued, "We're both married. We'll always be. Resign yourself to it!"

"You don't intend to petition, then," he said slowly.

"I forgot that hope long ago." She couldn't meet his eyes. "So long ago even the memory is as dusty as the chapel room——"

"Oh, Anne, it's dusty—and remote—because you've made it that way! But it's not too late!"

"It was too late before we'd even met!"

An exclamation of pain escaped him, and he walked toward Anne to take her in his arms and give her courage. She had been too long under her cautious father's training, that was the trouble, and she was afraid, as she had been at Montrichard before he had kindled her enthusiasm. She had always been cautious—even as a child she would warn him against the mischief he planned, and yet she had always wanted him to continue. She couldn't really mean their hopes must be abandoned now—when they were so close to triumph.

But Anne stepped back and sharply evaded his arms. She was afraid of them—afraid they might weaken her resolution and make her break her vow to her dying father.

"No!" she said. "No! I can't change my father's plans—not for you nor myself!"

Louis stopped short, looking at her intently, absorbing a second terrible shock. She no longer loved him! Or, if she did at all, it was a less important love than her attachment to her dead father. The years of separation had done it, he thought numbly; her father had won again!

"Your love has grown very small, Anne," he said shortly. "Or is it all gone, and you have lied about that too?"

"Louis—no—I do love you, but——"

He smiled wearily. "I see—you love two things, and I am second. Well, you have the right to the choice, but, Anne" —in spite of himself his urgent love forced him on to another appeal—"it's the wrong choice. Look at your father's life—is that your goal? To live alone in this miserable little room"—he looked around scornfully—"scheming for power

—so busy stamping out revolts you can't enjoy spring days or have a life of your own—a husband and a family."

"I have a husband!" she reminded him sharply.

After a long silence he said quietly, "Yes, I see you have —and you wish to keep him."

She met his eyes and they looked at each other steadily, while Louis faced and accepted the bitter thought that now he would never have Anne and nothing that he could say would change her mind, because her love had dwindled until there wasn't enough left to fight for or with. Louis broke the silence with a weary sigh as he bent down to pick up his gloves before he spoke.

"I'll never find the words—there aren't any to tell you how sorry I am. Up to now I've had only one thought—to free ourselves so we could marry."

"Put it out of your mind—forever."

"Then I have only half a plan left—to free myself, so I can marry and have children for my name."

"Put that out of your mind too. The king will be forced to oppose your divorce."

Louis shrugged indifferently. "My decision is as firm as yours. The king can have his sister back again—with her money."

"No, Louis."

"Yes, Anne, yes!" He wanted to hurt her now. "Did you know the Duke of Brittany had offered me his daughter? I put it off because of you—I laughed and said we'd have to wait till Ann-Marie was older—her name is Ann too!"

He watched her to see if she winced, but she only smiled in a superior fashion, as though he were talking nonsense.

"Perhaps," he told her, "it won't be so hard to forget you as I thought. She's very sweet—and if I can't have one Anne, why, then I'll have another! And she's heiress to all of Brittany—think how your father will curse in his tomb when he hears that Orleans and Brittany are united!"

Anne made an impatient gesture. "How freely you betroth yourself for a man with a wife!" She walked around the desk and came toward him, her face softening. "You're angry at me, and I don't blame you. I should have told you—I meant to when you were here, and then—it was so wonderful to be loved and have you near me—that I couldn't do it. I'm sorry—it was only because I loved you."

Anne's lips were trembling and her eyes appealing.

Louis spoke eagerly. Perhaps her father's influence wasn't so strong as he thought. "If you really do—then let's fight! Anne, we can win—I promise you——" But even as he finished the words she was shaking her head.

"It's impossible." She reached out and put her hand gently on his arm. "But, Louis—don't find another Anne. I'm the only Anne you need. We can still be together—not quite as we had planned it. We can't marry, but it wouldn't matter either to Jeanne or Pierre if we take what little love we can safely share."

She couldn't stand the thought of losing him altogether, and who was there to stop them, now that her father was gone, from enjoying the pleasures of their love? There was her conscience to tell her it was wrong, perhaps, but she had reached a point, trained by her father, where she could convince herself that anything she wanted was right. She didn't admit this to herself, but she was already justifying her proposal in her mind, basing it on the fact that since kings must marry for reasons of state, their hearts were granted permission to love outside the church, and since she was now, in a sense, a king herself, she had that permission too.

Her life, she thought with exultation, was just beginning. She would have the power of the throne, the glory of Louis's love!

The muscles in his arm had tensed suddenly as he pulled away from her. "This miserable hour!" he said wildly. "Won't it ever end! A bribe! Was that still another echo of your father's voice—or is it your idea?"

She backed away, startled at his reaction.

"The price of Orleans is going up!" he said scathingly. "Jeanne's dowry is a part of it—and your body is to be the rest! It's a tempting offer. I'm sure your father would think any man who refused it was a fool." His voice grated angrily. "Well, I'm a fool!"

"Louis—don't be angry——"

"I'm not angry—I'm bankrupt, that's all! My whole life —my plans—seven years thrown away—for your cowardly little love! I said your love has dwindled, but I didn't realize how very small—and how very cheap it is!" He quoted her words savagely: " 'What little love we can safely share'! Why, you're like your father, always wanting everything— and wanting it safely, too—never daring to pay for it with courage. We might have had everything, Anne—our whole lives together—but now to hell with your little love that can be safely shared!"

Anne stood rooted to the floor in a searing humiliation, and then she lashed out furiously. "You're a peevish boy who whines for what he can't have and then pushes away the hands that try to bring him comfort."

"Comfort!" he spat out the word. "Comfort! I'll never understand you, Anne! Would it be comfort to come sneaking to you in the darkness when Pierre has done with you? A proud love that would be! I think my honor would die of it!" He felt as though he had died already to have her so belittle his love. He didn't want her for a snatched hour here and there, like a pretty village maid for a night's pleasure. He wanted her for his wife, forever his, only his.

Anne was trembling with a rising fury. "Oh, love and pride and honor! Just words and posturings in men! I'd come sneaking to you, past a thousand wives if you'd been forced to them! I'd walk naked to you through the sunlit roads of France! My honor would not be touched! Go back to your daydreams, you—boy! You're not fit for reality!"

Louis was intolerably stung. "Yes, I'll go, and I'll never trouble you with my childish love again—but as for the regency, I'm not daydreaming! I'll convoke the States-General, and they'll confirm my right. You'll find that some of my friends can't be bribed!" He strode toward the door and opened it.

"Take care, Monseigneur!" she called ominously after him. "Once you start on that course—remember that no soft memories will make me merciful to treason!"

"Our soft memories," he told her sharply, "are as dead as your father! From this moment on, we're enemies, and no mercy asked!"

He reached for one of the gloves that hung at his belt, jerked it free, and hurled it across the room at her. It struck her skirt and fell at her feet. Without taking her eyes from his, she stooped and picked up the gauntlet, the symbol of the enmity now between them.

"And no mercy given!" she said as he slammed the door behind him.

12

"The bitch! The highhanded, treacherous bitch!" Dunois raged, prowling around the long table in the council chamber at Blois, where the members of the Orleanist party had gathered.

Louis sat at the head of the massive table, turned sidewise in his chair, one knee crossed over the other, his forehead resting in his hand, hardly listening, while he stabbed idly at the table with a sharpened pen. Eugène and Georges sat on either side of him, Eugène chewing unhappily at his fingernails, and Georges talking in an undertone to the Duke of Bourbon, who felt that this last insult to a duke's rights must be answered. The Duke of Lorraine was there, gaunt and gray, and Louis's cousin, the Duke of Alençon. The Duke of Mayenne and the Duke of Anjou added their weight, which was considerable, to the council, but whereas they sat and talked and planned, Dunois found it impossible to be still. He walked around the table one way, stopping to kick an empty chair and to talk to Louis, and then around the table the other way, looking with growing impatience at the sitting men.

"Are we to sit here forever and admire each other's scars and dimples?" he asked explosively.

The men who knew Dunois smiled at his outburst, but the more pompous were annoyed.

"What more have you to suggest?" the Duke of Mayenne asked sharply. "We've convoked the States-General."

"And in the meantime Anne sits on her little brother like a brooding eagle on her eggs. And the longer she sits, high and looked up to, the harder it'll be to pull her down," Dunois answered, glad to have an argument if he couldn't do anything more active.

"Patience, Dunois," advised Georges, knowing full well his soothing advice would bring a snort of disgust, which

256

it did. "The Duke of Mayenne is perfectly right." He bowed politely to the duke, who returned the bow and felt better. "There's nothing we can do until the States-General!"

"But that'll take months!" Dunois exclaimed, aghast. "And all that time Anne will have the resources of the Crown to use in her favor. You may as well toss a farewell kiss to the regency if we do nothing but sit on our tails and wait for the States-General!"

Louis didn't look up from his table-stabbing, but he agreed with Dunois. His friends reported to him the favors Anne was granting everywhere to cement adherents to her claims. Certainly he had no such resources to use. His only hope was the early convening of the States-General, and that wasn't likely. It would take months for them all to dare to assemble, and Anne would do all she could to delay it even further, using the time and the money to get her great advantage. The queen mother was no help to him in the battle, for she had no party, no money, no inclination, nothing at all but a desire to get this earthly life over with as quickly as possible and go on to the greater glories that must surely be coming.

"I suppose," the Duke of Alençon suggested smoothly, his olive skin glowing with dislike of Dunois and his rudeness, "you're impatient to give us some infallible plan of action?"

"It wouldn't have to be infallible to be better than this," Dunois answered shortly.

"Well?" prodded Alençon as Dunois hesitated. "What startling thing do you advise? Had you thought of calling on the English for help? Or abducting the king from under his sister's skirts?"

"Why not abduct the king?" Dunois asked, goaded.

Alençon laughed. "It would take a braver man than I am to venture under the Lady Anne's skirts!"

Louis stood up abruptly. Georges and Eugène stood too, and together with Dunois they gave the impression that the council was adjourned. Alençon was somewhat disappointed; he had looked forward to making Dunois look foolish, but they walked out of the hall, all anxious and worried. Louis turned at the door, went back to his seat, and threw himself down into the hard wooden chair, accepting with indifference the jolt it gave his body.

He looked straight ahead of him with somber, unseeing

eyes. They had all sat here in this room for almost four hours, talking and swearing, making and unmaking plans, and all he had heard of it had been the times when Anne's name had been mentioned. She had been called all kinds of names, and he hadn't moved a muscle. It would have been ridiculous of him to object. He laughed with wry humor, seeing himself rise in dignified hauteur during one of the worst outbursts against her and saying, "I'll appreciate it, gentlemen, if you'll refer to our mortal enemy in more kindly phrases."

His laugh faded quickly, and his eyes focused on the table before him. Surely there had been no need to gouge the oak paneling like that, he rebuked himself, and then he saw what his pen had scrawled, mixed with savage jabs. "Anne," he had written. "Anne." A tall slim "A" standing apart, two "n's" close together, and a little loop of an "e." Would he never forget her? Would it always be like this, the mention of her name, the memory of her stabbing and gouging his mind as he had scarred the table?

"I'll forget," he told himself. "This will pass, and I'll be able to forget her. But when?" he ended despairingly.

The States-General finally convened, so at least some good grew out of Louis's disaster. Anne was furious that the House of Lords had been reorganized to meet this emergency, but she didn't dare antagonize all the dukes by forbidding it, since force of that kind would have swung them all over to Louis's side. She knew her hope of being confirmed as guardian depended on how indulgent and generous she seemed now. Later she would make them pay.

Louis realized his chances were small, and when the deputies met on January 7, 1484, the results were only what he had expected. The clever wording of the dead king's will enabled the deputies, the majority of whom had been bribed by Anne with some favor or privilege, to evade the awkward question of the Duke of Orleans's rights. There was to be no regent at all, he was soothingly told, so he needn't feel the honor had been taken from him and given to another. Since the king was thirteen, he would soon reach his majority, which was fourteen years, so it would be enough if his sister would be his guardian, as she had been all his life, and initiate him into his duties, for which position her past life had so ably fitted her.

Of course there were days of bitter arguments and re-criminations before the vote was taken, but when the final decision was reached, among shouts of jubilation from one party and hissing indignation from the other, Anne had won.

She stood in the great hall, before the huge marble table of justice, and made an excellent speech, with enough flattery and gratitude in it to tickle the vanities assembled, but not so much to indicate that she found it anything but natural that they should reach so sensible a conclusion. She smiled on her young brother with tender maternal pride and told them what an excellent king he would make, liberal and understanding. Carefully, she didn't mention her father at all, for he had stepped on too many of their toes.

The deputies found her entrancing. So young and beautiful a woman to have so much intelligence! It was a rare combination, and the king was fortunate to have her at his side. She finished her speech in a furor of excitement and swept out dramatically, glowing with triumph, her brother's hand in hers. She passed close to Louis and surveyed him with arrogance as she drew Charles protectingly close to her, although Charles somewhat spoiled the effect of the tableau by smiling confidingly toward Louis.

Louis returned the king's smile warmly and then changed the meaning of it as he included Anne. He tried to look contemptuously indifferent to her victory, but he was burning with anger against her, and his blood was racing, too, when she passed him by and the faint odor of Spanish musk came to his remembering nostrils. It seemed it would take a long time for his senses to grow away from her.

Louis and Dunois rode to Brittany again. "One good thing, anyway, Louis," Dunois pointed out, "now you won't have to disappoint Duke Francis. We can draw up the marriage papers while we're there."

Louis nodded in silence.

The duke was delighted, and Ann-Marie was in heaven. She followed Louis around with her eyes and herself whenever she could, and her uneven dimples came and went with fascinating suddenness.

She liked to talk with Dunois, for they shared the same hero, and Dunois, in the manner of a brusque and masculine grandmother, was glad to tell her all about Louis.

"Is he always so gay?" she asked, for she loved Louis's

humor and the way he saw laughter in small, apparently serious things.

"He laughs a good deal," Dunois said, "and a good deal at himself." Too much lately, he was afraid, for there was a bitter, self-mocking note that had crept into the laughter.

"Why should he laugh at himself?"

"He's beginning to blame himself for his defeats, which is ridiculous"—Dunois spoke hotly—"for if one man attacks a whole kingdom, there's no disgrace if he fails before he wins."

"You know he'll win, though, don't you?" she asked, knowing the answer but wanting to hear it.

"Ultimately, there is no doubt of it!"

The coronation for the new king was set for May fifteenth, and Louis's part in it was to be an important one, as he was next in line to the throne after the king. But he refused to go.

"If my rights as heir presumptive to the throne may be so easily passed over, I don't see that my presence is so essential," he wrote in a letter to Anne.

Couriers almost tripped over each other back and forth with letters, politely urging notes from Anne and politely refusing notes from Louis.

"It would be a scandal throughout France," she wrote, "if the Duke of Orleans weren't there on his famous white horse, to ride in triumph through the city."

The horse was, in fact, a notoriously beautiful one, and it was often borrowed to take part in pageants and parades. Louis laughed and wrote: "I've dispatched my white horse by messenger to Rouen." But he still refused to go.

Anne postponed the ceremony to the twenty-second, and more couriers raised the dust on the road between Rouen and Nantes.

She wrote again: "The ceremony, owing to many things, has been delayed until the twenty-second of this month. I'm glad this necessity has arisen, for I think it will give you time to see that no matter what your personal feelings may be, you owe France this duty."

His answer was: "If the ceremony were postponed until doomsday, it would still not give me time to see why duties should be so unbalanced. France owed me a duty."

The ceremony was delayed again until the twenty-fifth. Anne was determined Louis should be there, for if he re-

fused, it would stir up the question of the regency again.
She used stronger tactics.

"My brother has asked me to say this to you, that if you
are not in Rouen for the ceremony on the twenty-fifth,
he'll take it as a treasonable action against himself."

Louis laughed and flung the letter down. "My brother
says to say this to you! My brother thinks it's treason, does
he? Your brother, my dear Anne, thinks nothing at all that
you don't put in his mind!"

Duke Francis was worried. "You'll put yourself in the
wrong from the first day of the new reign if you don't go.
Why not go and hold the crown over the boy's head—what
harm will it do?"

Dunois started to protest. "Are we always to yield——"

But Louis broke in. "Of course I'll go. I expected I
should have to, in the end, but it has been amusing to
harass them a little. I'll go and ride my pretty white horse in
a most gallant manner, and I'll crown our little dunce with
his jeweled cap and then everyone will be pleased."

So he wrote mockingly: "I've been wrong to refuse the
honor, and I see now I should be cruel and ungrateful if
I added more discomfort to the king's life, which I am
sure is uncomfortable enough now. Tell your dear brother
I'll be in Rouen on the twenty-fifth of this month, delighted
to see him and to render him any service." He added a
postscript: "How fortunate circumstances conspired to post-
pone the ceremony!"

Before he left for the coronation his marriage contracts
with Ann-Marie were signed. This seemed to have a soothing effect on the Duke of Brittany, but Louis felt he was
traveling in a circle. His petition for divorce was dormant,
owing to the king's determined stand on the subject. Anne's
letter to the Pope had been strong and threatening, and it
pleased her to know that Louis was helpless because of her.
Her love was turning so bitter that only a continued harrying of him gave her pleasure.

The glittering coronation took place as planned. Louis
rode at the head of the procession on his huge white horse
and later held the crown over Charles's large, unsteady
head. Anne looked at him with cold animosity when he
bowed and told her again how glad he was the delay had
given him time to change his mind.

The months went by. Anne was King of France, and a

strong king, as her father had been, to the surprise of the dukes. Even those who had supported Anne in her claims to the regency were beginning to be uneasy at her strength and growing arrogance. They had expected, at her father's death, to come back into their old privileges, but she kept them as subject as her father ever had.

Feeling a rising tide in his favor, Louis convoked the States-General again, glad for the excuse, because the oftener it met, the more chance of its being firmly re-established.

He rose to make his complaint in a waiting silence. Dunois sat beside him, his big hands clenched in his lap in an agony of nervousness. This speechmaking was hard; Dunois preferred a fight, but Louis stood there, assured and bold, his dark eyes looking sharply about the room, counting his friends and his enemies, and his tanned face flushed with excitement.

He began speaking with easy nonchalance, his voice unhurried and friendly. "I haven't brought you all from your homes to plunge you into the midst of another argument as to the regency. Over a year ago you debated and came to a conclusion, using your full knowledge and experience. I leave it to your own minds and consciences whether it was a just decision, and I pass on to events that have followed.

"When the regency was given to Anne of France——" He was stopped by cries of protest, as he had expected to be, and he looked around in startled amazement.

"Oh!" He appeared to understand the cause of the cries, and he began again when he could obtain silence. "I beg your pardon, my lords, I was so intent upon explaining to you, my mind forgot the formalities. I should say, of course, when the 'guardianship' of the king was given to the Lady Anne, there were many of us who agreed that it was a sensible conclusion. She knew the business of France and she could initiate him into his duties. Gradually she could give more and more government into his hands; gradually she could bring him into daily contact with us, his subjects. But"—he paused—"the king has reached his majority, my lords, and other kings have ruled most competently at his age with a little advice from older men, but our king is not ready for the task, because he has been kept in absolute ignorance of every phase of his duties and privileges." The wind was rising, an uproar was coming, and his voice rose above it in audacious strength:

"My lords, Anne of France has kept our king in her pocket!"

The storm broke; the windows of the hall rattled with the noise and tumult. Swords were drawn and "Treason!" was shouted. Men surged around Louis, some in support and some in anger. Dunois stood with his back to Louis, his sword ready and willing. Louis did not touch his own sword, but struck one out of the hands of a man brandishing one in his face. He sprang up onto a table, shouting for silence, but the meeting had to be adjourned for the day, since the argument was so heated and general that everyone was talking at once.

When Anne heard of it, she exploded in furious anger. "It's treason," she said. "No less than treason! How did he dare!" She turned in anger on her informers. "Why didn't you have him arrested?"

Hurriedly she prepared a paper for Louis's arrest on the charge of treason and sent off a troop of soldiers to arrest him.

If she had sent fewer men, she probably would have succeeded, but a whole troop of horsemen riding fast and on king's business was bound to be noticed. Louis heard of their coming; he had his own spies and couriers—they were a necessary part of every duke's equipment—and he slipped out of the château close to Paris, where he had been staying while the States-General was convening, and rode off with Dunois for Blois.

They laughed and joked all the way, delighted to have goaded Anne into making such a mistake, for it wasn't treason to complain in open States-General meetings against any kind of wrong.

Anne realized her error the next day, when she was calmer, and she let the charge against him die out as quickly as she could, glad that he had eluded her guards; but she was bitter against Louis for having driven her to making such a mistake. Now she had given him cause for real complaint against her.

As to his charge that she kept the king prisoner, she thought it wise to have the king answer to the States-General himself. Charles spoke the words she had made him memorize, praising his sister and promising them more

of his company, but sent them home unsatisfied. Louis was
ordered to remain at his home and attend no other public
meeting without permission.

Louis's mother had returned from Cleves, and her visit
had done her some good. She was frankly an elderly lady
now, but more peaceful and contented than he had ever
known her. Past the torments and needs of love, she could
look back in amazed wonderment at the sufferings of the
woman she had been. She saw very little of her husband,
but sometimes after dinner, if he had been present, they
sat and talked together and it was all very ordinary and
unexciting, so that she could almost laugh when she looked
at him and thought of what he had meant to her. She could
have laughed if Louis hadn't been injured because of that
meaning.

De Mornac was showing his age too; the pleasures of the
table were his main physical enjoyment, and he had thick-
ened and shortened. He enjoyed talking with her. She remembered all the things he remembered, and the care of
Orleans was a common interest; but he didn't marvel, as she
did, at the lack of excitement between them. That was only
to be expected.

Serious news came suddenly from Brittany. Duke Francis
had finally answered the army of French spies and agents
with force, and the regent had declared Brittany to be in
revolt against the king. This was an excuse, of course, for
absorbing Brittany more closely into France and subduing
it, and it was only what the duke had expected. Louis and
his promised help were needed at Nantes.

The four friends, Georges, Eugène, Dunois, and Louis,
gathered at Blois for council together. Georges was cautious, as usual. "You'll be in open revolt against the king
if you go."

"*If* I go?" demanded Louis. "Of course I'm going. I'm
gathering my equipment—we should be ready to leave on
Wednesday, isn't that right, Dunois?"

"Wednesday it will be," Dunois said with enthusiasm.
"Wednesday at noon."

"But it's true," said Eugène of Angoulême uneasily, for
he had been entertaining some thoughts of going also.
"You'll be accused of treason."

"Well, I've been accused of treason before!"

"But this time it will be true," Georges continued. "You've

gathered together an army, and Anne will of course say you direct it against the king."

"And I'll say," Louis countered, "that I don't direct it against the king, but at an unjust regent who is as harsh to the king as she is to his subjects."

"And she'll say——" Georges started, but Louis broke in with a surprising amount of sharpness, for he was irritated to the end of his patience.

"Oh, she'll say and I'll say—what does it matter what any of us say? A friend needs my help! Wednesday it is, Dunois, at noon," and he turned and went quickly out of the room, leaving his friends to make their own plans.

Dunois was going, of course, eagerly. Georges would go back to Rouen, where he was now a bishop, and Eugène, hesitant, as usual, vacillated between thoughts of going with Louis and more prudent thoughts of remaining at home. He decided finally to be prudent.

Louis and Dunois rode off at the head of their assembled armies bound for Nantes. Max rode bravely along too, having exchanged his valet's livery for a soldier's uniform, just for the trip and the novelty of it. On the way they encountered small groups of Anne's agents and a scattered fringe of her army, but they found their way easily through them and arrived at Nantes a few days before Anne herself, at the head of a larger army, rode to the closed gates of Nantes and demanded entrance.

"In the name of King Charles VIII, King of France, we demand admittance."

The gates stayed closed, but a parley was held. If the king himself should enter the city, with his own guard, but without the regent, the city was his and all his subjects would do him loving homage, but to the regent, who had sternly and unjustly persecuted Brittany beyond even a king's right, there were only high walls, a closed gate, and resistance to the death. That was the final message.

Uneasy hours followed, and then, as anxious eyes watched from all the towers and walls in Nantes, Anne and a small guard rode away, but her army remained. They camped about the city walls and laid siege with ominous earnestness. Anne rode to Paris, and before a Court of Peers she brought charges of treason against the Dukes of Brittany and of Orleans. They were sent notices to appear and answer the charges.

That was an empty formality, and when the day came on which they were to appear, there was only silence in the great hall when their names were called, three times each, before the marble table of justice.

The besieged city of Nantes was well stocked with provisions, the city walls were strong, and they had a good supply of men and weapons. There wasn't much fighting, only now and then when some of the Breton party slipped in or out of the city through the surrounding lines of soldiers, but life in the castle was worried and the air was stagnant with arguments.

Duke Francis was aging and weakening, and his friends quarreled among themselves. He had had one serious disagreement with Sire d'Albret, a hard-bitten, gnarled old soldier with a large military following, whose support was needed.

"This marriage of your daughter to Orleans is ridiculous," the Sire d'Albret had begun with rude vigor. "It must be forgotten quickly. She must be married to someone who has no wife to get rid of first."

"I've promised my daughter to the Duke of Orleans and I won't repudiate my word."

"Oh, promises!" D'Albret was contemptuous. "Be honest with yourself and with us; you haven't long to live, and when you die, you leave a young, unmarried girl to fight for Breton independence. Orleans couldn't be more married if he had ten wives, and besides, we none of us like the notion of a Frenchman at our head. We want a Breton, with strength and followers. I always thought you intended your daughter for me; I took many of your words to mean that, or perhaps I wouldn't have brought you so many men. I'm not so rich that I can afford an army for my own pleasure!"

The duke was furious. "Not one of my words could have meant such a thing, for it never occurred to me. I know what your life has been! I hear the men laughing and trying to count all of your bastards; I could never have thought of you in the same day with Ann-Marie!"

The duke was annoyed to find that many in the castle supported D'Albret's suit, but he wouldn't consent, although it led to dissension and weakened his party. Louis saw that his friend was dying, and, as at every other crisis in his life, he found himself bound and helpless by the power of the dead king. The siege of Nantes he would manage well enough, but the state of siege his marriage was in was another thing.

One evening he stood alone on the roof of the castle, leaning against the parapet and watching the darkening sky. The lights flared up in the castle courtyard, and he looked down idly at the men going about their evening tasks. He could hear their voices but not their words. Now and then a horse would ride over the cobblestones and a rider slip off and go into the castle. There were lights encircling the castle, in wider and wider rings. They were the lights of the city, in the homes and on the streets. Around that was a border of darkness, the walls of the city, and then, even beyond that, were the encircling lights of his enemy's campfires.

Anne of France, his enemy! They had laughed and played together when they were children, kissed when they were older, but now he was in a besieged city, her soldiers waiting for him. He sighed heavily and bent over to rest his chin on his folded hands.

He heard footsteps and turned to see Ann-Marie finding her way carefully to him over the uneven stones. She came to his side and leaned against the parapet.

"You don't seem very cheerful tonight," she said.

He turned and smiled down at the white oval of her face in the dark. A fur cloak was around her and a fur hood framed her face. Only a few strands of her hair moved a little in the night breeze.

"Perhaps you can make me forget my gloominess."

"What is it makes you sad? This enormous army?" She gestured widely, making it seem rather a small army after all.

"Surely," he said lightly, "it would take more than the army of the regent!"

"Perhaps," she said maliciously, "you were thinking of the regent herself."

"And would that make me sad?" he evaded.

"I've heard it said that it does." She calmly met his look of annoyance. "Though why it should," she added in a burst of contempt, "I can't imagine. My father says she looks like a fox."

Louis laughed before he thought. "She doesn't look in the least like a fox. She's very beautiful."

"My father says she's not half so pretty as I am."

"She could be very beautiful and still be only half as pretty as you are," he said, smiling at her, and her look of sparkling pleasure was so enchanting that he was startled into observing that what he said was really true. She was almost fourteen now, an adorable mixture of childish sweetness and a girl's appealing loveliness. There was quick intelligence in the dark, brilliant eyes, and the soft purity of her rounded cheeks was edible as a pink peach. Her throat and arms were soft and round, and her waist was slim and firm below the outline of her small, curved breasts. Altogether what he said was very true, and he repeated it reflectively. "She could be very beautiful and still be only half as pretty as you are, so your father is right."

Ann-Marie was never one to let opportunity pass. "My father says I am as intelligent, too."

Louis considered that in amusement, while she waited for as favorable an answer as she had received to her previous remark. In a judical manner he finally said, "Almost. Perhaps."

It was the Duchess of Brittany who haughtily inquired, "In what way, may I ask, does her intelligence surpass mine?"

The Duke of Orleans bowed and answered, "In only one respect, Your Grace. She doesn't boast about it."

"Oh!" said an abashed child. "How horrid of you!"

"On the contrary, how horrid of you." Louis smiled.

Ann-Marie looked at him and then her dimples deepened. "How horrid of me," she agreed. "But you haven't answered me. You were looking toward France; were you thinking of her?"

"It would be hard not to, when her army surrounds us with a necklace of bonfires."

"It isn't much of an army," she said complacently. "We'll defeat it when the time comes."

"When the time comes. We must wait for D'Albret to assemble his complete army, and he isn't so eager to help as he was."

"He thinks my father should promise me to him before he sends for his army, but if he waits for that, we'll never see it."

Louis regarded her. "You wouldn't be delighted to marry the brave D'Albret, I see."

"I couldn't," she said with satisfaction. "I'm promised to you."

"But I, God help me, am far from free, and I don't know when I shall be."

"I'll wait!"

"You're very sweet," he told her gravely, and she answered him with a look of adoration. They turned and stood side by side, looking out over the parapet, over the city and the city walls, over the campfires, to Tours in France, both of them thinking of the woman who was regent there.

Although he told himself time and time again that Anne was his enemy, still he couldn't forget her. If her father hadn't left them this troubling question of the regency, things would have been so different. But now they would never be together. Never, never in this life! He sighed, and Ann-Marie, beside him, read his thoughts and was furious.

"Why should he be thinking of a woman whose face is like a fox's when I am here and he is going to marry me?" she asked herself furiously.

She was terribly jealous of the regent, although never of Louis's wife—that shadowy twisted figure who was only an obstacle, never a woman with emotions.

"I'm too young," she thought. "If I were one year older, I'd know how to make him forget her quickly enough. But he only thinks I'm a child because he is older. If he weren't married to that hunchback, we'd be married now and he would find out I'm not a child. He'd kiss me——" She looked down sidewise through her lashes at his folded hands upon the parapet, his strong, nicely shaped fingers, and she shivered with the warmth of her thoughts that had no words to them, only feelings.

Winter partially broke the siege; Anne's army returned to France, leaving many of the towns they had taken garrisoned and protected. Louis left Nantes too, with his men, hoping to recapture these towns, and his winter campaign was most successful, mainly through its surprise element, for the enemy had expected to be in peace for the winter. Louis recaptured three of the large towns and some of the small ones before Anne even knew of it. With these victories there was celebration and a new hope in the château at Nantes; the dying duke summoned up his waning strength to help plan a spring campaign that would surely secure

Breton independence and Louis's divorce, but when the spring came, Anne sent with it a large army marching under the command of La Trémoille, already famous at twenty-eight for his military genius.

He came in April, marching directly toward Nantes, knocking over towns as he went as though they were ninepins. He took Châteaubriant, Ancenis, and Fougères among the large towns and many more of the smaller ones.

Louis was on the march too, headed directly toward La Trémoille, although he didn't know it. The Breton army had left Nantes for a surprise attack on St.-Aubin-du-Cormier, which they expected to recapture from the French. It was a patchwork quilt of an army. Bretons, English, French rebels against the regent, Navarrese and German mercenaries, each group with a different leader and different ideas of how the campaign might be won. Louis commanded the Breton lancers and the remnants of the French rebels; the mass of Bretons were under the sulky d'Albret, who was still of two minds about helping at all; the Navarrese were under the Maréchal de Rieux, Duke Francis's close friend; the small English contingent was commanded by Lord Scales; and the German contingent, consisting of eight hundred horsemen, was commanded by the Duke of Orange.

After much wrangling this army had straggled forth, and Louis, riding at its head, turned to wave farewell to the confident girl and her apprehensive father. Ann-Marie, in the confidence of youth and love, expected him back in brilliant victory without even considering an alternative. Duke Francis had every confidence in Louis, but he had been through enough battles to know that while neither side ever expected defeat, one of them was sure to receive it. Of course the town of St.-Aubin-du-Cormier wouldn't be fully garrisoned, but one way to court defeat was to set out with a divided command and a divided army, as Louis had.

Max waved a sulky good-by, annoyed at the loss of his soldier's uniform and Louis's stern command to stay at Nantes until Louis returned for him, because, as Dunois said, "As a soldier, Max is a fine valet!"

So he stayed behind, promising to guard Louis's new porcupine coat—a copy of the old one—with his life.

Marching and arguing with every step, the armies drew closer together, but their first warning came when the two advance guards met. They stood and fought, a few men from each side riding quickly back to the main body to prepare it for battle, and while La Trémoille made single, decisive steps toward attacking, the Breton army spent its time disagreeing.

"Retreat," insisted d'Albret, "retreat to Nantes while there's time."

Louis spoke urgently. "It's too late now! They'd overtake us and cut us to ribbons from the back. Strike quickly before they're quite ready."

"Yes," agreed the Maréchal de Rieux, and Orange and Scales agreed. "Our only hope is to attack quickly."

D'Albret refused to give his troops that order.

Dunois stood up close to d'Albret, smoldering with rage. "Has the regent paid you to keep us here—arguing—while La Trémoille advances?"

D'Albret spoke loudly, so that even the foot soldiers in the front ranks could hear. "That's a strange accusation coming from you. Everyone knows you've just been to make your peace—and Orleans' peace—with the regent! A separate peace, of course, and when this battle begins, you and Orleans will ride out of it and leave us to be ruined alone!"

The foot soldiers began to murmur, passing the rumor along from row to row, until the whole Breton army was an ocean of tossing, gesticulating hands and roars of disappointed anger. Dunois had just returned from France, and Louis was a Frenchman; there was that much to build upon. D'Albret did the rest.

Louis wasted no time answering d'Albret. Time, valuable time, was passing. He dismounted from his horse, gave it a slap of sudden dismissal, and it went galloping in startled surprise some distance down the road. On foot, Louis walked to the front of the Breton lines and shouted over the tumult.

"That's a lie, and you should know it! I'll march into this battle with you, and those who don't wish to be struck down before they have even landed one blow for your duke and your independence had better follow me! Those of you who wish to die with spears in your back can follow d'Albret."

The tumult rose again, but he did not stop to see which way the sympathies lay; he gave the command "Forward! In the name of God and the right! Forward!"

He started to march, Dunois falling in beside him. They marched as though they had an army at their back. After a while Louis looked back to see what numbers he could count on, and his heart sank when he saw that almost half the Breton army had retreated with d'Albret.

He called a halt hastily and prepared for battle. The German horse troops were spread out protectively across the front, backed by what was left of the French horse, but before they were ready La Trémoille attacked. His heavy cavalry came at a furious charge, spears leveled, crashing through the lines of the Germans, cutting through to the rear ranks and attacking from the rear, while others galloped after the retreating d'Albret. Taken between two lines of spears, the Bretons were skewered to defeat, while Louis, Dunois, and the Duke of Orange stood on foot and fought hopelessly.

Orange, seeing how the battle was going, tried to save his life by flinging himself into a heap of the dead, for he saw La Trémoille's Swiss mercenaries massacring every prisoner. Louis and Dunois stood together in the noisy heat of battle, determined to dispose of as many as they could before they died.

Then Dunois fell, wounded and unconscious. Louis groaned aloud at the sight and stood over him, trying to protect him, swinging his heavy sword desperately with both hands while the muscles across his back and shoulders had turned to fire. The Swiss closed in around him, delighted to have a great French seigneur at their disposal, to hack to pieces with their murderous axes, and he could see his death in the eyes that gleamed out from under their helmets. But all Louis could think of was his friend lying there, being kicked and trampled by horses and the careless feet of the Swiss.

"Dunois!" he kept saying in low, urgent tones, as though Dunois somehow must hear him and know that it was Louis's one great desire to go to his help.

"Dunois!" he said, as his sword swung slower and slower, less powerfully with every stroke, and his breath came gaspingly, sounding loud and hollow in his reverberating head-piece.

Louis knew he was dead as he sank to his knees under the blows of the Swiss, and he shouted out loudly a farewell to his friend—"Dunois!"—with his last conscious breath.

He would have been dead in a moment, butchered in a frenzy of blood delight, but one of the French cavalry came riding by and recognized him for the valuable prisoner he was. Shouting to the Swiss and cutting his way as carelessly through them as though they had been enemies, he reached down and pulled Louis up onto his horse, while the disappointed Swiss yelled oaths after him and turned to find another victim, of which there were surely plenty.

Louis was alive, but a prisoner. And there were others that had been rescued from the Swiss, among them Dunois, the Prince of Orange, and d'Albret, too, but with this crushing defeat, the rebellion was over. After the battle, still unconscious, Louis and Dunois were taken to the Château of Sable, where they were to be held until a peace treaty could be negotiated.

The Treaty of Sable was quickly ratified and signed, on April 20, 1488. Duke Francis, by its terms, was forced to acknowledge himself the aggressor and the vassal of France. His daughter could not be married without French consent; he was to assume the cost of the war, while the French kept and occupied the towns they had won. At this price the sentence of treason and confiscation of his land was revoked and he was able to go home to die, a brokenhearted vassal of France.

The others drew varying degrees of punishment. Dunois was given a few months in prison and some of his privileges were withdrawn. Orange was sent into exile for a while, but he was used to that. De Rieux was pardoned, Lorraine paid a stiff fine, and d'Albret was rebuked, although La Trémoille laughingly said to Anne that d'Albret should have been decorated for service to France.

Louis waited for his own treaty to be made with the regent. He expected his punishment to be heavy; he expected to lose privileges, much of his wealth, and some of his land, but he never expected what he received.

No one could have known about that but Anne.

13

Louis was worn out after the battering events, aching with half-healed wounds and weary in spirit, when they came to the Tower of Bourges, the most formidable of French prisons. It was almost evening, and the great stone building looked unbelievably grim in the fading light. He looked up at the tower as he and the guards rode in through the gates and the many horses' hoofs echoed in the empty courtyard. Anne had taken no chance, but had sent him with a large escort.

He wondered how long it would be before he would be free to walk out of those big, bolted doors that opened now to let him in. His sentence was indefinite, but emphatic. Treason, of course. He slipped achingly off his horse into the midst of waiting guards that closed around him, and together they all walked up the stairs, but at the door most of them dropped back, and he passed in, preceded by two and followed by two. He heard the doors close with a creaking, dismal finality. He waited in a room that was cold and empty, with his two guards, while the other two went into an adjoining office and attended to the formalities for his reception. Then they came back, accompanied by the keeper of the tower, and in a heavy silence of mind he followed up a stairway, through a long, poorly lit hall, up another stairway, and then to the door of a room. The soldiers stood aside for the jailer with his keys.

The stairs and the hall and the sound of their feet reminded Louis of another hall. At Linières.

He remembered how they had stopped outside a door, as they were stopping now, and Madame de Linières had turned to him in the dark hall and asked him to be kind to little Madame Jeanne because she suffered so much. . . . He remembered with shame how her eyes had dropped when she saw his scorn and how her hand had gone out to open the

274

door, the same hand that locked him in later. He was to be locked into a nightmare again, and he wouldn't be able to escape as he had then. He remembered how he had felt as his horse had run swiftly along the black roads, the air moist and refreshing against his face. To be free like that now!

The door was open, and the three of them stepped back to let Louis and the jailer pass in. Automatically he walked through, knowing it would be a futile and unnecessary indignity to be hustled through by shouting guards if he should refuse. The keeper of the tower followed him in, put a lantern on the table, said something about coming back in a moment, and went out. The door was closed and locked; the men's voices came unevenly through the small window in the door. He heard the stumbling of their feet down the hall. At last he couldn't hear even that, and in the widening and deepening silence he was alone!

Louis flung down his cloak, picked up the lantern, and walked with it around the room. In one wall was a high window, barred and small. One wall was entirely bare but for the scratchings on it. There was a wooden bench, or perhaps it was meant to be a bed—it was quite long—and he stumbled against a straight wooden stool that was evidently a companion piece to the scratched and scarred table. He lifted the lantern to inspect the other sides of the room, and the wavering light showed him something against one of the remaining walls that made him catch his breath in a sudden short gasp. He stood striving for control. He had been put into a room with an iron cage in it! He regarded it with eyes of incredulous horror, while the muscles of his body twitched in an instinctive recoil. Louis walked back to the table and put down the lantern, trying to assure himself that it was only coincidence, it couldn't be meant for him.

He heard the noise of returning footsteps and pulled the stool up quickly to the table and sat down, struggling to seem calm. By the sound, several men were coming, but only the jailer entered the room. Louis looked up at this man who held his immediate future. He was tall, thin, and almost entirely bald; his skin was muddy, and there was a cluster of deep pockmarks on one cheekbone. His clothes were wrinkled and soiled, he had a sour smell, and about him altogether was an air of moldy disuse, as though he had been born and raised in one of the damp, sunless rooms of his prison.

He looked at Louis and spoke to him with enough respect. "Monseigneur, I am Guérin." Louis acknowledged the introduction silently and Guérin went on. "I'll attend to your needs."

"Thank you, monsieur. Perhaps it will be well to find out now whether my conception of my needs and yours is the same."

"Anything within the limit of my orders, Monseigneur," Guérin offered.

"I'll see that you're well compensated if you'll arrange the things I wish to be sent to me. Clothing, of course. These things"—he looked down, smiling, at his disheveled clothes —"look and feel as though I'd worn them throughout the entire war, which is almost true."

Guérin shook his head, interrupting Louis. "I'm afraid that can't be arranged, Monseigneur. I'll bring you some clothing—not so elaborate and fine as yours would be, of course." Louis looked at him sharply to see if the man had intended insolence, but Guérin seemed to mean nothing more than he said. "But I think you'll find them sufficient to your needs."

It wasn't beginning well, but Louis went on. "And then, of course," he said, "I'll require paper, pen, and ink. There are many letters I must write immediately, and you can arrange a courier for me, I have no doubt." His voice came to a stop as he saw Guérin again shake his head.

"I'm afraid that can't be arranged either, Monseigneur. I have very strict orders."

"You mean I'm not allowed to communicate with anyone?" Guérin bowed in assent.

"That's ridiculous, and I think you're mistaken. Whose orders are those?"

"Madame Anne of France has signed the order for the king, Monseigneur."

"Is it also by Madame Anne's orders that I'm not to have clothing?"

"Yes, Monseigneur."

"And visitors—I can see I'll not be allowed them."

"No, Monseigneur."

"But books—some pastimes?"

"No, Monseigneur," with the impassive respect that was becoming maddening. "I'm sorry."

Louis felt a wild need to know the worst; he looked directly at Guérin and asked the question tensely. "Is it also by Madame Anne's orders that I've been put into a room with an iron cage in it?" If he wasn't mistaken he saw a flicker of amusement in Guérin's eyes.

"Yes, Monseigneur."

Louis looked quickly away. It was unbelievable that Anne could do that to him. He rose and steadied himself against the table.

"I must ask to see your order!"

Guérin shrugged his thin, narrow shoulders and his eyebrows made a line of weary acquiescence. "If it will make you more resigned, I see no harm in it."

He went to the door and, as though he had expected something like this, quickly came back with a big, thick scroll of paper which he unrolled and held so that Louis might see it. As he came back into the room two guards came in, too, and stood on either side of the closed door, silent and prepared for anything that might happen.

Louis leaned forward, his eyes rapidly scanning the paper. Anne had taken no chance that there should be any mistake; she had written out all the instructions. He saw his future life written down in her black, strong handwriting: no letters, no visitors, no exercise, no books, not even musical instruments. Bread and water twice a day for food, and every night—the words blurred before his eyes—in an iron cage! There at the bottom, black and definite under the seal of France, it was written: "Anne of France."

"Unbelievable!" his heart said, in an anguish of tearing pain.

He looked up and saw all of their eyes on him, Guérin's in cool observation, one of the guards in pity, and the other in awkward embarrassment. He tried to brace himself into some dignity.

"I see," he said in a labored voice. "It was I who made the mistake."

They were silent, but they continued to stand in readiness, and then, his bones melting, he realized they were waiting to put him into his cage for the coming night. He thought of resistance, but saw how futile it would be.

"Why are they here?" he asked Guérin, pointing to the guards.

"To execute Madame Anne's order, if necessary."

"Monsieur Guérin, may I speak to you alone for a moment?" Louis thought, without much hope, of bribery, and he wasn't surprised at Guérin's answer.

"It would be to no advantage." He walked to the dim corner where the black, barred cage waited and, taking a key from among his many, he unlocked and opened the creaking small door through which Louis must crawl. "I must ask you to go into this now, Monseigneur. I hope you won't make our duty more painful by resisting." He waited, holding the top of the door in his hand.

Louis looked around, saw the three men, the closed door with more men outside, and knew he must obey. He gathered up his cloak, wrapped it around him against the bite of the iron bars—a motion he half expected them to prevent—and in continued silence crawled through the small opening, scraping his forehead and bruising his wounded shoulder as he squeezed through. He turned in the cage and settled himself as comfortably as he could in the small confines that allowed him neither to stand, sit, nor lie down, but only to crouch. He avoided the eyes of the guards and of Guérin, for it was surely one of the most humiliating moments of his life. Although he was heir to the throne of France, used all his life to deference, respect, and the most fastidious kind of life in luxury and beauty, he was caged now, inferior to every free peasant in the land. He closed his eyes until the cage door was creakingly closed again and the booted feet tramped out of the room. He heard the room door close and lock, but only when he could no longer hear the retreating sounds did he open his eyes again.

Guérin had taken the lantern with him but had left a candle in a bottle holder, and Louis's first thought was of fright when he saw it. What if it should topple over in the night, set fire to the table and chair, and he should be roasted alive in his cage! His skin would burst open and the blood would come pouring out, like a dead lark being roasted on a spit. He tried to close his eyes against the thought, but his heart pounded in the unreasoning terror that comes to man when he isn't free to run from danger.

Uncomfortably he tried to shift his weight away from the bars that pressed so cruelly into his wounded shoulder and aching sides. He found relief for a few minutes, but soon again his muscles were aching and the bars had found another tender spot to bruise. He had had almost no sleep at all for several days, and he hoped he could escape for at least a little while into a half doze, but pain soon displaced all thought of sleep, or even terror at the candle. Louis crouched and shifted and turned, but there was no relief in any position. He tried to control himself, especially for the moment when he felt eyes on him through the window in the door, and he remained quiet in the same position while he counted to one hundred slowly, then turned into a new position for the same length of time, watching the candle and trying to judge by it, and his counting, how fast the night was progressing.

Finally, his muscles and his wounds aching with an ache that was beyond endurance, there was no such thing as time, only an eternity in which he was alone with himself and the iron cage. The room was a red mist of pain, and the fierce yellow light that swayed and flickered in the midst of it was Anne's face. In a surging frenzy that was madness, he crashed his fists against the bruising bars of the cage and shouted at the leaping face of flame.

"Anne! Anne!" he shouted again and again, and hate for her grew to the bursting point when he saw how indifferent she was to his pain.

She nodded and danced, shook her flaming head, and said, "Take care, Louis, no soft memories will make me merciful to treason!"

Soft memories! Children beside a pond, talking of the day when they would be rulers of France. Children, tumbling and wrestling the day he had proved she wasn't a boy. A girl crumpled into her mountain of skirts under her father's displeasure on a wedding day at Montrichard. The terrace at Amboise when she had kissed him—and lied. Her voice, softly in love: "No, I haven't forgotten my promise." The sigh and the pressure of her hand in the dance. Her consenting, deceiving eyes. The kiss at Tours before his world had fallen under her decision. Soft memories. Soft memories.

"No soft memories," the flame hissed. "Take care, Louis! Take care! Take care! Take care!"

His maddened mind concentrated on the brilliant flame that was her face. If he could reach it, he would kill her!

He remembered once he had wanted to kill someone else, he couldn't remember who, but it had opened a door! This door must be opened before he could kill, and this door would never open. Never open.

"Take care, Louis!"

In the morning, when Guérin came to let him out, he was slumped into unconsciousness, and Guérin had to call a guard to help pull Louis out of the cage. He sprawled limply, face down on the floor, and since the bed was only a board on legs, they saw no point in lifting him to it. Guérin brought in his breakfast—a piece of fresh bread and a jug of water—leaving it there on the table. The guard looked thoughtfully down at the unconscious figure and did what he could for Louis's comfort while Guérin watched amusedly.

"You're wasting your pity," he said. "He'll never see daylight again. He is here till he dies, which won't be long."

The guard stolidly continued to lay the cloak over the limp body and placed the water close to Louis's hand so he could reach it easily. "He's human, and he didn't do anything worse than Orange or Lorraine or Brittany, and they're all free as air."

Guérin laughed. "Especially Brittany," and then, more briskly, "Come along now; you hang over him like a mother with a three-day-old baby. The lady on the throne isn't so anxious for his comfort."

Sometime during the morning Louis went from unconsciousness into restless sleep. And sometime in the morning, he woke, dazed with the pain of cramped, protesting muscles. He blinked, his eyes heavy and red, looking about the room, surprised to find himself released from the cage he had been sure would never open again. The cloak fell from his shoulders as he sat up, and he wondered who had put it there. It couldn't have been Guérin. He saw the water close to his hand and drank it gratefully, thoughtlessly leaving none of it for later thirsty moments, then he pulled himself up. He wasn't able to stand completely upright, and he took only a few hobbling steps before he was glad to sit down on the hard stool. He saw the bread on the table, and after a while he reached out and began to eat it slowly.

The future was a black abyss into which he couldn't see. How long he was to be imprisoned, he didn't know, but if this treatment was any gauge of her displeasure, Anne meant to keep him here forever. A blank incomprehension of her feelings was one of the worst things he was enduring. Enemies, yes, he could understand that, but there should never have been brutality between them. Such bitter hate from one who had loved him saddened him past his physical pain. He knew his friends were working for his release, but he feared as long as Anne was in control he would never 'be free.

He sat for a while longer and then rose and walked stiffly around the room. Guérin brought him water with which to wash, cold water in a shallow basin, and some other clothes to wear—a coarse dark tunic and a harsh wool shirt. He instructed Louis as to his bodily necessities and left him. Louis was alone then until late afternoon, when Guérin returned with Louis's supper—a larger piece of bread and another jug of water. Louis had been a little refreshed by the cold water on his face and neck and hands and a little rested by the day, and he was able to smile wryly when the elaborate meal was placed before him. He looked up at Guérin, hoping to share the joke, lonely for companionship after the isolated hours, but Guérin's eyes were cold and hard, and Louis looked quickly away again, his amusement gone. He crumpled the bread and ate it, washing it down with sips of water, and when he had finished he was still hungry. He had never been hungry before when he didn't know that he could satisfy his hunger, and he wondered if Anne knew what it was like.

When he had finished he sat in thought. Thinking of the disaster to Brittany, he relived the rebellion, wondering at what point he might have saved it. But he could find fault only in what he had seen then; too many minds in command. What unhappiness they were enduring now, the confident girl and her white-haired father! He wished he could know about them, and he thought he would try and beg a little news from Guérin, provided Anne had not told him to let the prisoner live in a darkness of mind as well as of body.

Guérin didn't come back until it was night and time had come for the cage again. The same two guards came with him and stood just within the door, waiting. Louis looked up heavily at them, and his mind cringed away from the thought of another night in hell.

He spoke to Guérin. "Monsieur, can you give me news of the Duke of Brittany?"

Guérin replied readily, "The Duke of Brittany is dead, Monseigneur."

"Dead? How?"

"His heart stopped," Guérin said calmly.

"And his daughter?"

"She's well enough, as far as I know," the man answered indifferently, walking to the cage and indicating that Louis should follow.

Louis rose. Duke Francis was dead, and that was best for him; but Ann-Marie was alone now, alone and in subjection to an enemy. She was no weakling, she would fight for herself, but she was so young and alone. If he could have been there to help her! But he wasn't, and the cage was waiting.

Guérin had the little door open and ready, and Louis walked to it, but at the very last step his body refused, as a horse refuses a jump instinctively, almost beyond the very last second. He swerved away from the cage and stood facing the men.

"I won't go into it! If you are men, you won't make me! I won't go into it again!"

Guérin nodded as though he had expected this rebellion; he signaled to the guards and all three of them advanced on Louis. He backed into a corner, trying to grasp the stool as he retreated, to use it as a weapon, but his hand missed it and they were suddenly upon him. He fought with panic-inspired strength, striking, gouging, kicking, even biting when he could, beyond all pain, like a trapped animal struggling to release itself.

He heard with satisfaction the groan of one man as he was flung backward over the chair and table and went crashing to the floor. With all his strength Louis smashed his fist into Guérin's stomach, and the sudden strangled grunt told him how much it had hurt. But the other guard was behind Louis and was forcing his left arm backward and upward. The already wounded shoulder made him nauseous with pain, and the arm went farther and farther upward so that he expected it to crack with the strain. The sweat was rolling down his face, and he set his teeth against the agony as he tried to free himself, kicking and throwing himself backward upon the guard. It was no use. He couldn't get free.

Guérin was back, and the other guard. As Louis thrashed about with his feet and his free arm, his body was entirely unprotected, and Guérin retaliated with a strong blow of his own. Louis slumped forward, his wind gone, and the guard released his arm as he fell. He lay there, not unconscious but helpless, and the three of them took him and forced him, almost piece by piece, into the little cage.

They were all sweating and gasping with the exertion. Guérin was furious with his own pain, and they treated Louis far from tenderly, tearing away one entire side of his tunic as they forced him in. They slammed the door and locked it, stood glaring at him and feeling their bruises, then left him. This second night was worse than the first. He went completely insane, pounding, battering his bleeding hands against the bars, yelling at the world, but especially at Anne and Guérin, crashing his head backward against the bars, hoping to stun himself into insensibility, or, better yet, death.

"Duke Francis is dead. Fortunate Duke Francis," he thought. "Death couldn't be so bad, not so bad as this."

The noisy, insane night went by somehow. Morning found him in a half coma of exhaustion, and he had to be vigorously hauled out by the guards, who weren't so solicitous this morning.

The third night Guérin entered with four big men, all grim of face and expectantly brutal-looking. Louis knew resistance was even more useless than ever and went meekly into his iron bed without a word to anyone. That night was bad too, although he spent it in a dull silence, but it passed, day came, and then shortly it was time for the cage again.

Time went by, divided into only two parts, the time he spent out of the cage and the hours he was in it. Some nights he prayed for death, but his body was too young and strong to be defeated, for as his wounds healed—and they did, miraculously, in spite of their cruel treatment—the cage wasn't so painful, and he slowly began to build up resistance against the nights. He entered the cage quietly, saving his strength to last the night. Sometimes he dozed, but usually he slept during the daytime, and since he was allowed no exercise beyond the walking and bending he did in his room, he required less and less sleep. Through the day and the long hours of the night he lived in his thoughts and his memories. The future, if it existed at all for him, was blank.

He thought of his former pleasant life and the luxuries he had carelessly accepted. He thought of Anne—her love, her hate, her power. He thought of his mother—her sweet weakness, her blind marriage, and her cruel disappointment. He thought of his father, whom he had never known, and the twenty-five years he had spent in an English prison. He thought of dimpled Ann-Marie in Brittany, and even in the torment of mind and body he smiled. He smiled at the memory of Max, too, and was glad Max had stayed in Brittany. Perhaps in some way he could help Ann-Marie, if only to make her smile. He thought of Dunois and his loyal friendship. He thought of Georges and hoped he wouldn't be punished for his share in the divorce. He thought of Eugène of Angoulême, whose spasmodic rebellion against his marriage had come to an end with Louis's defeat, and who had taken his childish wife to live with him now. Louis knew that if he were to be released at all, it would be through these friends.

He thought of Jeanne, too, and began to realize some of the suffering she must constantly endure. He spent twisted nights and prayed for death; Jeanne's entire life was twisted, but she endured it, with pity to spare for others. To his affection for her he now added respect and humble admiration. He wished and wished he could recall that first cruel night at Linières. He didn't think that, once having suffered cruelty himself, he could ever be cruel to anyone again.

All his life as a prince of the royal blood he had been cared for so well, down to the smallest detail, by so many friends and servants that the world had seemed a thing created for his own use; but now there came to Louis, in his enforced hours of loneliness, the understanding that he was only one in a world where the needs of others were as important as his own. He was only one out of thousands of prisoners who suffered as he suffered, no more and no less because he was a prince. He was only one out of thousands who had fought in the crimson battles, and he had been so near death he could almost say he was only one of the thousands who had despairingly died.

He remembered now the bodies on the battlefields, owned by pain and soon to be claimed by death, and he winced

when he tried to count how many of them he had placed
there out of his own decision to rebel.

He remembered now the bodies on the battlefields, owned
by pain and soon to be claimed by death, and he winced
when he tried to count how many of them he had placed
there out of his own decision to rebel.

In his pain and loneliness, Louis began to understand the
universal importance of life, to understand what it was he
had done so lightly. In a bitter regret that always remained
with him, he vowed, if he were ever released from this
prison, that he would never again let his personal desire
lead others to death. His rebellion would be patient resistance, involving no other person's life.

At Blois they couldn't tell Louis's mother of his imprisonment, for Mary, once of Cleves, later of Orleans, and now
Madame de Mornac, was dying. She lay, small and
shrunken, in the huge bed, canopied and hung with tapestries, the bed to which she had come as a young, docile
bride, where her children had been born, where her husband
had died, where she had lain with a lover, and, now, where
she was to die. She was far removed from the agitated hus-
tling of anxious people about the room; their words floated
in the air about her, but they were only remote sounds
without meaning. There was only one meaning in the world
to her now, only one necessity—not to breathe deeply. She
breathed in little, shallow, quick breaths, giving her whole
frightened attention to the task, and yet knowing that it was
not enough air for her lungs, that in a moment she would
have to gasp deeply and then the sword that hung over her
would be plunged for a shattering instant completely
through her, to be withdrawn again by a merciless hand.

Attendants wept, nurses and men of medicine jostled
each other about the bed, priests administered extreme
unction, de Mornac stood, looking down at her with pity,
wishing he could help her, and Marie-Louise knelt beside
the bed in prayer, but Mary knew none of these things. She
didn't think of her life with Charles, peaceful and yet un-
satisfying, of the strange years with de Mornac, hours of
joy that almost compensated for months of pain, nor of her
children, nor of her God. She thought only of the moment
when she would have to take that deep, agonizing gasp for
breath. She counted the little shallow gasps that came with

each pounding throb of her heart. Sixteen of them she could endure and then she must breath. Sixteen, then the sword. Sixteen again, and then torture. Only fourteen this time! Sixteen, and then death turned the sword harmlessly away.

14

As Louis grew in reflective understanding, Anne grew in an entirely different direction. Although Charles was eighteen and well past his majority, his natural deficiencies, added to the deliberate subjection in which Anne kept him, made him as dominant a figure as a young chicken in a cage of foxes. Although it had been Charles who had been crowned king and Charles whose signature was necessary on some documents, it was Anne who held the crown in place and Anne who held the pen for him to sign. Sometimes she didn't even stop for his signature, but signed her own large "Anne of France" which everyone obeyed without hesitation.

And yet it was more than Anne who did these things. Behind her always was the dark shadow of her father. His hands were on her shoulders, keeping her steadily moving forward toward his goal; his training made her competent; his ideas were firmly planted in the strong soil of her mind; his beginnings carried her on toward the end.

There weren't enough hours in the day for what she had to do. England was a centuries-old and ever-present menace. A fine balance must be preserved if peace were to be maintained, and peace was more necessary to France, which had been so badly invaded, than to England. It would take years for the scars from the Hundred Years' War to heal, but there were always those around the thrones of France and England who felt they owed it to their honor to be constantly engaged in war. It was profitable for them—loot and lands and ransom made up part of their income—but it wasn't profitable for the country, and it took many hours of Anne's day to smooth out acts of provocation on either side so that honor wouldn't become so deeply involved there must be a war to avenge it.

There was always Savoy and Milan, too, to engage her attention. France felt it had a hereditary claim to these wealthy states, and there were always machinations and stratagems going forward to force that claim.

And there was Charles's marriage to consider. The king had been betrothed and married when he was very young to the baby daughter of the now-dead Mary of Burgundy and Maximilian, Holy Roman Emperor, but the child—Margaret of Austria, she was called—had not yet been crowned queen nor had the marriage been consummated because of her age. Anne was beginning to wonder if this marriage wasn't a mistake and if a better one couldn't be arranged for Charles. While the status of Margaret was carefully preserved, Anne's eyes went roving around the country, to see what more profitable marriage there might be.

But France itself, its civil uprisings in the final struggles of the different princes to keep their rights as independent duchies, was her greatest concern. It was her dream, as it had been her father's, to nationalize France, to weld it into one powerful country under one all-powerful leader, and she went about it much as her father had done, as he had taught her to do. She descended to treacheries he would have thought clever; she ascended to bold heights he would have dared; she bribed and bought things he would have thought valuable; she made sacred and holy promises, as he had done, and was as slippery and adroit at piously evading them; she incurred debts honorably, and dishonorably repudiated them in a way that would have called forth his admiration. She was all and more than her father had been, for she added, to what he had given her, her feminine subtlety and a better understanding of character. All that she lacked, and it was a galling lack, was his secure position.

She had beauty, too, and when it suited her purpose she could gain her point by using it discreetly. But she was contemptuous of men, chaste and moral because of that contempt. She remembered Louis with a rankling, envenomed love, hating herself because she couldn't hate him, treating him with cruelty for the perverse, painful pleasure it gave her.

Her life, for all the millions of important things that clamored for her every hour, was sour and unhappy. When she laid herself down wearily into her bed, often it was almost dawn. When she closed her eyes, it wasn't to quiet peace and darkness, but the lights and events of the past day would be on her eyelids and she would go through it all again, reassuring herself on some debatable point, preparing herself for the morrow's debatable points, and in exasperated weariness wait for sleep to come to her before the vision in her mind should change from impersonal questions to the heart-stabbing picture of Louis's face.

When Anne saw that sleep was far away, she deliberately encouraged herself to think of other troubles, of which she had enough. Charles was beginning to give her a great deal of difficulty, and it wasn't so easy any more to keep him thoroughly subjugated to her will, ready to sign amiably what required his signature and to say "Yes" when "Yes" was needed.

She had to keep a close eye on his companions, undermining and removing those who might encourage him to have an idea of his own. His majority made her position more difficult, for there were many around the court who would have been delighted to gain control of the king and see her power vanish.

She sighed and laid cold fingers on her hot eyelids, thinking of the angry way Charles had reproached her when he had heard for the first time of Louis's imprisonment. He had come flinging petulantly into the room, his prominent light eyes red with angry tears, where she had been busily engaged in pacifying the Duke of Mayenne and his friends for the revocation of some of their ancient privileges. Charles had made it very embarrassing for her. In the midst of the silence, while all had arisen at the king's entrance, and before she could dismiss the gentlemen and take care of Charles alone, he had begun to whimper and bluster his complaints at her, and she knew it had made her prestige suffer, for the duke and his friends had exchanged glances that read, "So! The regent is on her way out, and a king is on his way in!"

When they were finally alone, Charles stormed at her. "Why wasn't I told about Louis? I might never have known, the way I'm kept under lock and key, if his cousin Dunois had not told me! He asked me why I'd done such a thing, and I hadn't even heard. You make me into a fine fool of a king!"

Anne looked at him in the angry way that usually

brought tears to his eyes, and she thought it would give her great pleasure to see Dunois in prison also.

She folded her white arms across her breast, her long fingers shining with jewels, leaned back in the chair, and surveyed him in the cold imperious way he hated. "You're forgetting too many things, Charles. Your father made me guardian to act in your interests, and I don't like to see your ingratitude—nor your stupidity."

Charles was still too angry to melt as he usually did. "My gratitude has nothing to do with it. I want Louis released immediately!"

He spoke with unusual authority, but she saw also that he had come to her first, when he might have ordered Louis released without her. She felt safer.

"If you're too stupid to see Louis's release is the same thing as your death, I suppose you really deserve that I should do as you ask."

She looked her contempt for his slowness of mind, and she noticed with satisfaction that his anger had yielded to bewilderment. She felt safe in seeming to acquiesce, reaching for pen and parchment.

"I'll write you out his release and you may sign it now. Would you like to take it to him yourself, so he can accomplish your death a little sooner than he would otherwise?"

She began to scribble on the paper, waiting for his voice to stop her. It came, uncertain with fear.

"Wait, Anne! Have you heard something to make you think Louis is planning my death?"

The fear and the bewilderment in his vacuous face would have moved anyone not so familiar with its phases as Anne. She half laughed in an annoyed way and pushed the paper from her, flinging the pen down onto it, so that a smear of ink was across the large white space and the few hurried words that might have been Louis's freedom were left unfinished.

"My poor boy, I hate to think how many times you might have died if I hadn't been so eternally vigilant, and your father before me. Even you, inexperienced as you are, must surely see that Louis has gone too far in his treason to retreat now."

Charles defended the cousin he had liked so well. "Louis only fought for his right to be my regent. And I think I might have been much happier if he'd won. You treat me like a baby still."

"If you weren't a baby, you'd see that I represent you and those who rebel against me, rebel against you!"

"But they all did! Orange and Brittany and Lorraine and Dunois and Angoulême—many of them—and yet they're all free but Louis. Why was his treason worse?"

Anne looked at him as though she couldn't believe there could be so much blind stupidity in the world. "Because, my poor child," she said pityingly, as though she spoke to an idiot, which she often thought he was, "neither Orange nor Brittany nor Lorraine nor Dunois nor Angoulême nor any of the others is heir to the throne after your death, and Louis is! He's committed treason so far; what would keep him from committing more and possessing the throne?"

Comprehension came slowly to Charles and tears welled up slowly with it. Anne pressed her advantage.

"Have I ever had a thought in my life, since our father died and years before that, except to look after you? Have I, Charles?"

"I haven't been very happy," he said in answer, feeling very sorry for his unhappy life.

Anne sighed. "Nor have I! But you're child enough to expect happiness. I'm old enough so that I'm satisfied if I can keep you alive. It doesn't make me happy to put Louis into prison." That he was in an iron cage, also, no one knew. "Once I was as fond of him as you, but I can't let affection for anyone keep me from looking after your safety. I'd put you into prison, too, if I thought it was the only way to keep you alive."

She could accomplish even that, Charles had no doubt, and his affection for Louis was giving way to fear.

"You know something to make you think Louis wants to kill me?"

Anne pulled open a drawer and looked in it for papers, presumably proof that Louis was plotting such a thing, but she wasn't able to find them. She talked as she looked.

"I have the proof somewhere. He's gone too far to retreat; he must go forward. If he's free, it won't be long before you're dead and he is king. I guard you as well as I can, but if you open the prison gates, I can't be responsible for your safety!"

Anne abandoned her search for the nonexistent papers

and went to Charles. She put her arms around his shoulders and drew him to her.

"I'm sorry you're unhappy, my poor little brother," and she was sorry for him.

Watching his foolish, pitiful face, she thought again for the thousandth time how much better it would have been for both of them if he hadn't been born a king and she hadn't been born a woman. At her words of sympathy, tears spilled out of his eyes and he laid his large head on her shoulder. He was sad and alone in a world where the cousin he loved wished to kill him and where the only person on whom he could rely for his existence kept him so sternly apart from life. If he were really king, he supposed it wouldn't be much better. Anne was the same as king now, and she said she was unhappy. She looked unhappy. Her eyes were tired and there were shadows beneath them, and there were two lines on either side of her mouth that had come quite suddenly. There was no happiness in the world, Anne said so. The tears were pouring from his eyes now, and he was glad to feel her familiar arms around him. Anne, between satisfaction at having him under control again and annoyance at such weakness, consoled him as best she could.

This scene with Charles wasn't the only trouble over Louis's imprisonment. The Pope, now Innocent VIII, activated by Georges and the Bishop of Orleans, wrote to reprove her; but she paid no attention, and the new Pope was too much in need of France's help against Ferdinand of Naples to dare to be too harsh. Louis's friends were working everywhere for his release, but Anne was surprised when Jeanne came hurrying to Tours to see her sister as soon as she had heard the news.

"Anne, how could you be so cruel as to imprison Louis? When are you going to release him?" Jeanne's large, beautiful eyes in her ugly face accused her sister.

Jeanne was dressed in her usual somber clothes and the big dark cloak that she always wore, no matter what the weather, held concealingly around her. It was always painful to see Anne's beauty and to know that if she had been more fortunate she might have had beauty, too, and Louis might have loved her. Always in her mind was the picture she had seen in the mirror on her wedding day, her sister at her side. She reproached herself for her envy, but it was the only impiety she couldn't control. She wore Louis's ring on a little gold chain around her neck, hidden beneath her dress, and no one but she knew it was there; but it felt warm and comforting against her skin, and at night, when she was alone, she would take it out and slip it on her finger, sometimes smilingly over two of her fingers together. Then she would take out Louis's letters—he had written regularly until he had been imprisoned—and she would read them all over. And, with his ring on her hand, she would proudly know that even if he would never be her husband, he was her good friend.

Anne was startled by this attack and showed it. It was surprising that Jeanne should feel so, after Louis's contemptuous treatment of her. "Why should you care?" Anne turned the defense into attack. "He hasn't been a devoted husband to you, for all that you come to me like his loving wife!"

Jeanne quivered and then hardened into rigidity. "I am his loving wife," she said quietly, "but neither of those things is right. I have no right to love anyone." She looked down at herself, her eyes traveling sadly over her body and then to Anne's eyes who avoided her gaze. "A fine vessel to carry love in! It was a wicked thing for my father to do, and I think he's answering for it to his God. Anne—Anne, you'll have to answer to your God one day too!"

Anne replied with annoyed finality, "Very well, I'll answer to my God, but not to you! I'll have no more of this discussion. Return to Linières today, and I had rather you wouldn't return until you are resigned to it!"

Jeanne saw clearly that there was no more to be said to Anne, so she pulled her cloak more closely about her and started for the door with as much quick resolution as her shambling walk would allow. "I'll speak to Charles," she said.

Anne went to her with rapid, strong steps and grasped her arm in a tight clasp, delaying her at the door.

"You'll do no such thing! I have enough trouble with Charles to keep his foolish brains from rattling him to disaster!"

Jeanne could hardly believe the words she heard. It couldn't be possible that Anne should have become so rigid a ruler over her own brother and sister. She was shocked at the way Anne was changing.

"Do you mean I am not to see my brother?" she asked in amazement.

"I mean you are not to see Charles!" her sister answered with conclusive finality.

Their eyes locked in a depth of intensity, and Anne was the first to look away. She called for guards to escort Jeanne to her carriage, taking no chances that Jeanne would disobey, and Jeanne limped away in angry humiliation, making the long, bumpy journey back to Linières in shame for Anne's hardness and regret that she had accomplished nothing for Louis.

Anne redoubled her care to keep Charles away from all of Louis's friends, so that the suspicions she had planted in his mind should grow to venomous maturity.

Forced at last by his persistence to grant Dunois an interview, Anne looked across the desk at the strong, stocky figure of Louis's cousin and hated him. He stood in a characteristic position, his legs placed firmly apart, his arms folded across his chest, no slightest trace of the deference that should have been shown to the regent-in-fact, only belligerent animosity. Well braced against time and interruption, he was there for an accounting, not to sue for favors, and the steady gray eyes over the long, straight nose accused her.

"Well," she began, and her usual arrogance was tempered, to her annoyance, by some apprehension. Certainly Dunois was no more capable of disturbing her plans than Jeanne, but with them both she felt a shamed sense of being naked before their eyes. They saw the motives that were hidden to everyone else. Their perceptions were too keen for her explanations.

"Well, it wouldn't be hard for me to imagine what it is you wish to see me about. It is your cousin, of course."

"Yes. I think this comedy has gone far enough!"

Anne's smooth black eyebrows rose in polite inquiry. "Comedy? Perhaps you'll point out to me what's amusing about treason?"

Dunois made an impolite sound of scorn. "Save your little song about treason for younger ears than mine. You know where it's effective; you should also realize where it makes no impression. You took Louis's place—he fought for it, and he lost! He won't fight for it again, especially since there's no need for a regency now that the king has more than reached his majority." He smiled significantly and she flushed. "Now let Louis go!"

Anne rose to her feet in anger. "You go too far! You may leave now, and I won't see you again on this or any other subject."

She walked to the bell rope to pull it and turned back to eye him with hot enmity. He had only a moment before the door would open and guards would come, and he poured into it all the acrimonious reproach he could.

"I go too far?" he echoed incredulously. "It's you who've gone beyond all reason—and why? He's never done anything wrong—except to love you!" he said stingingly. "And why, I could never figure, for you have no more heart than a painted picture! The most draggled whore out of the lowest street in Paris is worth ten of you! At least she gives something—while you take everything—his heart—his life —and throw him into a dark cell to rot! You kept him hoping with your lying promises, you threw him away for the regency, you goaded him to rebellion, and now you have him at your pleasure! Are you going to kill him too? If you do, I warn you there will never be a safe place in France, nor in all this world, for you! There will never be a place I can't find you! Now! Cry treason if you like, since the word comes so easily to your false tongue!"

And Dunois strode out of the room, slamming the door behind him. By God, it had been good to throw a little truth against that white arrogant face!

But on his horse, riding rapidly out of the courtyard, his fury began to sink into gloomy despair. It had been a great satisfaction to pour out his anger over her, but talking wouldn't get Louis out of Bourges. Dunois pulled the horse down to a walk and began to ponder other ways of bringing about a release, since he was certain it would never come through Anne.

She had been so infuriated by his astounding words that she had wanted to arrest him, but, thinking better of it, she let him go. It would only have caused her more trouble with Louis's faction, and there was trouble enough now. She would make Dunois pay for his rashness in other ways, and if her life and power depended upon it, she wouldn't release Louis now.

Dunois's shocking words came back to her: "No more heart than a painted picture!" And suddenly she put her head down upon her arms and cried as she hadn't cried for years. "No more heart than a painted picture!"

That was what Dunois thought, and she wished it were true. Better to have no heart at all, so she could go about her work, the things she had to do, and not carry this heavy, aching emptiness within her!

15

In Brittany, Ann-Marie's dimples had scarcely seen the light of day since Louis's imprisonment and her father's death. She had always, in a childish way, looked forward to the time when she would be ruler of Brittany. But when she had seen her father's beloved face in that last quietness, with the shadows on it that gradually deepened like the coming of night in a silent street, and his white hair gleaming silver in the light of the tall candles at his head and feet, her breath came in one great strangled sob and she sank to her knees beside him. The hands she clutched were cold and unresponsive, and the blue eyes that used to shine with laughter and love at the sight of her were closed. So many things she wanted to tell him welled up into her aching throat, so many things she might have told him but that she had carelessly laid aside for another day that would never come now.

After his burial, when the solemnity of death was removed, soldiers, politicians, courtiers, and troubles descended on Ann-Marie in a surging flood. Peace with France must be adjusted and the indemnities of the war must be met, prisoners exchanged and ransomed, Brittany's soldiers paid and disbanded under the agreement of the treaty, and private grievances must be judged and settled.

The late Duke Francis had taken as much care with his Ann as the late king of France had given to his daughter, so that they should both be fit to rule when the time came. Although it came sooner to Ann-Marie and she began her reign after an inauspicious defeat, she plunged in and did her best, helped and advised by the trusted de Rieux. She did very well. She had intelligence, bravery, and humor, and she was loved and respected in a court that was more open and honest than the intrigue-ridden palace of France.

Although the Bretons had been forced to acknowledge

the sovereignty of France and had promised that the
Duchess of Brittany could not marry without French consent, those things were words on paper, forced on them, but
not in their hearts. Breton independence had suffered a set-
back, but one day there would be another ending to the
story. When the details of the war had been settled, the important matter of Ann-Marie's marriage was brought up
without any consideration for French approval.

There had always been a section of the Breton court
which had opposed Ann-Marie's betrothal to Louis, and now
that he was imprisoned and married, too, even those who
liked the idea when he was free agreed it was hopeless. But
still Ann-Marie clung stubbornly to her betrothal to Louis,
although she had received no word from him since his
imprisonment. She sent couriers with messages which they
were forced to bring back, undelivered.

She sent for Max, a sad and dejected Max, who could
scarcely show his uneven teeth in a smile, much less manage one of his cheerful grins. The thought of his master in
prison, and without any of his clothes, not even his scarlet
coat, was terrible. He brightened a little when Ann-Marie
gave him a message to Louis and a large purse of gold to
use in delivering that message, and in an elaborate disguise
designed by himself he rode out for Bourges. He took with
him the scarlet coat, carefully packed in a flat leather case.

While she waited and waited for Max to return, suitors
were submitted to the stubborn Ann-Marie. There was this
gentleman of Brittany who would fight for Breton independence, or this duke from England who would bring them
English support against France, or this Spanish gentleman
who might be very useful, or this duke from an Italian
state who might make France more lenient. She maintained
her betrothal to Louis, but as the pressure became stronger
and stronger all the time, a dismal premonition came to
keep her company.

Even in her bed at night, when she thought she should
surely be free from gentlemen who wished to marry her,
her maids, bribed by one faction or another, would talk to
her about it.

"Look at this!" Madelon Boisvert, her youngest lady-in-
waiting, whispered to her, pushing something small and
metallic into Ann-Marie's hand as she was getting into bed.

"This" was a miniature of an almost impossibly pretty

young man in long golden curls, painted in pastels on ivory and framed in jewels.

"He's mad about you!" Madelon continued in a sibilant whisper which everyone in the room could hear, but the other ladies-in-waiting did not interfere.

It was only fair that Madelon should be allowed a few minutes to earn her bribe. Their turn would come too, for they were well organized.

"There's a note behind the picture. He is waiting for an answer."

Ann-Marie took the miniature and looked at it, tolerantly weary.

"Who is it now?" she asked with a sigh of impatience. "This isn't the one you said was mad about me yesterday."

Madelon was disgusted at the very thought of the other one who had met with so little favor, although she had extolled him frenziedly at the time. "That old goat! No, this is the Duke de Neuville!"

Ann-Marie laughed with real amusement, and her dimples rejoiced at the unusual exercise. "Madelon, you are delightful, and such a liar. I must know who painted this. Do you know?"

Madelon did not know, but she had to smile too. "If he could make the Duke de Neuville look like this," Ann-Marie continued, "I must have him paint some of me, and die of delight at my own beauty. Go away now, and take this thing with you."

Madelon took the miniature that could also be worn as a locket, after she took the picture out and replaced it with one of her own young men of the moment. She was not at all surprised or dismayed, but pleased. She had the locket, the bribe, and the prospective business of more suitors.

All the ladies-in-waiting said good night to their mistress and withdrew to the outer room, their white starched Breton hats flocking together at the doorway like large white birds. They talked and whispered for a while and then gradually left for their rooms in the castle, leaving only two women who remained in the duchess's antechamber all night.

When she was alone, Ann-Marie got up from her bed again and went to the high window that looked out across Brittany to France and a high window at Bourges.

What was happening there? she wondered desperately.

Why hadn't Max returned with a message? If her longing eyes could have traveled the distance to Bourges, they would have seen Max, sitting dejectedly on his horse, looking up at the high blank tower, and, in a sense, as far away from Louis as she was.

Max had spent all the money in the purse and stolen some more to use for bribes to get the message to Louis and secure an answer, but whether the message had really been delivered, Max couldn't be sure. The bribed guard assured him it had been slipped through the barred opening in Louis's door, together with material for an answer, but when weeks and months had passed and the guard had no answer for Max, and Max hadn't even seen Louis's face in a barred tower window, although he had ridden around the tower a thousand times, he could see that it was hopeless and he rode to Amboise to consult with Dunois.

Ann-Marie couldn't know this, but she sensed Max's failure. She knelt there on the window ledge in the moonlight and pulled her robe down over her bare feet, listening to the sounds that came up out of the night and thinking of Louis. She could hear the neighings and stampings of restless horses in the stables, and someone from the garden side of the château was playing a guitar and singing. Someone serenading Pauline Deslys, perhaps; she drew serenades as sugar drew flies. Ann-Marie could hear the words, the man's pleasant voice rising and swaying in a sweet melancholy, and she found in them a sad appropriateness.

"My heart is far away, beside my love,
My heart will ever stay beside my love,
If I may never be beside my love
I pray you, bury me, beside my love."

Ann-Marie sighed and thought that surely there would not be much comfort in being buried with her love. She wanted to be alive with him. She turned and left the window, but the singing voice followed her for a little as it began a new song.

"My lady is fair; she has gold in her hair,
My lady is wise; gives a kiss with her lies,
My lady is cruel; wears my heart like a jewel,
My lady——"

But whatever else it was his lady might be—and so far it was quite descriptive of Pauline—Ann-Marie didn't hear, for she had pulled the covers over her head. It was too reminiscent and too descriptive of another lady, her greatest enemy, Anne of France.

"It cannot be postponed forever," her councilors told her, and when the Maréchal de Rieux added his grave voice, Ann-Marie knew it was true. "You must marry and secure the succession. You must marry!"

"You must marry, you must marry," it went on like a tune all the days. She evaded and pushed it away until everyone's nerves were taut, hoping that time would release Louis. Fifteen months had gone by since he had been imprisoned, but she had not had a word from him. A messenger had finally come from Max, explaining his failure and telling her it would be useless to send any more messages and bribes. Louis was guarded too well.

A note from Dunois was included, telling her not to despair, that they were working steadily for Louis's release and it must come soon.

Finally a suitor offered himself who pleased almost everyone, and even, to some extent, since she was desperate, Ann-Marie herself. It was Maximilian, Holy Roman Emperor, whose first wife, Mary of Burgundy, was dead and who was free for a political marriage. He was important enough for the Breton pride, even if he was impoverished from his hopeless struggle to keep the empire together. He pleased Ann-Marie because he couldn't come in person to be married, and it might be months or years before he could come to consummate the marriage, and when he came she would find a way to refuse him.

Since Ann-Marie couldn't leave her throne to go to him and he couldn't come to her, it would be a marriage by proxy until circumstances changed, marriage for its title and its advantages only.

It would be an easy marriage to slip out of when Louis was free. It gave Ann-Marie freedom from pressing suitors, title, help, and glory, and was no hindrance to her hopes of Louis. An ideal marriage, certainly.

The marriage papers were drawn up, the bridal clothes and stealthy celebrations prepared, quickly and quietly, so that France wouldn't know and object before it was too late. And, in the presence of many witnesses, Maximilian's proxy, an elderly gentleman who was aghast at his own importance, gravely bared his skinny leg to the knee and crawled into the nuptial bed, touching Ann-Marie and thus symbolizing the consummation of the wedding.

The proxy was blushing with pride at his performance, while Ann-Marie's dimples were fighting to be released, for she found it all very funny. Some of the disappointed suitors were hopeless and some were not, figuring, as Ann-Marie did, that it wasn't much of a marriage.

It took months for the news to filter through to France, more months for indignant couriers to ride to Brittany, drawing forth explanatory couriers from Brittany to France. Through all these months Louis crawled out of his iron cage in the morning and crawled into it at night, hungrily and sparingly eating his bread and thin soup, growing leaner and wiser, with no word other than Guérin chose to give of the world that had almost ceased to exist for him.

Almost two years of imprisonment went by, and then one morning Louis didn't crawl out of his cage but lay, uncomfortably huddled, sprawling from one side to another when Guérin reached in and shook him. With his usual unconcern, Guérin call a guard and together they dragged Louis out, his arms catching in contrary limpness on the door and his head bumping as they pulled him onto the floor. Together they lifted him onto the bed and Guérin sent the guard for the doctor. The jailer was sure Louis was meant to die, but, as a prince of the blood, necessary formalities must attend his death.

The doctor came and pronounced it a fatal fever, which was no more than Guérin had decided. Louis was bled, while the jailer left to write a report and sent it by fast-riding courier to Anne, who had demanded weekly reports and had left instructions that in case of emergency she was to be notified immediately.

A fatal fever! The words brought a fever of uncertain anxiety to Anne. Her father would have rejoiced! The Orleans duke, the last of his name, was dying, and Orleanais would soon belong to the Crown. But with the Orleans duke would die Louis, whom she loved and hated and harried, and without whom the world would be barren. When the fever had burned and consumed him, there would be only a blackened, empty place where she couldn't go either to torment or to be tormented.

And there would be a scandal if he died, and Jeanne to accuse a shrinking conscience, Dunois to fear! In a conflicting surge of so many motives that she didn't even try to separate them, hurriedly she sent her own doctor to Louis.

In rigid poise she went through the days, controlling Charles and the kingdom with undiminished competence, preparing herself for the storm that would break with Louis's death. Three times a day couriers came in breathless haste from Bourges with a detailed description of the prisoner's condition.

"Hopeless," they kept saying, "fatal it certainly is. No body so weakened can withstand such a fever; bleeding didn't abate it. It is only a question of time; God's will must be done."

But it became evident that God had other plans for Louis, for even while they continued to maintain stubbornly that he was as good as dead, weakly he came out on the other end of his dark tunnel of fever and feebly began to ascend into life again.

When he opened his eyes after his hot, mumbling dreams were gone, he found himself in another cell, three doctors looking at him in surprise, no signs either of Guérin or of the iron cage, and, unspeakable luxury, a mattressed bed under him! He lay peacefully with growing strength while he wondered if all his comforts would vanish when he was well. But they didn't—mainly because some talk of Louis's illness had gone around the court and had brought Anne the unhappy few moments of a meeting with Dunois. She had refused him an interview, but he had come upon her unexpectedly and, knowing he had only a second, he poured everything he had to say into it.

"If Louis dies in his cell like a dog in a ditch, there'll be hell to pay, and you'll pay it! If he dies, prepare for death yourself!" His voice was menacing, and he walked on before she could answer.

Jeanne came, too, and assailed Anne. Listening impatiently, Anne had a thought worthy of her father. Since Jeanne felt so hotly that more care should be given Louis, why shouldn't Jeanne herself be allowed to give it? Why

shouldn't Jeanne be sent to Louis, and perhaps his lonely
need for human sympathy might accomplish the purpose
her father had tried to attain at Linières with drugged wine
and locked doors?

Anne was shocked at herself for having such a thought,
and it made her realize abruptly that she had gradually
coarsened and that she could now plan coolly, with no feeling at all, schemes that would never even have entered her
mind before she had been regent. It was a callousness that
was useful to a ruler but not becoming to a woman. Well,
since she was a regent and wanted to continue as one, she
had better ignore her womanhood if it threatened to interfere.

So Jeanne, in wondering surprise and gratitude at the
happy signs of relenting on Anne's part, was sent to
Bourges. Timidly she entered the room in which Louis lay,
and though it was a bower of luxury compared to his first
cell, she glanced around in pity and horror. Louis had
weakly raised himself on one elbow and was staring at her,
trembling and excited to see a friendly face.

"Jeanne!" he exclaimed. "My dear Jeanne," and he
stretched out his hand to her.

She hurried to the side of the cot as fast as her twisted
leg would let her, and there were tears in her eyes as she
saw how thin and pale he was.

"Oh! How ill you have been!" Then quickly, to cheer
him, "I've brought you things to make you more comfortable, and news of everyone."

"Tell me all of it!" he said eagerly, and then, wonderingly,
"How were you allowed to come? No one else has been
here!"

"My brother and sister gave me permission," she said. "I
asked to come when I heard how ill you were."

"Jeanne! How good of you to travel all this way. Tell me
everything—I know nothing of what's been happening. How
is Dunois—have you seen him? And what has happened in
Brittany—do you know if the duchess is well? And where
is Georges—still at Rouen? Tell me everything!"

He leaned back, weakened by his excitement, and hastily
she answered his questions.

No, she hadn't seen Dunois, but she knew he was working hard for Louis's release—so was Georges, who spent his

time between Rouen and far-off Rome. He was rising rapidly in the church and might soon wear the robes of a cardinal. The Duchess of Brittany had defied France and married Maximilian of Austria.

That was a surprise, although he had known Ann-Marie could never maintain her betrothal to him. Still, why, of all people, Maximilian of Austria? He would be no help to her. She needed someone closer beside her in Brittany. He sighed.

Jeanne had noticed he hadn't asked for news of his mother. Did he know she was dead? Jeanne wondered.

"Your mother——" Jeanne began gently, but he nodded, and she could see he knew.

"That was the only piece of news they gave me," he said, "and in a way it was just as well she never knew about my defeat."

Quickly, to keep him cheerful, she talked on, giving him all the news of France while she sent for the baskets she had brought from Linières. Louis exclaimed in pleasure when the wonderful luxuries were carried in. Luxuries to him now, when only a few years ago he would have accepted them thoughtlessly as the barest of necessities.

She had brought clothing and bedding. Louis surveyed the well-made white shirts with appreciation and smiled at the sight of sheets, smiling even more at Jeanne's surprise when he told her it was over two years now since he had seen one.

Then his breath came sharply when he saw the contents of one of her boxes.

"Books!" he said wonderingly. "Do you think I'll be allowed to keep them?"

The wildest anger Jeanne had ever known filled her when she realized how cruelly he had been kept from anything that might have made his life endurable. Words of denunciation were piling up in her mind, and Jeanne longed for the moment when she could drench Anne and her meanness with them.

"Certainly you may keep them!" she said in a tightly controlled voice. "I'll send you more when I know your tastes a little better."

Eagerly he told her his preferences, excited at the thought of a wonderful future that would contain books, blankets, clothes, and even sheets, but no iron cage. And when he

saw something else she had unpacked and a little shyly held
out to him, he exclaimed with pleasure. It was a guitar.

"How wonderful! And how thoughtful of you!"

Jeanne blushed with pleasure. To give him, at last, something he loved and wanted, as he had given her his valuable
ring and even more valuable friendship.

"I thought it would be a companion for you, something to
speak to you."

How well she had known his greatest need—another
voice to speak to him in the lonely hours! He looked at her
searchingly and realized again her never-ending thoughtfulness for others.

She was smiling at him and reaching for a small basket.

"Here is something else to keep you company!" And,
raising the hinged lid, she drew out a plump white cat, a
red ribbon around its neck with a little silver bell attached.

Louis laughed and reached eagerly for the soft, furry
animal whose dangling legs clawed wildly at the air and
who meowed in protest. Once in Louis's arms, it settled
contentedly down, and as Louis's fingers tickled the little
pink-and-white ears the cat tucked its forepaws under it,
closed its eyes, and purred loudly.

"This is almost the best of all!" Louis told her delightedly. "Something living—that I can talk to! Has he a
name?"

"Not yet."

"I'll call him Max!" Louis said, as the cat moved and the
silver bell on the red ribbon jingled. "Max Poquelin, because
I miss my Max. Of course you wouldn't know anything
about him—but perhaps, if you should be allowed to come
again, could you find out from Dunois what happened to
Max?"

Jeanne nodded. "Max Poquelin. I'll remember to find
out."

Jeanne remained three days at Bourges, and Louis found
her presence very comforting. As the early darkness came
to the already dim room, they sat by the light of a small fire
in the grate, which Louis never tired of watching and finding beauty in, having been so long deprived of warmth and
beauty. They talked of books and travel more than the
present world, for there was too much to constrain them
both from speaking of Anne or the king.

They never discussed the divorce, but once Jeanne said

suddenly, as though perhaps she would never again have a chance such as this to tell him that as far as she was concerned he was as free as he wanted to be, "I trust that someday you'll be happier with another than you've been with me."

And he didn't know what to answer—for, friendly and pleasant as she was, still she wasn't a wife for him or any man.

When Jeanne left she went back to Linières, not wishing to see Anne yet. She wanted to be alone, and as she thought of it more she decided not to go to Anne with recriminations at all, for it might anger her and Louis would suffer for it. He might be deprived of his books and his fire and his blankets again, and she couldn't bear to think this might happen through a mistake of hers.

Left in comparative paradise with his new comforts and his three-day oasis of companionship in the desert of loneliness, Louis felt well-being and strength welling up in him like red wine filling an empty decanter. Before the warmth of his fire, after a savory dinner of rabbit stew and fresh warm bread, he lounged on his mattress bed, stroked the purring cat, and read the books he had never read as a boy. Coming to him in his maturity, ripe and eager for the pleasure they would bring him, they were as savory and nourishing as his dinner.

Jeanne sent every book in her library to him, but since they were mostly lives of the saints, she sent a message to Blois, directing that a certain part of Louis's father's library be sent to Bourges. Hungrily, Louis read them all.

He read the Greek and Oriental philosophers—in translation, because he had never studied Greek or Persian. In stumbling Latin, which he improved by practice, he read the Roman poets and historians, dazzled and excited by the wealth of wisdom he had so foolishly ignored. In his own language he read novels and dramas and fables and poetry —every book that came was read at least once.

History was his favorite reading and he was impressed with the constant repetition of like events. He had thought, somehow, that his own case was so extraordinary, that his own age was so efficient and sophisticated, and it was an interesting surprise to read of lives that paralleled his own. "There is no new thing under the sun," he read in the

Bible, and his pride in his own age was considerably chastened by the accounts he read of the Chinese dynasties, the wonderful Persian courts, the sophisticated Greeks and the efficient Romans.

"History is philosophy learned from examples," he read in a book by Thucydides, and though he couldn't pronounce the writer's name, he agreed, and, fascinated, studied the examples of history, especially interested in the histories of different forms of government.

He had always taken the divine right of kings for granted, but he couldn't read long without wondering just how divine right entered into it. Looked at dispassionately, was it the best form of government to depend on the lottery of birth for an efficient leader? How often did countries suffer under a madman's reign? And if a king was a madman, was he still also divine? Was election of a leader better, or did that system have as many errors, with election a forced thing, as it had been in Milan, when Sforza had taken the throne by divine might? Voraciously he read to find the answer.

He read the historians of his own times, especially curious to read Philippe de Commines's many articles on the dead king Louis had so hated. His face fell in furious lines as he read Commines's glowing eulogies, and more than once he swore and hurled the book across the room. But he forced himself to retrieve it and read on about this wise, brave, generous, unselfish king he couldn't even recognize.

Acidly he spoke to the cat: "Max, does it seem to you that Commines would have written all these loving words if the king hadn't paid him well and flattered him that he was a great writer?"

Max purred and considered answering but fell asleep instead, and Louis read doggedly on. He came to a good, well-expressed paragraph, nudged Max awake, and read it to him, commenting on it.

"Commines writes well, no doubt of that, and he seems sincere. But of course, Max, you know he only saw the best side of the king."

Max nodded thoughtfully.

"Of course I've only seen the worst side, so maybe I'm even more prejudiced. He was certainly shrewd—and if you can once agree, Max, that his goal was wise, then he had to

ignore our desires for the ultimate good of the country."
Louis thought awhile, and Max yawned.

"But I don't agree that it's a wise thing—taking the long
view, Max—to ignore everyone's needs, because they'll only
rise in revolt, and more is lost to the country than is gained."

Max fully agreed.

These arguments with himself and Max were very stimulating to Louis's mind, and they helped him see a little
deeper into the dead king's character. Up till now it had
seemed only a dark, poisoned well of personal hate. That
there had been poison and hate in it he still saw, but there
had been a motive, too, and, understanding that, he understood Anne better.

Power and personal hate went together much too often,
history told him, and he made a vow to himself that if he
ever emerged and had any kind of power again, he would
never use it to avenge personal grievances.

When it grew too dark or he was tired of reading, he
drew out his guitar and delighted in the voice that answered
him at the commands of his fingers. He put some of his
father's poems to music, sang them to Max, and smiled ruefully over the irony—poems written in captivity by the
father set to music and played by the imprisoned son. And
when it grew late and it was time for sleep, there was no
creaking door, held open by Guérin's dirty, pitiless fingers.
For Guérin was with him no more! Louis hadn't seen him
since the illness, and could only assume he had been passed
on to some other unlucky devil along with his keys, his un-
interested eyes, and his iron cage.

Louis had a new jailer; his name was Gourney, and the
contrast was great. Gourney was large and powerful, but
his strength had no menace in it. It was the large, rather
lovable strength of a bear, amusing and unfrightening. He
was as kind and interested as Guérin had been cruel and
callous, and he did everything he could think of for Louis's
comfort. He offered himself as a partner at cards whenever
Louis wanted companionship. He talked intelligently and he
searched about for news to bring Louis. He admitted
Jeanne's boxes and messages when they came, and was distressed when he wasn't permitted to allow Louis exercise in
the courtyard.

Together with the jailer's kindness, the many comforts
and pastimes, Louis's health swiftly returned. And with the

books to fill his mind with a new maturity, the quiet hours for introspection and growth, the years in prison were, in many ways, the most valuable years in Louis's life and the Tower of Bourges became a tower of strength.

16

Charles, his meager, unkingly body unfortunately clothed in brilliant orange silk that made his light eyes and hair look even paler than they were, sat gloomily in the recessed window seat, looking down into the gardens at Amboise, where his nine-year-old wife played, rolling a big blue ball at her excited little dogs in happy ignorance of her strange life to come.

Anne, within the room, meditatively surveyed Charles, and then she walked to him, her big black-and-white striped skirt swaying and gleaming in the light of the sun that poured in through the casement windows. She placed her arms about his shoulders, standing behind him and looking down over his head at the childish Margaret of Austria at her play.

"You aren't very happy about your little bride, are you?" Anne asked kindly.

Charles shook his head dismally but didn't answer. His father had planned the marriage with his usual contempt for happiness.

"She's much too young," Anne remarked ruminatively. "You need the companionship of a girl of your own age, and we need an heir. I never did think it was a good marriage."

Charles looked up at her in surprise, taking care not to dislodge her arms from his shoulders. He needed all the affection he could find, and the moments Anne gave him were far apart.

Anne smiled into his puzzled eyes. "You need someone who's young and pretty, someone who'll amuse you——"

That was exactly what he needed, and Charles's eyes were alight with the thought.

"Because we've made a mistake is no reason for you to suffer from it forever," Anne said, and stepped back as he

311

rose excitedly from the window. "I've been thinking that we're not committed so deeply. She's only a child and she's not been crowned queen. I think we could do better."

"If we could, Anne, if we could!" Charles excitedly stammered, and she smiled maternally at his eagerness.

"If we could?" she asked indulgently. "You'll never again doubt my interest in your happiness, will you?"

In confusion that he ever had done so, he overwhelmed her with love and promises. She accepted his caresses smilingly.

"I've been thinking about it for a long time, Charles, and I've been gathering together a list of eligible brides for you. You and I will talk about them, and look at their portraits someday soon, and you can take your choice."

"You have portraits, Anne? Let me see them. Now!" He took her shoulders and urged her in the direction of her workroom, where he knew the miniatures must be, and she allowed herself to be urged.

Through the halls they went, Charles laughing and talking with more animation than he had shown in months and Anne falling in with his mood as she seldom did.

At her desk he stood in impatient eagerness while she found a little group of miniatures. She handed them to him one by one, telling the bride's name, country, and dower, and watched his face growing disappointed and gloomy again as he scanned the miniatures, for she had deliberately gathered together an unattractive group of ladies, not one of whom looked even remotely amusing.

When he came to the last one he looked up at Anne and laid them down with a sigh.

"I'm as well off now as I'd be with any of these," he said unhappily.

Anne looked surprised and picked them up to look them through.

"They're not exactly beauties," she admitted, and then, puzzled, "but I thought there was one you'd like. She was young and dark, and I thought rather pretty." Anne shuffled them through again while Charles brightened with a renewed hope. "Oh no!" she suddenly remembered. "I remember now. I laid it aside because I felt it would be impossible!"

"Who was it, Anne?" he asked anxiously. "Let me see it anyway. Why was it impossible?"

Anne looked in another drawer and found a small miniature, which she handed to Charles, watching his face. The portrait was that of a young girl who smiled sweetly and mischievously straight into Charles's eyes. Her dark brown hair was shiningly painted over shell-pink cheeks with pinker dimples in them, and her rose-colored lips curved over a delighted thought. Charles was instantly certain that if anyone had ever been created to amuse him, this girl was the one.

"Who is she, Anne?" he cried. "Who is she?"

"Ann of Brittany," she answered, with malicious delight in her eyes.

"Ann of Brittany!" Charles looked up startled, from the picture. "She's betrothed to Louis and married to Maximilian!" The incongruity of the statement didn't strike them, royal marriages being complicated things sometimes.

"Yes," said Anne, reaching for the picture as though to put it away, but Charles clung to it. "She's married to Maximilian. But we're gong to dissolve it in any case. As for Louis—she may as well forget him!"

"Then why can't I have her?"

She pondered the question. "Well, I suppose it could be done, but I hoped you'd find an easier bride!" She tried to give him the others to reconsider, but he backed away from her with the miniature of Ann-Marie clasped tightly in his hand.

"None of those—no! You could do this for me, Anne. You must!"

She looked her displeasure at his insistence. "Charles— it's too hard—it would take months——"

"But you will, Anne?"

She sighed in exasperated yielding. "Oh, I'll try if you insist."

She watched his transports of enthusiasm with amused eyes, and when he left her to go rejoicingly out for a ride into the forest, she tossed the worthless miniatures back into the drawer and then sank down into a chair and took up the ivory painting of Ann-Marie. She studied the sweet young face and the laughing eyes of the Breton duchess.

"Perhaps," she remembered Louis's voice saying, "perhaps it won't be so hard for me to forget you as I thought. Ann-Marie—yes, her name is Ann too—is very sweet."

He had said that when Ann-Marie was a child; now she was a woman. Had Louis given his love to this smiling picture? The question clutched at her heart like a sharp-nailed hand. Why should she care what he had done with his love? she asked herself in disgust. But she did care, cared with a burning, distorted, antagonistic love that was the most important thing in her life.

Well, no matter what he had done with his heart, Louis's body would never know Ann of Brittany, or any other woman, as wife!

Anne shook her head at the miniature. "You'll never have Louis! I'll never release him to marry you or anyone else. For a husband you'll have Charles!"

The miniature smiled a mischievous, knowing smile, and Anne, in a sudden gust of fury, brought her fist down heavily on the pink-tinted ivory face, watching it crack and splinter into many pieces. The eyes were separated and the mouth had been broken in half, but the smile was still there!

Ann of Brittany herself didn't smile when she received the envoys from France with the proposal that she accept their king in marriage. In a rage at the arrogant way in which the message was delivered, as king to vassal, she arose to terminate the interview and delivered herself with fervor of her sentiments toward France.

"King Charles is an unjust prince," she said boldly but formally, "who tries to despoil me of the inheritance of my fathers! Has he not desolated my duchy, pillaged my subjects, destroyed my towns? Has he not entered into the most deceitful alliances with my allies, the kings of Spain and England, endeavoring to overreach and overrule me? And have I not, by the advice of all of you"—turning to her own councilors, who were aghast at the force and frankness of her speech—"who now counsel the contrary, just contracted a new solemn alliance with Maximilian, King of the Romans, approved by you and all my people?" She swept to the door in a furious dignity and turned there to deliver herself of her final anger. "And if I were free to marry— you all of you know the man I'd choose!"

And out she stalked, her fur-banded skirts swishing with indignation, leaving her own counsel and the envoys from France in an awkward silence, with the echo of her young and courageous words hanging in the air between them, to be gradually disseminated by the smooth, false diplomacies of the elderly men.

"France," they said, smiling at the very absurdity of the

whole affair, "in no way considered that the recent ridiculous exhibition between Ann-Marie and Maximilian constituted a holy marriage."

And the Pope had sent along a little notice to endorse this opinion—an annulment of her marriage. Therefore the girl was as free as the air and should be grateful that she hadn't been punished for her disobedience to the Sable treaty but was being offered the most glorious hand of His Christian Majesty in marriage. Ann-Marie's councilors quite saw the honor and lenience and were sure that with time, and the matter having been properly presented to Her Grace, she would shortly be willing to receive contracts of marriage to read and amend. In mutual courtesy and dislike, they parted, and the steps toward the marriage were in motion.

Ann-Marie's councilors were with her constantly, urging the marriage, and in an aloof and quiet despair that amazed them all, she held them off. She clung desperately to Maximilian, and through him to Louis.

"No!" she kept saying. "No! No, I won't do it! I'll hear no more of it!"

The Maréchal de Rieux, who knew her better and loved her more than any of them, counseled her that this marriage with France was her only choice.

"My dear child, you saw how rebellion against France ended only a few years ago. You wouldn't start all that again, would you?"

Ann-Marie looked at him with the tears that no one else ever saw in her eyes. "We can't rebel against a country that isn't sovereign to us."

De Rieux smiled. "There's no use hiding behind words, Ann-Marie. I'm only advising you as your father would do if he were here."

"I know—I value your advice!"

"Because we claim Breton independence doesn't mean we've achieved it. France is our sovereign"—she looked a protest, but he continued—"by might, if not right. If she chose to invade us again, she has a perfect pretext. We've disobeyed the Treaty of Sable by your marriage to Maximilian, but she chooses to invade us by peaceful means, by marriage, and it seems to me, my dear, in justice to every soul in Brittany, you've no choice but to accept."

Ann-Marie sat in motionless stillness, still refusing the

thought of marrying Charles. Louis couldn't be caged forever. Time was her good friend, and she would descend to any trick to keep him with her.

Charles was hurt at Brittany's furious rejection of him, and Anne used the incident to further his dislike of Louis.

"For your sake," she said testily, "Louis should have been imprisoned at his birth! He has consistently used his freedom against you, although I suppose we mustn't blame him if he's so charming Brittany clings to a memory even if she hasn't seen him for three years."

Charles's eyes clouded at the thought of the pretty Breton's memories of Louis. "She'll forget about him when we are married," he said vehemently.

"I don't know," she said absently. "Once loved, he isn't easily forgotten." Then, quickly, "At least that's what I've heard."

"But she must do as we say," he said, anxious that Anne shouldn't give up.

"It might take an army to change her mind." Anne watched him speculatively.

"Well, then, we'll send an army!" He spoke militantly, but he appealed to Anne in the next breath. "That's what you'll do, Anne?"

"It would be poor policy to let Brittany think she can disregard us," she said thoughtfully.

When Dunois heard the rumors of the proposed marriage, he asked for an interview with the king, but he wasn't surprised to see Anne beside her brother.

Dunois plunged in. "I've begged for Louis's release so many times and offered so many different terms that I've completely exhausted our resources, but now that this Breton marriage is of interest to you, may I offer another kind of ransom?"

Anne coldly nodded permission, disliking his choice of words very much.

"If Louis were free and broke his betrothal to the Duchess of Brittany, she'd see she might as well obey France," Dunois said.

Charles was sulky at the thought of being so unwelcome to the duchess, and Anne was very angry at Dunois's rude frankness.

"We don't need such miserable bargaining," she said, rising. "The duchess will shortly see it's to her advantage to make this marriage. And Louis will remain where he is! That's all either of us have to say!"

And Dunois, muttering savagely to himself, was soon outside the palace. He had sent to Rouen for Georges, who was waiting to hear the outcome of the interview.

"I should have gone myself, Dunois," Georges said sighingly, settling his round girth into a more comfortable position. "You speak so bluntly—say things that do more harm than good."

"I only said what was the truth!" Dunois protested, and the Bishop of Rouen groaned at such a mistaken amount of zeal.

"We'll get nowhere with Madame Anne; we may as well stop trying. We'll find the king alone sometime."

Dunois returned the groan. "It's just as easy to find a horse without a tail! I've tried for almost three years to see the king alone!"

Georges somberly meditated the problem. "I haven't been to court for more than a year—I may be able to see him. I won't ask; I'll wait my chance."

They stayed close to the court, and while Dunois waited, as he had been told to do, in impatient silence, Georges wandered the corridors at court, attending chapel when the king did, going to the entertainments in the evenings, bowing smoothly to the king and Anne as though he hadn't another thought in the world but enjoyment. He made no attempt to gain an interview and spoke to no one about Louis.

After almost three weeks of this, he had his reward!

Anne, the king, and a small part of the court were journeying from Tours east to the castle at Nevers, breaking the trip at Sancerre, a little town only a few miles from the tower of Bourges. Georges traveled with them; Dunois trailed behind.

Georges relied on the disorganization of the trip to give him a few moments alone with Charles, and promptly enough, the morning after they had arrived at the old inconvenient château of the Count de Sancerre, who was overwhelmed by the pleasure of His Majesty's visit, Charles, in an aimless mood, wandered out from the room Anne had appropriated as her temporary study for the three days they would be at Sancerre. Since she had summarily dismissed him to go about his business—"As though I were a child who plays with dolls," he had resentfully told her—he was in a perfect state of mind for Georges's advances.

After the polite amenities had been taken care of, Georges smoothed the uneven robes down over his rounded front and launched his attack. His pink, plump face was pleasantly sympathetic.

"I hope you'll forgive my solicitude"—he spoke gently, with priestly accents—"but I've been worried that you're not well."

"Not well?" asked Charles, surprised but always interested in sympathy, especially this, which seemed so sincere.

"Perhaps I shouldn't have mentioned it"—Georges hesitated—"but I thought perhaps you'd let me help. I know a physician in Rouen who's a miracle man; perhaps you'll give me your permission to bring him to you."

Charles laughed in a bewildered way. "But I'm not ill—what made you think I was?"

Georges seemed overwhelmed with embarrassment. He looked at the king in anguished humiliation and then around the hall to see if they might be heard by other men standing about and talking. Charles, all curiosity, took pity on the discomfited man and urged him into a little alcoved room where they might talk without being heard.

"I've been most indiscreet," Georges confessed in great confusion, "but I beg Your Majesty to believe it was only from an earnest desire to help you. Forgive me for my stupidity—let's speak of something else."

Charles was annoyed and insistent on continuing the subject. "Why did you think I needed a physician?" he asked in his most royal tones.

Georges stumbled unhappily into the explanation. "Well, I've heard and seen how your sister keeps you—secluded from work and pleasure—and I could only think your health wasn't strong. I saw how listlessly you received your sister's entertainments, and although, with all respect to her, the court does seem unusually dull, I was surprised you asked for nothing more lively. Naturally I thought you must be ill, for I know how the normal young man loves gaiety, remembering my friend Louis. You remember his charm and gaiety, of course?"

"I remember," said Charles wistfully, sinking down into a chair, while Georges moved closer and hovered over his prey, like a fat benevolent spider weaving a web.

"If he had been your regent, as he wanted to be, I think life would have been very different for you."

"Perhaps I would have had no life at all," Charles returned stiffly, remembering Anne's words.

Georges looked pityingly at the king. "How you've been poisoned against Louis!"

Charles stirred restlessly. "My sister doesn't like me to speak of him to anyone."

Georges smiled. "But of course she doesn't. It's better from her point of view to keep you away from Louis's friends, who are your own, so that you'll never learn the truth. And never learn what people say of you," he added.

"What do they say of me?" the king asked sulkily, fearing it wouldn't be nice.

"It is not my opinion, but that of all the court, that you're a weakling who doesn't dare to rule alone!" Georges put out his hand placatingly as Charles started to sputter furiously. "You see, this is what your sister doesn't like you to hear—what others are saying of you. She'd like you to be content with your position, but I know you're not a weakling, I know that when you see the truth you'll act. Face the truth, Your Majesty! She keeps you virtually a prisoner, but face this truth also. If you liked, you could order guards to arrest her and they'd obey you."

Charles listened with startled eyes while Georges hurried on, speaking smoothly and with power.

"You wouldn't do that, for you owe your sister much gratitude for the wonderful way in which she's reared you." Charles agreed with that, and had more trust in such an impartial friend of Anne, Louis, and himself. "But when you came of age, did she turn the kingdom over to you, as Louis would have done, with encouraging words and promises of aid when you required it? You know she didn't! She talks of Louis's power, to keep you from freeing him, but what of her—she's taken the throne from you!"

Charles sprang to his feet in rising indignation, either against himself or Anne or this round little man who dared to say such things! The blood came to his face and made his eyes bloodshot and furious. Georges gauged the king's fury and knew the crisis had come. Whether he turned now against Anne or against Louis was within Georges's own power of eloquence. There was a very fair chance of the combined wrath of Charles and Anne alighting on his own head, but he didn't hesitate. To strike a good blow for Louis's freedom was intoxicating, and he continued without any time for fear.

"Speech like this is what she's kept you from—from friends who dare to tell you the time has come to free yourself from her domination! What is your life? Lonely and aimless, without affection and gaiety, but above all, without the right to govern your own country!"

Charles's head was nodding in agreement, and Georges pressed on.

"It's within your own power to have all these things she keeps from you. She isn't the king—you are! You have hundreds of unknown friends who sympathize and love you, who wait only for your signal to crowd about you with their support. Will you refuse to take what every other king enjoys? Just because a woman with no other power but what you give her tells you to do so?"

Charles knew whom he was angry at now. It was his sister, and he began to stride about the room in nervous indecision.

"I've endured it long enough!" he muttered. "As though I were some child who played with dolls!"

"It is infamous!" Georges agreed with fervor. "Everyone says so."

"Well, everyone shall see I'm not to be a puppet king much longer!" Charles turned and shook his fist menacingly at Georges, who agreed that everyone must soon see. "I'll act suddenly and take her by surprise!" But he couldn't think on what project he would act so suddenly.

Georges's heart was beginning to pound so violently he imagined he could see his robes jerking with it. This was the time to attempt Louis's release, and whether he would be able to carry it through without interruption he didn't know. Someone might already have reported to Anne that her brother was in earnest conversation with too good a friend of Louis! Georges sent a prayer to his patron saint and promised the cathedral at Rouen an entirely new altar before he plunged back into the battle of words.

"You mustn't think of arresting your sister!" he said urgently. "She has only been mistaken, and let her greed for power overcome her love of you. I could never," he said pleadingly, "bear to have it on my conscience that I had come between brother and sister. Think of some other way of asserting yourself and showing her and everyone else that you've come to your kingdom at last."

So Charles let himself be dissuaded from arresting Anne, not that he had thought of it for a moment and not that Georges wouldn't have enjoyed seeing it done. But it was an impossibility and they both knew it, although they pretended to each other that they didn't. Charles was in the market for some other startling way to exhibit his new manhood, and Georges offered him some wares.

"You could proceed to the state prison and release all the prisoners," he said tentatively, as though he thought none too highly of the idea himself. Releasing all prisoners was often used by incoming kings to procure popular sentiment for themselves.

Charles shook his head. "Too far to go—and too hot to stand the stench when we get there!"

"Have a great ball at Amboise, a really magnificent affair," Georges suggested, his brows horribly wrinkled in the great effort to think of something to please the king. "Have a masque—do all kinds of lighthearted things. I wish I weren't so sober a person, I could think of things to brighten your life, but unfortunately I'm not Louis of Orleans——" The thought seemed to strike him like a thunderbolt, and he stopped in the midst of his sentence, staring at Charles in great excitement. "But of course! OF COURSE! It's the perfect gesture to show your new freedom. Release Louis!"

He offered it in perfect faith of its being delightedly received, and for a moment it was, but then Charles shook his head.

"He's in the way of my Breton marriage," he said. "Perhaps when I'm married I'll free him."

"But," almost stuttered Georges in his eager excitement, "see how perfect it is! Free Louis, show Anne your power, and Louis himself, I promise it to you, will release Ann of Brittany from her betrothal. He had no way of knowing you wanted her for yourself, or he'd never have thought of it for a moment. I'm a son of the Church, Your Majesty," he said, falling into humble deference, "and I consider my promises sacred. If you free Louis, as in your heart I know you long to do, I promise you he'll go to Brittany himself to further your marriage. I promise it to you, I, Georges d'Amboise, Bishop of Rouen!" and in solemnity he made the sign of the cross over his promise.

Charles was impressed; he hesitated, and Georges assumed his consent.

"It'll be wonderful," he said, his round face all smiles, "to see Louis at your feet, giving you his grateful thanks. He's been so long away; you must have forgotten how amusing he is."

A new thought came to him, and he laughed aloud while Charles waited in eagerness to hear what else there was to this wonderful plan. "You said you wanted a sudden surprise; it comes to me like an inspiration. Free Louis yourself! Let's ride to Bourges, it isn't far, and it's early morning still. We could be there by noon—you could see him yourself——"

The action appealed to Charles, and the thought of so exciting an adventure in a morning that had been cheerless warmed him into impulsive co-operation.

"We could ride out now," he said, "as though we're just going for a ride into the forest, and when we're free from sight we can take the road to Bourges and put spurs to our horses as though the devil were behind us."

Georges thought that the devil might be, but he was all admiration.

"It's easy to see," he said, eying Charles with respect, "what an excellent king you'll be. You put your plans into such quick and decisive execution!"

Charles swaggered under the admiration, wondering why, when it was so easy, he hadn't asserted himself before, and they walked down the stairs, the king adding more dramatic details to the plan in a whisper and laughing loudly about the wonderful hunting they were going to have in the forest. Georges grew more and more uneasy at the bluster, fearful that someone might become suspicious of the not very cleverly hidden double meanings in the king's speeches.

In the courtyard Georges urged the grooms and attendants to more speed, while he anxiously looked over his shoulder toward the castle for any unwelcome approaches. At the same time he laughed and talked with the king, keeping him in a warm and enthusiastic mood. When at last they rode out of the courtyard Georges was consumed with a desire for more haste, but feared it might be suspicious, so the control he put upon the horse's speed took more and more strength of will.

They rode decorously into the forest, and quite by chance,

the king thought, they encountered Dunois, who had been waiting there in hopeful suspense. Dunois was seized with uncontrollable excitement when he saw the king riding out at last with Georges, and when he rode beside them for a way and gathered the story from them both, he was all surprise under the king's eyes, but he and Georges exchanged one exhilarated look of delight.

Dunois was sent on ahead to warn Louis and give him the details of his release, and the rest of the party, when they were well out of sight of the towers of Amboise, put spurs to their horses as though the devil were indeed behind them.

Georges relaxed his tightened nerves, and while he continued to bathe the king in admiration, at the same time he surreptitiously sought to alleviate the discomfort he was suffering from the streams of cold perspiration that were trickling down his back.

17

In the tower room at Bourges there was silence as Louis and Gourney sat intently over the chessboard that lay between them on the square wooden table. Louis leaned negligently on one elbow, watching with amusement the perplexity on his opponent's face. The pleasanter months since Louis's illness had brought a calm humor to his lean face, and the two years of hardship before that had left their marks, too, in the strength and endurance that were evident. He was comfortably clothed in one of the white shirts Jeanne had sent to him and which, unknown to him, her own fragile fingers had happily stitched. His tights were of sturdy wool.

Gourney's matted dark brows were close together over his large, crooked nose; his huge hands hovered uncertainly over the pieces on the board and he sighed.

Louis smiled. "Are you in difficulty, monsieur?"

Gourney dropped his hands into his lap and looked up in despair at Louis. "If my life were to hang upon it, I could not remember where each one goes. Can this one"—picking up a piece—"go here?" laying it down where he thought it ought to go.

"No," answered Louis, picking it up again, "It may move sidewise, or forward, or backward along unoccupied territory as far as it likes, but it may not pass over occupied space."

"Of course, of course!" said Gourney, annoyed with his lack of memory. "You are very patient, Monseigneur. I think you must have told me at least one thousand times. Do you think I shall ever remember?"

Louis leaned back in his chair and laughed. "Well, we are ideally situated for that purpose. We have years at our disposal, and you may ponder one move for a month if you like. It took some time for me to learn it. My uncle taught me when I was seven. He was devoted to the game; this would be a paradise for him, no duties, no interruptions, only chess. It is a shame I could not change places with him; this would suit him very well."

"Sometimes I think I would not mind exchanging places with you either. There are certainly many worries that you do not have."

Louis considered that, still smiling. "There are times when I do not mind my situation any more, but there are many more times when I stand on that little stool and look out of the window, and I see dogs running and fighting, a man working his land with a woman carrying his food to him, children playing and old people walking slowly in the roads, and I'd be glad to give my life if I could have only an hour of their freedom." His voice was grave as he finished, and his smile was gone.

"I hope you will have more than an hour of freedom very soon." Then, wishing to divert Louis, Gourney spoke cheerfully. "I think it amazing that you should have learned this game so young."

"It is easier for children, you know; the Romans proved that they have more retentive memories."

"Then if I were a child I would know where these pieces move, but since I am a miserable forty-seven, I shall have to ask you to place them again for me."

"Certainly, monsieur. Perhaps if you could think of them as persons, with a definite purpose, you could more easily remember their powers."

"Perhaps," Gourney doubtfully agreed.

Louis smiled at the doubt. "Well, we shall start with this piece." He picked it up in his fingers as he talked, illustrating the moves. "This is the king; there is only one, of course, like our king Charles."

"King Charles, with due respect."

"The king can only take one step at a time, this way, this way, this way, and this way. He usually stands behind the queen or some other powerful piece who protects him. Now, this is the queen, only one of her, too. We have no queen as yet——"

"Call her Madame Anne de Beaujeu; she is practically queen," Gourney suggested.

"Madame Anne it is, then. With more than due respect," Louis added wryly. "She has great power. She may move sidewise, forward, backward, or diagonally, also over

unoccupied territory. And there are two of these pieces—
they are gentlemen of the realm, knights, if you prefer—
and we could call this one the Duke of Orleans. He has
very curious privileges; he may jump two spaces forward
and one to the side over occupied territory. He is a very
impetuous fellow, this Duke of Orleans, and he comes suddenly from nowhere and lands here—in Brittany."

Louis was amusing himself with the analogy, and he put
the piece down with a warlike emphasis that bounced all of
the pieces on the board, and Gourney looked up with
startled understanding.

"I wish he hadn't done that; he's likely to be taken."

"But you see he is protected by this other gentleman of
the realm; we'll call him the Duke of Brittany. And they
are both protected by this soldier, who shall be named the
Sire d'Albret."

Gourney leaned back in his chair, shaking his shaggy
head in disapproval. "I am only a novice at this game,
Monseigneur, but it seems to me they've bitten off more
than they can chew."

Louis laughed in agreement. "How much better is your
judgment than theirs, for you see what happens." He illus-
trated again with the pieces. "The soldier d'Albret has a
most changeable mind, and suddenly, without troubling to
tell the two gentlemen that he has withdrawn his protection,
he calls away his soldiers and starts home to paint his stables
or to betray a woman, whatever he had been doing before
he left. Here, you see, are the gentlemen, their main support
gone, protecting only each other, and all around them are
the queen's soldiers. It is the queen's move and she has her
choice. The Duke of Brittany is a little too large to gobble
in one gulp, but the Duke of Orleans she has been wanting
for some little time, and she sends her soldier, La Trémoille, with rows and rows of protection solidly at his back;
they close in on the helpless gentleman of Orleans and—
here we are!"

He removed the Duke of Orleans from the board and
handed him to Gourney for safekeeping, while he looked
about the room and gestured toward the little, barred
window with a wide smile.

Gourney followed the direction of his eyes, and together
they inspected the place to which Louis's unfortunate experiences had brought him.

"It is not so bad as some I have seen," offered Gourney, in defense of his hospitality.

"I know that very well! Compared to the room where I spent two years of misery, this is paradise. And compared to my former guard, the sweet Guérin, you're like the keeper of the holy gates himself."

"That Guérin!" said Gourney with vehement dislike. "He gives our profession a bad name!"

Louis's smile came quickly as it always had. "Now that I come to think of it, it seems an odd profession for so kind a man as yourself? How did you happen to enter it?"

"My father was keeper of the keys in this same tower," Gourney explained, "and his father before him. My eldest son will take my place when I retire." Gourney smiled indulgently. "He's five years old, and his favorite game is keeper of the keys. He has a set of old keys and locks the children in the cellar and barricades his mother in her room —refuses to let them out till they swear allegiance to the king!"

Both men laughed, then Louis said wistfully, "Your sons must give you endless pleasure."

"Whatever it is they give me," Gourney sighed, "it often seems endless." Then he returned to the subject. "This doesn't have to be a cruel profession. It's the person who makes a prisoner of you who's cruel. Now I, for instance, could never send a man like you, we're not speaking of criminals, you understand—to prison for nobody knows how long, but it has been almost three years now, has it not?"

"Very nearly."

Gourney spoke from deep conviction. "I could never put anyone, criminal or not, into an iron cage. When I first saw one, it didn't seem so horrible to me—it had no spikes nor barbs, like some things I've seen—and out of curiosity I crawled into it to see what it was like." Gourney and Louis exchanged a wry glance of understanding. "I soon saw! I couldn't sit or stand or lie down. I crouched in it as well as I could, the iron bars bruising wherever they touched, and a few moments seemed an hour. I twisted into a new position, hoping for relief, but soon my muscles were screaming, and I crawled out thinking a whole day must have passed—and I had only been in it much less than an hour!"

"And there's no doubt but the knowledge you could leave

it whenever you liked made it more endurable for you. I spent every night for two years in one, and the door was locked. You're right to think it's torture fit for hell. The first nights were the most terrible; I remember I prayed for death."

They sat in a moment's somber silence and then Louis went on, seriously but not morosely. "And yet those years brought me something I might never have found without them, something I'm glad I have learned."

In a pitiless room, he had been taught pity. He knew and respected the endurance of bodies, and he had learned patience of mind.

"I've often marveled at the calm, patient way you take this life," Gourney said admiringly.

"It's had its value," Louis said slowly. "Oh—and one other thing I've learned. When your body has been in almost constant pain for a long time, and then that pain is suddenly lifted, a certain selfish greediness for life goes with it. It seems enough to be merely in comfort, your body warm and free from pain, your mind free to read or think. There are so many things now that give me infinite pleasure, small things I can never accept thanklessly again." He smiled. "My plain supper tonight will be an epicurean's feast. I'll eat it slowly and enjoy it, and my bed—— Gourney, have you ever slept joyfully and reverently?"

There was a sincerity in Louis's face and deep emotion in his voice. Gourney shook his head pityingly.

"When I go to bed"—Louis's voice was full of awed pleasure—"I lie stretched out at full length on my back, with my arms flung over my head. Then I turn and I'm on my side for a while, with my warm blankets over me, and I know if I like I can rise and stand before the window and look out for a while, or I can sit before the fire and warm my hands at it. That doesn't seem very exciting to you, I know, but to me it's breath-taking, exquisite bliss!" He laughed lightly, but he meant it.

"Still there must be prisons, you know," Gourney said mournfully in the stillness that had followed Louis's words.

"Must there be?" asked Louis from a great distance, and then, recalling himself, "Yes, of course there must."

"And there must be keepers, but that isn't to say they can't be human. They must follow their orders, which are sometimes stricter than they'd prefer. Now you, for instance

—I'd like to have been allowed to take you out into the air, at least for a walk in the courtyard. It would have been good for you after your illness. I applied for that permission, knowing if I had your word of honor you wouldn't attempt to escape, but the Lady Beaujeu wouldn't grant it, nor would she allow me to ask the king."

"I could have spared you the trouble. She promised me no mercy, and she's kept that promise enthusiastically."

"But for so clever a woman, it seemed to me that for her own sake she would have been more lenient. If our king shouldn't have children, when he dies you'll be king, and then where would she find herself?"

"She is also clever enough to see that I'll never be released—alive. Charles is already married to Margaret of Austria; there's no doubt when she is old enough Charles will have children. And she'll make doubly sure, for when Charles's first son is born, and I'm not an heir presumptive, a very sudden death will come to me."

Gourney stirred uneasily. "She'd never do that while I was here to protect you!" he said sturdily, but in embarrassment at his heroics.

"Then you'll not be here! So, Gourney, thank you, but don't petition favors on my account; it's completely useless."

Gourney bent back over the chessboard, pleased with Louis's gratitude, and they resumed the game. With names and purposes to add to the wooden pieces, Gourney was able to remember better what each was able to accomplish. He became very fond of the game, but all his life through he called the king piece Charles, the queen Anne, and the two knights the dukes of Orleans and Brittany. He never liked the soldiers, who were all d'Albrets on one side and La Trémoilles on the other, and he always gave d'Albret an extra bump as he set it down, in punishment for his treachery.

The game progressed in silence, so that the sudden clatter in the courtyard attracted both their attentions. There were never many visitors to Bourges. Gourney got up quickly from the table, walked to the stool under the high window, and mounted it to look out. Louis turned to watch, and as Gourney peered out from between the bars a sudden surge of excitement went through his large frame and his huge paws tightened on the window ledge. He got quickly off the stool, turning and beckoning Louis to come and look.

"You have a visitor, Monseigneur! I think it's your cousin, the Count of Dunois."

"Dunois!" Louis was at the window in a few steps and mounted the stool to see for himself. "It is! It's Dunois!"

Gourney hurried to the door in a flurry of excitement. "I'll unlock the upper doors. Perhaps he has good news for you!" And he left, running in his eagerness, while Louis got down from the stool, walking about the room nervously, his eyes on the door and his ears alert to hear the first sounds of Dunois's approach. His excitement mounted as he heard men's steps and men's voices growing louder, and in a fever of eagerness he watched Gourney open the door. He heard Dunois's deep, brusque voice before he saw him.

Dunois was speaking to Gourney. "I suppose I'll be lucky if I find Monseigneur in?" he asked, laughing, but there was an excitement in his voice that contradicted the jesting words. In a moment his strong bulk stood in the doorway and he was able to see what he had been striving for three years to behold, Louis's eyes in enthusiastic welcome.

They met in a strong embrace, Louis's arms about Dunois's large shoulders, Dunois's arms feeling the leanness in Louis's body and his eyes seeing the lines of strength and maturity in Louis's face.

"Dunois," Louis was saying, "it's wonderful to see you at last. Wonderful, and unexpected!"

They drew away from each other, embarrassed at so much emotion, and Dunois looked away from the mist in Louis's eyes, around the room, and spoke in pretended amazement.

"You do very well for yourself! While I wear my breeches out on the back of a horse, riding to Tours, to Brittany, to Amboise, to hell and gone, you sit cozy by the fire and pet your cat. You like this better than your other apartment I wasn't able to see?"

Louis laughed. "Quite a good deal better. The other had too much iron in it."

"Clever of you to be so ill you had to be moved."

Louis agreed with reservations. "It would have been cleverer if I hadn't been so ill I was almost completely removed."

"Nothing would have pleased Madame Anne better. She was hoping to hear that you had died from natural causes."

"Starvation and the iron cage—are they natural causes?"

"Yes, I think she would put them under that heading. But listen—Georges has accomplished, with his slithering tongue, what I never could do! He's bringing you freedom, Louis!"

Louis stood in a sudden chill of shock, the flesh prickling out all over his body in cold excitement.

"Freedom!" he repeated, staring at Dunois. "Tell me!"

"I rode ahead to prepare you—Georges and the king are following—they'll be here very soon. You'll be a free man this afternoon by the king's hand!"

"And Anne?"

"Madame Anne," said Dunois, his tone cutting, "knows nothing—and when she does, it will be too late. You'll be free and we will go to war before we will let her take you again!"

"Oh no! There'll be no more wars over my little problems."

"There won't need to be. Georges has goaded the king into acting for himself. I think he'll like the sample so well that he'll continue."

"There's no use trying to find words to thank you and Georges——" Louis was beginning, but Dunois, knowing there was much to say before the king arrived, cut him short.

"There are conditions to this release, of course."

"Conditions?" Louis looked at Dunois, who averted his eyes. "I can see you don't care for them much—so I won't either."

"What does it matter, if they bring you freedom? This'll be news to you—but Charles is planning a marriage, and he needs your help for it!"

Louis was surprised. "He *is* married."

"He *was* married. It's been annulled and the Austrian child will be very politely returned to her father, Maximilian. Madame Anne has another lady in mind for her brother."

"Who?" asked Louis, wondering in what way his help could be needed.

"Ann of Brittany!" Dunois said unhappily, looking away from Louis's start of annoyed surprise.

"But Ann-Marie's married too!" Louis protested.

"No—the marriage has been annulled by the Pope and France. But she refuses to marry Charles, because she considers herself still betrothed to you. That's where you must help."

This was more than Louis could understand. He had heard of Ann-Marie's marriage and had felt that she was now entirely lost to him, even if he should be able to regain his freedom. However, he had understood the pressure and necessity that had made her marry. What he hadn't understood was that she had married Maximilian to protect her betrothal to himself. He had never considered her love more than a child's hero worship, and he didn't know how desperately she had fought to stay free.

"But I can't make her marry Charles if she doesn't wish to! If my freedom depends on that condition, I refuse it."

Dunois was aghast. His blunt, strong face showed his horror at the thought of Louis's refusing the freedom it had taken three years to obtain.

"That would be insane," he said vehemently, "to throw away your freedom for nothing! Madame Anne will take the Breton for her brother any way you look at it. She has a large army ready to march on Brittany, and the marriage will be a part of the treaty that follows Brittany's invasion."

"Brittany invaded again!" Louis remembered the outcome of the last invasion and felt old.

"So you must persuade Ann-Marie to submit for the sake of all the Bretons! Even if you were free, you can't ever marry her. There's another condition to your freedom," he added grimly, knowing he was going from bad to worse.

"What is it?"

"You must recall your petition for a divorce."

"You're a positive treasure chest of conditions today, Dunois," Louis said with wry thoughtfulness, lowering himself slowing into his chair, picking up the pieces on the chessboard and regarding them with great interest.

At last Louis spoke quietly. "The gift is nullified. To give me my freedom and at the same time to take away my life's object—what have I left to hope for? If I accept these conditions, I accept defeat from the dead king. I think it would be easier for me, Dunois, to remain here until I die than to admit defeat at his hands."

Dunois was growing frantic. The king would soon be here to find a very lukewarm welcome, or even a complete refusal unless Louis could be persuaded back to eagerness.

Dunois wished he possessed George's slithery tongue at this crisis.

"It won't be a defeat, Louis, it'll be another lost skirmish, but we should be used to those by now."

"By God, we should!"

"What's one more to discourage you? We haven't come to the decisive battle yet, and when we do, do you want to be sitting here moping in the dark? You must take this chance we've given every hour out of three years to snatch for you. Think of Madame Anne—she'd love to see you die here! This is the first thing the king has ever dared to do without her, and for the sake of all of us you must see he's encouraged to act for himself!"

Louis didn't answer. He picked up the queen piece and rolled it thoughtfully in his hands. Dunois thought of the king and Georges, galloping closer with every second, and then suddenly he felt relief, and annoyance at his own denseness. He hadn't yet used his most powerful piece of persuasion.

"Think of Georges, then, if you won't think of yourself!" he said urgently. "Where will he be if you refuse to leave? Both the king and Anne will turn on him—he'll reap the entire punishment. And I'll inherit what's left over."

"I can't let that happen," Louis said slowly, and he put down the queen piece with decisive emphasis. "But it shouldn't have been promised that I'd help seize Brittany."

"She'll seize it anyway!" Dunois cried in frantic annoyance at Louis's reluctance. "Sitting in this murky hole has addled your brains! I tell you, I swear it by every martyred saint who ever sizzled on the fire, she's ready to take it by war; I've seen her army and it waits only for her word. You saw what happened once; you saw the siege of Nantes, do you want to see it again?"

"No."

"Then you must discourage the Breton! Go to Nantes, as Georges promised you would, and make her see it can't be avoided. It has to be a marriage, Louis—there are no two ways about it; there is only a choice of marriage by peace or by war."

"Such a marriage!" Louis protested. "Charles is no more fit for marriage than his poor sister Jeanne."

"Kings are kings, and whether they're sickly fools besides has no connection! I'm not saying it's right to marry Ann-

Marie to our imbecile—I like her as well as you do—but
we're in no position to question the rightness of a king's
desires. Someday we may be. The king's learning to walk
alone; you must be there to guide his steps. This isn't defeat; it's a chance at victory! God's teeth!" he exclaimed as
he heard the sound of horses galloping into the courtyard.
"They're here!"

He leaped up on the stool and looked out the window.
"Louis—look—there's your freedom getting off his horse."

Louis looked out and down. The height foreshortened the
figures, but he could see that Georges's rapid waddling walk
was nervous and eager. Charles was strutting proudly as
they walked up to the big door that was already open for
them.

There was his freedom! He would ride a horse again—
feel the fresh wind in his face! He would walk on yellow
autumn leaves and feel their crispness beneath his feet! He
could lie on his back underneath a willow tree and look up
at the sky. He could go in rooms and close doors—or leave
them open, as he chose! He would be free!

And yet—Ann of Brittany. How could he keep the
promise Georges had made for him? He couldn't. He shook
his head. Dunois saw it and worried. He started to speak,
but the cell door was opened, and in the doorway stood
Charles, red-faced and panting, Georges behind him!

Louis looked at Charles steadily for a second. Some of
the questions he had been asking himself about the divine
right of kings had a negative answer here in this silly, fickle
man who had been born King of France. Evidently it was
only a good system of government when the accident of
birth that made a king was also fortunate enough to give
him intelligence and stability. A king must be more than a
man, for on his whims a country depended for its life, his
words were formed with a royal breath that made them
commands, the destiny for thousands hung open the breath
of kings——

Then he was conscious that his face must be reflecting
his derogatory thoughts, for there was an ominous stillness
in the room. Georges flashed an apprehensive glance at
Dunois—the silly smile had begun to fade from the king's
lips. Then abruptly the silence changed, as Louis came
quickly forward and dropped to his knee before the king.

In this crisis he could have refused his freedom, but he couldn't fail his friends.

Warmth and relief poured back into the room as he deferentially took the king's offered hand.

"Your Majesty," he said gratefully, "thank you for my freedom!"

18

At noon, when the silver gong had been sounded for lunch, Anne emerged from her temporary study and descended the long dark staircase to the dining hall, talking with her secretary.

In the dining hall she walked alone among the small group of bowing attendants to Count de Sancerre's table, where she would sit with her flattered host, the king, and Pierre.

Charles didn't come, and she was informed that he had gone hunting. That was quite unusual, since she generally made his plans for him, and she didn't enjoy her luncheon when she was told that Georges d'Amboise had gone with the king. She considered what she would say to Charles when he returned, as she disdainfully pushed pink slices of ham and juicy wedges of venison pastry about on her plate with her gold knife.

Pierre came and sat beside her and they talked a little, not for the pleasure they found in each other's words, but for the appearance of family solidity. Pierre bent his blond head over his plate, not seeming to find any enjoyment in the food, but it was there, so he ate it. He was like that, his wife thought, with the contempt that had grown dim and familiar and a part of herself. If a plate of muddy, uncooked thistles were placed in front of him he would eat them, with no question in his blue eyes. He would think, if he thought about it at all, that someone's—anyone's—decision was more likely to be trustworthy than his own. He was a very healthy man. His cheeks were flushed with the sun and his eyes were clear; his yellow hair was crisp and curly and his walk was strong and upright. He was sturdy but not fat, although well into middle age. However, his diffident, uneasy manner detracted from his strength, and in spite of his well-made and handsome body, he gave an impression of timidity. He was frightened of his wife, ashamed of his position, suspicious of his friends, and uncomfortable with women. He did as he was told and asked only that he be allowed to slip through the rest of his life with a minimum of pain and trouble.

"You haven't eaten very much," he said to his wife.

She looked at him, said flatly, "That's true," and got up to leave the table.

She returned to her study with indigestion and an uncomfortable mind. When the afternoon wore away and still the king didn't return, her imaginary speeches to him became more and more angry. She dismissed her secretary, and he went thankfully away, much as the ill-fated Oliver le Daim used to slink out of her father's presence on the bad days. Le Daim was long since dead. He had been executed by Anne's orders as a concession to the nobles who had hated him for his closeness to the king, her father.

Continuing her work alone, Anne felt a distinct uneasiness chilling her. With Georges all day, there was no doubt but that Charles would be seriously unsettled again about Louis. She listened for sounds of the returning hunting party, and when she heard the clattering shoes of the horses on the gray stone-paved courtyard she hurried from the room and down the stairs, her full skirts trailing on the stair treads, tumbling down after her. Her white hand on the banister slid rapidly along, and as she came out into the lower hall a new clamor reached her ears. Men were shouting in excitement, and ahead of her, out of the carved doors that were held open, she could see them hurrying, dukes and courtiers, servants and soldiers, all moving toward a group of men who had only just alighted from their horses. She couldn't imagine what it was about, but a premonition of disaster came to her.

She swept even more rapidly out the doors onto the gray stone portico that overlooked the courtyard, her eyes searching the moving, shouting group of men for Charles, fearing an accident. Then she saw him, and she breathed a little easier, for he was standing beside his horse, laughing and shouting in animation, an animation that she feared, since it was joined to the laughter of Dunois and Georges. And then she stopped so suddenly that she almost over-balanced herself, for there in the midst of the congratulating, shouting group was Louis, his hair black and his face white in the late afternoon sunlight.

Some instinct must have told him she was there—some element in his body that always reacted to her presence—for he looked up to the top of the stairs where she stood, over the heads of the excited crowd, and they exchanged a look, as they once had over the bowing heads in a ballroom years ago. But there was no loving welcome in her eyes and no happy confidence in his. Between them was the shadow of the stone tower of Bourges and the iron bars of a cage.

She couldn't sustain his look, and she turned abruptly before anyone else should see her there. She went in a sleep-walker's daze back to her study, to walk about, picking letters up and putting them down without seeing them, to straighten her desk into an order she immediately disarranged, and all the time to hear the shouting in the court-yard that gradually diminished and to see the dark eyes that had looked at her.

She felt physically ill with a heavy nausea and a headache that beat at her with dizzying fierceness. A suspicion she had been trying to evade for some weeks turned into a horrible certainty. She was pregnant. Her knees melted under the dreadful truth, and she sank down into the chair before her desk, staring down at the polished surface. Why should this have happened to her? She had never wanted children, had taken care to see that she had none, and now, at a time when she least of all wished to be distracted from the affairs of the kingdom, she was in this disgusting condition. She thought of the things she might still do to evade it, but she felt grimly that if she had conceived, after all the pains she had taken to see that she didn't, then she would bear the child, too!

‚ Charles came to her after a while, bringing Louis with him, flanked by the triumphant Dunois and the wary Georges. Anne had put aside the thought of her pregnancy for a later, less crowded moment. She would need all her wits to deal with the problem of Louis's freedom. She would have to wait until he could be forced into a provocative act; in the meantime her position wasn't so strong as it had been. Charles could be subdued again, but it would take time and trouble to keep him that way, now that he had tasted the sweets of power. How little time she had to spare, and how little energy, especially with this new drain to be put upon her strength. She made a savage, pulling gesture with her clenched hand, as though she would like to drag the forming child from her body. What a wretched jest, to have been born a woman! So bitterly to need a man's impregnability, a man's inheritance, and to have instead this open body, this inferior position.

Charles swept in with a grand air, presenting his results of the hunting expedition with a braggart pride that annoyed everyone. Certainly Louis's freedom was too vital a thing to be cheapened by a sportsman's pride, but Charles had no diplomacy and not even the sensibility to see it was needed.

Anne spoke cool and formal words, treating this act of Charles's as though it weren't a surprise to her at all.

"Monseigneur," she said, her eyes not quite raised to his, "we hope you've used the past unfortunate experiences to good advantage. We hope now you've been pardoned that you'll be able to find contentment in conditions as they are and not attempt any more rash schemes for your own advancement."

Dunois stirred and muttered, Georges's smile was hard and set, but Louis answered reflectively.

"I've thought over the past experiences, and for *many* of the things that have happened I'm sorry."

That wasn't exactly satisfactory to Anne, but she accepted it as repentance for his past sins. "I'm sure you are. There are ways in which you can prove your sincerity and your gratitude to the king for his free pardon, and I'll summon you from Blois when we have returned to Amboise and are ready to see you. Until that time we wish you to remain at your home."

Charles began a protest, but Anne stopped him with a look. His humiliated, flushed face aroused pity in Louis, but Louis didn't at all mind having to remain at Blois, although it was technically a further reprimand. He hastened to agree.

"Thank you. I'll be glad to rest for a while at home." He turned to Charles. "I appreciate your understanding my need for quiet, and I'll wait eagerly for your summons."

Charles felt a little better, a little more like a king, although he would have preferred to keep Louis close to him at court, for he felt he would need continual reminders of his kingly act. Now that he was back with Anne again, his bravery was dwindling.

Louis was dismissed; he bowed again to Anne and left, followed by Georges and Dunois, but the unlucky Charles was requested to remain a moment with his sister. When the door closed behind the three men, he stood before Anne, his knees beginning to turn liquid. She eyed him for a moment in sharp dislike and then she began.

"What have you done, you stupid fool?"

And soon, under the acid of her tongue, the act that had seemed so splendid and golden tarnished and was a senseless, dangerous thing.

Louis, Dunois, and Georges turned their horses' heads toward Blois and raced, the three of them, for the joy of it until Georges's soft fat protested and he drew his horse to a panting halt. Dunois and Louis stopped and, turning, rode back to him, calling him a tender little lady but loving every pound. They all stood together in a little circle in the road, their horses moving about, rump to rump, jerking at the bridles, eager to race again.

Georges drew quick shallow breaths, and Dunois laughingly remarked, "You act as though the horse had been riding you!"

Dunois showed no signs of exertion, but Louis was tired, too, having been so long kept from exercise, and he was glad to be riding more slowly, the three horses keeping sedately abreast. Louis tried to express some of his gratitude, but they shouted him down and threatened to put him back again if they heard another word on the subject. Nevertheless, they were pleased at his sincerity, and the entire world seemed practically perfect to them now that Louis was back to share it with them.

When the towers of Blois came into sight, Louis couldn't speak for the emotion that shook him. He had never thought much about his home, its beauty or its value to him, except as a possession that might be taken from him by another's greed, but distance and absence had made its outlines clearer to him. He had often looked out from Bourges and in his mind had seen the high towers over the willow trees, the shaded gardens that sloped down to the Loire, and the small village that drew its protection and sustenance from the stone château of the Orleans family.

Now he was home again and it was as friendly and familiar as though he had never been away. The winding road led from the village up the hill to the castle through the blossoming hawthorn trees, and the wild hares scurried across from one side to the other. Then came the more formal avenue of poplars that led directly into the courtyard, overlooked by the tall, oblong windows of the château.

There was no one of his family to meet him at the door. His mother's presence he felt, and as he looked through the beautiful luxurious rooms he saw her everywhere, sitting in that chair, her young blond head bent over her embroidery; in the little salon, running about with him, playing games with Marie-Louise and Pierre; on the flagstone terrace, overlooking the river, and he was glad to remember her that way, instead of in later, unhappier years. Even de Mornac was no longer there. Aging, and unable to manage all the work, he had taken his considerable savings and gone back to his home in Gascony to finish his life in comfort and indulgence. Dunois had secured another steward, Alexandre Larat, who showed no signs of being de Mornac's equal.

But Max's grinning face was there, and that helped make it a home-coming. Max practically wept when he saw the very plain clothes Louis was wearing, and he was in despair later when he tried to assemble a more fitting costume. None of Louis's clothes fit him any more—not even the red coat with the golden porcupine. Louis had lost weight and his figure had changed. Max was consoled when Louis gave him most of the clothing and told him to order new. The first thing Max ordered was a copy of the wonderful coat.

Louis ranged over the whole enormous house, amused with the extent of the home he had taken for granted for so many years, and now, after the cramped years in prison, seeing it with new eyes. In the luxurious months that followed he enjoyed all the things that he had missed, including the company of Georges and Dunois. He gained a few pounds and hardened them into muscles with constant exercise. When luxury lost its bright novelty, for it was no longer essential to him, and Georges had gone back to Rouen and Dunois to his home, Louis began to think of the future again.

One of his first concerns had been to send a courier to Brittany with news of his release and word that he would be there himself at an indefinite time when he was allowed to travel, and his second concern had been to send a messenger to Linières with the news and his gratitude to Jeanne for her comfort during his imprisonment and her part in his release.

Eyes at court grew round and big as Anne of France grew that way too. She kept herself rigidly at work, sparing herself nothing, and when she was ill she was quietly and thoroughly ill in the prayer closet adjoining her study. Then she returned to her work with stern composure. There was plenty of amusement at her expense, for she wasn't well liked.

"I'll wager," one silken lady whispered to another behind a flirtatious fan, "that she didn't even enjoy the beginnings."

"It's hard to tell," the other one returned, "what the great lady enjoys. Perhaps when she lays down her pens and keys and takes off her virtuous-looking dresses, she's as playful and coy as I know you must be. Perhaps she giggles and pretends she's a little white rabbit pursued by the big strong hound, and perhaps she runs round and round the room in her pink skin with Pierre panting after her!"

But that "perhaps" was too much for the ladies, and their laughter broke out high and sharp, squealing in uncontrollable mirth at the impossible picture, and Anne, from the other side of the room, turned reproachful eyes on such undignified levity.

The hour came at last. It was a girl, to Anne's bitter dismay. She suffered the birth pains almost indifferently, she was so glad to have them at last, and was back at her desk in a week, very tightly laced and more exhausted than she would admit, but back, anyway.

Anne was ready now to proceed with the Breton marriage, and she summoned Louis to Tours for an interview with herself and the king.

"Monseigneur," she began, speaking for Charles as usual, "you remember, of course, the promises you and your friends made us?"

Louis remembered, but wished he didn't. "Of course I remember, but I know you won't need my interference. Naturally the king doesn't wish to have others manage his suit."

He knew he was only whistling in the dark, and Anne's

derogatory smile showed him how little she thought of his hopes.

"On the contrary, Brittany is being stubbornly foolish, and I think it's very possible we'll have to proceed to war unless someone can be found to convince the duchess she's being very stupid. My brother believes you're the man to persuade her."

He turned appealingly to Charles. "Won't it bring you more trouble than good to marry such a reluctant country?"

Anne raised her eyebrows and her shoulders in an expressive gesture, as much as to say, "You see. Just as I told you. He's trying to evade his promises."

Charles frowned, walking back and forth, turning to look backward at Louis in displeasure. Louis knew he was in trouble, but he went on, for his little Breton's sake.

"I hope you won't think I'm trying to break the promises my friends made for me. I wouldn't have made them myself, since I feel the marriage isn't a wise one. I know the Bretons—I know them well."

"We're quite aware of that fact," Anne spoke coldly.

"I know their independent spirit. You'll have nothing but trouble and revolt if you force this marriage."

Charles waited for Anne to answer, but she said nothing, leaning back in her chair and smiling, well pleased with Louis for the effect he was producing on Charles. Louis knew that and wished he could be alone with the king. His words might have some persuasion then. At any rate, he had to say them, alone or not.

"Let Brittany stay as it is. You can take it—you understand I don't doubt that—but it will give you only trouble, and you won't keep it."

No one answered him. Anne was leaving the burden of this interview to Charles, who had brought it on himself. Let him see, now, how he liked Louis at freedom! She smiled to herself and on them both, and it was hard to say which one found her the more irritating.

"Are you trying to repudiate your promise?" Charles finally demanded, facing Louis angrily.

"I'm only trying to point out that you'll be making a poor bargain. You'll have a bride who's thinking only of her own country, not yours. She'll be homesick, resentful, and unpopular. You'll have a province at some distance from you; it will take money and money and more money to keep because it will be in a continual state of minor revolt against you until the moment comes when it explodes!"

Anne's amused laughter came, blunting the point of Louis's words, and Charles repeated his angry question.

"Are you trying to evade your promise?"

There was a moment of silence, and then Louis spoke the inevitable. "No, Your Majesty. If that's what you wish, it will certainly be better for everyone if I can persuade the duchess, although I doubt if I can——"

"That's the only point which we don't doubt," Anne assured him. "I think it's very wise of you to go. I think the king wishes you to proceed there immediately, and to be certain everything goes smoothly, my brother and I will follow you and station ourselves close by—in our town of Châteaubriant."

The Breton town of Châteaubriant had been ceded to France under the Sable treaty.

"With an army?" Louis asked, looking directly into her eyes. She didn't turn away, although her eyes flickered for an instant, and he could see the light of malice there.

"It would be safer," she said. Although she didn't say why it would be safer, she gave the impression that Louis might dare to plunge himself into a new rebellion. "If you'll prepare to leave tomorrow, my brother and I will leave the following day. And we wish you'd make it very clear to Brittany"—she rose and spoke imperatively—"that we've waited long enough for a consent it isn't necessary for us to have at all. Our patience is wearing very thin, and we expect their duchess in immediate—*immediate*—marriage, or there will be reprisals for their disobedience!"

With these words loud in his mind, Louis rode to Brittany; and, face to face with the Duchess of Brittany, the words seemed even more cruel and ominous. Ann-Marie came running toward him in her eagerness, and he was amazed at the change in her. There was none of the child left. She was a woman, a graceful, lovely one, whose eyes held a deep welcome for him, deeper even than he knew, and whose warm words made pity for her come up in his throat. He took both her hands and held her away from him, inspecting her, and she stood in sparkling happiness under his gaze, knowing full well that she was a pretty sight. Her dress was a deep rose satin, and her dark hair was worn in a style very attractive to her provocative little face.

It was parted in the middle, braided, and the braids wound in flat wheels over her ears.

"What have you done to her?" he asked.

"To whom?" she smiled, bewildered.

"To my plump little friend with the dimples. These last lonesome years I thought of her so much—now I find she isn't here any more."

"Are you disappointed?" Ann-Marie asked in some surprise, for there was regret in his voice, and she was piqued that he should prefer a plump little girl to her present self, when her own greatest wish had been for more maturity so she could make him forget another woman.

"No—far from it," Louis replied. "But I need those dimples in my life."

She smiled and the dimples came, not the deep ones in the round, childish cheeks that he remembered, but suggestive shadows of coquetry and mischief in a face that had been refined by experience and maturity.

"I haven't used them much since my father died and since you were imprisoned, but now you're free, they shall be too. Come and sit here, Louis"—she drew him by one hand toward a small settee before a crackling fire—"and tell me everything that's happened since I saw you."

"I'm sorry I could never send you any messages. I knew how anxious you must be, but no matter how I tried——" He shrugged.

"I know," she agreed, "I tried too. There seemed to be no bribe large enough."

"They were all too frightened to take any."

"It's over, anyway," Ann consoled him, laying her hand softly on his, and he took it gratefully. "You're free! You can get your divorce here, and we'll marry."

Radiant with expectancy, she looked at him, shivering with happiness when he raised her hand to his lips and kissed it gently. She swayed toward him, instinctively raising her lips to meet his, her eyes half closed in a thoughtless and complete surrender, but they opened again in an amazed painfulness of incompletion when she saw him turn jerkily away from her, his face strained and his lean jaw line tight. He released her hand and stood up, looking down at her with a pity she couldn't understand.

He looked at her young, dark-haired beauty, and what he had to do appalled him! He thought desperately for an alternative. He could stay, in rebellion again, and pursue his divorce from here, close the gates of Nantes and stand the siege. That was what he wanted to do. And he knew it was impossible. The French Army would take them in two weeks or less—it was already there, waiting at Châteaubriant, forty miles to the north. War would only bring Brittany death and a bitter treaty. The end of the war would see Ann-Marie ignominiously married to Charles, with the bitter knowledge that it had all been for nothing.

"There is no way to say this gently, to make it pleasant, because it isn't, but, Ann-Marie, I must tell you I've been sent by the King of France to persuade you to the marriage."

Ann-Marie didn't move, nor did her eyes. She felt as though her muscles would never move again, they were so numb with the shock.

"I know what you're feeling." Louis's voice was somber. "No one should know it better than I! I can't even attempt to console you. I can only say it's inevitable, and someday you'll be glad you didn't offer useless resistance. If I were free to marry you, you know how happy it would make me. But I'm not free, and sometimes I think I never will be." His voice stopped. There was no use piling words upon words, and he couldn't stand the look of pain in her eyes. He sat down beside her and took her hand again, feeling how cold and nerveless it was, stroking it in an agony of desire to do something to help her.

But she snatched her hand from him as though he were the most distasteful thing in the world. She turned on him a look of such scorching contempt that although he had expected anger from her, he was surprised at its intensity.

"I should have known!" she said, her distinct words intense with venom. "I should have known that you're French first and then a man! You wanted Brittany, for yourself, if you could, and if not, then you'll help some other Frenchman steal it." She stood up, her body prickling with the returning blood that had been so suddenly chilled. She put her cold hands to her aching head. "How childish and naïve I've been! We have a saying here in Brittany, and I must have forgotten it. We say, 'Leave your heart and your jewels at home when you travel to France!' But see what a fool I've been. I didn't even go to France to be robbed; obligingly France comes to me."

"I expect you know your words hurt me, and they're not true!"

She turned her head from him in contemptuous unbelief. "You can go now and tell your king you've entirely failed, except that you've relieved my mind of a mistake concerning yourself. We can call this interview closed!"

Experience had given her a true imperiousness, and even her voice was impressive.

"Oh, Ann-Marie let's not make this worse by deliberately misunderstanding. Surely you can see my position. An army has followed me—a large one! It's only five hours ride away. Think before you subject your country to invasion again. Remember the men who died before!"

"I remember them," she said, "and there wasn't one who died for Breton independence who regretted it. We'll continue to fight, and if we die, then we'll die, but we won't be submitting to cowardly fear, as some others have done."

"You mean that's what I've done, of course," he said steadily. "Very well, then I've submitted to it. I'm ready to admit it's easy to be brave for oneself—easy to fear for you. There's no help for it, Ann-Marie. Marry on an equal basis with France and you'll gain many advantages."

"The advantages will be an imbecile husband, an exile life in France, and nothing to do with my country's government," she said stiffly, and Louis sighed.

"I couldn't make a gallant out of Charles if I tried. But you'll be forced to marry him in any case. That's all I'm trying to make you see."

"Well, you've failed, then, for I've quite finished with the subject and I'll ask you to leave Brittany tomorrow with my answer." She walked to the door and he quickly followed.

"Ann-Marie, will you consider it overnight, before you come to a decision?" he begged.

"I have come to a decision." She walked out of the room.

"Well, may I see you before I leave tomorrow?" he asked urgently, following her.

"If I have anything further to say, I'll let you know," she answered, unmoved, and continued on her way to the stairs.

He watched her go, her pretty figure moving swiftly and erectly down the wide hall and up the long flight of stairs, disappearing, as the landing turned, without looking back. He was completely miserable, and he went to find the

Maréchal de Rieux, who was waiting to learn if Louis had succeeded.

"Perhaps you'd better go and talk to her," Louis said, sitting down wearily in a chair across from the older man. "I've done nothing but harm."

De Rieux, gray with age and depression, sighed.

"She's too brave, too brave altogether. She refuses to think Brittany would be defeated. To me it's so plain that we're already defeated I wonder how anyone could not see it, but she's young and hopeful."

Then, after a moment, de Rieux spoke energetically.

"We must save her, Monseigneur, you and I."

Louis looked at him earnestly. "How?"

De Rieux spoke in a quiet voice. "The king and his sister are at Châteaubriant, expecting an immediate marriage. I could ride there myself—no one knowing—and bring the duchess's consent to the marriage. I'd urge a hurried wedding, there at Châteaubriant, for tomorrow. I'd say everything should be in readiness, for my duchess is following, and I'd say you're bringing her."

Their eyes were deep in concentrated understanding. "How?" Louis asked again.

"Somehow! I'll wrangle over the papers and do the best I can for Brittany. I trust you to bring Ann-Marie."

"And if she refuses even after she's there? She's young and angry—I doubt whether she'd submit."

"She couldn't refuse then." De Rieux spoke harshly, but it was easy to see how he felt. "She'll be helpless. Nothing but enemies all around her." He sighed again, thinking how he would appear to the girl who was almost his daughter. Louis, too, sighed when he thought of her desperation, to find herself so enclosed, nothing but enemies all around her and two of the men she had loved counted among them.

"But it is all we can do!" de Rieux said as much to himself as to Louis. "How do you think Charles will treat her?"

"Charles is very eager for the marriage," Louis said miserably. "There is no harm or cruelty in him. He's affectionate—and I think he'll do everything he can to make her life pleasant." Louis thought about it, and then, in a surge of fury against the whole situation, he said, "If he isn't kind to her, I'll kill him!"

De Rieux felt a little better. Ann-Marie wouldn't be so friendless as she thought in France, and he could rely on

Louis to watch over her. He came again to the details of their plan with increased determination.

In her room Ann-Marie walked the floor, her hands twisting into one another so that the rings cut her with their sharp corners. Months, years of love, looking toward this one moment—Louis's freedom—all scarred and soiled now by his refusal. All he wanted was Brittany, and she had given too much. He had never loved her. He loved Anne of France, and he had come to Brittany to spite that love. He had thought he had only to come and say, "I gave my part in you to Charles," and she would meekly go and do as she was told. He had yet to learn how she was made. Men couldn't hand her over from one to the other at their will, not the Duchess of Brittany!

"I have nothing more to say," Ann-Marie informed Louis decisively the next evening. "I wouldn't have received you this evening if the Maréchal de Rieux hadn't asked it of me as a favor to him. But there's no use going over the ground time after time!"

"And does his opinion do nothing to strengthen what I've said?"

"There's no one I trust more than the maréchal, but he's an old man, and pessimistic." She spoke in dismissal. "You've said what you came to say, I have answered, and let that be the end of it."

They were in her large council room, alone. He had waited there for her almost an hour before she had come to seat herself at the head of the long table, in the thronelike chair that was hers by right of inheritance. She had greeted him with formality, but she was dressed in one of her favorite gowns—a long tight-bodiced black velvet dress, the deep square neckline cut low so that it showed the two round white hillocks of her breasts. The trailing sleeves were embroidered with pearls and the neck was outlined in them. The tall headdress was becoming to her dark eyes and fresh young skin, and the velvet on it was also embroidered with pearls. About her wrists were heavy twisted bracelets of the same milk-white jewels. She had decided he should remember her at their last meeting as a beautiful woman, but what she couldn't read was his grim thought that she had chosen her jewels appropriately. Pearls before swine!

He was in his traveling clothes—dark olive-green vest and

jacket, with breeches, hose, and boots almost of the same color—and she wondered for a moment if he had dressed carefully to impress her also. If he had, she was reluctant to admit, he had succeeded, for she liked his looks. Yes, liked everything about him; she admitted more—his throat and his hair and his eyes, his lean cheekbones, his brown wrists, the straight line of his back, his slim, flat waist, his white teeth in his sudden smile—how would she ever forget all of that?

"Unfortunately, I have more to say," he told her, "and you'll like it even less."

Ann-Marie looked at him sharply.

"The Maréchal de Rieux has gone to Châteaubriant, to bring them your consent to the marriage." Louis hurried on without waiting for her comments, which wouldn't have come anyway. She was too stupefied. "We finally decided there was nothing else to do. He's arranging the contracts, and you are to follow immediately with me!"

He spoke sternly, knowing his wrath was going to descend on him anyway. It wasn't a thing that could be made pleasant, no matter what words he used.

The wrath descended. Traitor was the least thing she called him. She refused, of course, to accompany him as he had known she would.

"Ann!" he said angrily, his face determined. "Listen to me for a moment and stop this childish ranting. You sound exactly like I did when I was nine." That stopped her most effectively. "I'm resolved to take you to Châteaubriant. Will you come, or must I carry you?"

Her surprise came in wild laughter. "Carry me? You'd carry me as far as that door!" She pointed with shaking fingers. "What would happen when you opened it and I called for my guards?"

"They won't come," he told her, hastening on to make the picture completely clear to her. "They won't even see us, for de Rieux has carefully picked men with closed eyes. And in the courtyard it's the same. You see, we've anticipated your objections; we've anticipated what you'll say and think of us. We know that someday you'll see that we did what we had to, to save you."

"Save me!" she broke in, in impotent fury and anger. "Drag me to my destruction, you mean. As long as I live, Louis, I will never forget this night! Know that now!"

"I know," he said in grim agreement. "I know all you're thinking, for I thought it once myself. And my resistance led to war and death and a prison cell, which I'm determined to keep you from!"

She didn't really imagine he could carry her to Châteaubriant by force; it was too fantastic. Here in her own city, her own château, her own guards—— But she retreated before him, beyond the large chair, and stood in defiant anger.

Louis looked at her as he advanced. She was lovely in her flushed anger, her cheeks pink with it, her throat and breast rising and falling rapidly with her excitement, the dark eyes wide, and it was almost an inhuman task to take so much unwilling loveliness to another man when it might be willingly his. He could take her to Blois—— Then he laughed at his hopes of keeping her safe. No, there was no way out of it.

He walked steadily toward her, but as he advanced she retreated further, her hands coming up to hold him away. As she stood against the wall, no further retreat was possible, and he swooped quickly down on her, gathered her full skirt into his arms, one arm about her waist, including and pinioning both her arms, and his other under her knees. She struggled furiously, her teeth clenched, and he thought for a second, before he steadied himself against it, that he was going to drop her. But all he dropped, as he hurried toward the door, was her tall headdress that fell, dangled for a moment by its long streamers, and then rolled on the floor. He hoped, as he knocked on the door for it to be opened, that one of the guards would have sense enough to pick it up so it wouldn't bear too eloquent witness against him.

Only the guards then on duty in the lower hall and in the courtyard had been prepared by de Rieux, and whether or not others might come before they could get safely away was the difficulty. As the door opened he looked down at Ann-Marie, saw her taking a deep breath, and knew she was planning to cry out as soon as they went into the hall.

"If you scream, Ann-Marie, someone'll be killed," he said hastily, but he could see she was too angry to listen.

"I hope it'll be you," she fumed, struggling in his tight arms.

He saw that he must stop her screams, and he shifted her weight so that she slid a little further down into his arms. The arm that had been around her waist was under her shoulders and her neck, and the hand was laid firmly over her mouth as he walked out of the room and down the long, dark hall toward the courtyard and the waiting horses. This new position left one of her arms free, and with it she did her utmost to make him set her down. She pounded with her clenched fist against his face, which he turned away from her blows, and she clawed at the hand that was tight over her mouth until Louis thought that kidnapping a woman wasn't so easy as it might sound. He wished fervently that he had another hand.

The few guards along the empty hall stood in rigid inattention as Louis strode hurriedly along with his struggling burden, but Louis was tense with uneasiness. They might find it too much for their Breton loyalty to see their duchess carried off under their noses so unwillingly. De Rieux must have been very convincing, Louis thought, when they came out into the courtyard with no interference.

He set her down, still holding her close to him, and since it was impossible to put her on her horse and keep her quiet at the same time, he gestured to one of the two men de Rieux had assigned to him to lead Ann-Marie's horse until they were out of the city. Then he told the other soldier to hold her while he mounted.

It gave him a pang, settled in his saddle, to see her in another man's tight grasp, the dark eyes blazing fury at him over the gloved hand, and quickly he leaned down to draw her up with him. She had just a moment, in the transferring from one set of arms to the other, for one deep breath and the beginning of a scream before Louis's hand closed over her mouth and he held her tightly against him on his excited horse. They set quickly out, and Louis thought he had never heard so much noise in all his life. To his anxious ears the sound of the horses was magnified. The walls of the castle seemed to echo with ominous sound, but somehow they were out of the gates of the château, galloping through the dark streets of the sleeping city, then through the shadowy gates of the town, out onto the even darker road, all without interception.

They didn't stop, but rode on, Louis's horse leading, and he was at last able to take his stiffened, aching hand from Ann-Marie's stiff, aching face. He settled her more comfortably into his free arm and held her close, looking down into her angry face. The wind was cold in the spring night, and Louis turned in his saddle to call for the cloaks he had provided. Durand, one of de Rieux's most trusted men, came riding alongside for a moment, holding out the heavy cloaks, helping Louis to arrange them about his own shoulders and to encircle Ann-Marie with one. Having done that, Durand dropped back and they rode on in silence.

Ann-Marie made no motion to help Louis with the cloak. She sat stiff and unyielding against his body, her head against his shoulder. Although it would have been faster if she were on her own horse, he continued to ride with her warmth against him.

Fury and humiliation, wonder at the incredible daring, had possession of Ann-Marie's mind, but her body was beginning to tell her an entirely different story. Held so close to him that she could feel every breath he took, a sweet excitement slowly pervaded her, seeping up into her resentful brain and postponing her anger. "You can always find time to be angry," it told her. "This will be the only time in your life you'll be so close. Take what you can and forget what's coming. Perhaps you'll never get there!"

One of her arms was free now, and it dropped down behind Louis's back. It could have continued to fight and resist, but it stayed there quietly, hoping he wouldn't notice its compliance.

In silence they rode, not so fast now, the dark space on either side of the road, lit only here and there by the flares of an inn, slipping past them in coolness. Sometimes the low voice of Durand behind them would call out some words of direction or caution to them, and then there would be silence again. Far in the distance they heard the melancholy wails of restless cattle, and now and then scampering animals crossed the road in fright.

They stopped once on the road where fresh horses waited for them, held in readiness by four dark figures, and almost without any words the transfer was made. It seemed to be taken for granted by all of them that Ann-Marie would again be drawn up before Louis on his horse.

Two more hours of riding brought them almost within sight of the outskirts of Châteaubriant, and Louis let the other men gallop past him as he slowed his horse so that he could speak to Ann-Marie.

"We must change horses soon," he said. "You must ride your own horse into the castle courtyard———"

Ann-Marie straightened and put her hands on his shoulders, her eyes pleading. "Louis, don't do this to me! You'll regret it!"

His face tightened, and his breath came all the way from his heart. "I have to, Ann-Marie! It's your only safety!"

"I don't want safety. Did you? When you were forced to marry, didn't you know it was wrong?"

"Yes, but——"

"If you had been older—as old as I am now—would you have yielded?"

Louis was uneasily silent. He knew that he wouldn't have surrendered without a battle. She read his thoughts and pressed the advantage. "Do you think I'm less brave than you? I'm not, Louis—we're very much alike, you and I, and if we fought together, we could win!"

Her moonlit face was close to his own, and her arms slid up impulsively around his neck. She pressed her breast tight against his so that the hard buttons on his coat pressed into them both, and their lips were together in a kiss that amazed him with its wild, sweet feeling and left her with a longing to melt into him. After a moment she drew her lips slowly away, but his tight arms pulled her back. Châteaubriant—the waiting king—the horsemen galloping on the dark road ahead—he forgot them all.

Then, when he remembered, rebellion, excitement, and courage began to surge through him. Impossible now to be cautious and cold!

"Ann-Marie—if I could get you to Blois——"

"Yes?" she asked eagerly.

"We could stand siege there—with my friends to help—and we'd defy the regent to come get you!"

"Oh," she gasped, "Louis—yes! Yes!"

"Brittany would be untouched—Anne would need her armies to fight us—we'd have the advantage of time—we'd be well stocked—well locked—ready for her——" Louis laughed a low laugh of jubilant excitement, and Ann echoed it joyously. Then he sobered, looked down at her warningly. "We'll be outnumbered—the chances will be against us—and we may never get there. It's a long way! And if we're taken—you know it means our heads!"

She returned his look stanchly. "I'd rather have no head at all than one that hung in shame!"

Admiration for her warmed him. Here was an Ann to

fight for! One with courage, not caution, in her veins. One who would choose death before an imbecile marriage! With her strong loyalty beside him, they would take their chances! Hastily he began to plan. They were approaching a fork in the road; one branch led up to the Châteaubriant castle, the other to the town. The Breton escort had just passed the fork and were riding at a good pace, leading Ann-Marie's horse toward the château. Louis shifted Ann-Marie in his arms, holding her firmly with one arm, reining the horse with the other, and when he came to the fork he turned the horse's head toward the town and gave him a strong touch of the spur.

The animal responded nervously, and Louis urged him on, faster and faster, huddling low and holding Ann-Marie close against him, anxious to make as much distance as he could before Durand and the other horsemen realized that Louis and their duchess had taken the wrong road. For a while there was no sound in the night but the horse's thumping hoofs and his heavy breathing, and then faintly behind him Louis began to hear the sounds of pursuit. Forcing the tiring horse for all the speed that was in him, Louis kicked his feet free of the stirrups, shifted Ann-Marie's weight again, and bent to warn her.

"Cling tight to me! At the next bend in the road we'll slip off——"

He could feel her head nodding against him and her arms tighten. He raised his left leg completely out of the stirrup and over the back of the horse, slowing the pace for a moment, and then, wrapping the cloak hastily around Ann-Marie, he slid with her to the road, and the startled horse went galloping on in final obedience to the last goad of Louis's spur.

They landed in a rolling heap on the soft ground beside the road, and, without rising, Louis continued to roll and scramble with her, until they were completely hidden in the underbrush. They lay there, panting and too stunned to feel any bruises, listening to the receding sound of their galloping horse—listening to the approaching sound of the puzzled Breton escort.

They could hear Durand's shouts now. "Turn back!" he was calling, "turn back! That's the wrong road!"

But Louis's horse, terrified now by the sounds of pursuit, was racing along the road, almost out of hearing. Louis hoped and prayed it would gallop straight through the town, leading the Bretons after it, getting lost in the winding streets.

Warm and close, and lying half under him, Ann-Marie laughed with excitement, and Louis smiled down at her. He could barely see her face; the moonlight through the leaves above them showed him her sparkling eyes, the shadow of a dimple. He leaned closer and kissed the dimple, then rose and carefully pulled her to her feet.

"You're not hurt?" he asked softly.

She shook her head, and they stood brushing the leaves and mud from their clothing. She adjusted the cloak around her while Louis took his bearings.

Then he drew her along hastily. There was no time to be wasted. "We'll cut through this woods—we'll come out behind the road—there'll be inns—we'll have to get horses —buy them or steal them——" Reassuringly, he felt for his money belt. It was still there, and full, thank God. "It'll take four days—traveling day and night—to get home—I'll send a courier on ahead to rouse Dunois and the others— better let me walk ahead and bend the branches back."

He preceded her through the dark woods, and they stumbled hastily along the moist, uneven ground. It was a cool night, and the mist was damp on their faces. A fog was rolling in, stealing their moonlight. After ten minutes' walking Ann-Marie's feet, in the dainty black velvet slippers, were wet through, and the pearls that once decorated the slippers were now decorating the path behind her. Her breath was quick and labored. Louis turned to smile encouragingly at her.

"Would you like to rest a moment?" he asked.

"Oh no," she said breathlessly, "I'm all right." And that, she thought, was certainly an understatement of the fact. More than all right, she felt superbly happy. Her blood was singing with the excitement of the kisses and this adventure in the night. She couldn't remember once in her whole life ever having been alone, like this, outside the castle walls, without dozens of guards clattering around her. It made the forest seem a strange, new place, very exciting. She felt as though Louis and she were the only living people in the world, and all the vague noisy discussions of France and Brittany and armies and independence seemed far removed and unimportant. She smiled contentedly. If her feet wanted to hurt, let them! She would be content to trot after Louis in her tightest slippers to the end of the world.

She almost felt she had accomplished that deed when they came out of the woods and approached the straggling out-skirts of the town. It was late and most of the few houses were dark. A few flares lit the road and a small inn tossed lights and voices out of the open doors into the darkness as Louis and Ann-Marie walked swiftly along the uneven road, careful to stay in the shadows.

"Draw your hood about your face," he warned her, "or you may be recognized."

She obeyed, but said reassuringly, "Who would expect to see the Duchess of Brittany alone—at an inn—at midnight?"

"No one," he agreed. "And that's our only advantage— the improbability—but there's still the chance. Close your cloak at the throat, too," he told her. "And you have too many jewels on—slip off your rings and bracelets—no use tempting thieves."

She stripped them off, all but one ring, and under the shelter of her cloak she twisted it so that the big emerald stone turned inward and only the wide gold band showed, like a wedding ring, on her outer hand.

"Our story is this," he prepared her hastily. "We're trav-eling from Nantes to—Paris, and our horses were stolen from us by highwaymen, and all our luggage with them— and we must have horses to take us the rest of the way— and a private room for you to rest and dry your clothing while I arrange for the horses——"

They were almost at the inn now, and they paused in its dark shadow to finish their fabrication.

"What's our name?" Ann-Marie asked quickly, enjoying the story as though their lives didn't depend on the plausi-bility.

"I'm the Count—— No, we'll not be titled. I'm Mon-sieur Rolande—I'm a French merchant—I have leather shops—two of them, in Paris."

"And I," said Ann-Marie ecstatically, "am Madame Ro-lande. I married you for your money and your black eyes— and I have children—two of them—in Paris."

He had to laugh. "What are they, Madame Wife, boys or girls?"

"One of each, I think," she said judiciously. "Yes, one of

each." Then she shivered happily and caught his hand. "Oh, Louis—think—someday we will!"

He sobered as he bent to kiss her hand. "God willing——"

Then he put her hand through his arm and started toward the steps of the inn. There was a chance that the Bretons had discovered the horse was riderless. There was a chance that they had come back along this road and inquired at the inn. There was also the chance that they might be inside now.

Louis thought quickly how he would meet those chances. If the Bretons came, he would spin a story about falling off the horse—and then he would have to evade them again later. If the innkeeper was watching for them, he would tell him the same story. But the chances were just as even that the Bretons were searching miles away and that the innkeeper would see no reason to doubt Monsieur Rolande's unhappy story. Especially if the tip were large enough.

He pushed the door farther open, held it for Ann-Marie, and she passed through. They stood inside and looked around for the innkeeper. The room was big and dark with carved wood paneling. An open hearth at one end was flaming with fire and sputtering at the fowl that roasted above it.

A few soldiers, in the Breton uniform, lounged at a table, drinking and throwing dice. Two middle-aged travelers impatiently watched their supper roasting. A few villagers stood at the bar drinking ale and talking to each other and the elderly barmaid. It was an orderly room, and the warmth felt comforting to Ann-Marie, who was shivering a little now in her damp clothes.

After a quick, reassuring look around, Louis advanced toward the bar, Ann-Marie still on his arm. The soldiers and the travelers turned to watch them as they passed, and Louis was proud of Ann-Marie's poise and control. Her only fault was her carriage, which was too regal for a merchant's wife, but that was too old a habit to control in a moment.

Louis spoke to the barmaid in a pleasant and carrying voice. "Where's the innkeeper, if you please?"

The barmaid turned and shouted in the direction of the kitchen, and in a moment a plump, clean man, who was a good advertisement for the comforts of his hostelry, came hurrying out.

Louis told his story, once losing his temper and swearing at the highwaymen who had taken his best horses—with the silver saddle, too, mind you—and then apologizing to his wife for the swearwords used. The innkeeper was sympathetic. It wasn't the first incident of highwaymen around there, and it wouldn't be the last, either. Something had to be done—the roads weren't safe to travel any more. Yes, he had horses that could be bought—fast ones—and good padded saddles for the lady. He would send round to his man at the stable—right away and yes, he had a beautiful room for Madame to rest in while the horses were made ready.

He led the way upstairs. Ann-Marie, conscious that everyone was watching, demurely kept her cloak close around her and her eyes down as she followed the innkeeper. Louis followed her, to see her safely settled before he went to the stables.

The Breton soldiers looked up to the balcony, watching the innkeeper open the bedroom door for Madame.

One of the soldiers muttered, "Damn Frenchmen—they have all the luck!"

"Frenchmen!" said another, his eyes resting on Louis in a long puzzled stare. "He looks like——" and then he paused uncertainly.

"Who?" they asked.

He shook his head, irritated that he couldn't remember. "Somebody," he said.

They laughed, and since Ann-Marie had passed out of sight they returned to their dice, but the one soldier kept looking after Louis, in an annoyed way, trying to remember.

When the innkeeper had lit the fire and showed them how comfortable the bed was, he went out and left them alone, promising to have the coach and horses ready for them to leave in an hour.

Alone with Louis and an enormous feather bed that seemed to fill the room with meaning, Ann-Marie felt a flurry of embarrassment. But pleasant embarrassment.

"Better take your things off, Ann-Marie, and dry them at the fire. We'll be traveling all night—and it's cold—you don't want to arrive with a fever. I'll go hurry the stableman."

He left her, ran hastily down the stairs, and passed through the downstairs room. As he did he realized that one of the Breton soldiers was watching him intently. He smiled politely as he passed by, and the puzzled expression on the soldier's face suddenly changed. Louis strode on out, and while he talked and hurried the stableman he wondered about the Breton soldier. Could the man have recognized him? Possibly from years ago at the siege of Nantes? And if he had, was there danger in it? He didn't think so, because the Bretons had liked and trusted him—all but d'Albret and his men. God grant this wasn't one of d'Albret's men!

When he returned to the inn, ten minutes later, the soldier was gone. Louis felt distinctly uneasy. Well, there was nothing for it but to be on their way as soon as their horses were ready and their clothes dry.

He was too busy worrying to think of knocking at the door, and when he abruptly opened it Ann-Marie whirled from the fireplace and instinctively clutched a white linen chemise to her half-dressed body.

"Oh—I'm sorry," Louis said hastily, and half started to go. "I'll wait downstairs."

"No, don't," Ann-Marie called quickly. "I was just startled, thats all. Come and dry your things too."

So he came toward the fireplace, glad for its warmth, because he was chilled and wet. He tried to keep his eyes away from Ann-Marie, but he was extremely conscious of her, in her beautifully embroidered white chemise, her feet and ankles bare and rosy in the firelight. She had scrubbed her face—it was flushed and shining—and she had loosened her dark braids so her hair fell softly around her shoulders.

He took off his jacket, hung it close to the fire, sat down and kicked off his long boots and stood them on the brick hearth. Ann brought him a glass of wine, its rich burgundy color as warm and heartening as its taste.

She had a glass for herself, too, and wordlessly they raised their glasses in a toast—a toast to themselves and their good fortune in the coming battle. She sipped hers, smiling over the rim of the glass at him, looking provocative and sweetly bold.

"Monsieur Rolande is a very lucky man to have you for his wife, madame," he told her. "You're brave and beautiful and——"

"And what?" she asked invitingly.

"And very young—to be in such danger. Ann-Marie," he said suddenly, "there's still time to withdraw to safety!"

"Safety," she said scornfully. "Safety is for the dead! And I'm not dead—tonight!"

She put down her glass and with a quick movement slid into his arms. No—she wasn't dead. She was the most alive creature he had ever held.

The feather bed was deep and soft and warm, and when he roused himself from it to smile at a drowsy-eyed Ann-Marie beside him, he realized with a shock that more time than he had thought had gone by. Almost an hour—and it could have been years, for somewhere in that time one Anne had slipped out of his emotions and another Ann had claimed full possession, one who would love without caution or selfishness, who could be a queen and a woman. His true Ann-Marie.

She would be his wife—she would be his duchess and maybe one day his queen. She would be the mother of his children—and then he cursed himself for daydreaming as he sprang up. She would be none of these things unless he could get her safe to Blois.

He stamped into his boots and pulled on his coat. "The horses must be waiting——" Still struggling into his coat, he opened the door, took a glance down into the lower room, then whirled back in, closed the door, and hastily called, "My God, Ann-Marie, dress quickly and come! Hurry!"

She sat up hastily. "What is it?"

"D'Albret! He's downstairs! He may have seen us——"

Ann-Marie gasped and slid out of the white tumbled bed, ran hastily, slim and naked, across the room to her clothes at the fire. "What would he do?"

"I think he'd betray us by force of habit," Louis said scornfully. "I don't know what he'd do, but let's take no chances." He thought quickly. "I'll bring the horses around to the back—dress, and see if you can slip down without being seen. There must be a back stairs—God damn it!" he swore bitterly. "Why must this bedroom door open in full sight of the whole world!"

He went to the window and looked out to see if there might be a retreat that way. It was much too high, with a paved courtyard below. He went to the door again, opened it a little, and peered out. He nodded in relief.

"He's gone now—and if he's gone to make trouble, we'll

be out of here before he gets back with it. Come as fast as you can—I'll be waiting."

Downstairs he paid the innkeeper and hurried out to the stables. He was furious there to discover that the horses weren't saddled. He started angrily toward the coachman, who stood in the darkness near the horses' heads.

"What's the matter, you idle fool!" he began, and then he felt a crashing blow on the back of his head and across his shoulders. He staggered and turned to meet his attacker. There were two of them, and he grappled with them in the darkness as a coachman leaped up onto the seat of a big clumsy carriage and, whipping the horses harnessed to it, drove it noisily out into the courtyard.

When Ann-Marie came running out a few moments later, hastily dressed and with most of the laces and loops still undone and her hair rolled loosely under her hood, she heard sounds from the stable, like scuffling and stamping horses, and men's angry grunts, but the coachman called to her, "Madame—here—quickly!" and the coach door was open, so she drew up her skirts and reached up to the high coach step, wondering why Louis had changed his mind and decided to travel by carriage, which was so much slower and less comfortable than horseback.

The interior of the conveyance was dark and smelled musty; she felt a sudden sense of panic, and then from the stable she heard Louis's frantic shout: "Ann-Marie—be——"

Then his voice was abruptly shut off. She drew back to leap down, but a long arm from within reached out and pulled her into the coach, slammed the door, and while she sprawled on the carriage floor the coachman shouted and whipped his horses and the coach lumbered out of the courtyard.

Dazed, she felt bruising hands pull her up onto the seat, and as they passed the flaring torches at the courtyard gates, in the fierce flickering light she saw d'Albret's face.

His mouth was set in a furious grimace as he held her by the shoulders and shook her. "If you've got to throw yourself at a Frenchman," he said bitterly, "it won't be Louis of Orleans!"

"Where are you taking me?" she gasped apprehensively.

"To Châteaubriant," he said shortly, "and your waiting bridegroom—if he'll have you now that you've already given

Louis of Orleans what you should have saved for your husband.

After the bruising journey to Châteaubriant, d'Albret pulled Ann-Marie hastily through a dark rear courtyard and, unseen, except by a few of his soldiers, they entered the dark castle by a hidden entrance. Implacably he drew her along a private passageway to a little upstairs study, and she found herself face to face with Anne of France! Anne of France was regally dressed and alone. She nodded to d'Albret and quickly dismissed him, then she turned slowly and the two Annes were alone together.

Neither spoke for a moment. Anne of France took her time looking the Duchess of Brittany up and down, taking in every detail of her loosened hair, her disordered dress. Her eyes were critical and knowing. The Breton stood proudly under the scrutiny, making no effort to repair her dishabille. Then they looked into each other's faces, the two women who loved Louis, and they hated each other. Between them stood their knowledge that both of them loved the same man.

"We welcome you," said Anne of France coldly. "We're delighted you came to your sudden decision to marry my brother without further resistance."

"I came to no such decision, madame, and I never will!" Ann-Marie said sharply. "I was brought here by force—by a subject of mine, who has evidently turned traitor and become your subject!"

Anne of France held up her hand abruptly. "You forget your subjects are all subjects to France—including yourself."

The Breton smiled. "That is an argument not yet settled. I'll protest this to the Pope, and I'll tell him what I tell you now—I'll never marry your brother."

Anne of France was puzzled, trying to reconstruct the events that must have happened between the time the Maréchal de Rieux had brought the duchess's consent to the marriage and the assurance that the duchess was coming, accompanied by Orleans, to the moment when she had received a breathless courier from d'Albret saying that he would soon be there, bringing the duchess by force, and Orleans would be his prisoner.

"Why do you repudiate the consent the maréchal delivered to us?"

Ann-Marie hesitated. If she said that the Maréchal de Rieux had come without authorization, he would be punished by France. If she only knew whether Louis were still free or taken, she could give a wiser answer.

She evaded, "It was never my intention to come here."

"I see! More of Orleans treachery!"

"No—he insisted it would be wise for me to marry France. He kept his promise."

"What changed his purpose?" Anne asked sharply.

A slow, reminiscent smile faintly crossed Ann-Marie's face, and she answered softly but with pride.

"Perhaps it was a kiss!"

Anne winced with jealousy. Ann-Marie saw it, and her dimples flickered in triumph. This haughty regent should see that there were many different kinds of victories and that the Duchess of Brittany was not so helpless as it seemed. Louis, in loving her, had given her a proud weapon to use and prevent a hideous marriage.

"Perhaps it was more than a kiss," she continued, "because Louis and I are married!"

"Married!" Anne echoed in dismay. "Impossible!"

"Not formally," Ann-Marie admitted. "We'll have it legalized in time, when he has his annulment. But," she said, smiling blandly, "when the king knows that Louis and I have lived as man and wife, he will not, of course, even wish to marry me."

Anne of France quivered with hate and jealousy. That this woman—this Breton slut with her hair hanging down her back and her dress torn—could stand there so proudly and boast that she and Louis were lovers!

"I don't believe it," she said flatly.

Ann-Marie laughed. "You prefer not to. Yet you know it's true. Louis loves me!"

Anne turned abruptly away, recovered rigid control, said flatly: "Whether it is true or not, you will still marry my brother!"

Ann-Marie was shocked. "I am Louis's wife, and I shall tell the king I am."

"No," said Anne of France. "You will not tell the king. He will never be told!"

Ann-Marie stared at her in disgust and turned abruptly

toward the door. "Where is the king? Take me to him at once!"

Anne of France didn't move. She watched Ann-Marie and then asked quietly, "Have you wondered where Louis is?" Then she enjoyed the look of anxiety that crossed the other's face.

"Where is he?"

"On his way to Bourges. To be locked in the tower—and an iron cage!"

Ann-Marie caught her breath in terror. She had wondered all the way to Châteaubriant, in the rocking coach, what had happened to Louis. She had pounded her fists against d'Albret's inflexible shoulder and demanded an answer, but he had just cursed her and refused to say. Now, looking into the angry eyes of her enemy, she knew.

"Will you kill him too?" she asked sharply.

"Perhaps," Anne answered coldly. "Perhaps. He'll be tried for treason!"

"Tried for treason," Ann-Marie said sharply, "but convicted by your jealousy—because you're still in love with him!"

Anne was stung to fury. "Fling your love at his worthless feet if you like, but don't touch mine!"

The Breton smiled knowingly and nodded. "I thought so. You still do! You wouldn't be a woman if you'd forgotten so easily."

"You sicken me! If it were true, you should feel ashamed of me and all our sex! Are we dogs," she asked furiously, "to worship humbly—to lack the strength to snatch back our love if we find he's not worthy of it? If that's to be a woman, then I'll not be one!" Her contemptuous voice calmed her a little. She walked close to Ann-Marie and spoke, looking straight into her eyes. "I feel two things for Louis of Orleans, and love is not one of them! I miss the love we might have had—that's true enough—but I'm contemptuous he didn't have the strength to take it."

"You offered it to him, I have no doubt!" Ann-Marie said with a twinge of jealousy.

"His honor choked," Anne said with mincing unpleasantness. "His little pride refused the compromise!" Then she began to rage again. "But he was proud enough in war. His honor didn't wince when he saw men and beasts—and land —all broken for his own desires. Pride and honor in a man!" Her tone was scathing now. "Fight and kill, and be victorious or die, and if you die, then you were wrong, and that way it's solved!" She stopped abruptly.

Ann-Marie looked at her thoughtfully. "It won't solve your love if you kill him. Let him go free!"

"Why?"

"Because"—she sighed deeply and said what she had to say—"I'll marry your brother if you do."

They stood and looked at each other in silence again. Then Anne of France, without moving her eyes, gestured toward a desk in the corner of the room. "There are the marriage contracts. De Rieux has drawn them up—they're ready for your signature."

Ann-Marie shook her head. "A release for Louis first!" As her opponent hesitated, she added, "On my sacred honor, as Queen of Brittany, I promise to marry your brother in exchange for Louis's freedom."

Anne of France moved swiftly to the desk and reached for paper and pen. Ann-Marie came to stand beside her and prompted the wording of the release so that it had no date, but on presentation—at any time—it would revoke any previous orders and secure Louis's freedom. Anne of France smiled as she obediently worded it, because she could read the other's lack of trust and fear that, once the Breton was married to Charles, Louis would be rearrested. Both papers were signed, the release and the marriage contract.

Then Ann-Marie said, holding the precious paper tightly in her hands, "I'll ride with this to Bourges myself. I'll set out tonight."

Anne of France shook her head. "You'll set out tomorrow. Tonight you'll be married to the King of France."

Ann-Marie was taken to a room to dress in borrowed clothes for the wedding, and then she was presented to her bridegroom.

Charles was delighted with her. "Madame," he stammered in excitement, "I thought no one in the world could be as beautiful as the pictures we've had of you, but I see now how wrong I was."

Ann accepted his flattery unsmilingly. She thought of saying the pictures she had seen of him had been quite the contrary, but she was too tired, too miserable, to make barbed speeches. When she stood beside her large-headed bridegroom in the little chapel, she shivered with revulsion, thinking of him as her husband, and to reassure herself her hand crept toward the bosom of her dress, where she had carefully tucked away the valuable paper. Bitter as the marriage was, Louis's release was worth it.

When the bishop said the final words that made them man and wife, Anne of France stirred with triumph. Man and wife. Never wife to Louis. Never again. She almost wished Louis could be here to see the wedding; it would be a pleasure to watch his face. She looked forward to seeing the Breton's face one day soon when she found out that Anne of France had lied. Well, not lied exactly, but just said what she had hoped was true, that Louis had been captured by the two soldiers d'Albret had left behind to seize him. Two of them should have been enough, since they had taken him by surprise. He probably was on the way to Bourges.

But he wasn't. He was awkwardly slumped forward on a horse's back, on the road to Châteaubriant. The horse trotted, then walked, then trotted as Louis shook himself out of his dizzy coma and relapsed again. He was bleeding profusely from several knife wounds in his back, and there was other men's blood on him too, because he had left behind one dead soldier and one dying. He lay forward on the horse's mane, clinging to it, till finally his hands relaxed, the puzzled horse stood still, and Louis plunged face forward onto the road and lay there very quietly, not knowing that in the chapel at Châteaubriant he had lost another Anne.

19

As Queen of France, Ann-Marie was even more miserable than she had expected. She moved through the elaborate, tedious formal wedding at Langeais and the coronation with composed dignity. Her travels through the cities of France were triumphant, shouting receptions, for the people were delighted with her youthful beauty. She accepted their delight with charming appreciation, but within her was one voiceless cry of pain. Brittany was far away and Louis was lost to her. He was at Blois, recovering from his wounds. Treacherous, lying Anne of France was close, watchful eyes sharply intent and triumphant over the success of her trick, and Charles was close, oh, much, much too close!

Marriage with him was more terrible than she had imagined in her worst nightmares, and sometimes it took all her strength of will to keep from screaming out against Charles's inept love-making. But she was also sternly enough trained in the duties of royalty to know it was a necessity. Kings were often enough required to force themselves into feelings as repugnant for the sake of an heir.

Charles was disappointed in the marriage too, unhappy at her reluctance and ashamed that he couldn't make her love him, and their relationship was a very uneven thing. Weeks when it seemed to her he didn't leave her for a moment would be followed by sulky weeks in which he paid no attention to her beyond minor rudenesses. Now and then there would be intervals when they would be friendly but not intimate. Ann-Marie strove to achieve that as a perpetual relationship. She couldn't resist a feeling of pity and contemptuous liking for the friendless king. He wasn't a king at all, she soon saw, but that was no reason why he shouldn't be! With her own energetic ability, she couldn't remain idle, filling her life with social activities as some women did, concerning themselves entirely with the

latest cut in skirts and bodices, the latest gossip and the latest
gentleman, and she turned to the thing that she had been
trained to do—govern a country, although it was only hers
by unwilling adoption, or abduction. Naturally Anne of
France objected, and there began a struggle between the
two intelligent women for the possession and guidance of
one weak masculine mind.

Anne of France was now the Duchess of Bourbon, for
Pierre's four older brothers and their children had died,
leaving the large province of Bourbonnais to Pierre and
Anne, and their children after them, provided the children
were boys. But Anne and Pierre had still only the one child,
Suzanne, so Bourbon would return to the crown now, when
Pierre died, and the little clause the dead king Louis XI
had insinuated into Pierre's marriage contract would bear
fruit, fantastic as it had seemed at the time to Oliver le
Daim. So many of the things he had planned, impossible
though they had seemed at the time, had come about. Burgundy and Picardy were crown property now; Brittany had
come by marriage; Bourbonnais and Bourbon's smaller properties would come at Pierre's death, Orleannais at Louis's
death—plans far in the future when King Louis had made
them, but most of them realities now.

The work in the study became the work of a trinity, two
strong minds and one necessary puppet. In almost every
question of policy the two women automatically disagreed,
and then it became a tug of war between them to influence
the king to one or the other point of view. Charles often left
the room at the end of the day feeling like a battlefield,
smooth, angry insults echoing through his mind, seeing their
two faces in his mind's eye, looking at each in controlled
fury and then turning to him with their confusing questions.
Sometimes, in the heat of argument, they untactfully forgot
that he was there at all and flung words back and forth at
each other over his head, while he sat petulantly resentful
that he should be the king and yet be so ignored. On those
nights his wife had a harder time placating and encouraging
him, for it was borne in on him too harshly how much more
intelligent they both were, and he sank into a listless forget-
fulness of all the cares of the throne, feeling that he was
less than adequate to them.

When the queen knew she was going to have a child she
cried wildly before she went to tell her husband the welcome

news. She had wanted a child, many children to grow up in strength to their heritage, a throne, but she had wanted them to have another heritage, a dark-eyed, charming father with a quick smile. She hadn't wanted Charles to be their father, life had decided that for her and now she must make what she could of it. At least it would do a great deal for Charles's pride, and France would be delighted with a dauphin. Those things were valuable and she didn't underrate them, but they couldn't check her tears.

Charles was extravagantly pleased with the idea, and after the long, annoying pregnant months were over he was hysterically delighted when a son was born. He was christened Charles-Orlando.

Louis was summoned to the christening ceremonies and told to bring his wife Jeanne with him. He hesitated about going. He knew Anne of France wanted him to be there to see his Breton Ann-Marie with another man's child in her arms. He hadn't been to court since Ann-Marie's marriage, although his wounds had long since healed.

He considered disobeying the order and not going, and yet he wanted to see the queen. So he went, but he didn't take Jeanne with him. When the king and his sister reproached him for not bringing his wife, he repeated the words that were coming to be his credo.

"I have no wife!" he said.

Charles and Anne exchanged a look, and later, in the king's study, a three-cornered duel began.

Anne of France began it: "I've never met such stubbornness!" she fumed. "He must be forced to acknowledge Jeanne as his wife. He must bring her here, to court! And she must live with him at Blois, not stay there at Linières as though they weren't married."

Ann-Marie spoke quickly, her worried eyes on Charles. "The king knows what to do, madame, without your telling him. I have the utmost confidence in him."

"Yes," said Charles, "I'm king and capable of handling this!"

"And after all, madame, in all the years that you were regent—or guardian, call it what you like—you tried to force Louis to acknowledge a wife, and you couldn't succeed." Her tone was triumphant; she couldn't hide her pleasure in Louis's strength of will.

Anne whirled on her. "You speak as though it were something to be proud of—that he insults the king's sister!"

"And that wouldn't be right!" Charles murmured.

"His marriage was so forced," Ann-Marie said, "he feels he has the right to extricate himself if he can. I can't help but admire his strength of will."

"We all know how you admire him!" Anne answered pointedly. "It hasn't been forgotten that you were once so attracted to him you betrothed yourself, although he had a wife. It is said that attraction hasn't yet disappeared."

"And, by God, it hasn't!" Charles muttered miserably.

"I only tell the queen what the court says, so she can guard her tongue—and her eyes—a little better!"

Ann-Marie bowed. "Thank you, madame, for your advice. I'll save my defense for my husband's ears—he knows the loyalty I have for him."

"Yes," rallied Charles. "She's never given me cause to doubt."

"And never will, if you keep Louis far enough away! He must take Jeanne to Blois to live! The longer he denies her, the stronger his position! Tell him he faces imprisonment if he refuses!"

Ann-Marie looked directly at Charles. "How would you like to have Jeanne for your wife?"

"I wouldn't."

"Then how can you blame him? The wisest king would leave her there at Linières. That's what she wants—a quiet life—and Louis visits her now and then!"

Anne laughed scornfully. "You mean that's what he wants. Don't think for a moment he's forgotten a divorce. He says he has no wife—he says it high and low—and think how laughable it makes us look! A king's sister, married to him, with the Pope's blessing, in church. What constitutes a marriage, if that's not one?"

She asked it directly of the queen, and the queen's eyes answered her. Ann-Marie was remembering a marriage without a bell, book, or candle, in a little village inn—in a feather bed! Anne turned abruptly away from the lovely answer in the queen's softened face.

Charles was muttering. "He really shouldn't go about and say he has no wife. It makes my sister a—well, what?"

"If she were a normal girl, it would be different," the

queen said. Ann-Marie had dreaded meeting Jeanne, but once she had, the two liked each other and were becoming firm friends, for they had the same qualities of honesty and directness.

Charles sighed. "I wonder if there'll ever be an end to this talk about Louis."

Anne spoke quickly. "Put him back in Bourges, and there'll be an end."

"Oh God," Charles moaned fretfully, "I wish he'd never been born. Do what you will, Anne—you'll do it anyway in time!"

"Charles," said the queen anxiously, "you've let yourself be pushed!"

He got up petulantly. "I don't want to talk about it any more," he said angrily. "I hate this room!" And he went out, banging the door behind him.

Anne rose and went to the desk. The queen watched her as she opened a drawer, took out a long official paper, and deliberately prepared a pen to sign it. The room was very quiet.

Then Ann-Marie spoke. "If that's an order for Louis's arrest, you'll waste time signing it."

Anne of France looked across the room at her. "Why?"

The queen walked closer, and they stood facing each other, as they had one night at Châteaubriant. "Because I will use the order for his release—I've kept it—the one you gave me—surely you remember the bargain we made. A fair bargain, wasn't it? My marriage—for Louis's freedom!"

Anne was the first to look away. She turned, tossed the pen down on the desk, and stood looking down at it, thinking. For the present it seemed to be a deadlock. She carried the poison; the queen carried the antidote!

The next day the queen was conscious that her rooms had been searched. She was in a panic till she discovered that the paper was still where she had put it—in a very clever hiding place behind the brick and marble fireplace, toward the top, well above reach. Standing on tiptoe on the desk, she pulled the paper out and tucked it down the front of her dress, not daring to leave it in the rooms again because they might be even more thoroughly searched while she was away all afternoon and evening at the tournament being held in the fields outside the castle to celebrate the dauphin's baptismal ceremonies.

She worried about what to do with it. She couldn't carry it about with her forever, and if she left it in her room, sooner or later Anne's spies would find it. She knew full well that all her letters were opened and read and sealed again before she saw them, and Anne was probably given a full account of her every action during the day, and possibly a fairly accurate surmise of her thoughts.

During the afternoon she had half a moment alone with Dunois, and impulsively she told him about the release and Anne's search for it. He immediately suggested she give it to him for safekeeping, but she hesitated. Not that she couldn't trust him, but it would be a dangerous thing for him to carry. They couldn't say very much, for they were both conscious of Anne's friends around them.

He left her to prepare for the tournament in which he was to joust, saying carefully as he left, "Get it to me somehow, and I'll keep it safe."

She thought about it through the early afternoon, thinking that if she could get the release to him carefully enough, so that no one knew he had it, he would be in no danger from Anne. But how? She went to the tournament considering that one question.

The celebration for the dauphin was an extravagant one. The field had been leveled and turfed; tiers of seats, covered with cloth of silver, had been erected; pavilions and tents of cloth of gold were scattered about the grounds; bright banners were flung out; sharp-tongued trumpets called from one end of the field to the other, and in answer to the sound of trumpets, the men in their shining armor rode their strong-chested horses out onto the field of honor for the admiration and amusement of the ladies who sat, gorgeously gowned, in the boxes and hotly refused to obey the king's order that they abandon their huge headdresses so that those seated behind them could see.

The queen sat in her box, acknowledging the homage paid her by the horsemen who galloped up to her, and looked around for Louis. She hadn't had a word or a moment alone with him since he had come. She didn't expect it. She could see him, though, on his horse, talking to Dunois. She sighed a little.

They both looked toward her, and then Dunois, after a final word to Louis, rode across the field toward the queen's box. Dunois was a glittering picture of strength in his silver armor with the bar sinister proudly decorating his crest. He rode his favorite horse, a huge black brute that pranced sidewise, and as Dunois reined it in before Ann-Marie it reared up on its back legs, pawing the air with its shining gold shoes.

Dunois laughingly pulled it back to earth and made it bow to Ann-Marie. Then he drew it as close as he could to the box and smiled at her.

"I have a message from a friend of yours," he said.

Ann-Marie looked quickly around. Anne and her friends were in the next box, watching, of course, and listening too.

Dunois ignored them and said calmly, "Do you remember Monsieur Rolande at all?"

The queen nodded. "Yes, I remember Monsieur Rolande —very well."

"He thinks of you a great deal, he asked me to say. He lost his wife, you know."

"I know."

"But he expects to—find her again someday."

Ann-Marie looked down at her lap and shook her head just a little. "Madame Rolande is dead," she said.

Dunois refused to accept that. "Oh no, just lost!"

The trumpets sounded over the field, announcing the next contestants in the tournament. It was Dunois's turn to meet Legendre and see which one could unhorse the other with a single spear thrust. Dunois looked forward to the test, because Legendre was one of Anne's favorites. Before he turned to ride away he leaned closer to the queen but spoke clearly.

"May I have some token of yours—like the knights in the Golden Age begged from the fairest lady of the court?"

The queen smiled and looked down at her magnificent costume to see what could be detached with the least harm to the ensemble. She wore a Breton scarf of sheer embroidery about her bare shoulders, caught in front with a cluster of diamonds. She quickly unpinned the brooch, and as she did she felt the crackling paper she had hid in her bosom. The quick thought flashed through her mind that here was a chance to give it to Dunois, before the court and yet hidden from them. Nervously she half drew it out, thinking to wrap it in the scarf as she gave it to Dunois. Then she looked toward Anne's box. Anne's sharp eyes were on her, and they seemed to read every thought. Then Anne leaned forward and whispered to Legendre, who was paying her his homage.

Ann-Marie tucked the paper hastily back into her dress again and waved the scarf carelessly as she handed it to Dunois. He bowed and thanked her as he took it, tucked it into the open end of his chain-mail gauntlet, and, spurring the horse, galloped off to his end of the field, the scarf fluttering as he rode, its gold embroidery glittering in the sun.

The tournament went on. Dunois and Legendre were to gallop straight at each other from the far opposite ends of the field, lowering their spears as they passed in a gesture of salute, then, when they had galloped the full length of the field, they were to turn and charge and, with one spear thrust, try to unseat each other. The trumpet sounded, and they began their preliminary gallop. As they drew closer to each other, their speed was breath-taking. The big horses carried their heavy burdens of men and armor as if they weighed nothing. A hush was on the arena, and only the sound of the pounding hoofs and metallic clash of the armor was heard. As the two drew closer they began to lower their spears in salute. Then, when they were only a few yards apart, Legendre's horse faltered and swerved closer to Dunois. Legendre's spear seemed to waver and change direction, and then things happened too fast for the spectators to comprehend! There was a crashing, rending sound, the screaming of Dunois's horse, and Dunois himself fell heavily to the ground, rolled over twice, and ended on his back, the broken spear imbedded in his chest through the broken chain armor.

There was a moment's terrific gasp, then women screamed and men ran out on the field. Louis was the first to reach Dunois's side; a crowd gathered quickly around. Legendre came galloping back furiously, slipped from his horse, and began to babble about an accident and his horse tripping on the uneven ground.

Louis paid no attention. He was prying the dented, broken helmet from Dunois's head, and when he had it off —Dunois was already dead!

Louis couldn't realize it, looking down at the head he held in his arms. Dunois's eyes were open; they looked wide and astonished. It was so sudden it was unbelievable! One moment he had been in full strong motion, life in every vein and artery, and now he lay in irrevocable quiet.

"Dunois!" Louis said in tones of such regretful horror that the men around him were hushed for a moment.

Louis stared numbly down, incredulous. It was impossible that Dunois was dead—impossible. Louis could still hear the echoes of his strong voice. Surely he would begin to stir in a moment, open his eyes and mutter, "God's curse!" He still looked so strong and vigorous; that was what made it so unbelievable. His face was brown and still warm from the heat of his galloping charge—not gray and pinched as it had been in Italy, when Louis had feared his death might come at any moment. He hadn't died then— he had died as he always said he would—in France—on a fast horse—with a spear in his hand!

Louis hardly felt the hands that pulled him to his feet. He watched in a daze as Dunois was picked up and carried from the field. His horse was led away; his spear, his gauntlets were picked up—but the queen's scarf, which he had worn so gallantly onto the field, didn't leave with him. Ann-Marie's scarf was gone.

Ann-Marie saw that. She stood in frozen horror, gripping the edge of the box to keep from falling, and slowly turned her head toward the next box and Anne. Anne wasn't watching her now; she was talking in agitation among her friends, expressing her regret over such a terrible accident and discussing whether the tournament should go on or be stopped.

Was it an accident? Ann-Marie was wondering with sick horror. And was it a coincidence that the scarf, which Anne might have thought concealed Louis's release, was gone? The queen didn't think it was either an accident or a coincidence, and she felt with certainty that if she had given the paper to Dunois, it would be in Anne's hands now! The queen turned and left her box.

The tournament went on after a while, but neither Louis nor the queen knew it.

Louis walked away from the field in a daze of grief, turning and twisting in its iron grip. He sank down on a fallen tree, his head in his hands, in a heavy throbbing pain. He thought of Dunois's face again, so full of life and yet dead, and he groaned between clenched teeth. It was unendurable.

He felt a light touch on his arm and looked up in surprise. He had heard no one coming. Ann-Marie was beside him, her eyes dark and glittering with tears.

"Oh, Louis," she said brokenly. "I loved him too——"

She began to sob, and he put his arms around her waist and drew her close to him, resting his head against the sweet comfort of her breast. They stayed that way, careless whether the whole court saw them.

"I loved him too," she kept repeating, and when her tears began to shake her with their uncontrollable grief, he stood up and let her cry against his shoulder, and, in comforting her, his own pain became more endurable.

When she returned to her room she sent her maids away and took the paper out of her bodice, looking at it gravely. It had cost Dunois his life, even though he hadn't had it. The thought that she might be in some measure to blame for his death overwhelmed her with bitter regret.

The room had been thoroughly searched again while she had been gone; she could tell by a little trap of fine thread that she had arranged and which was now disturbed. The room would be searched again and again, she knew, so she looked around again for a better hiding place but finally decided that the old one up under that tall ornate fireplace was as good as any. Standing on the desk, she carefully returned the paper to its concealment and got down, tugging the desk away from under it. If Anne's spies had already searched the room and hadn't found it—it was as safe a place as any.

Georges came to officiate at the funeral mass. His plump hands were folded in sadness, and at the close of the service he and Louis walked out silently, missing the bluff laughter and the generous presence of Dunois. They never became used to missing it.

20

Now that Charles was king, he decided he would like to be an emperor too. "Emperor of the East" was the empty, glittering title he coveted, and it was being offered him by an Italian coalition headed by Ludovico Sforza and the corrupt Borgia Pope Alexander VI, in return for helping them take Naples and fighting the Turks.

France had a fairly legitimate claim to Naples through an inheritance from the dukes of Anjou. Of course claiming and possessing were separated by a wide gap, and this gap Charles, with the encouragement of his new mistress Etienne de Vesc, thought he would like to bridge with a triumphant war.

He went about it in his usual erratic way. He bought neutrality from Henry VII of England, Maximilian of Austria, and Ferdinand of Aragon, paid them in towns and huge sums of money, ignoring his sister's and his wife's advice in his consuming desire to be a great and conquering prince, leading his army into victory after victory.

The queen didn't object as much as Anne did, for although neither of the women thought highly of the idea, Ann-Marie was more of a Breton than a French queen and she preferred to see Charles lead his armies into Italy rather than into Brittany, where revolt was brewing again.

It was a popular war with the court and all the people; they thought it about time France set out for glory and conquests and ransoms.

Louis, because of his rank and popularity with the dukes, was chosen as second to the king, although he had his doubts about the success of the campaign and didn't trust the king's allies. He objected that it wasn't safe for Charles to lead the army into Italy himself. It was certainly putting his head into a lion's mouth. Louis earnestly warned him not to venture so far into the home territory of treacherous men like Sforza, the Medici family, and the Borgia Pope. They would battle each other to capture the French king, hold him for enormous ransom, or even see that he never lived to leave Italy. Charles disregarded Louis's warning, thinking Louis wanted to lead the army himself. Louis had no such desire.

The court was in a panic of preparation and Charles was in a seventh heaven of delight. Life was beginning for him at last. He had a son, he was about to have another, he was leading his army off to glowing victories. He was enjoying kingship to the full, since he had added a mistress to the pleasures of royalty. The queen looked the other way, tried not to notice Etienne's arch air of triumph. Ann-Marie was relieved to be free from connubial duties. Her days were bitter and long. She had only the knowledge of Louis's love to sweeten them, and she would never have anything more than that, just the assurance that he loved her. The days would go by, and the years, and they would never be together. Years without love were long!

Anne of France found her life was bitter without the smallest pleasure to sweeten it. Her quick eyes watched Louis and Ann-Marie jealously, and every time she saw his eyes upon the queen she quivered, remembering that he used to look at her like that. She reasoned with herself, told herself that the feeling she had for Louis, whether it was love or hate, was only habit. She had let it grow upon her, and she must halt it before it ruined her. And even as she reasoned she knew she was too late. Habit or not, it had ruined her. She tossed in weary anger half the nights, hating Louis and Ann-Marie, and herself most of all.

"You'll be careful, Louis?" Ann-Marie asked, looking seriously up at him from her seat at the end of the long ballroom. The chair beside her was the king's, but he wasn't in it, having excused himself to his wife an hour ago to go in search of a last loving farewell with Etienne, for tomorrow the army set out for Italy.

"I'll be careful, Madame Rolande," he assured her.

He wanted to bend and kiss her, but the scandal about them was bad enough, after the day of Dunois's death when the court had seen them embrace. He thought wryly it was ridiculous that he was allowed to touch only the women who meant very little to him. The two he had really loved he had rarely caressed.

"You must be careful too," he said, and she flushed. She was more reticent and didn't speak of those things so easily as the French. The fact that they loved one another and yet she was subject to another man's body embarrassed them both.

But she answered steadily, "That's an exchange of promises."

That was their farewell, but he had a different one from Anne of France. She stopped him as he was about to pass her and asked in smiling mockery, "And so tomorrow you set forth to cover yourself with glory?"

He smiled too. "Naturally! And yet past experiences on the battlefield haven't always found me successful."

"Is that true?" she questioned, politely incredulous.

"You have of course forgotten that little melee at St. Aubin-du-Cormier, but for some reason it's impressed upon my memory."

"Oh yes, St. Aubin; of course I remember. But," she assured him kindly, "then you were fighting against brother Frenchmen; I think you'll find it easier when your enemies are only Italians."

"Thank you," he smiled. "Your encouragement is soothing."

Her voice was still kindly. "But then you have so much encouragement, it seems superfluous to add mine! There's Madame Valentin, and de Porte, and"—she named over six of the most notoriously loose women of the court and then added—"and my sister-in-law, of course, has always been so interested in you and so encouraging!"

His smile ended very abruptly and his silence was a reproach. She herself wasn't pleased with her remark now. To see him angry at her because of another woman wasn't the same thing as annoying him for political reasons.

"And your wife?" she asked, her smile gone too. "Have you been to Linières for her encouragement also?"

He returned her gaze directly. "I've been to Linières," he told her, "to see my friend Jeanne. As for wife, I have none!"

He turned rudely away and left her. That was their farewell.

The next morning, to martial music, the waving of banners and kerchiefs and gloves, the army set forth to war, the glorious war that would capture Naples and whatever other Italian states that were available. Beyond that there was Constantinople and the inevitable infidels, plus the high-sounding title of Emperor of the East. It was a foolish quest, some of them realized, and yet the thought of Italian conquest was always attractive.

This present war was grotesquely complicated. It was a war within a war within a war. Charles didn't realize he was being used as a cat's-paw by Sforza and the Borgia Pope. Secret treaties lay under secret treaties, but boiled down to the essence, Charles and the French Army were being lured into Italy with promises of help and reward from Sforza. After they had used up their army in conquering Naples, Charles and his army would be taken prisoners.

The French Army marched easily toward Naples, conquering as they marched, but getting farther and farther from home with every step. Louis was left behind at the town of Asti, for he and a portion of the army had succumbed to a fever and had been too ill to go on. To his sickbed came disturbing facts his spies brought him, facts he had feared all along. Charles and his army would soon be trapped by the overwhelming forces of Sforza and Charles would be a prisoner. Louis got out of bed and, still feverish, began to plan Charles's rescue. He sent for reinforcements to come from France; he sent couriers to Charles to inform him of the truth and tell him to retreat as fast as he could. With his reinforcement Louis marched directly upon Sforza, to take his attention from the king's retreat so that Charles would have time to hurry over the mountain passes into safe territory close to home.

Louis's sudden attack was very successful. He took several towns, among them the strategically placed city of Novara, and kept Sforza's army in check there while he prayed for the king to hurry.

But the king was in no such haste. His indecisive mind couldn't comprehend the situation. Louis was put to his wit's end to keep the thirty thousand men of the enemy forces so busy they weren't able to get through to stop the king, but finally, after almost two months, Charles and the army passed safely over the mountains and reached Asti. Louis in his turn expected relief at Novara, for provisions were low and he was in a state of siege. Charles was safe, close enough to France, while Louis, with fewer and fewer men, was stranded at Novara. But Charles had only to send a contingent of his large army and everything would be saved. Louis waited for the relief, expecting it hourly.

He wrote to Georges in a hopeful vein:

"Our enemies' camp is still where it was, close to the town. They run and we run. Today we made a sortie and some were killed on both sides. Thank God we keep our hearts up while awaiting our rescuers, the king's army, and it doesn't seem much harm can come to us, since they're approaching. Written at Novara, this twentieth day of July, by the hand of your Louis."

But the king's army wasn't approaching. It was very hot, and the king had seen a woman who had made him forget there was a siege at Novara. Furthermore, he had had messages from Sforza, who protested he couldn't imagine what had made Charles leave Italy so precipitately and why had the Duke of Orleans turned on the king's own allies? Did Orleans mean to take Milan and Naples for himself? The fact that Sforza had poisoned the Duke of Milan, his nephew, to assume the throne, failed to influence Charles against Sforza, although by this time most of the French nobles had seen and understood the true situation and realized from what Orleans had saved them. They begged to be allowed to take some of the soldiers and march to Louis's relief, but Charles couldn't decide.

July melted away into August, and August, with men dying from hunger, intense heat, and fever, passed into September, and still Charles made no move to go to their relief. It required a decision, either for or against Sforza, and he wasn't accustomed to making decisions. Anyway, Novara was some distance away, he couldn't see it, and what he couldn't see he could never imagine or take very seriously.

But at the news that the walls of Novara had given way Charles was at last forced into action, an indecisive action. He didn't send relief, but he arranged a peace treaty, which was signed at Verceil. So the siege was dropped, a peace was signed that most of the men felt was dishonorable, but Charles didn't want to be Emperor of the East any more. It was too hot.

Two thousand men never came out of Novara at all, and

the five thousand who did were wracked with disease and weakness. They marched loyally to Verceil to greet their king, only five hundred of them able to carry arms, and when they staggered in, many of them having dropped on the way, King Charles greeted them with hysterical fervor and praise. He tearfully distributed food and money among them and even more tearfully watched some of them die from sudden overeating.

When Louis saw the number of men Charles had with him—twenty-five thousand Swiss mercenaries who loved nothing better than a fight, and also the original French Army—a flood of fury rose in him against the thoughtless mind that had left seven thousand men to starve in a walled-up city when Charles could have taken the city for himself, ruined Sforza, and taken the duchy of Milan in the bargain. Louis could barely speak to the king, he was so bitterly regretting the lives lost so needlessly. The whole war had been handled in such a reckless, extravagant way and abandoned halfway through when a little courage and determination would have won it.

Louis paid the indemnities of the entire city of Novara and the wages of that city's garrison out of his own pocket, for King Charles seemed to have no idea of that necessity. Once the soldiers were out of his sight he entirely forgot that a town and its inhabitants had been tortured so a king could take a whole skin back to France. Charles traveled back in hazy discouragement; his emperor's crown had drifted away into the fantastic dream from which it had come, and although he talked now and then of coming back later and retaking Naples, those around him shook their heads grimly and privately vowed to have nothing to do with another undertaking led and managed by so poor a soldier. Louis couldn't keep back some words of anger and resentment, so he traveled back in disgrace.

In dreary, discontented defeat the French Army returned to France and the Italian campaign was over. Nothing had been gained. Louis and a few of the others had distinguished themselves for personal bravery, and as Louis's reward for saving the king's life he was allowed to pay the cost of the siege of Novara.

21

Disheartening news waited for Charles at home. The little Prince Charles-Orlando, never very strong, was dying, and the baby the queen had been expecting had died before it was born. Ann-Marie was desolate, and when Charles-Orlando finally ended his helpless little life in shrieking convulsions, she fainted away and was ill for many weeks.

Between the disastrous death of the dauphin, the still-birth, and the wreck of the Italian hopes, the court was clothed in black for over a year. Charles had no sense of proportion. Having been excessively gay for some months, now he was going to be as lavishly miserable. His orders were very explicit. Everyone wore mourning. Entertainments and gaming in the evening were forbidden at the court, instead of which a dismal-voiced bishop read to them from pious books. Laughter wasn't encouraged. In this atmosphere of continual reminder the queen couldn't seem to heal her grief, but continued to hear the wailing screams and see the pain-tossed body of her little son.

Charles's grief was loud and extreme. He wept and prayed with her in a black-draped room before an altar with the child's picture upon it; he bemoaned and accused both himself and Ann-Marie for the wickedness they must surely have committed for God to so punish them. He allowed themselves no pleasures and distractions, beyond slipping away by himself to cry on Etienne's less grief-stricken bosom, and he encouraged the queen to fast and pray for another child until her weary body was weak and her mind light and dizzy.

Charles's sister did nothing to discourage this intemperate grief, for it very effectively kept Ann-Marie from the business of the throne, and without the queen behind him, Charles found it all too tedious. But when Louis saw the pale queen, dressed in heavy mourning robes that she could hardly support, her thin hands shaking with the lightest effort, he blazed with fury.

He went directly to the king, trying to smooth down his own anger as he went, for he knew he must be friendly and flattering if he were to have any result.

"Monseigneur, I'm worried for you," he told Charles sympathetically. "You will ruin your health."

"That must be as God wills," Charles sighed, seeing himself in patient, brave pain and approving the picture.

"As God wills, yes, but you must turn to your friends for consolation—not keep yourself shut up with grief for a companion. God gives us time in which to forget."

"Forget?" Charles looked displeased. "Can we ever forget our children's deaths? If you were a father, you wouldn't say that so easily."

"I realize, in a small way, what you have suffered, and your patient bravery is a miracle of endurance. But I'm afraid you'll strain yourself too far, and I don't think you realize how ill the queen is!"

Charles's eyes were annoyed and questioning. "And if I don't realize, you think you're better able to understand?"

"You're so worn out with your own grief. She's a woman and hasn't your strength. She has had physical illness to bear as well as mental—I know you'd see it for yourself if you hadn't so much on your mind, but question a physician about her. Perhaps if you took her away for a while, it would help her to forget a little what happened here."

Charles faced Louis in stern, fanatic rebuke. "When we sin, God sends punishment. It can't be run away from!" Then Charles turned the defense into an attack.

"It's very easy for you to talk lightly. You turn away from your lawful wife, throwing back your vows at the Holy Church, and you live in great sin. I don't know how much longer God will let you continue your wickedness."

God or Anne? Louis thought, and shrugged, irritating Charles to his usual imperative ending.

"Go and bring your wife to court!"

Louis went to Blois cursing Charles. What was especially irritating was the fact that in a few months, perhaps when it was too late, Charles would have laid aside this pious, God-fearing role and be ready to assume another equally intemperate attitude. There was no constancy of character to him—every hour found him a different man.

The death of the dauphin had made Louis heir presumptive again, and in such a position it was extremely dangerous for him to beg for more cheerfulness for the court and the queen. His enemies, including Anne, didn't hesitate to say of course he was cheerful, he was one step nearer the throne again, and there was only Charles to keep him from it.

Anne of France was always glad to suggest to the king that she had heard shocking rumors. She never was explicit, but she warned Charles to watch his food carefully and add a few more guards to the men who watched in his antechamber throughout the night.

Louis guessed all that was being said, but when the formal period of mourning was long over and the palace was still dismal as a tomb, Louis decided something must be done. It was maddening and degrading, Louis thought, for so many people to be dependent for their lives and happiness on a madman's whims. Here were hundreds of people living together in the palace, kept there by the desire and needs of royalty, glad to be there, of course, and dependent upon the royal family for their daily bread. They worked for it in different ways, and their private lives should be their own as long as they attended to their duties satisfactorily. Mourning was custom and necessity, but on this occasion it had grown into a creeping, dusty shadow that had laid its darkness over the whole castle, stifling laughter, insulting intelligence, and injuring health. This dust must be swept away. Ann-Marie must be freed from it, or her health wouldn't survive. He saw he must do the freeing, no matter what trouble it brought on him. Other nobles had protested to Charles but had been sent to their estates and told that if they didn't find it gay enough for them at court not to come back. They had been fined for insolence into the bargain. It wouldn't be an easy matter to bring gaiety back to a court where the king opposed it. Luckily for Louis's plans, however, envoys from Spain and the Pope came to France, important envoys who hoped again to interest Charles in the infidels, and these representatives required entertainment and hospitality.

Charles wanted to include them in the mourning, but was persuaded from that by Louis, who convinced him that some slight lessening of the sadness was necessary, or the envoys and their majesties would be insulted. A ball was planned, a sober one; only black was to be worn, the music wouldn't be lively, and Charles explained the reason for solemnity even in the midst of festivity to the envoys. They nodded sympathetically, competing with each other to see which one might look the saddest.

For the first time in over a year Ann-Marie and the ladies of the court dressed themselves for a court ball. They wore black gowns, and the queen's was of course, black, but it was embroidered with gold threads and it had a very old-fashioned but beautiful golden collar that stood up around her neck and framed her face and head. She was tremulous with excitement and a respite from her harassed mind. It was a somber room, filled with the black-clothed, quiet-speaking courtiers, the music slow and grave, and no one was to dance. They stood about in uncomfortable groups and watched the queen sitting quietly in her chair and the king talking in a side, alcoved room to some of the envoys. It was a very sad imitation of a ball.

Louis's arrival caused a stir, for he was dressed in his favorite scarlet coat, an exact copy of the one Dunois had given him years ago. His hose were white satin, and the brilliant red and white stood out in bright relief against the dark clothing of the other courtiers. His face wore his most expectant, charming smile. He went directly to Charles and bowed, presenting his respects. Charles turned his back deliberately on Louis as he was speaking and walked disapprovingly onto the terrace, where he stopped to debate with himself as to what Louis's punishment must be.

Louis continued to smile as though he hadn't noticed the king's displeasure and walked to Ann-Marie, who turned at the sound of his voice and caught her breath in sudden wonder at his dazzling appearance. Her eyes closed involuntarily and she was back in a little sitting room in Brittany with Louis standing in the same bright colors against the door, looking at her in surprise. She had thought him the handsomest man in the world then. She opened her eyes to look at him and found she thought so still. There were lines in his face he hadn't had then; he had more years and experience in his countenance now, for he was thirty-four years old. He seemed taller and leaner and more unhappy, but his eyes, with their look of understanding, gave her strength and encouragement. She felt a breath of Brittany wind in her nostrils; it refreshed her and she smiled back at him, forgetting death for the first time in over a year.

When he asked her if she would begin the dance with him, she put out her hand unquestioningly and followed him onto the floor. With one of her hands in his, his other only lightly resting at her waist, they began to move slowly into the graceful steps of the dance. After a moment another couple moved out, taking courage from their example, and then another, and very soon the room was full of dark-clad figures revolving slowly about the colorful pair in black and white and scarlet. In the little center circle of the room, reserved for the kings and queens to dance, Louis and Ann-Marie swayed and turned, Louis smiling down into her eyes and Ann-Marie, unsmiling but happy, looking up at him.

Louis made a gesture to the musicians and the music began more gaily. Faster and more lightly he moved with Ann-Marie, and the dancers followed his lead. Excitement and movement were loosening tongues that had been cautious for so long. Laughter broke out now and then, stopped in surprise at the unaccustomed sound, and then, taking courage at the music and the sight of the bereaved queen dancing, it came again, high and clear in feminine joy, lower, more rumbling, in masculine response. "Enough of sorrow," it said. "It doesn't help to grieve. And if we all laugh together, we can't all be punished!" Following Louis's initial step, the men and women of the court laughed and danced, and the wall of dreariness that had been built about the queen went down before their mirth.

Louis spoke, after he had surveyed the growing gaiety with great approval. "Madame Rolande, I'm angry at you! You've eaten your dimples."

Ann-Marie smiled, and he nodded.

"Much better!" he said. "But I'm still angry. These people look to you"—he gestured about the room—"they're your responsibility, and you mustn't think only of yourself." He could feel her stiffen in resentment, but he didn't care if she were angry at him if it brought back her own strength. "Charles will never think of them, and it isn't right they should be dependent for their pleasures on his whims. Promise me you won't let this gloominess go on."

She didn't answer for a moment, then she said firmly, "I promise."

Louis was content. He knew her determination, and when it was roused she was more than a match for Charles's uncertainty. They danced on in silence, observing with satisfaction the smiles about them. A taste of this will make them ready for more, Louis thought, and smiled back at his friends.

Anne of France was not present. She had gone to Bourbonnais, so there were no black looks to follow them about the room in malicious understanding.

The dance was almost over when the musicians suddenly stopped playing. The dancers, swaying on for a few steps, came to a gradual, bewildered halt, but when they saw the king surveying them all from a point close to the orchestra, they knew he had ordered the music stopped. The room was in absolute silence, heavy and embarrassing, while Charles walked through the bowing people, straight to the middle of the room where Louis stood with Ann-Marie. Louis watched him come and knew that a public reprimand and some sort of punishment was approaching with him, but Louis stood erect and smiling with a secure amusement. He had done what he had come to do; this little furious man was too late.

Charles stood before them, his pale, prominent eyes red with anger.

"It's interesting to see, Monseigneur," he said loudly, "how pleasant you find the dauphin's death, but it seems most indiscreet to flaunt it in our faces."

He turned and glared at Ann-Marie too, but whatever reprimand he had for her would come when they were alone.

Louis answered quietly, "The year is over. I assumed the mourning was concluded, or has the custom changed?"

There were some slight murmurs about the room, of not quite brave enough encouragement, and Charles's anger mounted at the attempted justification.

"The mourning will be concluded when I have declared it so, and nobody else shall take that liberty upon himself! The custom of obedience to the king hasn't changed, and I consider you've been insolent to the point of treason, Monseigneur."

Louis's face didn't change at the word; he had heard it too often. He was in danger, but there was nothing he could say. Charles hesitated, wanting to arrest Louis but not quite daring. "You will go to Blois, and you will remain there until you have my permission to leave it. We will dispense with your services as governor of Normandy, and when you return to court, if you do, I expect a thorough apology for this conduct and I expect you to bring your wife with you!"

Louis didn't speak, only bowed and left the king's presence and the ballroom, but there was so much contempt in his face and body that Charles was almost bouncing up and down at his insolence. Ann-Marie was blazing too. She didn't wish a family scene at that moment, and she excused herself with an equal contempt and insolence.

"You have guests here from Spain, madame." Charles tried to stop her. "Have you forgotten that?"

"I think you are the one who forgot!" she said, and went to her room, where she walked about furiously, thinking of what Louis's desire to help her had done to him. She blamed herself for slipping into such a listless condition, and she awaited the king's coming with eagerness, for she had a large collection of home truths to offer him. She was thoroughly aroused. She took off her black dress and threw it into the cupboard. The mourning was over.

Louis rode to Orleans, and the weight of disgrace and trouble gathering about him should have been heavy on his mind, but he was singing as he cantered along the dark roads, well content to trade the governorship of Normandy, the public disgrace, for the look of returning strength and courage in Ann-Marie's eyes.

22

Louis was kept away from court for two years, during which time Ann-Marie had misfortune after misfortune, for she lost another boy a few days after its birth and a little girl barely drew breath before it died, but neither death touched her so much as her beloved Charles-Orlando's, and through the grief she did not again succumb to hopelessness, but fought with success to keep the court, if not herself, from permanent mourning.

The state of the country was one of great unrest and dissatisfaction. At the close of the Italian wars the soldiers had come back, many of them ruined by fever and most all of them ruined for peace. Unable, some of them, to find work and food, to pick up where they had left off, they roamed the country as brigands, discontented with the king and the government that did nothing for them. Some of the less lawless marched to the king's palace and demanded relief. Some of them had been paid off with written promises and now came demanding their fulfillment. The working people were burdened to the last measure of their endurance by the heavy taxes that were required to pay for the silly, costly war. All this discontent Charles found convenient to lay at Louis's door, never for a moment admitting it might be his own fault, and there were always those who were willing to swear they had done this or that treasonable deed at the instigation of the Duke of Orleans. Louis was blamed for everything. He gave up refuting the charges. It was too hopeless, trying to defend himself against a hailstorm of foundless accusation, and the final foolishness struck him as so ridiculous that he burst into laughter, cruel and horrible as the charges were. He was accused by some of having poisoned the queen's babies, but at least that one charge he was sure even the king would not credit.

He was recalled to court and ordered to bring his wife
with him. This, the letter said in Anne's black handwriting,
signed with her name and the king's, was his last chance to
acknowledge Jeanne as his wife. He was to bring Jeanne to
the castle at Amboise in August, where the court would
resume residence after their months at Tours. If he did not
obey the king and bring his wife, he could expect imprisonment, without trial, for treason!

Jeanne heard of it and came limping to Tours to plead
for Louis. First she went to Anne, because she knew her
sister was the instigator behind the command.

"What makes you harass Louis so?" she persisted, following after her sister as she walked impatiently away. "Why
is it that you let him have no life of his own? How can it
matter if I live at Blois or stay where I am happier?" She
walked quickly around to stand in Anne's way so she must
listen. "Anne, never in my life have I seen a thing become
so poisoned as your love for Louis. Yes, I know, to others
you say he is treacherous, or murderous, or wants to be
King of France—but to yourself what do you say? There
must come some moments when you're alone with your
conscience. What do you say to it? You haven't the excuse
you had when you were younger. You're no longer a girl to
be petty and revengeful. You're a woman and intelligent
enough to know you cannot play the wicked empress with
another person's life for personal reasons! It's wrong, Anne.
I've told you that for ten years, since you imprisoned
Louis."

Anne broke in with exasperation. "Is it only ten? It
seems to me I've heard nothing else from you since we
were born. I am wicked, I am cruel, I am harsh, I shall be
punished! Very well, I think I'll be glad to exchange a
rigorous punishment for this never-ending reproach from
you."

She turned and looked directly at Jeanne, and Jeanne
was surprised to see how unhappy her eyes were. Tortured,
Jeanne thought, by something she sees daily.

"I have always tried to be a good sister to you, Jeanne,
have I not?"

Jeanne nodded. There had been many ways in which
Anne had made life at Linières more pleasant, influencing
her father into a generous allowance after years of being
dependent upon Madame de Linières for every piece of

clothing she had possessed, and when Anne had been regent she had increased the allowance and made grants to Jeanne for the founding of a convent in which Jeanne had been interested.

"Then you must judge me by what I have been to you. You don't understand all the elements that enter into my quarrel with Louis, and whatever cruelties you think I've descended to, you must know that I've been driven to them by circumstances"—Jeanne shook her head, and Anne turned hers away, suddenly saying, in a low, shaken voice, as though it were forced from her—"or something in myself that makes me the most unhappy of women."

She left Jeanne without another word, and Jeanne stood looking after the straight figure that walked away so assuredly, that was so competent and clever and yet was the most unhappy of women. Jeanne's eyes were wet with the pity she had for everyone but herself, and she thought that although it might be Louis who was punished, Anne suffered too.

Jeanne sighed and limped to see her brother, who greeted her indifferently.

"My brother, I have never asked many favors of you, have I?" Jeanne smiled at Charles, but Charles did not return it.

"No, but when you do it's certain to be about Orleans. Why do you do it? I'll never understand it. He refuses to acknowledge you're his wife and you come and ask favors for him."

"Because I can't bear to see you so unjust." Charles made an impolite sound with his lips and turned away. "No, truly, Charles, I've never seen anyone treated with so little justice as Louis has been. Think over his life—one long weary trail of injustice—all the things that should have been his were taken from him. And now I've heard that you have taken away his personal guard, are sending his only friend, Cardinal d'Amboise, away from him. I know very little of the world, I've often been told, but I do know it looks very much as though you intend to arrest Louis. Do you?"

How he hated these questions that required definite answers! "Not necessarily. It depends upon his actions when we return to Amboise."

"What actions?" she persisted.

"We must see how this trouble in Normandy concludes," he said crossly. Normandy had been devoted to its governor and was demanding that the king reinstate Louis there. "And we must see whether he is ready to obey our orders."

"Orders concerning me?" she asked, knowing that was what he meant. "Charles, would you like to have me for your wife?"

He looked at her in surprise, and involuntarily his eyes traveled over her body, which she made no attempt to conceal, even letting her cloak fall back.

"I can see by your eyes that you wouldn't. Neither does Louis, and no one in justice can blame him. He's made no further effort to divorce me, why not let it continue as it is? It's no kindness to me to force me to leave Linières and go to live at Blois, or come to court. It would make me miserable, and everyone else too. It would be a very wise thing to let it drop. I am Louis's wife—at least I am the Duchess of Orleans. He comes to see me very often and we have the most pleasant visits. That is how I'd like it to be left. That's how a wise king would leave it, not force something that makes no one any happier and that any one of his subjects can see is wrong."

Charles was silent, and Jeanne saw happily that she had made a strong impression. "As to Louis and Normandy—he was popular there."

"He's too popular everywhere for my taste," Charles grumbled.

"You like him too," Jeanne protested, "or you would if you were allowed to. Everyone does. Use his popularity to bring contentment to Normandy and credit to yourself. They wanted a duke, and you'd sent him—it seemed the natural thing for them to accept your representative and love him. It had nothing to do with a revolt against you— it was a confirmation of your judgment. Be just, Charles," she pleaded, "don't let cowardly fears push you into injustice as they did your father and your sister. Be wiser than they have been! You mustn't be impressed too much with your sister Anne's wisdom. She's only a woman, you know, and she hasn't your masculine impartiality and judgment."

Even Jeanne was willing to use flattery on Charles when it might benefit Louis, and her hypocrisy was rewarded by his pleased smile and nodding head.

Later in the day, alone with Anne, he said with resolution and masculine impartiality, or at least he thought he gave that impression, "I've been thinking that we may have been a little too forceful in our ultimatum to Louis."

Anne dropped the letters in her hands and looked at him with nervous exasperation. "You mean you have been talking with Jeanne. She inflicted the same touching speech on me. You're so easily influenced, Charles, it's the most maddening thing in the world!"

She wished him to be influenced only by her words; she wished she could nail him down in a corner and keep him there.

He was stubborn, remembering that, after all, she was only a woman. "There's a good deal of truth in what she says, however, and we mustn't forget it. She doesn't wish to come here or to Amboise, or even to go to Blois. She prefers to remain at Linières, and I must admit I wouldn't like to have her at court very much. She's too depressing— and after all, Louis does go often to visit her. That's all she wants."

Anne rose, tense and irritated. To go over all this again, when she had convinced him a hundred times already, was almost too much! She was tired, and for one weary second she thought how it might be if she said, "Very well, let Louis go! Let him go to Blois—let him just visit Jeanne now and then, or let him go to Rome and let him have his divorce! Let him marry, let him love, let him die, let him go to heaven or hell, but let him leave me in peace! I'm weary unto death of thinking of him!"

Could she achieve some peace if she let him go? No! It was too late. The habit of years of pounding on one point filled her voice with purpose.

"You mean it's all he wants. Just because he's taken no steps toward a divorce for a long time, you mustn't be lulled into thinking he intends to keep Jeanne always. He says he has no wife. He says it everywhere—and you must stop to think once and for all how ridiculous it makes us look. She is your sister, a king's sister, she has been married to him by permission of the Pope, with the Church's blessing, she was married in formal ceremony"—she added it up in impressive forcefulness—"and then he says he isn't married. If they're not married, what constitutes a marriage in his eyes? Perhaps he thinks you haven't been married either, for he takes an amazing amount of interest in your wife."

"Be just, Anne. He brought her to me himself."

"Because he had to, you fool," she snapped. "Because I made him!"

They glared at each other, Charles's touchy dignity very much offended. She sighed. "I shouldn't blame you, I suppose. Jeanne has a very clever tongue, but you will not be looking after yourself, nor her, if you let Louis continue his repudiation. He would like to have both your place and your wife—there isn't much to stop him; I doubt if your wife would!"

Charles bridled with indignation, but he wondered too.

"You mustn't take Jeanne so seriously, Charles. She comes pure and pious from her constant prayers and she doesn't know much about the world that we must live in."

Charles remembered that Jeanne had admitted she knew very little about the world. He nodded slowly.

"She's so perfectly safe herself, she doesn't realize how we're forced to guard your life. She lives in a noble world where everyone thinks only of right and charity—all those things are very lovely and they have their place, but if you enjoy your life, I warn you, you cannot afford too many of those impulses. Jeanne will see someday that we were right, so don't think too much about our little nun, Charles. Just see to it that Louis brings her to Amboise when we go next week!"

So he was back where he had been before. As he talked to each one, it seemed to him the one who was speaking was right. There seemed to be truth in what each one said, but he found it difficult to decide which was the stronger truth. Of course if Anne was right and he was foolishly charitable, he might find himself minus a wife, life, and throne. It would be better to err on the side of caution.

The king's bedroom was dark except for the firelight in the gate. Charles, from the bed, watched his wife, who sat in a low chair before the fire, her dark hair long down her back and her slim hands held out to the blaze.

"If you're cold, Ann-Marie," he said petulantly, "why not come to bed?"

She didn't answer immediately but let her hands fall into her lap, looking into the fire.

"I'm coming in a moment."

He turned in the bed, settling himself more comfortably, feeling the smoothness of the satin sheets and the warmth of the blankets. He closed his eyes and still saw the picture of his wife outlined against the fire. She was lovely. Lovelier than Etienne now. She hadn't been so beautiful for a while after they had lost the children, but now, in a way, she was more beautiful than she had been when they married, although none of that beauty had brought him much pleasure. He sighed and made a wager with himself that she was looking into the fire and seeing Louis's face.

That Louis of Orleans! He was everywhere. In his country, near his throne, even in his bed. His wife loved him, his subjects loved him, his sister Jeanne loved him—there was only Anne, and she hated him with a hate that made up for all their love. Anyway, it was a relief that he wasn't unanimously loved.

His wife's voice came and won him his wager. "Charles, what are you going to do about Louis if he doesn't bring Jeanne to Amboise with him?" And he wouldn't, she knew that. It was what she didn't know that worried her—it was the puzzling question of why Anne had suddenly forced this ultimatum, threatening Louis's imprisonment when she knew the queen still possessed the order for his release. It was still safely hidden in the queen's room at Amboise— or presumably it was, since Ann-Marie had left it there when they had moved to Tours, feeling it was safest in a place that had been overlooked in so many thorough searchings. Ann-Marie worriedly contemplated the dreadful thought that it might have been discovered. If it was—and Louis disobeyed next week——

"Charles," she repeated anxiously, for he hadn't answered, "what are you going to do about Louis?"

Do something. Always do something. He stirred irritably. "I wish I didn't have to do anything but forget him. But we've been lenient as long as we can. There's a limit to patience."

"You know it'll make Jeanne miserable to bring her to Amboise. She hates the court. She'd prefer to stay——"

He didn't let her finish. "I've heard that touching speech myself. You mustn't take Jeanne too seriously. She doesn't know much of the world we live in, her own is so safe and quiet. . . . It's all very well for her to decide where she'd like to live, but that has nothing to do with it. Louis has married my sister. He can't continue to go about saying he has no wife!"

"Charles, I'm very fond of Jeanne myself, and if with my thoughts and hopes I could make her well, I'd do it. Then Louis would have no right to refuse her. But as it is, anyone would act as he does." Anyone with courage, her mind added.

"You think, then, he should be free?"

"No—but Louis isn't asking for freedom. He withdrew his petition for a divorce at your orders."

"And you'd like to be free too," he said sulkily.

She turned from the fire to look at him, but she couldn't see his face in the darkness of the room and the shadows of the bed drapes.

"You and Louis would both like to be free. Then you could enjoy my throne together."

She got up and walked toward him, answering quietly. This was no unusual mood. It came to him recurrently in a flood of self-pity. "Why do you let your sister poison your mind against me and Louis too? You and I have always been good friends, Charles; it would be wrong for you to let suspicions like that come between us. I've been your friend when you had none. I've gone with you to your sister and helped you to take your rightful place. I've borne your children." She sat down on the bed and reached out for his hand, which he had kept from her at first and then let her take. "We've been married for over six years, Charles. Surely you know me well enough in that time to know I could never be false to you."

"Yes," he acknowledged reluctantly, ashamed of himself. All that she said was true. "It wasn't a love match, was it, Ann-Marie?" he asked, trying to sound sarcastic but being wistful instead.

"How can I say it was, when you know it wasn't? But I can honestly say there's been a good deal more in it than most royal marriages. Your sister would like you to think Louis is trying to plan your death so he may have your throne and your wife. That's not true! He'd like to be free from Jeanne, that's true. Any man wants a normal wife and children, but he's made no attempt to free himself since he promised you. And how can he take your throne? You are on it, and your children will be after you."

"Children," he said unhappily. "I have no children."

"There's no reason why we shouldn't have more, Charles," she forced herself to assure him, but he pulled away his hand resentfully.

"How can we have children when you never come to bed until long after I'm asleep? Perhaps you expect to find them some morning in the fireplace where you look so long!"

"No, that isn't where I expect to find them. We'll find one soon, Charles, in our bed where the others were born."

Slowly she slid under the covers and settled beside him.

The object of all these discussions was in the forest, lying on his back on the shaded grass under an enormous willow tree that overhung a stream. He and Georges had stopped there to have their solitary luncheon after a morning supposedly devoted to hunting but which they had passed in leisurely riding and talking. Georges was to leave for Rome on the next day and Louis was to start for Amboise—alone.

Louis had satisfied his appetite in neat dispatch. Remembering his prison days, he was unable to waste food or to overeat. He finished and dipped his hands into the running stream; washed his face in the cool water, swallowing some of it as it ran over his hands, and then lay back in the shade to rest and watch Georges, who sat with his back against the tree and delved deeper and deeper into the luncheon hamper, as though he had promised not to bring it back until it was empty, no matter what superhuman appetite it would require of him.

Louis smiled to watch him. The plump, well-cared-for fingers brought food up out of the basket, applied it diligently to the busy mouth, and returned for another trip. Georges had put aside his cardinal's robes for the day and was in a hunting costume that tightly outlined his figure. Louis smiled at the protuberance that marked Georges's middle and then raised his head to look down at his own. He was relieved to see that he was as concave below the ribs as he had always been. He knew, from being much with Georges, that so many extra pounds were a nuisance, although Dunois, he remembered, had been as heavy as Georges and as active as Louis. Dunois!

The hamper was empty at last. Georges rose, washing himself at the stream, and came back to stretch himself puffingly at Louis's side. They lay on their backs, side to side, their arms pillowing their heads, looking up at the sky, and at the white clouds that were forming and re-forming, through the slim-fingered leaves of the willow tree.

"In moments like these," Georges observed, "life is very pleasant."

"And at others?" Louis smiled inquiringly.

Georges heaved mountainously in a disgusted sigh. "It can be endured."

Louis rose on one elbow and leaned over him, interested. "But you shouldn't feel like that. You've almost everything you've worked for. You're a cardinal. Someday I think you will be the Pope."

"I think I could be," Georges agreed in a sober agreement that had nothing to do with boasting. "Perhaps I shall. I'll be able to do things in the Church I've always felt needed doing, but still I'll only be Georges d'Amboise, who eats too much and sleeps too much and is too fat. None of it will bring me much pleasure. I don't know why it is that sometimes my life seems not worth the bother of dressing for, even though I have, as you say, the things I've worked for."

Louis's gaze was thoughtful on his friend's face. "It's because you have missed the essence of it. If I had never been in love, I'd certainly not think life worth the bother. I'd hang myself some bright morning."

"Oh, love!" Georges was skeptical. "I expect I've felt it often enough myself."

"I wonder. I've never seen you so much in love that you wanted to give up the Church for the lady."

Georges was startled. "No, there was never that much to it, for which I'm very glad."

Louis shook his head decisively. "That's where you make your mistake. That's why you find life so lifeless. It must be the most important thing, even if it makes trouble for you, or you have nothing. I've often thought how sad it is for you churchmen to deny yourselves wives and families."

The smile on Georges's face was wry. "I wouldn't go so far as to say that. The Borgia Pope has certainly an incredible amount of nephews and nieces that look exactly like him."

"It isn't the same thing at all. I'd be the last to say there was no pleasure in light loves, but there's a difference between pleasure and necessity. Until you've met the love that's a necessity, you have nothing more than a little amusement."

Georges was curious in his turn. "I'd never have said that love had brought you anything but trouble. It seems strange to hear you speak so well of it."

"Oh, trouble!" Louis smiled. "Trouble and love travel together. It's true I never chose very wisely, but—I could never choose. It always happened before I could think. And yet, no matter what happened to my love for Anne, I'm glad I had it. And now . . ." He paused, looking thoughtfully up at the sky.

"Now?" prompted Georges.

"Now I suppose you'd say it was almost the same thing over again. It can never bring me anything but unhappiness. And yet I don't feel that way—I'm glad I have it. In the strangest kind of way, I feel, although I've loved twice, that it's all the same. Can you understand that, Georges? I mean"—falteringly he tried to explain what wasn't clear to himself—"when I was very young I loved Anne of France and did for the longest time, even after I had met Ann-Marie and loved her too, in a way. Gradually, I don't know quite how it was, unknown to myself even, I changed, and now I can't remember a time when I wasn't thinking of my little Breton. It seems she is at last what I thought I had in Anne." He looked at Georges and laughed. "I expect that sounds strange to you. In the first place, you could never sympathize with my love for Anne. Neither could Dunois."

"Oh no, you're quite mistaken. Under different circumstances she could have been a lovely woman. She might have been almost all Ann-Marie is today, but her father was too strong an influence over her. We understood your loving her, only I think we saw the change long before you did. And then, too, I think the fact that the king snatched her away made her forbidden fruit and even more desirable. Dunois thought so too—he said the only reason he wanted you to marry Anne was to show her father that an Orleans always won!"

Louis smiled thoughtfully and admitted, "It may have had something to do with it."

They were silent for a while, thinking of Anne and the past.

"I wish I didn't have to leave you tomorrow, Louis," Georges said uneasily. "The storm is brewing."

"I know. I leave for court tomorrow—with a king's escort! But that has happened before and the clouds have blown over. There's no sense worrying about tomorrow today, and as you said"—he smiled at Georges and settled back into his comfortable position—"in moments like these, life is very pleasant."

23

In the king's carriage on the sunny road from Tours to Amboise a familiar three-cornered duel was going on.

"I wonder if he'll come alone," Anne of France wondered aloud.

"Who is he, madame?" the queen asked politely, although she knew perfectly well.

"Louis of Orleans, of course," Charles said pettishly. "What other person do we ever discuss? The very word 'man' or 'duke' or 'he' means Orleans to me!"

Charles looked out the small carriage window at the hot August day and was glad to see that Amboise was only a half mile away now. He was tired of being caged up in the hot, airless carriage, and he envied the soldier on horseback who rode in front and back of the awkward swaying vehicle.

"I don't know why I listened to you, Anne," he grumbled to his sister, "and let you box us all up together in this tomb!"

"You listened because you knew it wasn't wise for you to ride out in the sun—it's very hot today—it might have struck you down."

Ann-Marie stirred impatiently. "It's certainly cooler on a horse's back, with a breeze in your face." She spoke to Charles. "I think it would have been good for you. Your sister is overanxious."

"Why do I have to be so careful all the time?" Charles accused Anne peevishly. "Look at Louis—he used to play tennis all day in a broiling sun, and he was never struck down." He muttered under his breath, "Lucky for me if he had!"

Anne sighed and pointed out, "His health is more robust than yours—and it's necessary to France that you take care —both for your own self and your hope of heirs." Then she looked sharply at Ann-Marie. "And if I'm overanxious, it's because I'm interested in my brother's welfare."

"If you had not been quite so interested," the queen retorted, "and overanxious in his youth, Charles might have enjoyed better health now. And as to hope of heirs"—which was a very painful subject—"it's not due to the sun's heat they died, and we'll have more when it pleases God!"

There was silence in the carriage for a while; the only sounds came from outside—the horses' hoofs on the road, the squeak of rubbing harness, the clanking of armor, and the voice of the coachman commanding the horses.

Then Charles himself resumed the discussion. "I think he'll bring Jeanne with him."

"He won't," said Ann-Marie promptly.

"He'd better!" said Anne of France grimly. "This time he'll go to Bourges if he hasn't!"

"Why this time, madame?" the queen asked. "Has the situation altered?" She watched Anne's face worriedly.

"Altered?" Anne of France seemed to find the word itself amusing. "Yes, it's altered."

"In what way?" the queen persisted. Was the release she possessed still safely hidden—or did Anne of France intend to try and cancel it? She felt a flicker of fear. "How has it altered?"

Anne of France smiled and shrugged. "Oh, there are several kinds of alterations," she said smugly. "You'll see when you get to Amboise."

The queen saw the moment the coach clattered into the courtyard at Amboise. There was the sound of sawing and hammering, piles of loose lumber lay on the ground, and workmen in leather jackets hurried around busily. The queen looked hastily up toward her rooms. The whole wing was being altered; windows were knocked out; nothing was left of her rooms!

Anne of France was watching her consternation with malicious triumph. She spoke solicitously. "It's a surprise I planned for you—we've altered that whole wing of the château to give you a pleasanter suite—a nicer view. It was really time we had it done—the walls were rotting and the bricks in the fireplaces were loose and treacherous!"

With a sickening heart, the queen had to admit that Anne of France was thorough. And clever. She had torn out a whole wing in order to have a logical reason to search every inch of the room. And she had found the paper! Louis, never knowing what had held him safe all this time, had lost his security without knowing that either.

Charles was commenting enthusiastically on the work, wanting to go and inspect it all the moment the carriage had stopped.

"Later," his sister told him. "We'll send for Louis first!"

"Oh, him again!" Charles muttered furiously. "You tend to it, Anne; I want to watch them paint."

That suited Anne well enough. Indulgently she watched him go and, walking upstairs to her study, she sent a guard to summon Louis to her there.

But the queen, hurrying on panic-stricken feet, reached Louis first. Careless of who might see her, she inquired for his room, found it, knocked, and, in answer to his voice, hurried in, closed the door, and stood breathlessly with her back to it as though to keep danger out. Louis turned in surprise at the sight of her. He had just come in from his arrival; he was brown and heated from the ride, his full white shirt damp with his exertion.

"Louis," she said hastily, "did you bring Jeanne?"

She could tell by his amused expression that he hadn't.

"No, don't smile—this time you must obey—or you'll be at Bourges again."

"Well, I wouldn't enjoy that," he admitted lightly. "Although, for all the progress I've made, I might as well be there!"

"She's sending for you right away—you'll have to choose today."

Her earnestness dispelled his light manner. "If I have to choose, I'll choose as I always have, Ann-Marie."

"But this time it's really Bourges—and an iron cage—oh, Louis——"

He tensed, his muscles remembering, but then he shook his head. "My life has been a strange one, Ann-Marie—the years I've spent with just one purpose. Defeat for that dead king! If I let him force me to admit Jeanne is my wife, he'll win!"

"You talk about him as if he weren't dead!"

"He isn't dead." Louis's lips twisted ruefully. "Far from it. He's like a snake with its head cut off—they say the snake doesn't die till the sun goes down. Well, Anne of France— she's his power and his sun. His strength lives in her. They're strong—both of them! But in this one small thing they have no force that's strong enough!"

Ann-Marie looked at him with frightened eyes. "Louis—don't be so stubborn—so foolhardy—don't let them send you away—think of me! Don't leave me here alone in this country I can't think of as my own! Think of me!"

"I think of you," he said softly. "I think of you—and I think of the day when there'll be some sudden change in our lives—and Madame Rolande will be there again! I won't tie my hands so I'm not free to take her!"

She shook her head vigorously. "Don't say that to me! Don't think it. That sudden change—it could only be Charles's death—we mustn't wish for that!"

"I don't. I've never wished him harm—he's a sad and silly little king——"

He was interrupted by a knock at the door. Ann-Marie's heart stopped. She knew it was the guard. Louis smiled reassuringly at her and went to the door, opening it a little, keeping Ann-Marie shielded from the sight of the guard, who had come to tell him that Madame Anne of France would see him and his wife at once in her office.

Louis nodded, then leaned toward the queen; he kissed her gently and whispered, "Au revoir, Madame Rolande!"

And he walked out to meet his enemy for the final decisive battle of the war between them.

He was admitted to Anne's study, and he bent low in a mocking bow, his eyes smiling. "You sent for me, madame?"

"For you and your wife. We will wait for her to join us."

"I'm afraid it would take too long a time, since I have no wife!"

Anne exploded. "Why you persist in this insanity I'll never understand! You babble like a fool, 'I have no wife, I have no wife!' You have a wife, and the time has come when you must say you have! This time, if you disobey the Crown, you'll go to Bourges! You've spent three years there —think twice before you make us place you there again!"

"My choice is made."

"You stupid, stubborn fool! I'll break your will, or I'm not Anne of France! I'll take those words from off your mocking tongue!"

"You can tear the tongue out," Louis suggested. Then he came closer and looked at her intently. "It's hard to tell where your greed for Orleans stops and your hate for me begins! Maybe you don't know yourself! But hiding behind your talk of treason—and France—I can see your hate, black—and bitter. Why, Anne, why? What did I do that was so terrible? I loved you—I wanted you—not for an hour's comfort, but for all my life. Was that why you hated me? I thought of that comfort I'd refused—those hell-begotten nights twisting in an iron cage! I wanted you—oh yes, but not for love or comfort. I wanted your body to hurt and crush as you hurt me." His fury mounted as he remembered. "Night after night after night—that creaking iron door held open for me by your hate. It was bad enough that there should be enmity between us—but to add that cruelty—oh, that was evil, Anne! I'll never forgive you that."

"I don't ask for forgiveness," she said through shaking lips.

"No—you still need more revenge, don't you? More and more cruelty. Well," he said with biting derision, "take all you want—enjoy it—revel in my pain, but you'll never make me change my words. I have no wife, Madame Anne, I have no wife, if you see that I die for saying it."

He hurled the words into her face, and before the echo of them had died away a commotion was heard through the open door that led out into the corridor. Running feet and startled outcries shook the bewildered Anne from the spell of Louis's words, and they looked toward the door with puzzled eyes. Men ran past, colliding with footmen running the other way. A high hysterical scream repeated itself again and again from a far part of the house, and a soldier came hurrying into the room, gasping out frightened, unintelligible words.

"What is it, what is it?" they asked together, and Louis hurried toward the trembling man, intending to shake the information out of him if it wouldn't come any other way, but the man answered at last.

"The king, Monseigneur—he went up on a ladder and he fell. Some lumber fell on him and hit his head"—he pointed to his own with shaking fingers—"here, and he's dying, they say."

Anne and Louis exchanged one horrified look.

"Where is he?" Louis cried to the vanishing guard, and the voice came shouting back to them as they stood at the door, hesitating which turn to take.

"In the upper hall—where the workmen are—they say he's dying."

He was. His large, unsteady head, on which the crown had never been very firm, was badly hurt, and they laid him down on a mattress pulled from the nearest bed, for they were afraid to move him. Hurrying doctors came to him, and the curious courtiers watched while he lay still and unconscious.

The palace was in pandemonium. In the courtyard couriers rode off to all the countries of Europe and all the corners of France; more couriers waited for more final news. In the stables the horses were unfed and uncared for; in the kitchen the dinner went to smoking ruins; in the castle one faction whispered among itself and looked frightened, another faction looked eager; Ann-Marie of Brittany knelt beside her husband and prayed for his soul, while Anne of France knelt and prayed for her brother's life, for if it flickered out, hers would follow it very soon.

The King of France was dying.

24

The long glass doors stood open in the small salon at Amboise, but the sun was no longer brilliant on the polished floors. It came in wanly and brought with it shadows from the tall poplar trees behind which it was sinking. The room was quiet with expectant silence, and the nervous movements of the man who walked about in it sounded hollow and loud in the stillness. Louis paced the room, his mind a chaos of uncertainty and wonder. If the king died, as it seemed he must, then he himself would be king. His life would be completely reversed with dramatic suddenness.

He tried not to see the pictures his mind brought temptingly before him. He had seen Ann-Marie, kneeling beside her husband and praying in fervent sincerity for his soul and his life. Louis wished he might pray in equal sincerity, but he couldn't. There was no use deceiving himself.

There was a portrait of King Louis XI hanging on the wall. Louis studied his godfather's sharp, sickly face, the cold eyes, as he waited for the news that would decide his life. What a king that dead man had been! How little he had cared for the many lives he had wasted.

And then Louis began to wonder what kind of a king he himself would be—if the chance came to him. Was he fit to be a king? As dying men are supposed to review their lives in their last conscious second, Louis, in the last waiting moment of his life, reviewed his past.

He had been taught nothing in his childhood that would have been of value to him as a king. It had seemed pleasant enough at the time, his studies all frivolous ones, taught him by the tutors the king chose for him, offering him nothing to train and discipline his mind, and he wondered for the first time, his gaze going quickly to the painted eyes of the dead king's portrait, whether the tutors had been deliberately chosen to make him as silly a boy as possible.

"Of course!" he exclaimed aloud, surprised at his own stupidity in not having realized it before. "Of course!" he said again, scanning the sardonic mouth and the pinched nostrils of the painting. The king had thought of everything. What would it matter to him if the clean materials of boyhood were soiled and wasted to serve his purpose?

But strangely enough the king's two daughters, one by cruelly locking him in a little room, the other by generously sending the books he should have known as a youth, had given him a discipline and training that would help him to be a fit king for France. The years at Bourges would be invaluable to him if Fate decided he was to be king, for he could never forget the lessons he had learned there.

He turned swiftly as he heard the door open. Georges slipped into the room; his plump face was white and quivering with excitement and he was trying hard to speak through shaking lips in answer to the question in Louis's eyes.

He walked across the room, and when he came to Louis he knelt down. His voice came, shaken with uncontrollable emotion.

"It is with great pleasure I see I'm the first to wish Your Majesty a long and happy reign!" he said.

Louis tensed with shock at the words that ended his suspense. His Majesty. He was the king!

He waited for the rush of triumphant realization that would make it clear to him, but it did not come. It was too much to realize all in one moment.

He reached down and raised Georges to his feet, and they looked into one another's eyes. There was so much in them that Louis sighed in a complete helplessness to express it.

"It's more than fitting that you should be the first, for never, I swear it, Georges, has any man had a more faithful friend. If only Dunois could stand with us now!"

His voice was full of regret, and they both looked back into the past to salute the sturdy figure, feet placed well apart, arms across the breast of the leather hunting jacket, the blunt, strong face raised in courage and obstinate loyalty. It was wonderful to have Georges beside him, but that didn't ease Louis's sorrow that the other friend who had fought so long, and who would have rejoiced in enthusiasm to acclaim Louis King of France, had been in his silent grave for years.

"I wish he were here now," Louis said slowly, "to see that the law he tried to make has been enforced at last."

"What law was that?"

Louis smiled gravely and reminiscently. "He felt it should be in the Code of France that I should always have my heart's desire."

"You have it now," Georges sighed in content. "There are many who would like to pay their respects to Your Majesty. May I bring them to you here?" He said the words lingeringly, enjoying their deference.

Louis frowned a little. "Already? The breath has hardly gone from Charles."

"No one even pretends to grieve for him," Georges said flatly. "He was a fool of a king, and France is better off without him."

Louis had to admit the truth of that. And yet, silly as he had been, Louis had felt a contemptuous pity for him. He had had such a small, futile life.

"Well"—Louis hesitated—"if they wish to see me, let a few come—but no shouting—and bring only my closest friends."

Georges's pink face was sardonic. "Your Majesty," he said with gentle cynicism, "they'll all be your closest friends now!"

The bells tolled in muffled gloom, Latin dirges were mournfully intoned, and the casket of the late King Charles went slowly through the streets on padded wheels. Almost no one cared that he was dead, yet he had been a king and must be so honored.

Ann-Marie walked in a dream, her eyes darkly shadowed with her nights of crying and self-reproach, for her Breton conscience knew its duty and expected sorrow of her, yet the most she felt was a numb pity for her dead husband. She offered as justification to herself that she had been married against her will, that she had been a faithful wife, that sorrow wouldn't bring her husband back, but it made no impression on the stern religious upbringing she had received in her pious country. No evasive arguments could change the fact that she couldn't grieve. In her black-hung rooms at Amboise, where custom was to keep her for many weeks, she walked in her conflicting dreams, back and forth, back and forth, across the long dim room.

In his study in another floor of the castle the new king was pacing restlessly too, and then he turned abruptly to Georges, who was working on some papers at the desk.

"Georges!"

"Your Majesty?" Georges looked up. "Yes, Your Majesty."

Louis smiled. "How many thousand times a day do you call me that? I've been king for more than a week—I should think the novelty would wear off."

"I like to say 'Your Majesty,' " said Georges contentedly, "and know it's you, Your Majesty!" He laughed. "I never liked to say the words before. How titles do change, according to the people who wear them!"

"I have no complaint," Louis admitted. "I only wish someone else could say it too!"

"Dunois," sighed Georges.

"And Eugène."

Eugène of Angoulême was dead too; his aimless, moody life was ended. Louis hadn't seen him so often in the last years, yet he missed him now he was gone. Eugène's two children, Marguerite and Francis, had been left in Louis's care. He was their guardian and he visited them when he could. Little Marguerite was beautiful and intelligent, Francis was already imperious and demanding, but no one thought that one day he might be King Francis I.

"There are just the two of us left, Georges, and soon you'll be leaving me—to be Pope at Rome."

Georges considered a moment and then firmly shook his head. "I think I'll not be Pope," he decided. "I'll just be Georges d'Amboise, who eats too much and is too fat and who likes to say 'Your Majesty' too well to leave you."

They smiled at each other, Louis very well pleased with the decision. "You'll stay beside me and give me your good counsel as you always have!"

Georges laughed. "And you'll obey it as you always have!"

"Georges, I need your advice now. I must see Ann-Marie."

Georges looked shocked. "The custom of the court——"

Louis interrupted, "Yes, I know the custom. She must be sealed up until she makes herself ill. Her grief must be so deep she's not allowed to see a friendly face—that's the custom—but I haven't seen her since Charles's death, and I must talk to her."

"I'd advise you not to——"

Louis smiled. "I wished to be advised *where* I should see her—if you would request her to come to my study, or if I should go quietly to her apartments—"

Georges leaped up quickly for one of his weight. "I'll request her to come here," he said hastily.

Louis laughed. "I knew it would be wise to listen to your advice."

Georges threw him a disgusted look as he hurried out the door to the corridor. After he had gone the smile faded from Louis's face. He was worried about Ann-Marie. He walked across the study to the other door, which led through his sitting room to the bed-chamber of his temporary quarters, the suite he had always occupied as Duke of Orleans and in which he would stay till the coronation. Then he would move the court to Blois—there were too many disagreeable memories here at Amboise—and he would try to avoid ever staying long at Tours again.

Ann-Marie still occupied the royal suite and would till the mourning was over. Mourning! That's all she had had ever since she had come to France. No wonder it was hard for her to love the country. He thought of her now, as she must be, drowned in black again, in her black-draped rooms, with Charles's picture placed by custom on her altar, watching her reproachfully.

Thinking his worried thoughts, he had quietly crossed the sitting room and was slowly opening his bedroom door, but he arrested himself suddenly and looked in amazement through the barely opened door. A strange-looking figure was standing in front of the full-length mirror, turning and preening in self-admiration. The slight figure was almost concealed in a regal cloak of cloth of gold with a train, all of it banded with heavy ermine. On top of a shock of wild red hair a crown glistened with many jewels——

Max Poquelin had borrowed the costume of the King of France!

Louis caught his breath sharply—and then, as usual where Max was involved, felt laughter bubbling up. To control it he caught his lower lip in his teeth and watched Max, who, all unconscious of his audience, was acting the part with the same superb elegance with which he had once graced the

livery of an Orleans valet. He was majestic graciousness itself as he bowed loftily to the multitudes, only half losing
the slippery crown.

It wasn't, of course, the great jeweled crown of France
that was too heavy to wear but would be held over Louis's
head at the fitting moment of the coronation. This was a
smaller diadem, but still the king's crown, and one to be
held in awe and respect. Louis knew, by all the rules of the
divine right of kings, that he should stamp frighteningly
in, snatch the crown, and punish Max, but he had no such
impulse.

That crown had already been on worse heads—sillier
ones, less faithful, less honest, and he thought that France
would be very fortunate if the crown could always be worn
on a head as good as Maximilien Poquelin's!

Max was regally turning to hold out his hand to be kissed,
so Louis very quietly closed the door and walked softly back
to the study. That door he opened noisily, stood there a
moment having a loud conversation with an imaginary
Georges, then he walked noisily back to the bedroom, and
when he opened the door the robe was out of sight, the
crown was back in its velvet case, and Max, rather breathless, was lowering the hinged lid of a big carved chest.

"Your Majesty!" he said hastily, and scrambled down
onto his knees respectfully with a guilty conscience.

"Max," Louis said sharply, "you kneel as gracefully as a
wounded boar!"

"Yes, Your Majesty."

Louis found what he had come for in a small locked
drawer of his desk, started out, but turned at the door for
an added word to his valet. "Respect for your monarch," he
said sternly, "is a necessary thing!"

"Yes, Your Majesty," Max said humbly, thinking regretfully that things would be a little different now that His
Grace had become His Majesty.

Then Louis smiled. "But a small amount of respect will
be sufficient, and your usual amount of impudence will still
be acceptable!"

"Oh yes, Your Majesty." Max grinned happily and got
up. Louis laughed and slammed the door.

He waited impatiently for Ann-Marie to come, but it was
more than an hour before Georges showed her in and dis-

approvingly left them alone. She was dressed, as he knew she would be, completely in black, from the black wimple covering her hair to the full black satin skirt that covered her small feet. Her little white face looked pale and very tired, and under her dark eyes, swollen with crying, were shadows, like bruises.

She bowed before him, not from formality, he thought, but simply to evade his eyes. He could see how miserable she had been.

He took her hand and drew her upright, said quietly, "You're unhappy, Ann-Marie."

"Very," she said slowly. "Very unhappy. We wished him dead."

"No!" he exclaimed strongly. "That we never did!"

"Just a few moments before it happened—we thought of it!"

"You're thinking of the things we said—but if you must remember them, be fair—remember correctly. I said I'd never wished him harm, and on my life, that's true. Ann-Marie," he urged her, "think of all the plots that were offered to me—why, hundreds of times, all I needed to do was nod my head and Charles would have been killed to put me on the throne!"

She considered that and knew that it was true. If the Duke of Orleans had wished the king dead, Charles could have been in his grave years ago. But if they hadn't sinned in action, still their thoughts had sinned.

"Yet—we wished him dead," she repeated miserably.

He shook his head. "No—not even that is true. If I'd wished Charles dead, I could have let him die in Italy. It would have been much easier, and no blame could have attached to me in any way. I had warned him again and again, and when I knew the plots against him, I forced him to retreat—I fought and saw thousands of men killed so Charles could live! No—you can't ever say I wished him dead!"

Her face was very grave, but he thought it cleared a little. But then she sighed. "Yes—your conscience is clear. But mine! My husband is dead, and I can't grieve."

"It that your fault? I think it's his!"

"How do I know? I married him, loving you. I never tried to love him."

"Ann-Marie, you're tired and weak, you're torturing yourself for nothing. Punishing yourself won't bring him back."

She turned away from him and walked toward the window. "Let me go back to Brittany," she said.

He followed her swiftly and turned her to face him. "Why do you want to leave me now—when in a little time we'll both be free—and we can take the happiness that surely we deserve after all these years of waiting? Surely we deserve it," he repeated firmly. "You were a faithful wife——"

She shook her head. "I gave him so little—so very little." Her voice shook, and she forced it on. "They should have found him a more willing wife—we could neither of us ever forget it took an army to bring me to him!"

"How was that your fault?" Louis asked gently. "Once married, you did the best you could. Now," he said decisively, "it's over—and regrets for the past can't stop us, now that we're *so* close."

She hesitated and said miserably, "Let me go back to Brittany!"

He watched her face, which she kept turned away from him, and he asked again, "What is it, Ann-Marie, what troubles you?"

She thought a moment and then said heavily, "There's so much between us—so many things wrong——"

"What?" he demanded.

"Oh—my dead husband, for whom I can't mourn—and your live wife!"

"Why, Jeanne's no obstacle at all!" he said in bewilderment. "I have assurances from the Pope—the annulment will follow soon."

"I know you'll think I'm changeable—it's difficult to explain. I always thought it was right for you to get an annulment and marry again—and then I came here and met Jeanne——" She hesitated.

"Yes?" he prodded gently.

She turned to face him, really looked into his eyes for the first time.

"She was born in misery—her whole life's been one long affair of ridicule and pain—and somehow, now that I know her and like her, I can't be the one to take her place and push her aside!" Her voice rose to vehemence. "What's she ever done to deserve such a disgrace—to be flung back, unwanted—unloved—while all of France laughs at her?

Oh, I've never seen such a cruel, laughing court as France! Louis, let me go back to Brittany!"

He answered her slowly. "Once I was offered love I didn't think was right. I couldn't take it—and I won't try to persuade you against your conscience. We'll come together only if you think we should. But"—he strode toward the desk and picked up the letter he had brought—"this, I think, will answer one of your objections." He handed it to her. "It came from Jeanne today."

Ann-Marie took it slowly and bent her head to read the scribbled writing while Louis watched her sympathetically. He understood her scruples about Jeanne. His own pity for the poor twisted princess was deep, and he hated the father who had had so little human feeling that he could have put Jeanne into the humiliating position of being an unwanted wife, exposing her to this repudiation.

But he and Jeanne understood each other—she had understood Ann-Marie's honesty, too, and in a separate, less formal note she had suggested Ann-Marie might wish to read the letter.

Ann-Marie's eyes were moist with tears as she read: "My dear Louis, today I stood before the Pope and answered his inquiries about my marriage. I accept his verdict with contentment. You are no longer my husband—you never were—only my good friend. I trust and know that you'll be happier with another lady, and as for me, I'm not fit for worldly life and this world's not fit for me. I leave it soon to go into the convent of the Holy Mother—signed by the affectionate hand of your friend—Jeanne."

Ann-Marie looked up from the letter with tears in her eyes. "The world's not fit for her!" she murmured. "It's our loss, not hers."

He nodded, then reached out and very gently touched her cheek with his fingertips.

"Go back to Brittany if you like, Ann-Marie—stay there till the mourning period is over—and when the time is up— I'll come to you. By then you'll be yourself again—and you'll tell me it's right for us to marry, because you're the only one in all the world who can make me change the words I've said so often—'I have no wife.' "

He left it at that. There was no good in being persuasive, pouring words over her or trying to remind her by his touch of the love between them. She needed time.

There was a hurried knock at the door. Louis called, and it opened to show Georges's pink agitated face, his big round blue eyes. He spoke hastily but formally: "Your Majesty, the Lady Anne of France asks to see the king!"

Louis hesitated and then nodded. "In a moment," he said, and Georges went out.

Ann-Marie of Brittany spoke hastily. "I'll go—I don't wish to see her wretched face again. I've seen enough of it to last me all my life!"

She thought of the last time she had seen it, across the dead body of Charles. When Anne of France had seen her brother proclaimed dead, she had refused to believe it. She had leaned down and, in a fury of resentment, shook him by his thin, limp shoulders.

"Charles," she had said vehemently, in the commanding tones that had always so affected him.

"Charles!" she had commanded him back from death, but his head had dropped back in listless disobedience. In wild exasperation, she shook him, thinking not at all of his wretched life that had just ended, but of her own more valuable one that would be endangered now because she no longer possessed a king's power.

She had suddenly felt her hands struck away from him by stinging blows. She had looked across him, recalled from her absorption, to meet the furious eyes of the queen.

"Take your greedy hands away, you miserable woman!" Ann-Marie had said in a low voice that stung as much as her blows. "You've had them on him since he was born— you couldn't let him die without feeling them! Get away from him—don't look at him again—go!"

Under the queen's compelling eyes Anne had risen from her knees and gone to her room, where she had sobbed in fury and changed into mourning clothes, thinking all the while how she could save herself from the fury of the new king. There was no use running to Bourbonnais. He could arrest her there as well as here. She would just have to stay and face it out, counting on her friends to help her when the blow fell. What friends, if any, she would have, she didn't know. She had waited hourly for the king's summons. He hadn't sent for her. She had seen him at the funeral, but he hadn't looked at her. She had waited a week, the tenseness mounting, and then, haggard with strain, she had asked to see the king. With trembling hands she had dressed carefully and gone down to his antechamber to wait his pleasure.

When Georges told her she might go in, she stiffened herself to meet her fate. She had never lacked courage, but this was the first time she had ever been helpless, in an enemy's hands.

Georges announced her: "Your Majesty, Madame Anne of France——"

Louis watched the door open and thought wryly how strangely the tricks of time had changed their lives. He would never have thought, that day at Montrichard, when they had made their promise—one loving, careless boy, one loving, cautious girl—that one day they would meet here with all the strange past between them—and be His Majesty—and Madame Anne of France!

Anne advanced steadily into the room, conscious of his dark, intent eyes on her. Straight to him she went and dropped in a deep obeisance at his feet, her black skirts all around her in a big billowing dark mound.

Her head still bent, she said, "Your Majesty, I've come to express my hopes that you'll enjoy a long and happy reign."

"Thank you," he said.

Then her voice faltered as she looked up, fear in her eyes. She was still beautiful, but her beauty had sharpened; there were lines around her mouth, and the firm, tight set of her lips gave her a faint resemblance to her father.

He had never seen her humble before. She had always been erect and imperious. Ah well, it was easy enough to be brave when all the power was on one side.

"I'd like to say," she went on, "that whatever differences we've had in the past, I hope you'll believe—any action I took I sincerely thought was for the good of France."

You lie, Madame Anne, you lie! he thought.

"How was it good for France," he asked, "for me to bruise my bones in an iron cage?"

Anne had no answer for that.

"Did you ever wonder how it felt," he asked, "to be locked in a small cold room with little food and nothing but your dark thoughts to keep you company?"

Still kneeling before him, Anne felt the ominous quality of his words, and fear poured through her. She shouldn't have come and brought this on herself; she should have tried to escape. It was too late now. He would call the guards, and she would find out the answer to his question when she herself was locked in the same small room.

But in that room Louis had learned a lesson she couldn't understand, and he kept the first of the vows he had made to himself—never to use a king's power to avenge a personal grievance.

Impersonally, he took her elbow and raised her.

"Madame Anne," he said in a voice of cold politeness, not an atom of personal feeling in it, "whatever charges I may have held against you, the Duke of Orleans will never be avenged by the King of France!"

Then, indifferently, he turned and walked away from her, after a dismissing nod. She stared at him, then rose slowly and stood there in bewilderment.

"Is that all you have to say to me?"

Louis shrugged carelessly. "What else is there? Oh yes—you're free to go to Bourbonnais or stay at court, just as you like."

Suddenly it was more galling to her to be treated so indifferently than if she had been arrested.

"Which would Your Majesty prefer?" she asked.

He shrugged again. "It makes no difference to me."

She could see it was true, and yet she couldn't believe it. It wasn't possible, after all that had been between them he could care so little, either to love or hate.

"Is this a trick?" she asked. "Will your revenge follow later?"

He looked at her quickly. "No revenge," he told her. "No trick." And then he explained, as if to reassure her, "I'll admit that once I thought I'd use my power—if I ever had it—to hurt you as you hurt me—but now I've so many other things to think about—so much happiness is on its way—that I haven't the time or inclination to think of you!"

She continued to stare at him. "You've dismissed me from your thoughts, then—as though I had no importance in your life——"

"Well," he said frankly, "to tell the truth, it's hard to look at you now and think you once were important to me. You're like a stranger I might speak to in the street—and then later hardly recall we'd met."

"We met," Anne said slowly. "We used to love."

"Yes. We used to."

"And if I'd wanted, I might be your queen now!"

He nodded. "It might have been that way. I'm glad it's not. We're not mates, Anne—there's too much difference in the way we think and live. Maybe Fate saw that and kept us apart till the day I could see it for myself."

"I'm incredulous," she said in amazement, "when I look at you now—with all the fantastic things you'd planned! This odd world," she commented wonderingly. "I planned with caution—worked it out in tedious detail—plodded along, too heavy with reality to run like you—yet here you are! All your dreams come true—and I'm left with empty hands! Why were you right—and I wrong? What was my fault?"

"You didn't love," he said. "You spent your energies in hate."

She laughed derisively. "I loved," she said. "I loved you all the time—although it seemed like hate to you. I tried to make it hate——"

"Yes, you loved a little," he admitted, "but not enough. You loved me and power—and power more."

"I love you now!" she said desperately, frantically eager to recapture what she had lost. "Louis—I love you now! It's not a little love—it's all my life! I've been wrong—I've been cruel—but it was because I loved and I could never have anything I wanted—not anything! But, Louis, it's still not too late. Let the queen go back to Brittany—I can make you forget her. And Pierre"—she stumbled, frantically eager—"you could have him tried and executed for treason—and we'd be together, as we'd always wanted——" She stopped, halted by the look in Louis's eyes.

He was looking at her in grave astonishment, and he sighed deeply, then said sadly, with a sincerity that surprised himself too, "You have my pity, Anne."

She caught her breath in unendurable humiliation. "I thought you said you didn't want revenge! What could be more cruel than that? You *pity* me!"

"Your father's poison is still in you—you'll never be free of it! I'm sorry for you——"

She interrupted him furiously. Her pride was dying in anguish inside her; she had never been in such pain.

"What have I ever had from life to deserve this?" she asked furiously. "I've had nothing! Ah, I've had a little

power—so bitterly schemed for there was never any peace
nor pleasure in it! I've had a touch of love—the smallest
touch—to make me know how much I've missed! I've had
days of work—distasteful nights—endured because of my
father's plans! That's all I've had—and it's all come to
nothing now, since you're the king! If I'd been a man"—
her voice rose wildly—"oh God, if only I'd been a man!
But some malicious fate laughed and made me—with a
mind well fit to be a king —a girl instead—and Charles—
with a mind not fit for anything—to be the king!"

"Anne," he said pityingly, "you'll be more at peace now
that it's all over."

Was it possible, she wondered, for an iron cage to be as
bruising as his impersonal pity and the knowledge that she
had lost him—lost everything—when if she had only been
more daring, as he had been, she would have won, too,
and would stand beside him now, his queen and his wife!
But she had made her cautious choice years ago, thinking
she was being so wise.

She laughed hysterically. "Oh yes, it's over now! And if
my young years have been as dreary as a February day,
tell me what will the rest be like?"

Louis didn't answer.

"My work's all gone," she accused him, "the work for
which my life was trained! I'll sit at Bourbonnais and
watch you here—your queen and you"—the thought
stabbed her, and she faltered—"your queen and you! And
I'll think that once I had the chance to share your throne—
and your love!" She came to a dead stop, realizing it all.
Then she rallied a little and said in bitter self-irony, "And
now you pity me? Well, why not? Now *anyone* can pity
Anne of France!"

And, turning swiftly, she ran stumbling out of the room.

Louis watched her go in a saddened mood. He sighed
and turned to the window, leaned on the window seat,
and pushed the glass open, to air the room of the lingering
scent of Anne's heavy perfume. It was sunset and he remembered the things he had said to Ann-Marie, about the
dead king, who was not really dead, but whose strength
lived on, like a snake's, until the sun went down.

He murmured aloud in the quiet room, speaking to the
cold dead eyes he remembered so well, eyes that were like

Anne's eyes now, "Your sun has gone down—your power is dead now!" and then he realized that his usual emotion of churning hate was gone. The king's life had been as poisoned and unhappy as Anne's. Hate and revenge and schemes for power didn't make pleasant hours and peaceful days. Louis felt a contemptuous pity for the friendless life, the pinched miserly mouth, the veined greedy hands of his dead enemy, and then he realized they were enemies no longer. The war was over, Louis had completely won, and for the first time since that dead king had touched his life Louis was completely free of him, for now he was free of hatred too!

The bells were tolling again. The bells had played a large part in Louis's life, separating the chapters, marking the difference between happiness and despair, waiting and hope.

They had tolled first, the bells of Blois, when a son had been born to Duke Charles of Orleans and his wife Mary. They had tolled when a son had been born to King Louis XI of France and his wife Charlotte. Marriage bells had rung out when two princesses of France had married, Anne to Pierre de Beaujeu, and Jeanne to Louis of Orleans. Funeral bells had sounded for King Louis XI and the young Orleans Louis had thought it the most exquisite sound in the world, for it meant he was free to divorce. But the bells had lied.

Coronation bells for Charles VIII had really been coronation bells for Anne of France and Louis had begun the darkest period of his life. The bells had pealed out in strident victory over the Treaty of Sable that placed him in prison for three years, and then, even bitterer, the wedding bells had rung for Ann-Marie of Brittany and Charles of France. Bells of joy for heirs to the throne, then funeral bells, as they were buried, left Louis again heir to the throne.

And just as he was preparing himself for another ordeal at Bourges, the funeral bells for Charles had tolled and the coronation bells had made him King Louis XII of France!

But of all of them in his life, these were the sweetest. He looked up at them, swinging high in the tower, gleaming bronze against the blue of the sky. The bells of Nantes in Brittany, tolling back and forth, proclaiming his joy in

deep-voiced triumph. Their rapturous echoes were everywhere, in his ears, in his blood, and, as he turned to look
at her, beside him in the big carriage of state, in the eyes
of his wife, Ann-Marie!

Moonstruck Madness

Laurie McBain

Author of
DEVIL'S DESIRE

It was the age of Scottish highwaymen, royal intrigue, and dashing swordplay. And for beautiful, aristocratic Sabrina Verrick, it was an age of romance and adventure, as she was forced to travel among rogues and assassins, masquerading as a man, plundering the rich to defend her honor and home.

And then, at the point of a sword, she met Lucien, Duke of Camareigh, who in a blaze of fury proved himself her equal in daring. Together they would face vengeful murder and the stormy passions of history before uniting in the everlasting ecstasy of love!

AVON   ◆   31385 $1.95

MOON 2-77